SHIELDMAIDEN'S REVENGE

VIKING LORE, BOOK 2

EMMA PRINCE

BOOKS BY EMMA PRINCE

Viking Lore Series:

Enthralled (Viking Lore, Book 1)

Shieldmaiden's Revenge (Viking Lore, Book 2)

The Bride Prize (Viking Lore Novella, Book 2.5)

Desire's Hostage (Viking Lore, Book 3)

Thor's Wolf (Viking Lore, Book 3.5)—a Kindle Worlds novella

Highland Bodyguards Series:

The Lady's Protector (Book 1)

Heart's Thief (Book 2)

A Warrior's Pledge (Book 3)

Claimed by the Bounty Hunter (Book 4)

A Highland Betrothal (Novella, Book 4.5)

The Promise of a Highlander (Book 5)

The Bastard Laird's Bride (Book 6 — Reid Mackenzie's story) coming Fall 2017!

The Sinclair Brothers Trilogy:

Highlander's Ransom (Book 1)

Highlander's Redemption (Book 2)

Highlander's Return (Bonus Novella, Book 2.5)

Highlander's Reckoning (Book 3)

Other Books:

Wish upon a Winter Solstice (A Highland Holiday Novella)

SHIELDMAIDEN'S REVENGE

VIKING LORE, BOOK 2

∼

By
Emma Prince

**Shieldmaiden's Revenge (Viking Lore, Book 2) Copyright ©
2015 by Emma Prince**

All rights reserved. No part of this publication may be reproduced, distributed, or transmitted in any form or by any means, or stored in a database or retrieval system, without the prior written permission of the author except in the case of brief quotations embodied in critical articles and reviews. For more information, contact emmaprincebooks@gmail.com.

This is a work of fiction. Names, characters, organizations, places, events, and incidents are the products of the author's imagination or are used fictitiously. Any resemblance to actual events or persons, living or dead, is entirely coincidental. Updated 6/12/17

For Scott. Always.

1

807 A.D.

A flash of lightning sliced through the sky, followed almost immediately by a boom of thunder. The mast reverberated under Rúnin's fingers. He clutched the wood as rivulets of rainwater ran over his bound hands.

As the thunder tapered to a low moan, Rúnin could once again make out the shouts of the men around him. The crew worked frantically to row in unison, but the roiling sea wouldn't allow it. Heaving swells snagged the men's oars, ripping the wood from their hands.

Just then, the small vessel tilted down the back side of a wave and seawater surged over the starboard gunwale.

Rúnin had just enough time to draw in a half breath before the wall of water slammed into him. The force of it tried to drag his body away, and if his hands hadn't been lashed around the mast, he would have been washed overboard. The ropes dug deep into his wrists and saltwater stung the raw flesh. As his head broke free of the sucking wave, he distantly registered the terrified cries of several of the other men as they were pulled overboard. For once in his life, he'd been the lucky one, bound as he was to the mast.

He shook his head, trying to clear his eyes of the stinging seawater. Another bolt of lightning tore through the night sky. The murky outline of the shoreline floated for an instant in his mind before all went dark again. It felt as though Thor was trying to split Rúnin's skull with the smack of thunder that followed.

The crew's captain must have seen the shoreline as well, for he bellowed to the men over the noise.

"Just a little farther!" he urged. "We are almost to safety!"

The rowers groaned as they dug deeper into the churning sea. With the sail lowered against the fierce winds howling all around, the small crew only had their oars to battle against Aegir the sea god's will.

Rúnin squeezed his eyes shut for a moment as the captain continued to bark a mixture of threats and encouragement to the rowers. He was even more powerless than they were against Aegir's whims and Thor's might. Even having lost several men to the storm already, the captain refused to untie Rúnin and set him to rowing alongside the other men.

He blinked at the captain through the heavy rain once more. The man's hazy outline became distinct in another flash of lightning, but Rúnin's eyes flickered to the unmoving swell of a wave over the man's shoulder.

Nei, it couldn't be.

The gods couldn't hate him so much. But he had seen it clearly in that brief moment—not a wave frozen in place, but a large rock rising from the water. They were still more than a stone's throw from the shoreline, but the fjord they sought as the storm had broken upon them must have been more treacherous than they'd initially guessed.

"Look out!" Rúnin shouted at the top of his lungs, but the roar of thunder descended, drowning him out.

Rúnin flailed desperately, trying to get the captain's attention. These men didn't care about Rúnin's life except that it would make them a few coins, but if this ship went down, he would go down with it. He bellowed into the wind, but the captain never moved from his post at the front of the ship.

Another blinding flash of lightning revealed the rock once more right before the ship drove into it. Rúnin braced himself but the impact was so great that his head snapped into the mast. The sound of splintering wood and the screams of the men filled the air for a fragment of a second before thunder muted everything.

Rúnin's body lurched forward then whipped back against the mast. Seawater swelled all around him, and he could no longer tell the difference between the waves and the debris as his body was pummeled. A deeper crack sounded in his skull and reverberated through his arms, and he realized distantly that the mast had snapped like a twig.

He couldn't tell if he was under water or in the air, so he held his breath and forced his body to shimmy down the mast. His arms made contact with the jagged end of the thick mast, the shards of wood burying themselves in his flesh. But he thrashed lower until his bound hands slid free of the mast.

He kicked in the direction he prayed was up. His

head broke the surface just long enough for him to drag in a ragged breath, then another wave crashed over him. He could only hope that the waves wouldn't drive his body into the protruding rock just as they had the ship. He would fare worse than the sturdy wooden ship, which had splintered like a child's toy.

As his head cleared the surface once more, lightning illuminated the world for one blinding moment. With his head bobbing barely above the waterline, Rúnin could no longer make out the shore. But he saw men, some flailing wildly, others floating motionless. The ship had been reduced to little more than splinters. Wooden boards that had been so painstakingly carved and fitted together by a ship maker now bobbed all around in disarray.

Rúnin threw himself at the largest piece of wood within reach. The fragment was little bigger than his torso, but it buoyed him slightly. Through the haze of pain and the cacophony of men's screams and thunderclaps, he realized in the recesses of his mind that he needed to free his hands. He dragged the rope that still bound his wrists along a jagged edge on the boards until it frayed enough for him to pop his hands apart.

As the waves tossed him mercilessly, he clung to the boards. Time stretched and his only focus was to keep his battered body above water. Slowly, he registered that the rain was beginning to let up and the lightning grew more distant.

The screams of the men onboard had faded, but it was too dark to know if any of them had survived. He hoped they hadn't. Though it was a cruel thought, Rúnin's life depended on their death. If by some twist of the gods' whims they lived through this storm, Rúnin would remain their captive, for they knew his secret.

He let his mind slip as the waves pushed him wherever they willed. He drifted through his memories, taking stock of the hard but safe boyhood that had warped into the shadow-life he'd lived up until the ship's captain had discovered him and taken him captive.

The pain dulled as he wandered between consciousness and the blackness that surrounded him. Perhaps the gods hadn't abandoned him completely. They must still possess a sliver of mercy for him. 'Twas far better to die in Aegir's embrace than to be reduced to a thrall. And better to die the relatively quick death of drowning than to slip away quietly and solitarily in the forests—the death of an outlaw.

He sent a prayer of thanks to Thor before succumbing to the darkness.

2

Madrena screamed as she charged forward, eyes locked on her opponent. He waited until her sword was about to bury itself in his chest before sidestepping in the mud. Madrena tried to halt her momentum but the soft, wet ground underfoot wouldn't cooperate. She slid, barely keeping on her feet, and spun just in time to block her opponent's blow.

The rain-slick sword reverberated in her palms as metal met metal, echoing the thunder that rumbled to the south. She blocked another blow aimed at her left shoulder, but instead of retreating defensively, she twisted her wrist, binding the blade with her own. With a jerk of her sword, she sent her opponent's weapon hurtling through the air before it landed with a squelch in the mud several paces away.

Her opponent eyed her, frozen under the point of her sword. She flipped the damp hair clinging to her forehead out of her eyes. The rain held the chill of fall, but her blood was pounding hotly through her veins. She took a slow step forward.

"Do you yield?" The thunder was drawing farther away, but she still had to shout to be heard over it.

Just then her opponent flashed her a smile. It was all the warning she had before he kicked the sword from her hand, sending it to join his blade in the mud. Before Madrena could draw the axe at her belt, her opponent launched himself forward, catching her in the stomach with his shoulder and sending them both careening to the soggy ground.

They tumbled together for several moments, panting hard and struggling to find purchase in the mud. But at last Madrena saw an opening. Her opponent was trying to pin her face-down in the sodden earth, one arm wrenched behind her back. She flipped over in a flash so that she faced him. Then with all her might she thrust her torso up, sending her opponent tumbling over her head.

Madrena scrambled to her feet and drew the seax in her boot in one smooth motion. While her opponent coughed for the breath that had been knocked from him and struggled to rise, she dropped on top of him, brushing the short blade against his throat.

"Now do you yield?" she panted, mirroring his crooked smile.

"Ja," Alaric breathed, holding up his hands on either side of his mud-streaked face.

She stood and re-sheathed her seax.

"Aren't you at least going to help me up, sister?" he asked, propping himself casually on one elbow in the mud.

She raised an eyebrow at him but then after a moment grudgingly extended her hand.

Of course, Alaric yanked on her hand so hard that she went slamming into the mud next to him.

He roared with laughter as she wiped mud and sweat from her face and gave him her fiercest scowl. But her twin brother's rumbling laugh was infectious, and she couldn't stop the grin that spread on her face.

"Just remember that I bested you fair and square, Alaric," she said, dragging herself to her feet. "*Before* you resorted to dirty tricks."

"Are you a warrior or not?" Alaric asked sweetly, rising next to her. "You must be willing to do whatever it takes to win."

"You still think to give me lessons? This is the second time in a sennight that I've beaten you."

Alaric bowed his head in assent, but his green eyes flashed. "There is always more to learn."

She rolled her eyes and nudged him with her elbow in response. He thought just because he was six minutes older that he was so much wiser than she.

They both turned to retrieve their weapons from the mud. The blades would need to be thoroughly cleaned and dried, but then again, so would everything they had on them. The rain was finally letting up from a downpour to a soft drizzle, but she was already soaked to the bone, not to mention covered in mud.

She glanced down at herself and had to suppress another smile. Laurel would bend her ear about how much work it would take to get the mud from her sodden wool overdress, which was pulled between her legs and tucked into her belt to allow her to move more freely. But worrying about keeping life running smoothly in the village was Laurel's task as wife to the Jarl—just as it was Madrena's business to learn the art of warfare.

Once they had collected their weapons and done their best to wipe them on their clothes, she and Alaric walked to the slender opening in the steeply sloped mountain walls protecting the practice grounds.

"When I talk with Eirik tonight, you'd do well to speak on my behalf," Madrena said over her shoulder as they made their way down the narrow path leading back to the village.

Alaric quirked a dark blond eyebrow at her. "You plan to ask him again?"

"Ja." She felt her jaw clench despite the lightness of her mood just a moment before. "Fall is already upon us, and I'll not be put off until next spring yet again."

"You know what he'll say already, sister. Why do you torture yourself?"

She spun around, blocking the narrow path and forcing Alaric to halt. "I've proven I'm ready. And you'd better not tell him otherwise, unless you want me to best you again in front of the whole—"

Madrena froze as a distant shout echoed against the rocks overhead. She turned slightly, eyeing the end of the path where it opened onto the village. Naught stirred, but the shout had come from that direction.

She glanced back and saw that her brother was tense and listening on the path behind her. They made eye contact and each nodded slowly. From the look in his eyes, which shone like emeralds through the mud on his face, he understood her perfectly. She drew her sword, careful to get a good grip on it. The rain and another distant clap of thunder muffled Alaric's noises behind her, but she knew without looking that he too had armed himself.

Madrena stepped cautiously down the path,

straining to hear sounds of an attack. But despite her noiseless footfalls, she couldn't hear any activity in the village a mere stone's throw from where they moved through the sloping mountain walls.

At last, they reached the mouth of the trail, the rock walls falling away and the village spreading before them. Her eyes instantly darted to the water on the other side of the closely gathered thatched buildings, expecting an attack by ships. But no longships or large rectangular sails were visible in the harbor. She relaxed a hair's breadth.

Then the shout came again, but this time, she could make out the words.

"Come help! Shipwreck!"

Madrena slammed her sword back into its scabbard and broke into a run, not waiting to see if Alaric was behind her. He came level with her before she was halfway through the village, though. He had heard the cry, too. As a fellow voyager, her brother understood just how disastrous—and deadly—a shipwreck could be. It didn't matter if the unfortunate sailors were friends or enemies—not for the time being, anyway.

As they reached the docks in their sheltered little corner of the fjord, Madrena's eyes locked on the terrifying scene before her. Wooden debris floated as far as the eye could see. The still forms of several men bobbed face-down in the water. As if reminding her of the gods' penchant for destruction, a distant roll of thunder punctuated the grotesque scene. These men must have been caught in the same storm that had swept over Dalgaard not long ago.

A handful of villagers were already streaming from the shelter of their homes to help in any way they could.

Some were even wading into the shallows to pull debris from the water.

She heard a commotion off to her left where several villagers were gathered around a sea-tossed body.

"He's alive!" someone shouted. "There may be other survivors!"

Suppressing a shudder of fear for what the survivor must have lived through to wash up on Dalgaard's shores, she drove herself into the shallows, the mud on her skirts staining the water around her.

Ahead, she saw the flash of a bright red garment. Wading forward, she sent up a prayer to Thor that the man had survived.

When she reached the body, however, she had to repress another shudder. He didn't wear a red tunic. Instead, his skin had been nigh flayed from him, and what remained of his clothing had been soaked in blood. He'd either been torn asunder by the treacherous rocks that guarded the mouth of the fjord or shredded by the splintered wood from the dismembered ship on which he'd sailed.

She moved away, her eyes catching on another flicker of movement. Farther out in the fjord, a figure lay draped across a few wooden boards. She couldn't tell if the figure moved or not, but at least he wasn't blood-red and nigh skinless like his former shipmate.

Madrena waded until she was waist deep. As she drew closer, she made out the figure's dark head and tattered clothes. At last, she was near enough to grab hold of his foot and drag him behind her.

As she made her way back to the shore, she glanced over her shoulder. The man was face-down on the boards, but she caught sight of his back rising and falling slightly with his breath. Another survivor. Her stomach twisted. He was one of the lucky ones, but he might not feel that way when he came to.

Memories flooded her, and her chest squeezed painfully. For a moment, the chaos on the shoreline in front of her transformed into that horrible night five years ago.

Villagers running. Huts burning, the black smoke blocking the moon and choking her lungs. Her own screams ringing distant and hollow in her ears. The searing pain as the shadow-man leaned over her. The bear, its teeth black and curving on the man's chest.

She shoved the memories aside. These men weren't laying siege to the village. They were barely alive, not killing and raping and leaving naught but ashes and broken bodies.

Alaric called her name from the shoreline, bringing her attention back to the present. She waved with her free hand and pointed to the body she dragged behind her. Her brother plowed into the water until he reached her side.

"Another live one," she said, her voice clipped as she forced herself to breath, burying the pain as she'd become accustomed to doing.

She felt Alaric's eyes linger on her as he fell in at her side. "You all right?"

"Ja," she said quickly. Her brother knew her well enough that he'd likely already noticed and interpreted the fright that undoubtedly flickered in her eyes, despite the fact that she worked to keep her features unreadable. But he also knew not to push her to talk about it.

When they were close enough to the shore, Alaric helped her lift the man off the boards and dragged one of his arms over his shoulder as she took the other. The man groaned but didn't open his eyes.

Madrena studied him out of the corner of her eye as she and her brother half-carried, half-dragged him out of the shallows and onto the narrow strip of sand that lined the shore. Judging from his large frame, long hair, and beard, he was a Northman like them, but the head that slumped in semi-consciousness against his chest was dark rather than blond like most of the people in the western Northlands.

Would he be from the east, then? Her mind sparked at the prospect. Now wasn't the time to think about her hoped-for mission. She would have to ask the man later about the lands to the east—assuming he lived.

She grunted as she and Alaric shuffled up the steeply sloping beach. The man they hauled on their shoulders was heavy, his frame large and his body lean but hard with muscle. Even slumped and slack in a seemingly oblivious state, he rivaled Alaric and Eirik in size and build, except perhaps that he looked somewhat underfed, judging by the way his sodden tunic clung to his narrow waist.

Something brushed against her arm, and she looked at the large hand dangling limply over her shoulder. A piece of frayed rope hung from his wrist. She glanced over Alaric's shoulder and noticed that the man's other hand also bore a bit of rope. Strange. Something about this man didn't fit with a shipwrecked seafarer in the western Northlands.

Her thoughts were interrupted by the sound of Eirik's voice barking orders.

"Bring them into the longhouse!"

Madrena darted a glance to the left and saw that

several villagers were helping men in various states of consciousness up the gently sloping rise from the shoreline to the wooden longhouse in the center of the village.

The man draped over her shoulders coughed wetly. Madrena looped an arm around his torso to help ease his weight from her shoulders. He coughed again, spitting up water, and she felt the tightening and bunching of his muscular back under her hand.

Alaric hurried their pace toward Eirik, who had spotted them from the longhouse's threshold. Eirik's face was set with the grim concern of a leader, his hands fisted on his hips in the doorway.

"Has this one spoken?" Eirik asked once they reached the longhouse. His brows were low as his eyes flitted over the survivor slung between their shoulders.

"Nei," Alaric answered. "The others?"

"Not yet."

Something in his tone told Madrena that the presence of these outsiders made Eirik uncomfortable. It was his job as Jarl to protect his people. A handful of strange men in his longhouse clearly didn't sit well. But he couldn't simply turn them away either. She knew her friend well enough to be sure he was searching his mind for the honorable and just course of action.

Eirik waved them into the longhouse and followed in behind them.

"Eirik! What has happened?"

Suddenly Madrena knew the real source of Eirik's unease. Laurel, round with child, emerged from the Jarl's private chambers built on the side of the longhouse. She hurried toward them as fast as her large belly would allow.

Shieldmaiden's Revenge

"Laurel, I asked you to stay in our chambers," Eirik said quietly, but Madrena didn't miss the pinch of worry in his normally commanding voice.

"I cannot sit idly by when there has clearly been a disaster. Oh!" Laurel's gaze fell on Madrena and Alaric —or more accurately, the large man draped between their shoulders. Then her dark brown eyes swept over those gathering within the longhouse and huddling around the enormous fire in the center.

"I'll have a broth prepared," Laurel said even as shock widened her eyes. "And I'll send for all the dry blankets and clothes that can be spared from the village."

Without waiting for Eirik's approval, Laurel set off for the kitchens at the back of the longhouse as quickly as she could. Madrena would have chuckled at Laurel's determination to help the strangers who'd washed up on the shores of her adopted home if the current situation weren't so pressing.

Eirik watched her go for a moment before turning back to them.

"Leave it to Laurel to defy the Jarl and take charge," Alaric said to Madrena, but loud enough for Eirik to hear.

Eirik snorted at the tease but didn't deny it. Though he was clearly mad for his wife and their unborn first child, Eirik was stronger with Laurel at his side, and the whole village knew it. Madrena had been one of the last to trust Laurel, outsider that the woman was, but now she would defend Laurel with her life, just as she would Eirik and Alaric. Though Eirik looked at the moment like he wished his wife would involve herself less in facing this disaster, Madrena was grateful for her friend's eagerness to help. They would need all they could get, judging by the handful of dazed, injured, and semi-conscious survivors now filling the longhouse.

Eirik motioned them toward the warmth of the fire, and with a few more shuffling steps, they reached the rectangular fire pit. At last, Madrena and Alaric eased the man down to the ground, propping him against the warm stones that lined the pit.

Again, Madrena had a fleeting moment to examine the stranger. Her eyes swept over his face, which was mostly obscured by a dark beard, and once more took in his frame and the ropes around his wrists. He had the build of a warrior, though he bore no weapons. His trousers were worn and sodden, as were the leather boots on his feet. His tunic was in even worse condition. It was nigh shredded to pieces and barely hung together across his broad shoulders. There looked to be some sort of marking on his chest, but the tunic clung to his skin, obscuring it.

Alaric cleared his throat loudly, snapping Madrena's attention to him. He was studying her, she realized with an inward curse. She should know by now to keep her curiosity better guarded. She was a shieldmaiden, not some curious girl ogling this mysterious stranger.

Alaric's cough drew Eirik's attention back to them. "What in Odin's name happened to you two?" he said, taking in their wet, muddy appearance.

"We were practicing," Madrena said. "I bested Alaric again."

Eirik eyed her sharply, clearly anticipating the direction she was about to take their conversation.

"Eirik, I wish to speak with you again about a voyage to—"

"You already have my answer, Madrena." Eirik sounded more like the Jarl now than her friend.

"But that was before—"

"Now isn't the time. We need to see to these men, and I must decide what is to be done about them."

Madrena clenched her fists at her sides. Her brother had been right, of course. Eirik had already made up his mind long ago. But she wouldn't give up so easily.

"I deserve to be heard."

Eirik sighed and pushed a hand through his golden hair. He dropped his eyes, searching the floor for a moment. "As I said, now isn't the time. But perhaps we can talk this evening once these men are settled and I have some answers."

She nodded curtly, forcing her hands to relax. He'd listened before to her reasons for wanting to be granted permission to set out on her mission. She could only hope that this time she'd somehow convince him. She was ready.

Just then, Laurel reappeared in the longhouse with an armful of woolen blankets. As she shuffled by, Madrena snagged a blanket from the top of the pile. Alaric fell in beside Laurel, lifting the blankets from her arms and handing them out as they moved around to the other shipwreck survivors.

Madrena turned to the stranger she'd pulled from the icy fjord. He leaned against the stones of the raised fire pit, his head lolling against his chest. She draped the blanket over his limp form and watched him closely, waiting to see if he had the strength to drag himself from the fog of his own mind.

At last the man stirred. He coughed again and his eyelids fluttered, his brow furrowing as if he was in pain.

Madrena hadn't seen any injuries on him, but the sea could batter a body without leaving a mark. Her hand tingled at the memory of the feel of his muscular but lean back under her fingertips. No broken ribs that she could remember. Just hard, planed muscles.

"What...where...?" The man winced and clutched his side as he tried to sit upright. Madrena put a hand on his shoulder to still him.

He blinked up at her then. His eyes were cool blue but burned with an intensity that forced her to swallow.

"Freyja," he whispered roughly, his gaze locking on her.

She would have laughed at the ridiculousness of mistaking her for the goddess of sensuality and beauty if she hadn't been pinned by the man's vivid eyes.

"Nei, I'm not—"

He raised a shaky hand toward her, his gaze moving from her eyes to her lips. His fingertips grazed her jawline, the pad of his thumb brushing against her lower lip.

Madrena froze. She could have slapped his hand away, or even removed it all together with the seax in her boot, but for some reason she didn't stop his touch.

The man's fingers were cold, but her skin flared hot at the contact. Considering how large his hands were, his touch was surprisingly gentle, hesitant even. But his eyes burned into her, the haze of pain and confusion melting into awe and anticipation.

"Freyja, you have not abandoned me after all," he said, his voice hushed.

She blinked, forcing herself to break the spell. "You are not yet with the gods. You live."

The man squeezed his eyes shut, shaking his head a

little. He dropped his hand away from her face, though Madrena's skin pricked where he had touched her.

"How?" All the hushed joy now fell from his voice to be replaced with gruff flatness.

"You survived the storm and the shipwreck. You washed ashore in a village called Dalgaard." Madrena forced her tone to be level as well, yet her insides churned. Why should she be so affected just because a strange man looked at her with searing heat in his eyes and mistook her for the goddess of sensuality?

"Village?" It was as if the man had suddenly come fully back to reality. Both his voice and eyes were sharp now. He tried to stand but as he moved, he groaned in pain. Madrena pressed down on his shoulder and with little effort got him to sit down again. He cursed softly under his breath, either at the pain or his own weakened state, she wasn't sure. But his eyes, which grew more alert by the moment, quickly scanned the longhouse.

"You're safe here," she said, watching him closely.

"The others?"

"Many of your friends were taken by Aegir," Madrena replied, trying to soften her countenance. The man had just lost most of his fellow seafarers, after all. But she didn't do soft very well. And besides, his reactions seemed…off somehow.

The man muttered something under his breath again, but then his eyes returned to scanning the longhouse.

"Some survived," Madrena said quickly. "Where were you sailing from? What was your destination?"

The man turned those intense, searching eyes on her once more and she forced her features to remain still. If she hadn't been a trained warrior, she would have recoiled at the look in those bright blue depths. It was hard and assessing, guarded yet concentrated.

Before she could make sense of the man's strange behavior, Eirik's voice rose above the noise in the longhouse. He stood on the raised dais at the end of the room.

"I am Eirik, son of Arud, Jarl of Dalgaard," he said. "You men who were pulled from the sea—the gods have smiled on you. You have naught to fear from us. But I wish to know who you are."

Madrena turned slightly from the man at her feet and let her eyes roam the longhouse. From the looks of the huddled forms and clumps of villagers, about ten men had been rescued from the storm. Some were barely conscious, but others looked at each other warily. None of them spoke.

An uneasy silence grew heavy in the air. Those who had been rescued continued to eye each other, seemingly wordlessly discussing who would speak. At last, one of the men stood on shaky legs and nodded toward Eirik.

"We thank you for saving us, Jarl. I am Bjorn Storrisson, the *Wolf*'s second in command. We hope not to overextend your hospitality. As soon as we are all able, we will be on our way."

Eirik narrowed his eyes on the stranger. Madrena instantly tensed. The man had blatantly avoided Eirik's request for an explanation.

Slowly, Madrena's hand moved to the axe strapped to her belt. None of the shipwrecked men appeared to be armed, but that wouldn't stop a Northman bent on attack. These strangers couldn't have meant to be caught in that storm and shipwrecked, but they were clearly hiding something.

Shieldmaiden's Revenge

"Where do you hail from?" Eirik said flatly, giving the man and his companions no room to evade the question this time.

The man who spoke for the others waved his hand vaguely. "We are traders. We travel widely."

"Then where have you been most recently?" Eirik's jaw ticked. Madrena knew him well enough to sense his growing frustration.

"We were in the northeast," the man said casually.

Madrena's eyes darted to the stranger at her feet. Her intuition that he was from the eastern Northlands had been right. Her heartbeat hitched in anticipation. The man didn't seem to notice her gaze, however. His eyes were locked on the one speaking, Bjorn.

"And where were you headed in—the *Wolf*, was it?"

The man waved noncommittally again. "Jutland. To trade."

Eirik nodded slowly but kept his eyes on the man who spoke. "Very well," he said at last. "You can stay here and recuperate until you find transportation to Jutland. I'm sure you're aware that the *Wolf*, along with your cargo and many of your crew, has been lost."

The man nodded, though instead of thanking Eirik, his eyes flickered to the man at Madrena's feet. His gaze held an unspoken threat.

Madrena's fingers clenched around her axe's handle. She itched to pull it free and feel its comforting weight in her hand—but why? To protect the man she'd pulled from the fjord? He was with Bjorn and the others. Yet Bjorn's look was unmistakably threatening. And the man she'd saved had been evasive and nervous even before Bjorn spoke. Something wasn't right.

"You and your men will be more comfortable in one

of our outbuildings," Eirik said levelly, drawing Madrena's attention once more. "We'll have it arranged."

With a nod, Eirik stepped down from the dais and made his way through the crowd. Some of the villagers began helping the stranded men to their feet and guiding them out of the longhouse.

Just then Alaric reappeared at her side. They exchanged a look, and Madrena knew that he too had picked up on the strange exchange between their Jarl and the outsiders.

Eirik strode to them, his face unreadable. He took Madrena and Alaric each by the elbow and pulled them a few feet away from the man she'd saved.

"I want them watched," Eirik hissed in a low voice. "Set up a guard around the smithy. They're hiding something."

Madrena and Alaric nodded in unison. Eirik moved off again, his relaxed stance concealing his unease from those who didn't know him as well. Madrena forced herself to drop her hand from her belt and the axe she longed to draw. Eirik clearly didn't want to alert their unexpected visitors to his sense of suspicion. She wouldn't defy him, but she damn well would rather have a weapon in hand if the shipwrecked survivors were planning something.

With a little nod that communicated his intentions, Alaric slipped from her side and into the crowd filing out of the longhouse. She knew without Alaric having to say the words that he was going to inconspicuously recruit several warriors to stand guard over the smithy.

Eirik had chosen a fitting building for the survivors' temporary home—or prison. The smithy only had one door and the windows were too high and narrow for a man to pass through. And it was made of stone and mortar right up to the high thatched rooves. There would be no chance of escape.

Madrena looked down at the man she'd pulled from the sea. He had removed the frayed bits of rope from his wrists and thrown them into the fire behind him, where they drooped wetly in the flames. Angry red marks chafed his wrists where the ropes had been. He rubbed them absently as his gaze clashed with hers.

If she'd thought he'd been guarded before, now he looked downright flinty. She bent and pulled one of his arms over her shoulder to help him to his feet.

"Tell me your name," she demanded, no longer trying to soften her voice.

"Leave it, girl." His voice was so low that she almost missed his words.

She instantly bristled. Why would this man deny her a simple piece of information? And why did his own crewman shoot hostile looks at him? Was this man trying to warn her of something? Or was he threatening her?

Once he was on his feet, he shook his arm free of her shoulder. Though he moved stiffly, he fell in step with the others as they trailed out of the longhouse, leaving her behind to ponder the strange events of the day.

3

Rúnin didn't know where they were being taken, but he followed passively, as did the others. If the Jarl of this village wished to kill them all, he could have simply given the order. The man seemed good to his word to provide protection—for now—but Bjorn's behavior had clearly drawn the Jarl's suspicion—and that of the girl who'd been tending him.

The rain had completely stopped now, but the ground was soggy under Rúnin's boots as he shuffled from the village's longhouse to one of its outbuildings. Judging from the fact that they were being led toward what looked to be a smithy made entirely of stone, the Jarl suspected that they might try something. A hut made of stone rather than wood or sod was designed to protect against an accidental fire. But it also meant that there would be no easy way for him or any of the other men to escape, save climbing through the thatched roof.

Rúnin silently cursed Bjorn. The captain must have died in the storm, for Rúnin hadn't seen him among the other survivors. Bjorn had taken it upon himself to be

Shieldmaiden's Revenge

their new leader, though he clearly didn't know how to lie very well.

Then again, Rúnin wasn't doing so well either. The girl—nei, she was a woman—who had helped him was suspicious too. He clenched his jaw against the memory of her beautiful if mud-smeared face floating before him as he'd drifted back to reality. He'd mistaken her for Freyja and had nigh wept at the thought that the gods had embraced him in death. He should have known better.

Her pale, almost colorless gray eyes had bored into him with an unexpected sharpness when he'd slipped and shown too much fear to learn that he was in a village. The normal reaction would have been one of relief, joy even. He'd been away from people too long to remember how to fake such a response.

Rúnin balled his fists in the woolen blanket the woman had given him. He had thought that being on a ship headed for Jutland with the merciless slavers had been bad. Now he was stuck with those slavers in the middle of an unfamiliar village. Some people were afraid of the wilderness beyond the known borders of a village. But for him, the wilderness was his only shelter from the dangers of other people.

He pulled the blanket tighter around his shoulders, making sure it covered his chest. None in the village had seen his marking yet, otherwise they would have set upon him by now. There was still a sliver of hope for his survival. All he had to do was separate himself from the slaver ship's crew, find a way to escape the stone walls of the smithy, and evade any eyes until he was well clear of this village. Simple.

As Rúnin stepped into the smithy, he finally got a

good look at those who had survived. Besides Bjorn and himself, there were eight other crewmen. One of them looked to have a broken leg. He was hopping on his good side, his arms around two villagers. That was one less man Rúnin had to worry about. Two or three of the others were only semi-conscious. But the remaining men eyed him silently, daring him to reveal the truth to the villagers.

They should know that their secret was safe with him. They were all in the same danger now. For if Jarl Eirik so chose, he could sell them all as thralls in Jutland.

His eyes swept the smithy, hoping to find something that could serve as a weapon. Unfortunately, the Jarl must have ordered the smithy emptied for that very reason. Besides a simple wooden table and bench in one corner, the smithy was empty. The hard packed floor was swept clean, and the stone walls were bare of any tools.

One of the villagers was kind enough to light a fire in the blacksmith's enormous fire pit. Rúnin was grateful for the heat, but he didn't approach the fire. He retreated to one corner, hoping to evade notice.

As the *Wolf*'s surviving crew hunkered down on the floor in front of the fire, a few villagers passed around wooden bowls of steaming broth, along with some day-old bread. As a young man handed Rúnin a bowl and a hunk of bread, he felt Bjorn's eyes on him. Luckily, none of the villagers seemed to notice, and once the survivors had all been given food, they shuffled out, leaving the men to eat and rest.

As soon as the door was closed behind them, three men, including Bjorn, turned on Rúnin. He froze in mid-chew as the men moved in on him slowly. Rúnin's shoulder blades hit the cold stones in the corner he'd backed himself into right before the men launched at him. One sent a fist into his already bruised ribs. Rúnin dropped his bowl and bread with a muffled grunt. He blocked another blow aimed for his stomach but caught a fist in the chin.

He tasted blood and had to fight against the urge to lash back. It had taken a dozen of the *Wolf*'s crew to take him down the first time a fortnight ago when they'd found him in the forest. He knew even in his battered condition he could fend off these three. But now wasn't the time. There was nowhere for him to go even if he beat back Bjorn and his lackeys. He had to be patient.

"If you say aught, swine, you won't live long enough to be sold as a thrall in Jutland," Bjorn whispered next to Rúnin's ear. One of his men picked up Rúnin's hunk of bread and began eating it with a grin.

Rúnin met Bjorn's eyes and nodded slowly.

The men backed off, but Bjorn's eyes burned into Rúnin's. Rúnin forced himself to hold their stare, clenching his teeth against the fresh pain in his ribs and jaw. At last, Bjorn turned to converse quietly with the others.

"No one says aught about our…cargo," Bjorn said with a dart of his eyes toward Rúnin. "If they know what he is, they'll take him for themselves and either kill him or sell him and keep the coin."

Several of the men nodded, their eyes glowing in the firelight.

"But Bjorn," one of the men whispered. "What if the Jarl sells us as well?"

"That's why we have to convince him that we are simply innocent traders caught in an unfortunate shipwreck," Bjorn hissed. "The Jarl already promised us hospitality. He'll likely let us go in a day or two."

The men continued whispering, but Rúnin turned away. They were underestimating the Jarl. But Rúnin didn't care what happened to these men. He had to think about himself now. How could he separate himself from them and escape the well-built walls of the smithy?

By the time the fire burned low, the men had hunkered down on the floor with their blankets, some snoring. Rúnin had to pinch his leg to keep from falling asleep. Weariness racked him, but he couldn't miss what might be his only opportunity to form his own plan.

At last, he trusted that the others were deeply asleep enough not to notice his movements. He rose and glided silently along the stone walls until he came to a high, small rectangular gap in the stones that served as a window. No covering protected the inside of the smithy, for normally the blacksmith's fires would keep the building toasty warm, summer or winter.

Rising on his toes, Rúnin peered out into the night. Clouds obscured the moon and stars, but there was enough ambient light to make out a shadowy figure not far from the smithy. The figure glided through the night slowly until it crossed with another form.

Just as he'd suspected, Jarl Eirik had ordered that the smithy be watched. Rúnin's stomach sank as he added evading a guard to his impossible list of things he would need to do to escape this nightmare.

MADRENA WAITED until the embers glowed in the longhouse's fire pit, her mind churning. Laurel and Eirik sat on the dais, Eirik silently brooding and Laurel leaning on him, likely exhausted from the events of the evening. Laurel rested her dark head against his fair one. Though she had taken to the Viking life over the last year, her small frame and dark brown hair reminded Madrena that she was an outlander—like the strange man she'd tended to.

Eirik was clearly deep in thought about what to do with the secretive strangers in his village. Madrena couldn't untangle their unusual behavior either, but she had more on her mind. Today's storm only served as another reminder that fall was upon them. Time was running out for her to embark on her mission.

Madrena rose from her seat next to her brother slowly, determined to put her case to Eirik this night. Only the four of them remained in the longhouse, so she was at last able to speak freely.

Eirik's wearied eyes followed her as she made her way from one of the long tables to the dais. She knew Alaric watched her as well.

"I think you ought to hear what I have to say."

"Now isn't the time, Madrena."

She pressed her lips together and forced her voice to remain impassive. "It's never the right time, is it?"

Eirik stiffened but remained seated. "It's not every day that the remains of a crew from a shipwreck wash up on Dalgaard's shores. There are more pressing matters at hand this night."

"There was no shipwreck last year when you denied me my mission."

Eirik sighed. "My position hasn't changed since last year."

She felt the muscles in her shoulders bunch in frustration. "No matter what I do, you refuse me. Shall I remind you that I bested Alaric again today?"

Laurel raised her head, glancing between her husband and Madrena. "What is this about?"

Sometimes Madrena forgot that Laurel had only been with them a little over a year. She hadn't even told Laurel what had happened to her five years ago, and she doubted Eirik had either.

It was Madrena's burden to carry, not Laurel's. But Madrena saw an opening. Laurel had become one of Madrena's closest friends in the last year. Though she was an outsider, Laurel took to the Viking code of honor as if she had always been raised with it. She was a champion of goodness. Perhaps she would take up Madrena's case and convince her husband.

Eirik was watching her and seemed to guess at her line of thinking, but Madrena disregarded him and turned to Laurel. "I wish to go on a voyage," she said, then turned her gaze back to Eirik. "But he won't agree to it."

"Why? Surely she is capable of leading a crew," Laurel said, tilting her head to look up at Eirik questioningly.

Madrena's heart surged toward Laurel in that moment. Ja, Laurel was from the west, the land of the Angles, but she was the closest thing Madrena had ever had to a sister. If she hadn't been wound tight with frustration at Eirik, a smile would have softened her mouth at Laurel's endorsement.

"As I said, I beat Alaric on the practice field again," Madrena added, returning her attention to Eirik.

"I don't doubt you did. You two have been splitting victories for nigh a year. You think so much alike that I imagine half the time you anticipate the other's move."

She heard Alaric snort behind her, but rage flared in her veins. Friend or no, she took a step toward Eirik so that she stood over him.

"You question my abilities?"

Eirik rose slowly until he looked down on her. Though she was tall even for a Northwoman, Eirik stood more than half a head taller. "I am not insulting your skill. You have trained hard these past five years," he said levelly. "What I do question is the soundness of your plan."

That was his reason. That was *always* his reason.

"It's my right to seek vengeance," she hissed, her rage barely in check now.

"Vengeance for what?" Laurel spoke softly, clearly sensing the deep-running pain underlying the conversation.

"Now isn't the time," Eirik said gently.

"Nei, she should know," Madrena replied. "She's one of us. She's family."

Eirik gave a small shake of his head in warning. He was extremely protective of Laurel, especially now that she was large with child. Though Madrena didn't wish to upset Laurel either, for some reason her anger flared again. No one had shielded *her* from the darkness of the world.

Madrena felt a presence at her back and knew her brother had come to stand by her. He was one of the only ones who understood just how much it still pained her to discuss what had happened. He heard her screams of terror when the nightmares stole over her. He saw in her eyes the flashes of fear that still paralyzed her from time to time—he'd witnessed it just a few hours ago when the men had begun washing ashore in the fjord.

Madrena took a steeling breath and turned her gaze on Laurel. "Five years ago, the village was attacked by raiders," she said flatly.

Laurel's eyes widened and she stood. She had lived through a raid last summer, and the memories of the bodies, the smoke, and the screams likely now filled her mind.

Madrena cleared her throat and went on. "We didn't know the men, but we believe they came from somewhere in the east, or perhaps the north. Alaric left me behind in our hut to fight. One of the men…" She swallowed, forcing herself to go on in as close to a neutral voice as she could manage. "One of the raiders found me alone and raped me."

Laurel gasped and clapped a hand over her mouth. She stepped forward without thought and took Madrena's clenched fist into her small hand. Madrena let her, but she felt too numb to allow the comforting gesture to sink in.

"I wasn't always a shieldmaiden," she said to Laurel. "I only began training after that night so that I could defend myself. And so that I would eventually be ready to seek revenge."

"Madrena…" Laurel's voice held all the sorrow and compassion the words would have if she could have formed them. She squeezed Madrena's hand, her dark eyes brimming with tears.

Shieldmaiden's Revenge

A long moment stretched, and it seemed that all four of them were lost in their own thoughts. But then Laurel's delicate brows drew together.

"You seek the man who...who attacked you? But you said no one recognized the raiders."

Laurel was too kindhearted to voice the underlying question that plagued her, but Madrena knew her well enough to surmise the direction of her thoughts.

"And you wonder how I can possibly have my revenge?"

Laurel nodded reluctantly, so Madrena went on.

"Though you have learned much in the last year, you still don't understand just how important honor—and its vengeance—is in the Northlands," she said quietly. "That man...that man stole my honor and besmirched his own. Vengeance restores my honor and further diminishes his—both in the eyes of the gods and of mortals. He cannot go unpunished."

At the last words, she shifted her eyes to Eirik, letting the heat of her earlier anger spark again. "Revenge is rightfully mine to claim. Yet it is a revenge you seem determined to deny me, *Jarl*."

She never used his title. They had grown up together, and though he was Jarl now, she would have given her life for him long before that. It had been Eirik and Alaric who had stayed with her during the dark months after the raid, when she'd barely been able to get out of bed and the shadows played with her mind. And it had been Eirik and Alaric who had started training her to be a warrior. But now Eirik stood in her way, using his power to deny her mission.

Eirik's eyes flashed in annoyance at her. "It is my duty as Jarl to protect this village and its inhabitants. I cannot risk a ship and the lives of a crew this late in the season."

Madrena scoffed. "You could have allowed me to go earlier in the summer instead of waiting until fall's arrival to deny me."

His voice remained level even as hers rose. "Ja, you're right, Madrena. 'Tis not simply the season that leads me to refuse you."

"Then what? I have trained every day for nigh five years. I have bested Alaric, admittedly one of your best warriors, repeatedly. I'm ready."

"Are you?" Eirik's eyes assessed her flatly.

Anger surged through her veins, but before she could defend herself, he went on.

"Perhaps I have denied you because I don't believe you have thought your plan through well enough. You aren't even sure exactly where you're headed."

"I know enough about the man who attacked me to find him along the way," she shot back.

"And when you find him? What then?"

She inhaled sharply through her nose. "I'll kill him."

"And then what? Will his death stop the nightmares?"

"Stop it," she hissed.

"Will killing him undo what he did to you? Will it give you back what he took?"

"I said stop!"

Eirik's hard blue eyes bore into her. Tension crackled in the air around the four of them until Eirik spoke again.

"*This* is why I am denying your request to set out on this voyage. The revenge you seek is hollow. You haven't thought your plan through. And you are still blinded by rage. You'll never find satisfaction on this path. You aren't ready."

"Have you forgotten the ways of the Northlands?" she snapped. "What he did cannot be undone, but his dishonor must be known, and my honor must be restored!"

"I have come to believe that the gods see all," Eirik said lowly. His eyes flickered to Laurel, who gave him a little nod. "They know where honor truly resides."

Madrena's heart twisted. She couldn't deny that Laurel's presence had a positive effect on Eirik—on the whole village. And yet the fire that had once burned in Eirik's veins, the fire of battle and bloodlust, had dimmed, even as it burned brighter within her.

"You can't refuse me this!" she panted. The familiar desperation clawed at her insides.

"They are my ships and my men," he said, his voice cold. "I'll not endanger them." He took a deep breath and softened his voice ever so slightly. "You have suffered much, Madrena. I only wish that you could find a way to escape your pain. Seeking revenge rarely does so."

"How easy for you to say," she retorted. "Your cousin and uncle are dead. You killed Grimar with your own hands for what he did to you and Laurel. You've had your revenge, and yet you deny me mine. I can't decide if being Jarl has made you too soft to fight or too hard to care about your friends."

She regretted the words instantly, but her blood ran too hot to temper her tongue. Eirik had ruled with fairness and equanimity in the year that he'd been Jarl. But deep in her chest, it ached that he would refuse her the opportunity to seek vengeance. If she didn't leave soon, the snows would be upon them and she'd have to wait until next spring. She had waited five long, hard years. She would not be put off again.

Eirik stiffened and Laurel inhaled. "Is that a challenge?" he asked through clenched teeth.

"Not to your Jarlship," Madrena said quickly. "But to your judgement on this matter, ja."

She could sense Alaric's disapproval at her back. Normally her twin brother would take her side against anyone. It stung that he didn't speak on her behalf now. But both he and Eirik had decided long ago that Madrena had mistakenly placed her focus on revenge. She would not beg her brother for his support, though deep in her heart she longed for it. Nei, she had to accept that she was alone in this.

Eirik considered her for a long moment. Finally, he spoke again.

"You think you are ready?"

An unexpected surge of hope coursed through her. "Ja. I know I am."

"Best *me* then."

"What?" she blurted.

Alaric shifted uneasily behind her.

"Eirik, no," Laurel said softly. Did Laurel think Madrena would hurt Eirik, or the other way around?

Eirik went on, though. "If you can beat me, you can sail to the east with my blessing. But if not, you'll respect my judgement."

Anticipation spiked through her. She had never beaten Eirik on the practice field, but this was different. She didn't want to hurt her friend, yet this was her chance to satisfy the burning desire for revenge that had gnawed at her all these years.

She nodded curtly and turned on her heels without waiting to see if he would follow her into the open space outside the longhouse. Laurel protested, but her words wouldn't change things now. A challenge had been issued and taken up.

There was naught left to do but fight.

4

Rúnin's head drooped over his chest, his eyes barely cracked open. His jaw throbbed where Bjorn's man had hit him, the pain more acute than the ache in his ribs and limbs from the shipwreck. His mind hazed with fatigue and soreness, but he struggled against sleep. He needed to think, to form a plan.

He'd watched the shadows of the guards outside the smithy for what felt like ages. There were at least two of them, and they crossed each other within view of the narrow window every half an hour.

But he couldn't stay straining on his toes and peering into the darkness all night. At last he'd allowed himself to slump to the ground below the high window. His mind had roiled, yet he was no closer to a plan than he had been upon washing ashore in this accursed village.

The fire had reduced itself to embers long ago, and the *Wolf*'s surviving crew slept huddled together. Even Bjorn had at last turned his back on Rúnin, trusting that he was sufficiently cowed.

Voices, men's and women's, drifted through the fog

in his mind. He blinked. Had he imagined it? He dragged his head from his chest, forcing his legs to straighten as he pushed himself up the stone wall of the smithy.

The voices came again, clearer this time.

"...can choose the weapons." That was a man—a familiar, commanding voice, though less hard-edged than Rúnin remembered. Jarl Eirik.

"I don't need any. Do you?" The woman's voice was unmistakable as well—it belonged to the one who had saved him, the one whose eyes cut through him and whose face was the definition of honed beauty, even obscured as it was by dried mud.

"Don't be so hot-headed, sister."

Another man's voice, though Rúnin didn't recognize it.

"Madrena, please. Surely there can be another way," said a second woman who spoke with a strange accent. "Perhaps next year—"

"Nei, Laurel, I am done waiting."

Her name was Madrena. He whispered the word, feeling it on his tongue. He owed her his life—and yet her cool, gray eyes rang a bell of warning in the back of his mind. She was far too keen.

A long silence stretched, but then the quiet night air was filled with the muffled sounds of heavy objects hitting the soft ground. After several thumps and clatters, another quiet fell. Could they be discarding their weapons? But why? Rúnin had seen plenty of combat in his life, but this was different. This was a duel—one on one, Madrena versus her Jarl.

The silence was broken with a woman's angry, wordless shout. Rúnin shot a glance over his shoulder at his sleeping companions. Blessedly, none of them stirred. He stretched onto his toes and gripped the narrow built-in window to steal a glimpse into the dark village.

Through a gap between two huts, Rúnin saw two shadowy figures moving together in combat. One was clearly broader and taller, yet the other, the woman, was fast and light on her feet. *Madrena.* Why would she challenge her Jarl?

Before he could puzzle out the strange event he was witnessing, the man, Jarl Eirik, grunted as Madrena landed a blow to his middle. He stumbled back a few steps and she followed.

She was too eager, Rúnin thought with a frown, too impatient. As she launched forward to land a second blow, the Jarl spun and swept her legs. She toppled to the ground with a grunt but managed to roll out of the way before the Jarl could pin her. She came up on her feet quickly, and the two circled each other silently.

"This is madness." The second woman's mutter drifted to Rúnin, but no one moved to stop the two combatants.

The Jarl seemed to be in no hurry. He evaded several of the woman's feints as she looked for an opening, but he never struck back. Perhaps he was even holding back, but why, Rúnin couldn't parse.

Clearly Madrena withheld naught. After several of her attacks failed, she grew impatient and simply lunged at him, her shoulder lowered. He took the hit to his middle but pivoted with Madrena in his grasp. They both fell to the ground. The Jarl maneuvered so that he landed on top, pinning her.

She flailed, trying to break the man's hold on her. One shadowy arm shot up and caught the Jarl on the chin before he could capture her hands. He grunted as he took the blow but didn't budge. Her legs were still free, and she heaved with all her might, sending a knee into the man's back. He toppled to the side and like lightning she rolled on top of him, her hands going to his throat.

The second woman, who stood to the side with the nameless man, cried out, a hand coming up to cover her mouth. Neither of the two fighters on the ground broke their attention, however.

"Wrong, Madrena," Jarl Eirik croaked on his back. He pried first one and then the other of her hands from his neck. "You always try to match strength with strength."

In a flash, he rolled so that she was sent into the soft wet ground next to him. Before she could regain her feet, he set his knee into her back, pressing her to the ground. He grabbed one of her arms and torqued it. She gave a yelp of surprise and pain.

Rúnin had been put into a hold like that as a boy, back when he'd been training with the other lads to go raiding for his Jarl. If Jarl Eirik's angling grip was similar to what Rúnin had experienced, Madrena would feel like her arm was a hair's breadth from being ripped from its socket. Yet even still, she struggled against the inevitable, likely drawing even more pain upon herself.

Grudging admiration settled into Rúnin's chest despite the fact that the woman had been bested by her own impatience and rashness. Yet she fought on, huffing into the mud even though her Jarl didn't budge.

"Strength alone—or the force of your will and your rage—will not get you what you want," Jarl Eirik went on calmly as Madrena squirmed in the hold.

The Jarl maintained the lock for another long moment, as if making it clear to both Madrena and those who watched that she could not escape it. Then he released her and stood, waiting.

Madrena let out a muffled curse as her body went limp. She lay on the ground, rubbing her shoulder.

"You are not ready to lead your own voyage, Madrena," the Jarl said quietly. "You will not go east this year. I only hope that another winter will give you the time you need to let this plan of yours go."

Rúnin's head spun as he tried to understand this new information. This was clearly some sort of power struggle, but why did the woman want to go east? Why was the Jarl denying her? And what did she need to let go?

If the memory of her flashing gray eyes was any indication, Madrena wouldn't take this defeat well, though he didn't know her well enough to guess at what she'd do. A seed of an idea took hold, but before Rúnin could nurture it, his attention was tugged back to the shadowed figures before him.

Jarl Eirik extended his hand to her. She considered it for a long moment but then slapped it away. Both the woman and the man who had watched the exchange off to the side inhaled.

"Sister, don't—"

"Leave me alone, Alaric!" Madrena snapped, pushing herself to her feet. The Jarl moved away slowly, and Rúnin thought he saw him shaking his head. He guided the second woman toward the longhouse. The man called Alaric stood rooted, watching Madrena. She spun on her heels so that she gave him her back.

Without a word, he stomped off in the opposite direction.

At last, she thought herself alone, unaware of Rúnin's eyes on her. He watched as her shoulders slumped, the fight finally draining from her. He caught a muttered curse, but her voice was thick with emotion and he couldn't make out the words. She bent and slowly collected her weapons, repositioning each on herself deliberately.

She straightened then and stormed around the little clearing she'd just fought in as if trying to decide where to go. At last, she turned toward the smithy. Rúnin had to suppress a grunt of surprise, but there was no way she could have seen him in the dim window slit. She veered to the left, toward one of the shadowed figures of their guard.

"I'll take this watch," Madrena bit out.

"What was all that ab—"

"Don't concern yourself, Svenir," she cut in, her voice rising. "You and Findarr can go home. Alaric and I will cover the smithy."

The guard snorted but didn't press. Instead, he whistled softly. The other guard appeared from the shadows, and the two men moved off toward one of the huts on the far side of the village. The one called Alaric was nowhere in sight, though.

Madrena watched them go silently. At last, when they were long gone, all the tension drained from her body. To Rúnin's shock, he heard a wretched sob and watched as she slumped to the ground.

Rúnin swallowed. Hers were not the tears of physical pain. He doubted a skilled fighter like her succumbed often to such a thing. Nei, her muffled sobs were for some other loss, some deeper frustration.

He tried to block out the heart-wrenching sound and focus on what he had learned. She wanted to go east. She'd been denied by her Jarl and embarrassed in losing their battle. She was vulnerable now, angry and hurt.

Rúnin pushed down the flicker of guilt at the direction of his thoughts. There had been a time in his life when he would never compromise his honor by taking advantage of a woman who suffered—a woman who'd saved his life, no less. But the last fourteen years had beaten, starved, and frozen that honorable impulse out of him. He had to do whatever it took to free himself.

He bent and picked up a pebble from the smithy floor. After checking on the sleeping men behind him once more, he stretched toward the high window and chucked the pebble out. It landed with a soft rustle in the ferns outside the smithy.

It was enough to silence the woman's muffled cries instantly. Rúnin peered out the window, but she must have positioned herself against the smithy's stone walls out of his sight.

Taking a deep breath, he let out a whistle, barely more than a whisper. The village remained silent, as did the interior of the smithy. He risked another whistle, a little louder this time. From what he'd seen of this Madrena woman, she was warrior enough not to mistake the noise for a bird—it was night, after all.

Just as he inhaled and pursed his lips for another soft whistle, the tip of a sword hissed through the narrow window an inch from his eye. He stumbled backward, barely avoiding stepping on the sprawled foot of one of the *Wolf*'s crew. Regaining his balance and suppressing a curse, he eased back toward the window.

"I hear a little bird who is eager to lose his wings." The woman's whisper was only loud enough for his primed ears.

"Or perhaps he has a song for you, one you might enjoy hearing," Rúnin breathed.

"How can a bird in a cage help one who is not?" Her voice was skeptical, but the tip of the sword slid out of the window. He heard the soft rasp of the blade being re-sheathed.

"I saw what just transpired between you and your Jarl."

A tense silence hung in the air and he feared he had misstepped. She was clearly a proud woman. She might choose to kill him for drawing attention to her dishonor rather than hear him out.

"And I heard that you plan to go east," he added, sending up a prayer to any of the gods who'd listen to him.

"If you hear so well, then you know that I was denied the right to go voyaging." The bitterness in her voice was exactly what he needed. Now he just had to strike.

"And you will accept such a thing? Hmph. I had assumed warriors in the west behaved more like those in the east. They don't give up so easily."

"Don't try to manipulate me," she said coldly. Rúnin's stomach sank. He held his breath as he waited, hoping he hadn't gone too far.

"And what do you know of the east?" she asked at last. Rúnin had to clench his teeth to prevent an exhale of relief from sounding.

"I am from there. I grew up in a mountain village far to the northeast in Kvenland. I have traveled those lands extensively over the last several years." It was true enough, of course, but he'd never tell her why he'd been forced to roam the forests and mountains alone all these years.

He could practically hear her heart hitch at his words. He squeezed his eyes shut, willing himself to remain silent as she considered. It didn't matter why she wanted to go east. Whether she wanted to raid, build a name for herself, or simply explore, he'd use her to get out of this forsaken situation.

But he couldn't simply use blunt force, the way he'd seen her try to do against her Jarl. Nei, he'd never be able to force his way out—there were too many men who'd survived the shipwreck who would kill him before letting him escape. And he couldn't overpower all the warriors in this village who would rather keep him locked away until they could decide what to do with the men who'd washed ashore. He had to let her decide.

"You are plotting something," she whispered. "You can either tell me or my Jarl, but either way, you *will* tell."

He swallowed. Whatever he did, he couldn't underestimate her. She was still his best chance of escape, though.

"I want out of here," he hissed. "And you want to go east. I know the lands, and you clearly don't, otherwise you wouldn't be begging your Jarl to let you take a crew with you to go searching for whatever it is you're looking for."

She inhaled sharply but didn't contradict him. He'd guessed right thus far. But he still had to convince her to release him—without any of the crewmen or villagers realizing it.

"If you free me, I will serve as your guide. As I said, I know the land well."

"How do you know that you are familiar with what I seek?" Her voice was still incredulous, but the very fact that she would ask such a question revealed that she was giving his proposition consideration. He only wished he could see her through the narrow slit in the stones above his head. He'd just have to go on instinct in handling her.

"Try me."

She hesitated, seeming to choose her words carefully. So, she hid something as well, he thought with unease. Whatever she'd been fighting about with her Jarl, it was clearly more complicated than simply being granted a raiding expedition.

"I seek a village—a man, more specifically. I don't know his name, but he carries a distinctive tattoo. It is of a bear on his chest."

It was as if the room tilted on its side.

Rúnin leaned against the cold stones as he struggled to breathe. His hand instinctively flew to his chest, where underneath his tattered tunic, the old scar and the underlying marking felt hot and itchy.

He tried to swallow against the dryness in his throat.

"I-I know the man," he breathed at last. His voice sounded strained and distant to his ears. "I can lead you to him."

Another long silence stretched. Desperation surged through him. He prayed that his shock at the mention of the bear tattoo—and her knowledge of the man who bore it—hadn't piqued her suspicion and shredded any hope for this fraught scheme.

"Why are you so eager to escape?" she asked at last. "Are not these men your friends?"

"We both have secrets to keep," Rúnin said lowly. "Do not ask me about why I am with these men, and I'll not question you about why you seek the man with the bear tattoo."

"How do I know I can even trust you?" she whispered.

"You don't."

His heart hammered in his ears as he waited for her reply. He clenched his fists against the cold sweat that had sprung to his palms, willing away the memories of that bear tattoo. It seemed the gods would never let him escape his past, even if they were giving him a slim chance to escape this village and thralldom at Bjorn and the others' hands.

"What do you need?"

He exhaled, and his knees wobbled as relief and hope flooded him. "A new set of clothes and boots. Food. A horse for each of us. And a weapon would be nice."

She snorted softly. "You'll remain unarmed. And I doubt I'll be able to steal two horses."

"An overland journey on foot will take a fortnight—possibly more."

He heard an exhale of frustration on the other side of the stone wall. "Ja, I know. But it must be so."

The ferns rustled almost inaudibly. Rúnin guessed that Madrena had stood and was about to leave.

"I'll see about the rest. I'll be back—or not. You'll have to wait and see."

He would have laughed at her audacity if he hadn't still been wound tight with trepidation over his plan and aching all over from the events of the last day.

The faintest shifting of plants told him she was already moving away. He rose on his toes once more to peer out the window slit and caught sight of her shadowed form as she weaved through the huts. He let himself sink back to the floor, the cold stones at his back.

He'd done what was necessary, as he'd been forced to learn to do over the years. Of course he'd have to escape the woman as soon as they were alone and far enough from the village, but she didn't need to know that.

The thought of her seeking the man with a bear tattoo nearly stole his breath away again. He couldn't let that distract him. He'd lead her into the forest and then disappear. She could either hunt for Bersi on her own, or she could return to her village and do as her Jarl said —drop it, learn patience, and wait.

For some reason, he doubted very much that the woman with flashing gray eyes, the woman who'd taken on her Jarl in a duel, the woman who now plotted to spring a stranger from imprisonment and let him lead her into the wilderness, would back down so easily. Nor would she take Rúnin's betrayal well when it came time to abandon her.

He'd just have to make sure that once he was free of the slavers and this village, she'd never see him again.

His life depended on it.

5

Madrena's mind swirled as she made her way toward the hut she shared with Alaric. She hadn't gotten the opportunity to see the face of the man who'd whispered to her through the smithy's slitted window, but she recognized his voice. She wouldn't soon forget the rough, low timbre of the man whose life she'd saved—the man whose fingertips had felt like they'd left an icy mark on her skin where he'd touched her face.

She hoped she wasn't wrong, for something about the other men caused the hair on the back of her neck to stand on end. The secretive looks they'd exchanged in the longhouse didn't bode well.

There was no time to dwell on such trivialities, though. The man she'd saved needed her help, and she needed his. It could be as simple as that, couldn't it?

She skidded to a halt outside her hut. Was she truly going to trust some shipwrecked outsider whose name she didn't even know to lead her into the eastern wilds?

The way he'd inhaled and fumbled for words when she'd brought up the bear tattoo revealed more than he likely intended. Ja, she believed he knew of the marking, and the man who bore it, which meant he was likely telling the truth about being familiar with the lands to the east. She'd already guessed based on his dark coloring that he wasn't from the western Northlands, so he could be from Kvenland, the mountainous region to the east of which she'd only heard tales.

Her heart thumped loudly in her ears. Could she go through with this? Would she defy Eirik, her friend and Jarl, and set out with a stranger? Would she leave her brother behind without explanation? Would she embark on a lengthy and dangerous overland journey for the slim chance of actually finding the man who'd raped her, thus completing her quest for revenge once and for all?

She rubbed her shoulder, which was still sore from the bind Eirik had put her in. Hot tears of embarrassment and frustration sprang to her eyes once more. Luckily no one was nearby to see her swipe her hand over her cheeks and dash away the tears.

Eirik had proven in front of Alaric and Laurel that she wasn't as capable as she believed herself to be. He thought her too hot-headed, too impatient. But what did he know of the rage that still burned in her belly? What did he know of the pain and fear that had turned into determination and fury over the years? What did he know of the thwarted need to seek vengeance?

She had waited so long already. She'd trained until she bled, until her body ached, until she couldn't lift her sword any longer. This was to be her summer to go searching for the man who'd violated her, who'd stolen her youth and carefree spirit. No one would take that from her.

Yet Madrena hesitated outside the hut. If she were truly committed to this wild scheme, she had to do it right, be careful—else Eirik or her brother try to hamper her once again.

Her mind flew over all that she needed to do in the remaining hours of the night. Since she and Alaric always ate in the longhouse with Laurel and Eirik, they didn't store any food inside their hut. She should gather whatever food she could find in the kitchens at the back of the longhouse, then return to the hut for clothes. That way she'd be able to slip back to the smithy easier and with less chance of being spotted.

As casually as she could, she strode to the longhouse. The village was still, but no doubt some villagers remained awake behind their wooden or mortared walls, chattering about the strange newcomers who'd washed ashore that day.

Once she reached the longhouse, she made her way to the back where the kitchens stood. She listened outside the door for a moment, but all was quiet within. Holding her breath, she eased the door open and slipped inside.

She moved as silently as possible around the kitchen, filling a cloth with the morning's flatbread, some salted fish, small crabapples, and a wedge of cheese. It certainly wouldn't feed them for the entirety of their journey, but she could hunt, and she hoped her guide would know the plant life in those parts—if he truly knew them as he said he did.

Just as she was tying the ends of the cloth together to make a satchel of food, she heard voices coming from the longhouse and froze. She instantly recognized her twin brother's voice.

"...if they had been on their way to attack us."

"'Tis possible. That would explain their evasiveness," Eirik responded.

"Or mayhap they truly were just the unlucky victims of Aegir and Thor's wrath."

Eirik grunted in response to Alaric's suggestion, and Madrena could imagine that he was raising an eyebrow at her brother on the other side of the wall separating the longhouse from the kitchens.

"It may have been happenstance that washed them to Dalgaard's shores, but I don't believe for a second that they are innocent in this. Did you see the looks they were giving each other?"

"Ja," Alaric replied. "They seem to be hiding something. They likely fear that you will sell them as thralls in Jutland. They are strangers, after all, and they don't know your ways."

Madrena absorbed her brother's words. Most Jarls in the Northlands wouldn't have qualms about selling outsiders into slavery—after all, strong, able-bodied Northmen fetched a high price in Jutland. But the men who'd washed ashore didn't know that Eirik reviled the practice of slavery. Was that why the man she'd saved was so eager to escape? Did he believe he'd be sold as a thrall in Jutland?

That couldn't be all of it, though, for the looks that the others had shot at him spoke of some darker secret. She pushed the puzzle aside for the moment.

"Often, men's fears of what will be done to them reflect what they'd do to others, given the chance," Eirik said, his voice distant in thought. "Perhaps they are slavers themselves. That would explain their secretiveness. They don't want to lose their profit."

"Whatever the case, we can't keep them in the smithy forever," Alaric said. "What do you plan to do?"

Madrena heard Eirik sigh. "I don't know. I suppose I'll have to release them in the morning, though I don't want them lingering on my land."

Madrena's stomach clenched. If Eirik freed the shipwrecked men and made sure they didn't linger near Dalgaard, she'd lose her last chance to go east. Though she hated to admit it, she needed a guide, and that meant trusting—and freeing—her nameless ally. Time was running out.

Just as she rested her hand against the thick wooden door leading outside, Eirik's voice froze her.

"And what of your sister?"

Alaric's sigh was almost completely muffled by the wall, yet Madrena could hear the sadness in it nevertheless.

"She'll need some time to cool down."

"And then?" Now it was Eirik's turn to sigh. "You know her better than anyone. Was I wrong to challenge her?"

A long pause stretched.

"I don't know, honestly," Alaric said. "Madrena has always been stubborn, but you know as well as I that this is different. You were right to point out to her that her plan isn't sound. But it might not matter what either of us says or does."

"I only wish she could find peace."

The last was spoken so low that Madrena had to strain to hear it. Unbidden tears of frustration sprung to her eyes. Ja, somewhere deep inside her heart, she knew Eirik and Alaric only wanted to help. But she had sworn to herself and the gods not to rest until she exacted

Shieldmaiden's Revenge

revenge. An oath was not something she took lightly. It didn't matter that her friend and brother were trying to look out for her. She *had* to do this.

Forcing her feet to move, she slipped silently from the kitchens and crept through the shadows back to her hut. Once she was inside, she let herself ease the knot in her stomach with a few deep breaths. Now was the time for action, not brooding and tears.

She stoked the fire to have enough light by which to work. Then there was naught left to do but hurriedly pack.

Madrena threw the satchel of food, along with a waterskin and an extra shift and overdress, into a leather bag. Rummaging through the wooden trunk at the foot of her cot, she withdrew a curved fire-steel and flint stone, a bone and horsehair comb, and a few other small items to add to the bag.

She realized suddenly that she still wore her mud-covered sparring clothes, so she quickly stripped and changed into a clean linen underdress and woolen overdress, dry boots, and a fur-trimmed cloak. She didn't have time to wash the dried mud from her hair and face, so she ignored the crusty feeling and turned her attention to more important matters—her weapons.

Once she'd refastened her sword and axe to her belt and the seax to her boot, she tucked away a few more small blades for extra measure. She also snatched her hunting bow and quiver from the corner and slung them over her shoulder.

Then she had to turn to Alaric's things. He had a mattress and trunk of clothes and weapons in an added room at the back of the hut. In the low light, she rummaged through his trunk, suppressing the guilt at stealing from her brother. She found a tunic and trousers she hoped would fit the shipwrecked stranger, then grabbed a pair of Alaric's fur-lined boots and a thick woolen cloak near the door.

Madrena normally wasn't one for sentiment, but she spared a brief glance around the hut. Would it be the last time she saw this simple home? If she failed, ja, it would be.

With the bow, quiver, and leather bag over her shoulder and her arms full of Alaric's clothes, she eased out the wooden door. She kept to the shadows between huts as she made her way as quietly as possible back to the smithy.

Once there, she dropped Alaric's clothes in a heap and drew her seax. She crept toward the window through which the man had spoken to her and pursed her lips. Imitating his earlier bird call, she whistled softly.

An answering whistle sounded almost inaudibly from within. She snuck toward the smithy door, seax ready in case this was some sort of ambush.

As she swung the door open, the hinges squeaked, breaking the otherwise silent night. She froze, holding her breath and listening to hear if anyone from the village had noticed. After a stretching silence, she exhaled and cracked the door the rest of the way open.

A tall shadow loomed before her in the doorway. She took a step back, seax at the ready. Slowly, the man she'd dragged from the water emerged, hands raised to indicate that he wasn't going to attack.

Seeing him upright and moving under his own power, however, she didn't believe for a second that he wasn't a threat. He was as tall and broad as any warrior.

Shieldmaiden's Revenge

The darkness obscured his face, but his cold blue eyes flashed in the light of the half-moon breaking through the clouds overhead.

What had she gotten herself into?

She pushed her fear away, reminding herself that she could handle this sea-tossed, weaponless man.

"You're sure you want to leave your…friends?" she said, flicking her gaze to the men sleeping on the smithy floor through the open door behind him.

The man quickly closed the door behind him, and this time, the hinges were blessedly silent.

"They're not my friends," he said curtly in that low, rough voice. "Are *you* sure you want to do this?"

She bristled. "I'm here, aren't I?" She motioned with the tip of the seax to the pile of clothes not far off. "Get changed. We won't have much time until someone comes to relieve me of my guard."

The man moved past her toward Alaric's clothes. He positioned himself so that his back was to her and tugged off his tattered tunic.

Moonlight caught on more than a dozen crisscrossed white scars on his back. Those weren't from a battle, she realized. He'd been flogged, and hard enough to leave scars.

"What is your name?" she whispered, eyeing his broad back, the muscles dancing in the moonlight and casting shadows.

He glanced over his shoulder as he put his arms through the new tunic. "Rúnin."

She turned away as he pulled off his worn boots in preparation to change his trousers.

"And you are Madrena," he said softly over the rustle of fabric.

"Ja. That's all you need to know for now."

He grunted in response, but it sounded like it was more from pain than assent. She turned around and watched as he finished pulling on Alaric's boots and settled the cloak around his shoulders.

The clothes were a good fit, though Rúnin was slightly taller than Alaric. The tunic stretched over Rúnin's broad chest and shoulders, with the trousers fitting snugly on his lean hips. The cloak hung a few inches above the ground, but that would actually be better if they were caught in snowy conditions. Winter was still far off, though—or so Madrena prayed.

Rúnin balled up his worn, threadbare clothes and boots and tucked them inside a hollowed-out fallen log nearby. Clearly he hoped to buy them as much time as possible by obscuring their escape.

Uneasiness flitted through her stomach, but she wanted the same thing, strangely. It was odd to work with this stranger toward the same purposes, yet hide from each other their real reasons for doing so. There was no need for this man, this *Rúnin*, to know why Madrena wanted to go east. And as long as he held up his end of the bargain, he could keep his secrets as well.

"Let's go," he whispered.

She nodded curtly, though she waited for him to come even with her instead of turning her back on him to lead the way. She could only hope that her instincts to trust him weren't off.

Madrena re-sheathed her seax in her boot and they moved side by side in the shadows of the other buildings around the smithy. When they had cleared the last of the huts, she paused and turned to him.

"We'll have to cut south briefly to avoid the rocky

crags walling in the village," she said lowly. "Then we can turn—"

A flicker of movement in the side of her vision had her whipping her head around. She inhaled sharply as a shadow stepped out from behind a large tree on the outskirts of the village. Her sword was half out of its scabbard before she recognized her brother's golden head and glowing green eyes in the moonlight.

"What in Odin's name are you doing, sneaking up like that, Alaric?" she hissed.

"You're asking *me* what I am doing?" he shot back, his eyes sliding over her to where Rúnin stood to the side. Her brother had his sword fisted in his grasp as well. "What are you thinking?"

She intentionally dropped her hand from her weapon and stepped toward Alaric to create space away from Rúnin. Alaric positioned himself so that he had a direct line of sight to the man. Rúnin said naught, but Madrena could feel his eyes on her back.

"I'm leaving," she said quietly to Alaric. "This man says he knows of the one I seek. He is going to be my guide."

"*Are you mad?*" Alaric forced himself to lower his voice. "You don't even know him, Madrena. He's probably lying—he just wants to escape."

Madrena looked over her shoulder at Rúnin. He stood stiffly, his eyes hard and honed on them. She was taking the biggest risk of her life in trusting him. But she couldn't doubt herself now. She turned back to her brother.

"I need to do this, Alaric. I'm going."

"Madrena, this is insane—"

"I'm doing this, brother!" she snapped, though her

voice sounded more desperate than angry to her ears. She took a deep breath, racking her mind for a way to make her brother understand. She gripped his arms, locking eyes with him. "Do you remember that day five years ago?"

Alaric's face hardened and he nodded.

"Do you understand why I need to have my revenge?"

Her brother searched her face. "Eirik is right, sister. Revenge won't end your pain. It won't undo what happened."

"Then let me find my own way! You and Eirik have tried to protect me for too long. Let me do this on my own."

He stepped back, his gaze pinning her. His eyes, normally vivid emerald, were now as dark as the forest surrounding them. If there was anyone in all the world who knew her heart, it was her twin brother. Taking a chance, she dropped the hard flatness of a warrior she'd worked so long to develop from her features. She let her pain, her desperation, and her determination flash in her eyes, trying to communicate all that roiled within her to Alaric.

As if mirroring her, his eyes flared with sadness for the briefest of moments.

"Go," he said at last, breaking their stare.

Her heart surged to her throat. He clearly didn't approve, but he would not try to convince her to simply give up on her need for vengeance. Perhaps he understood at last.

"And what of Eirik?"

"I'll tell him you left, that you needed to be alone. I'll do my best to convince him not to go after you when he learns you've disobeyed him, and freed this man to boot."

"Thank you," she breathed, emotion tightening her voice.

Again, Alaric's eyes flickered to Rúnin. "If you hurt her, I'll kill you," he said simply. "Or more likely, *she'll* kill you."

Before Madrena could find the words to thank her brother again, he drew her into a hard embrace.

"I hope you find what you're looking for," he whispered before letting her go. Without another word, Alaric turned and strode toward the village, melting into the shadows.

She swallowed back the thickness clogging her throat at her brother's words and actions. She sent up a prayer for Alaric's protection, then turned to Rúnin.

His eyes penetrated her in the low light, seeming to glow vivid blue. She'd made her decision. Her fate now rested with the gods—and with Rúnin.

6

"What were you going to do in Jutland?"

This was Madrena's third approach in drawing information out of him. First she'd tried demanding, then she'd threatened him, but they both knew that she needed him if she hoped to traverse the mountains and rivers of Kvenland. Now she'd moved on to apparently innocent questions.

"Trade," Rúnin replied tersely.

She huffed next to him. "Obviously. But trade of what?"

"Goods."

Madrena made another little noise of frustration but dropped that line of questioning.

Silence settled between them as they continued to walk. They still had perhaps another hour of darkness before the sun rose, but they didn't have to discuss whether or not they would continue or break for a rest. Both of them had their own reasons for wanting to put as much distance as possible between themselves and the village—though like Rúnin, Madrena didn't seem particularly interested in sharing her reasons.

"What of Kvenland? You said you were from there."

She formed the name of his homeland hesitantly, as if she were somewhat unfamiliar with it.

"What do you know of the region?"

He felt her eyes on him and realized she was shooting him a glare.

"Answering a question with a question," she muttered. After a pause, she seemed to decide to play along, though.

"I know it is to the northeast of Dalgaard, though a mountain range separates the two."

He nodded. "And a vast gulf as well—the Gulf of Bothnia." At Madrena's little intake of breath, he added, "But the gulf can be skirted to the north with a few days' extra journey."

"What is your land like?"

Rúnin felt the old, dull ache rise from his belly to his chest.

Kvenland—its thick forests, flowing water, and snow-capped mountains.

Seterfell, his old village tucked away in the foothills, a place that had once been safe and quiet.

Aeleif, his mother, brushing the hair from his eyes, blinking back tears of sorrow after his father was slain.

He willed the memories away and forced his mind to return to the here and now.

"Kvenland is beautiful country," he said. "It does not lie so close to the open seas as your lands in the southwest, but we have the Gulf of Bothnia, perfect for fishing, voyaging—"

"And raiding," she cut in. Her voice had an edge, despite her attempt to sound flat.

"Ja, raiding as well," he said, eyeing her out of the corner of his vision. She kept her attention on the woods in front of them, but she held her shoulders rigidly.

"Much like Dalgaard, I'm sure," he said casually. When she didn't take his bait, he went on, more directly. "I'm surprised you aren't more familiar with the lands to the east. Surely your village's warriors go a-viking for your Jarl."

"We sail to the *west*." Her voice swelled with unmistakable pride at that.

He was glad for the darkness, for his eyebrows shot up involuntarily. As isolated as he'd been these last years, even he had heard the rumors about the lands to the west—a dangerous oversea voyage, but lands filled with unguarded riches and lush farmlands waited at the end.

"You've seen the lands to the west?"

"Ja. I will likely go again next raiding season, if—"

Madrena faltered, and he didn't have to ask why. She had defied her Jarl to set out with him to the east. She'd only be granted the right to go raiding *if* Jarl Eirik decided to forgive her. And *if* she survived this journey.

She cleared her throat and tried to recover her line of questioning. "Are there many villages in Kvenland?"

"Not so many. The land and the living to be wrought from it are hard." Rúnin thought back to all the freezing nights he'd spent on his own without the vital protection and shelter to be had in a village. Even those who hadn't been banished from society were molded into hard, stalwart people in the Northlands.

"And your village? What of it?"

Shieldmaiden's Revenge

His mind again flew to Seterfell.

"I left a long time ago." His voice sounded harsh, but he needed to put an end to these incessant questions.

A long silence stretched in which they both focused on weaving through the trees and finding safe footing in the dark. Now that they'd cleared the towering, rocky crags that walled in Dalgaard, they were heading roughly northeast, inland to the dense forests of the heart of the Northlands.

"You said those men weren't your friends," she said at last, trying a new tack.

Rúnin merely grunted in response. By Odin, she was persistent.

"Why were you traveling with them, then? Why did you want to get away so badly?"

"I could put the same question to you, girl."

"I'm not a girl," she snapped.

He snorted noncommittally again. Nei, she wasn't a girl. She was woman enough that he'd mistaken her for Freyja, an error which still rankled. Not because she wasn't fair enough to be compared to a goddess, he admitted grudgingly, but because he'd made a fool of himself, shown his vulnerability. In the face of her haunting eyes, curved pink lips, and smooth, pale skin, he'd forgotten for a moment that he could never let his guard down. He could never trust anyone—his life depended on it.

After another pause, he sensed her gaze on him in the dark. Those eyes were too sharp and canny by half.

"I suppose I don't need your version of who you are or what happened. I've pieced things together well enough."

He glanced sideways at her. Her voice had been

light, but her eyes lingered on him, nigh colorless and unreadable in the dark. What did she think she knew?

"Go ahead then," he said brusquely.

"You say you and those men were traveling to Jutland, but you and the others were cagey when my Jarl asked you why. I assume that means you were either lying or that you don't want anyone to know what you were trading."

Rúnin suppressed a curse. Apparently he hadn't been as evasive as he'd hoped.

"You are clearly guarding your information, which leads me to wonder what else you are guarding," she went on. "Perhaps you think that if my Jarl knew what you planned to trade, he'd take it from you. But whatever cargo you had sank along with your ship, so I can only assume that you are protecting the source of your trade, hoping to be able to return to wherever you came from and gather more. Is that why you are so eager to lead me to Kvenland?"

He didn't answer, but she didn't wait for him to. "Or perhaps what you trade wasn't lost in the shipwreck after all. A slaver ship's cargo is men—and several men washed ashore, including you."

She was getting too close to the truth. But he feared that if he tried to guide her away from it with another lie, she'd sense that he was protecting something. He was out of practice in lying—'twas safer to avoid people altogether.

He forced his aching body to relax, keeping his face a mask of neutrality even though the darkness gave him a modicum of protection. The silence stretched, with only the rustle of ferns underfoot to break it.

"We have a long journey ahead of us," Madrena said at last. "I *will* have answers."

She was back to her hard-edged warrior's approach. He almost smiled, thinking back to the memory of her charging her Jarl, taking him down despite his superior height, weight, and skill.

The admiration for her determination faded as he considered the threat she posed. She was relentless. And even though he planned to leave her at the first opportunity, he faltered at the thought of the hours ahead, with her questioning and prodding, demanding, and cajoling information out of him.

Perhaps if he gave her a crumb, she would be satisfied long enough to drop the questioning—and long enough for him to slip away. Besides, he needed her to trust him enough to turn her back on him. He could sense her growing agitation at his evasiveness. Those cold, colorless eyes would likely follow him the way an eagle tracked its prey if he didn't put her more at ease soon.

"As I said, I wasn't connected to those men," he said. "But you are right—they are slavers. I joined them when they came through the northeast looking for thralls to sell in Jutland. They needed crewmen, so I went along."

Not the truth, but not a full-blown lie, either. The captain and his second in command, Bjorn, had needed more oarsmen, and they were willing to force him into their service. But when Rúnin resisted and they saw the marking on his chest in the fray, they realized his true value to them was as a thrall to be sold for coin. He gritted his teeth against the memory of the beating they'd had to give him to subdue him.

"And the ropes on your wrists when I pulled you from the sea?"

Rúnin swallowed hard. He'd forgotten in his half-conscious state when she'd dragged him ashore that she'd seen the ropes. "I…I wanted off the ship, so they lashed me to my oar." That was a plausible explanation. He only hoped that she hadn't noticed his falter.

He felt her cool eyes on him once more. "You tried to rebel against your position as oarsman and leave the ship?" She snorted in disdain. "You're a deserter then. I suppose that explains why you wanted to get away from your crewmates."

His stomach twisted. He hated the lies, hated spinning a story to this honor-bound warrior that he was a coward, a man who would flee hard work, but it was necessary. If she found out the truth, her disdain would be the least of his problems.

"As I said, those men didn't consider me a friend."

"And that also explains the looks I saw them give you in the longhouse."

Of course she would notice Bjorn's threatening glances. He nodded, unable to form another lie.

"And what of you?" he said at last, racking his mind for a way to divert her attention away from him. He still needed to put her more at ease with him, and telling her he was a coward and a deserter wasn't exactly ideal. Perhaps if he could draw her out, she'd grow more trusting of him.

"That man on the outskirts of the village—that was your brother, ja?"

"Ja. He…he is my twin."

At the tightness in her voice, he softened his tone. "You two must care a great deal for each other."

He glanced sideways and saw her throat bob delicately in the light of the moon. She only nodded, so he was forced to search his mind for more to say.

"He doesn't approve of your desire to go east. Why?"

Was that color rising to her cheeks or just a trick of the clouds scuttling across the moon? Perhaps he had pushed her too far.

"That's none of your concern," she said flatly. He silently cursed himself for another failed thread of conversation. As a tense silence descended, he latched on to the memory of her shadowy figure sparring with her Jarl.

"Like me, you don't seem to mind defying those above you in station."

He regretted the words even before he sensed her stiffen at his side. By the gods, he was out of practice holding conversation with people. Fourteen years wandering alone in the wilderness would do that to a man.

"What I mean is, your Jarl seems like a good man. But you clearly had some misunderstanding with him."

"Eirik *is* a good man," she muttered, though her anger didn't seem to be directed at him for the moment. She brushed aside a tree branch with more force than necessary and it almost swatted Rúnin in the face, but she didn't notice.

Damn, he couldn't seem to form a single useful thing to say. "You fought well. You must have had a shieldmaiden for a mother," he rummaged at last.

"I've only been training for the last five years."

Rúnin halted abruptly with genuine surprise. "Truly?" From what he had seen, she must be an incredibly fast learner, for at several points she had nearly bested her Jarl, who had no doubt been training since he could toddle. "Why did you begin so late?"

Again, he must have misstepped, for she fell silent for a tense moment. "I had my reasons."

He had to break into a trot to catch up to her long strides. "As you said, we have a long journey ahead of us. Perhaps by the end we both won't have so many secrets."

It was another lie, for he would begin looking for an opportunity to abandon her and resume his travels alone in an hour or two. But an easier silence settled between them as they continued trekking through the night-darkened forest. Something about the idea of getting to know this hard, mysterious woman better sent an unfamiliar stirring in his chest.

~

As the thin, yellow rays of the fall sun touched the tops of the trees overhead, Madrena halted and turned to him.

"We'd better stop to rest. Just for a few hours."

Her pale eyes raked over him, and though his clothes were clean and new, he imagined that he looked bedraggled. After the captain and Bjorn, along with their men, had taken him more than a fortnight ago, he hadn't had an opportunity to bathe or shave the dark beard that now covered his face. He also hadn't slept in almost two days and had eaten barely more than a crust of bread in as much time.

He'd hoped to slip away before letting himself succumb to the vulnerability of sleeping in the presence of another person, but his body screamed at him that he needed rest.

"Very well," he said, motioning for her to take the lead in picking a safe spot.

It was his first real opportunity to scrutinize her in daylight and with a clear head. His memories of being dragged from the water and led into her village's longhouse were fuzzy. Her gray, nigh colorless eyes were the only things that had made an impression through his pain-hazed mind. Then they'd both been shrouded in darkness as they traveled. But as she strode past him and scanned the forest for a resting place, he let his eyes roam over her.

She was tall, even compared to other Northwomen. The top of her head would come up to his chin if they stood face to face. Her limbs were long and lithe, but not girlish. Nei, she was a woman, though her training had likely made her more firm than soft. Still, she wore a dress that revealed a narrow waste, the delicate curve of her hips, and the swell of modest breasts.

She moved gracefully, though the ease of her movements belied her obvious lethality. He'd seen her fight. He knew that she was capable of holding her own.

As she walked, the hilt of her sword poked out from her cloak. It was strapped to her right hip, which meant that she must favor her left hand, at least for sword combat. It likely gave her an advantage against her opponents since left-handedness was unusual. But then again, she was already unusual—a shieldmaiden whose delicate beauty masked fierce strength.

She turned back to him, and he had to quickly avert his eyes to avoid betraying the fact that he'd been staring.

"Let's head up this ridge and see if we can find some water," she said.

Her face and hair still had dried mud on them, as they had the day before when he'd first opened his eyes and seen her looking down on him. Her hair was light in color, but it was hard to tell the exact shade through the mud. Her eyes, so sharp and hard to read, pierced him.

He nodded curtly, hoping she hadn't noticed him assessing her. With another wave of his hand to indicate that she lead the way, he followed her up a steeply sloping hill to their right.

Once they reached the top, the sound of running water drew them to the east side of the ridge. A little creek wound down from the ridge's peak. They followed it downhill to the point where it flowed into a still, clear pond. The pond's narrow, rocky shoreline broke the sea of trees all around them.

"We'll rest here," Madrena declared.

After they both cupped their hands in the cold stream where it met the pond and drank their fill of water, they hunkered down in the dew-damp ferns just inside the tree line. Rúnin wrapped the thick wool cloak Madrena had procured for him tightly around his shoulders. He forced his eyes to stay open as she settled into the ferns a few paces away from him. He bit the tip of his tongue to stay awake until he heard the sound of her even breathing. At last, he let himself relax, and he fell into a deep sleep.

It wasn't until Madrena screamed that he was yanked from sleep's embrace.

7

"Nei!"

The shadow loomed over her, growing ever larger. Madrena tried to scream for help, but it sounded as though she were underwater.

Her skull vibrated as her head connected with the wood of the table, sending dull pain through her. The shadow pushed her back down against the table despite her struggles.

Wake up.

Her hands clawed wildly even as the shadow wedged her legs open. Her nails found purchase on his shirt. Fabric ripped, but she couldn't tell if it was the man's tunic or her skirts as he yanked up her dress.

The shadow's shirt fell away in shreds and her eyes locked on the bear marking. The tattoo sat on the man's barrel chest, right above his heart.

Wake up.

Blinding pain stabbed between her legs. She screamed and clawed, but the bear hovered near her face, filling her vision. Its mouth gaped with sharp teeth as the shadow moved over her.

"Madrena, wake up!"

A set of large hands was gripping her shoulders, shaking her.

With another scream of rage, she pulled her seax smoothly from her boot, feeling the comforting weight and coolness of it in her hand. As she blinked her eyes open, she pressed the blade against her attacker's throat. Eyes blurred with sleep, her heart hammered at the sight of an indistinct figure looming over her, squeezing her shoulders.

But it was daytime, and her nightmares were always shrouded in darkness. And she didn't lie on the wooden table in the hut she shared with her brother. Instead, she was gazing up at the undersides of towering trees.

The hands on her shoulders eased, but she kept her seax trained against the skin of the figure's neck.

"Madrena, it is Rúnin."

His low, raspy voice brought her careening back to reality. She blinked again, her eyes clearing at last. He slowly leaned back until he rested on his heels, hands raised in the air as he had done the previous night when she'd freed him from the smithy.

She glanced around quickly before re-sheathing her seax. "Sorry."

She felt the weight of his bright, sharp eyes on her and her cheeks grew hot.

"What was that about?" he said levelly.

"Just a nightmare." She shoved down the lingering panic from the dream, along with the embarrassment of having a stranger witness the terrors that still stole over her sometimes, hoping he would accept her casual tone.

Shieldmaiden's Revenge

"It happens." He shrugged, but his eyes remained riveted on her. She jerked her head toward him. Was he going to press her? Did he think she was mad?

A fleeting look crossed his blue eyes, as if he, too, had been haunted by night terrors. He broke their stare and stood before she could be sure of what she saw, though.

"If you'll allow the delay, I'd like to eat and bathe before we continue on," he said, motioning behind him to the pond. "I don't mind going out to hunt something up, but I'll need a weapon."

She stilled, considering. It was only natural that they would have to hunt on this journey, and that he would need a weapon if he was going to help her in the task. But she wasn't sure yet about arming him while diminishing her own weapons. Perhaps she was being overly cautious, but she wasn't quite ready to trust him with her hunting bow and quiver.

"We have enough food for now," she said, eyeing him carefully. "But I could use a bath as well."

She tilted her head back to assess the sun. It was a stunning fall morning, with only a few wispy white clouds overhead. Judging by the sun's slant, they had slept for a few hours—enough to take the edge of exhaustion from her mind and body.

"We can stay for another hour," she said, returning her gaze to him to assess his reaction.

He only bobbed his dark head and sat down a few feet away from her. She reached for the leather bag she'd deposited next to her before she'd fallen asleep and dug for the parcel of food. As she unwrapped the bundle carefully, she glanced up to find Rúnin's eyes riveted on the food. He looked half-starved. She tossed him half of one of the flatbread loaves and he set into it like a semi-wild animal.

Madrena watched for a long moment, trying to understand what his hunger meant. Her belly was empty as well, but she could control herself enough to eat slowly.

Something still bothered her about Rúnin, though he'd explained why the other men who'd washed ashore with him treated him like an outsider. Something about the ropes on his wrists, the long-ago healed flog marks on his back, his ravenous hunger…

She would do well to keep an eye on him. He could have hurt her while she slept, or tried to disarm her, though she'd trained herself to wake quickly whenever she felt her weapons shift. But he hadn't. Instead, he'd shaken her awake, breaking her free from her nightmare. Again, something didn't fit about him.

She ate in silence, occasionally tossing him more food. He devoured everything she gave him, and she imagined he would have eaten every last crumb in the folded cloth if she had allowed it. As it was, they had to make the food last, so she reluctantly packed it away.

"Would you like to bathe first, or should I?" he said at last, watching her as she set the bag aside.

"You go ahead. I'll fill our waterskin and look for some berries."

He stood but hesitated before turning to the water. "I'd like to rid myself of this beard. Can I borrow your seax?"

She felt one of her eyebrows rise involuntarily. Was he trying another angle to get his hands on one of her weapons, or did he simply want to shave, as he said?

Slowly, she lifted the hem of her dress and drew it up to reveal the bare skin above her boots.

His gaze darted down to her exposed flesh, his eyes widening in confusion until her hem was high enough to reveal a small blade strapped to the outside of her left thigh.

She mentally tucked away the realization that there had been a look of hunger—hunger of a different sort than that for food—in his blue eyes as he'd beheld her lithe leg. She was unpracticed in the ways of using her body against men—unless it came to besting them with sword and shield. Though she was no green maiden, his unguarded reaction to her sent a strange flutter in her stomach, similar to the one she'd experienced when he'd brushed her lip with his thumb and called her Freyja.

The flat look quickly returned to his hard features, though. The fact that he didn't try to advance on her or insinuate something sensual actually put her more at ease.

"You can have this," she said, unsheathing the tiny dagger from her thigh. The blade was no longer than her little finger. It would be enough to allow him to shave, but he'd be hard pressed to break skin with the thing.

Now it was his turn to raise an eyebrow at her. "Thank you," he said dryly.

She tossed him the dagger, and without taking his eyes from her, he snatched it from the air. Then he tipped it at her in a little salute and sauntered off to the pond's waterline.

Leaving the bag and her bow and quiver where they'd slept, she moved parallel to the pond, keeping her eyes on Rúnin while also sparing a glance for cloudberries in the underbrush. 'Twas late in the season for the little berries, but soon enough, Madrena's eyes lit upon the distinctive little flashes of orange-red dotting the bushes.

As she plucked a berry from its stem, her eyes fell on Rúnin again. He was at the shoreline a stone's throw away from her with his back turned. He'd already discarded his cloak and was now peeling off his tunic. In the slanting light of midmorning, the white scars on his back were even more visible.

Madrena absently placed a cloudberry on her tongue and let the sweet juice explode in her mouth. If she had been in Dalgaard, she would have dumped the berries into a pot of cream, letting the fruit tinge the cream with its tanginess and the cream suffuse the berries with smooth richness. The pure indulgence of such a treat collided in her mind with the image of Rúnin's hard, honed body before her.

The thought caught her off guard and she told herself to stop staring at her mysterious guide, but her eyes had a will of their own. Rúnin's back and shoulder muscles danced as he tossed the tunic aside. He was lean but still well built, with broad shoulders that tapered into a narrow waist.

He drew off his boots and she watched as his back rippled. Then his hands were working the ties on his trousers and a second later, the smooth, somewhat paler skin of his buttocks was exposed.

With her eyes riveted on his hard form, she popped another berry into her mouth. This one was tarter than the last, though she hardly noticed. Even from this distance, she could see slight discoloration on his thighs and ribs where he'd likely been battered in the shipwreck. Despite the bruises, he glided smoothly into the water, his flanks flexing as he walked. He carried himself like a warrior, yet he'd only mentioned being a sailor—or at least an oarsman. Rowing a longship would give a man muscles like that, but it didn't explain the deadly grace of his movements.

When the water lapped around his waist, he dove all the way in with a splash. His water-slicked head re-emerged, his dark hair dripping around his shoulders.

Just then, he partially turned toward her and she jumped in surprise. He'd caught her staring at him while he bathed.

Heat flooded her face and she cursed herself. Who was she to be blushing over a man like a silly maiden? If she wanted to look, she'd damn well look. She held her ground, forcing her feet to stay rooted in place and her eyes to remain locked on him. As casually as she could, she tossed another berry into her mouth.

He considered her for a long moment, his clear blue eyes cutting into her even from a distance. Then he chuckled, the sound drifting over the water to her burning ears. At last he freed her, breaking their gaze to dunk his head underwater once more.

While he was underwater, she hurried back toward her bag, bow, and quiver. Her earlier boldness fleeing, she made haste deeper into the forest. She didn't want to meet his teasing gaze when he stepped from the pond in a few moments—or worse, not be able to look him in the eye at all if he strode toward her naked and dripping wet.

She'd been training with the men of Dalgaard long enough to have seen it all, but Rúnin's presence was having a strange effect on her. She felt more acutely aware of his body than any man she'd encountered before.

Mayhap it was because he'd touched her as no man ever had. As his thumb had brushed her lip, he'd been captivated by a dumbfounded awe at her beauty. The lads in the village she'd dallied with all treated her as one of them—like a mate, not a vision of the goddess Freyja.

Whatever the reason, the last thing she needed was to be distracted by his lean, hard physique instead of focusing on her mission, she told herself firmly.

By the time she returned to the pond's edge, she'd collected two handfuls more of cloudberries and had cooled her heated cheeks enough to face Rúnin again.

He sat on a rock with the sleeves of his tunic rolled up, grazing the blade she'd given him along the underside of his chin. At the sound of her approach, he turned and she started yet again. He was almost done shaving the dark beard that had covered half his face, and she finally got a look at him.

His jawline was hard and firm, yet his mouth was surprisingly soft, relaxed as he was. He looked younger without the beard, though she guessed that he was still several years older than she—closer to Eirik in age. Although the beard had hidden his face, giving him an air of mystery, now that it was gone he looked harder, the cut lines of his jaw combining with his bright blue eyes to sharpen his features.

Blessedly, he made no mention of her earlier brazenness when she reached his side. She unceremoniously dumped one of her handfuls of berries on a rock near him as he finished shaving.

"Pleasant view, isn't it?" he said at last, his eyes on the pond.

She whipped her head to him and saw a quirk around his lips. Was he teasing her after all, or was he innocently referring to the pond?

"It is like most views in these parts," she said casually. If he was teasing her, then he could take her barb for it.

He didn't respond and instead stood from his rock and strode to the pond's edge, cupping water to splash on his relatively smooth face. The dagger wasn't sharp enough to give him a proper shave, and a shadow of dark bristle still peppered his cheeks and jaw.

When he turned back to her, he had the little dagger extended toward her, hilt first.

"Thank you," he said.

She shrugged and took back the blade, suddenly uncomfortable in his presence once again. His eyes seemed brighter, clearer now that he'd eaten, rested, and cleaned himself up.

He sat on his rock once more and went about eating the cloudberries she'd given him one at a time, savoring them. All at once she realized that he was waiting—waiting for her to strip and bathe as well. Would he sit there watching her as brazenly as she had watched him? The thought sent her insides spinning with a strange mix of embarrassment and anticipation.

She stood, dropping her bag and then removing her cloak. She deposited her bow and quiver on top of the cloak, followed by her belt with her sword and axe. She could feel Rúnin's eyes on her, but he remained silent.

As she pulled off her boots along with her seax, she

dared a glance his way. He was watching her, eating his cursed cloudberries with an expressionless face.

Just as she'd seen everything the warriors of Dalgaard had under their tunics and trousers, they'd seen everything under her dress as well. She thought herself long cured of modesty, for all the warriors would swim in the fjord after training on the practice fields, women and men alike.

She thought of all the men in Dalgaard like her brothers. But Rúnin didn't seem brotherly at all. For some reason, his cool, penetrating eyes set her nerves on end.

"Still enjoying the view?" she asked tartly.

His mouth twitched again, though it could have simply been from a sour berry. But at last he stood and ambled away from the pond.

"Don't go far," she said to his back. By Thor, she was acting like a silly girl, blushing and feeling modest, telling him to stop staring at her and then ordering him to stay close. But she couldn't have her guide wandering off. She trusted herself to find her way back to Dalgaard from here if she needed to, but she'd be at a loss if she continued further east without Rúnin.

Cursing herself quietly, she yanked off first her over-dress and then her shift. With the cool fall air teasing her heated skin, she made quick work unfastening the small sheath on her thigh then hurriedly waded into the pond.

The water was surprisingly cold, but then again, they were headed into mountainous terrain and fall was well upon them. The leaves on the birch trees lining the pond were already vibrant yellow.

Once she was in past her thighs, Madrena quickly dunked her head and scrubbed her fingers through her hair underwater. As she came up for air, she rubbed the last of the day-old mud from her face. It felt like a lifetime ago that she had been sparring with Alaric, rolling in the mud and teasing him about being the better warrior. Her heart tugged west toward Dalgaard.

This was the farthest she'd ever been from her twin. Of course she'd been outside of Dalgaard many times—most recently she'd gone as far as the lands to the west with Eirik and Alaric, the land from which Laurel hailed. But without the safe familiarity of being near her brother or friends, the world felt crisper somehow, the colors more vivid, her awareness heightened.

Or perhaps her senses were sharper because she was traveling alone with a secretive stranger whose eyes seemed to cut right through her.

Nei, it was because she was finally setting out to complete the task that had dogged her since that terrible night five years ago. She felt more alive than ever before. She would finally end the life of the man who'd tried to end hers.

She rose in the pond and squeezed the water from her hair. With a glance over her shoulder, she searched the tree line beyond the pond's rocky shore. Rúnin's large, dark form wasn't visible. She didn't have time to entertain girlish modesty, she chastised herself. Straightening her spine, she strode from the water, letting the cool air lap at her wet skin.

On the shore, she dried herself quickly with her spare linen shift, then donned her clothes and weapons.

"Rúnin! We'd best head out!" she called into the woods.

The forest remained silent except for the rustling of the wind through the tress.

"Rúnin!" she shouted, louder this time. Still naught.

Unease stabbed Madrena's belly. She quickly touched each one of her weapons, but all were accounted for. Then she rummaged through her bag, but except for her now-damp spare shift, everything was exactly as it had been before she'd bathed. And yet, her guide had vanished.

"Rúnin! Odin curse you!"

~

Rúnin crouched at the top of the ridge overlooking the pond. He held his breath, but he knew Madrena couldn't see him from here.

He should have already been sliding through the forest in the quick but silent way he'd learned over the years. He bit back a curse. He'd endangered himself by lingering. If he hadn't stolen a glance back at the pond a moment ago, he'd have already dissolved into the trees by now.

But he'd looked back and seen Madrena emerge from the pond, looking even more like Freyja, goddess of all that was sensual and passionate, than that first time he'd laid eyes on her.

Madrena's hair shone like pale yellow silk as it draped down her back, flowing with water. As she pulled it from her shoulders to squeeze the water from it, she revealed the tapering curve of her back, which narrowed into a slim waist. The flare of her hips was swallowed by the water, teasing him, making him long to see more.

Then she'd turned and strode out of the pond, and he'd had to press his lips together to keep from gasping.

Shieldmaiden's Revenge

She was more perfect than any goddess, Freyja's wrath be damned.

Her high, round breasts curved delicately from her chest, each tipped in the soft pink of dawn. As he watched, her flat stomach and then the narrow triangle of hair below came into view. Her hips swayed as she waded toward the shoreline, setting a hypnotizing rhythm.

He ripped his eyes away as she began drying herself and dressing, forcing himself to slip deeper into the woods. Of all the dangers he faced, why did he willfully linger just to catch a glimpse of such a beautiful woman? And why did that beautiful woman have to be the one to whom he owed both his life and his freedom?

It didn't matter that Madrena, hard-edged and secretive though she was, stirred something in him that he hadn't felt for a long time, something more than a bodily need. He wasn't safe around people, especially not a shieldmaiden who was far bolder and sharper than he'd realized.

He'd assumed he could use some sort of womanly modesty against her to conceal the mark on his chest while he'd bathed. But instead of turning away when he undressed and stepped into the pond, she'd kept her gaze trained on him. Those pale, unreadable eyes had assessed him, coming dangerously close to seeing his chest.

He'd underestimated her, and he couldn't afford to do so again. If she knew the truth about him, about why he was fleeing now, about just how well he knew the man she sought, it would end badly for one or both of them.

With a quick glance at the sun, he pointed himself

west. He'd have to cut back the way they'd come for a short distance, then travel hard north to be sure he'd avoid her. If she continued east, he'd be well away from her, and if she returned home, he'd hopefully have already readjusted his course northward.

"Rúnin!" Her voice was distant now, but her rage seemed to fill the forest all around him. He heard her curse him to Odin but didn't look back.

He'd done it. He'd survived the slavers' shipwreck, escaped Madrena's village and the slaver crew that was left, and now he'd slipped away from his shieldmaiden keeper.

It was unfortunate that he hadn't managed to take a weapon with him, but he'd deemed it too dangerous to approach her pile of clothes while she bathed. He pushed aside another reason that whispered in the back of his mind—that he hadn't wanted to steal from her, hadn't wanted to deprive her of her weapons or food in case doing so would somehow bring her to harm.

He could make do without a weapon. He'd managed before. Her shouts dwindled as he wove through the trees.

Were the gods smiling on him? He'd thought so many times over the last sennight that he'd finally been chosen for death, and yet here he was, only a little worse off than he'd been for the last fourteen years. He should have felt relieved to have escaped. But for some nagging reason, he was ill at ease as Madrena's voice faded behind him.

8

Rúnin sniffed the underside of the mushroom carefully. Then he checked the gills—not white, which, taken with everything else he'd already determined, meant it was almost assuredly safe to eat. He dropped the mushroom into his tunic, the front of which he held out to collect his bounty.

Five mushrooms and a handful of cloudberries wasn't exactly a bounty, but it would fend off the ever-present gnaw of hunger until he could rest long enough to make a rabbit snare. For now, he had to keep moving.

It had been two days since he'd left Madrena by the pond. Two silent, solitary days moving through the forest, the trees his only companions. He'd traveled west for a few hours that first day but had been making his way due north since then. Soon he would need to turn east if he was going to return to more familiar lands. The weather had cooperated up until this morning, but now low clouds threatened rain overhead. Thank the gods for the thick woolen cloak Madrena had given him.

He frowned as his eyes searched the forest floor for

another edible mushroom. Thoughts of the woman kept invading his mind, distracting him. Her visage floated back to him whenever he tasted a late-season cloudberry. She so often scowled, her pale blonde eyebrows drawn down over those nigh-colorless gray eyes. But then he would remember the look on her face as she fought against her nightmares—so vulnerable, so frightened.

"I hope you have forgotten me," he muttered to himself, thinking back on the disdain in her eyes when he'd lied about being a mutinous oarsman and the rage in her voice as she'd called his name after he deserted her. Strange. When was the last time he'd cared what another had thought of him?

He'd once thought himself honorable, but the boy he'd been had died under Jarl Bersi's hand. How brave he'd been as a lad of fourteen. How sure of right and wrong he'd been. If that boy were alive today, he'd condemn his older self as a coward, a dishonorable man.

But he lived today because of what he'd had to do, because he'd been willing to survive even if it meant dishonoring himself.

What did the gods think of that? They hadn't chosen him to join them yet—the time of one's death was fated, though naught else was. He made his own legacy with each action. It seemed the gods wanted to see how low Rúnin would go before stealing the life's breath from him.

He stuffed one of the mushrooms into his mouth and chewed quickly. Such doubts and worries hadn't plagued him in years. He thought he was free of guilt for doing what was necessary to survive after Jarl Bersi shattered his boyish certainty about the world. Why were these dark musings surfacing again?

Madrena's clear, hard eyes drifted to his mind. She was a shieldmaiden, a warrior, though she'd come to it relatively recently. Yet she clearly lived by the Northlands code of honor. Some wrong had been done against her, and she sought revenge. She defied her Jarl, yet it was in a quest of righteousness. But how did she know of Bersi and his bear tattoo? He had an inkling, but he hoped he was wrong for her sake.

Suddenly he realized through his swirling thoughts that the forest had fallen unnaturally quiet, with none of the late-season birds calling to each other in the trees.

A twig snapped behind Rúnin. He started, dropping the berries and mushrooms from his tunic that he'd so painstakingly collected. His head whipped around, scanning the forest wildly.

Shadows shifted a stone's throw away through the trees. Rúnin's heart leapt to his throat. So lost had he been in thoughts of the past and of Madrena that he'd made a terrible error.

Voices filtered through the air. He'd let people draw near him.

If he bolted now, he'd make too much noise. His only hope was to hide nearby and pray that whoever now shared the forest with him would pass along unknowingly.

The voices drew closer. How many of them were there?

Slowly, Rúnin eased backward, careful not to snag a foot on a root or fallen branch. He inched until he felt a wide spruce trunk behind him. He slipped around the trunk, crouching.

"...check the ones in the creek bed ahead and then we can return to Knorrstad."

Rúnin held his breath. Knorrstad was more than a day's travel on foot to the southeast. He'd been careful to give the town a wide berth for fear of being seen. Cautiously, he eased his head around the spruce's trunk.

Three men emerged from the shadowed forest, the ferns swaying at their feet as they strode purposefully. Rúnin ducked back behind the trunk. From the look of the men's animal skin hats and fur-lined cloaks, they were likely a group of trappers. But that was odd, because trappers were known as a solitary lot.

Ja, the gods may not have stolen Rúnin's life breath yet, but they seemed to find pleasure in threatening to take it at every turn. He squeezed his eyes shut, willing his mind to form a plan.

The trappers still might not see him. And if they did, he could flee. Or fight, if it came to that. Each man carried a bow over his shoulder, though Rúnin couldn't tell from such a short glimpse at them what other weapons they might have.

The men's voices suddenly stopped and Rúnin's heart clenched.

"What is this?"

The voice was only a few feet away on the other side of the spruce behind which Rúnin hid.

"An animal's cache?"

Rúnin's eyes darted to the front of his tunic. He'd dropped all the berries and mushrooms he'd collected, but he hadn't had time to hide the evidence of his presence. He gritted his teeth so hard that his jaw ached.

"Nei," another man answered, just as close. "A person's."

Rúnin's mind raced. If he waited to be found, there was no telling what these men would do to him, whether they saw the marking on his chest or not.

Trappers were known to prowl the woods, living by their own laws—which mostly involved taking what they wanted without qualms. He'd encountered one before many years ago. The man had come at him with a knife in the middle of the night. Rúnin had barely survived. The trapper hadn't. And these men traveled together. What purpose other than violence did a pack of trappers have?

His mind rioted even as his window to act closed. If he ran, he still had a chance to evade them.

He bolted, throwing himself headlong into the forest. Shouts of surprise rose behind him, followed by the sounds of the men's pursuit.

Rúnin cut hard to the right, then back to the left. Zigzagging would waste his precious lead on the men, but if they fired at him, he'd be a harder target to hit.

As if in answer to his thoughts, an arrow whizzed by on his right, where his body had been a second before. He needed higher ground. Pushing his legs harder, he dashed toward a sloping hill ahead. The ground grew rockier underfoot, though the trees remained thick, providing him with lifesaving cover.

The men shouted behind him. Their calls were dispersing. They were spreading out to try to surround him. He cursed internally. Another arrow shot past his head. The arrow landed with a thunk in a tree ahead of him. As Rúnin ran by, he yanked the arrow from the bark.

Suddenly, he veered to the left and dove behind an enormous fallen tree. He clapped a hand over his mouth to quiet his panting. His ears strained for sounds of his pursuers. One scrambled up the rocky incline behind him. He heard a rustling to his right and knew another of the men was moving in. He couldn't pinpoint the third's location.

He clutched the arrow shaft in one hand and felt for a rock with the other. One arrow and a rock. That was all he had against three armed men.

The forest stilled as the men paused, listening. Taking a chance, Rúnin threw the rock off to his left. It landed with a satisfying thump in the underbrush.

"Over there!" the man who'd been behind him shouted. He and the one to Rúnin's right crashed through the woods in pursuit of the noise.

Rúnin cautiously lifted his head from behind the fallen log. He caught a glimpse of brown wool and fur hats as the two men tore off through the trees. He stood, easing backward until they completely disappeared from view. Then he turned to slink back the way he'd come.

Just then, something flew at his head and he ducked just in time. The third trapper stood before him, bow drawn with an arrow trained on his chest.

There was no more time for evasion. Rúnin lunged forward with the arrow raised in his hand like a dagger. The trapper lowered his bow slightly and let another arrow fly, and this time, his aim was true. A stab of pain shot through Rúnin's leg and he stumbled.

"Drop it, unless you want another one in the throat," the man said, fitting an arrow in his bow.

Rúnin glanced down to where an arrow bristled from his right thigh. His gaze, muddled with shock and pain, shifted to his hand, which still clutched the arrow he'd hoped would save him. He straightened, wincing against the pain in his leg. Reluctantly, he unclenched his hand and the arrow fell to the forest floor.

Never taking his hard gaze from Rúnin, the trapper shouted to his companions. He kept his bow trained on Rúnin while the other two hustled to his side.

"What do we have here?"

Rúnin forced his mouth to work, hoping that his mind would follow suit. "I-I am from Knorrstad. I am a simple farmer. Please, don't hurt me."

"Why did you run from us?" the man with the bow aimed at Rúnin said flatly.

"I was…I was fleeing my lover's father. He didn't want me to lay with his daughter, but he caught us. I thought perhaps he sent you after me."

The other two men glanced at the one with the drawn bow. Apparently he was their leader. Rúnin's mind threatened to haze over from the pain in his leg, but he willed himself to focus on the man.

The man's eyes slid over Rúnin, assessing. "Those are unusually fine clothes for a farmer."

Rúnin had meant to thank Madrena for the well-made, thick trousers and tunic, the sturdy boots, and the fur-trimmed cloak. Now he wished he had his tattered, weathered clothes on his back once more. He fumbled to come up with a response, but before he could, the man with the bow lowered his arrow cautiously.

"Go fetch the cloak," he said to his companions.

"Please," Rúnin croaked. "It is all I have." He would beg them like a farmer would for such a fine garment, but if all they wanted was his cloak, perhaps they would let him go once they had it.

"Nei," one of the men said as they approached him. "You also have that fine tunic. I'll take that."

Panic surged through Rúnin's veins. He couldn't stop them from stealing the cloak. But if they removed his tunic, they were sure to see his marking.

As the two men drew closer, Rúnin took a pained step backward. "I will freeze out here without my tunic. Surely you can take pity on me."

Each man seized one of his arms while their leader walked calmly toward him. The stink of dead animals hung about all three men. The trappers must have fallen on hard times and resorted to forming this pack. How many other innocents had they set upon and robbed —or worse?

The leader halted in front of Rúnin, and now he could see that the man's fur hat was tattered and worn, as was his cloak. He reached for the ties at Rúnin's neck and his wool cloak fell in a pool at his feet.

"You're naught but gutless thieves," Rúnin hissed. Through the pain, he could see only one last play to save himself from having to reveal the brand on his chest that marked him as an outcast of society. If he enraged the men enough, perhaps they would beat him and leave him for dead. "The gods will spit on your corpses, for you have no honor."

The leader's fist flashed out, connecting with Rúnin's stomach and forcing the breath from him. Good. This was what he wanted, he thought as he gasped for air.

But then he heard the whisper of a blade being unsheathed, and he struggled to right himself in the other men's hold.

"Nei, don't, Harald," the man holding his left arm begged. "I want his tunic. Don't mar it."

Harald, the leader, toyed with his seax in front of Rúnin's face.

Shieldmaiden's Revenge

"And I want his boots," the one on Rúnin's right said.

With a sigh, Harald flicked the seax, indicating that his men could take what they wanted. He pressed the blade to Rúnin's throat as one of the trappers released his arm and tugged the boots from his feet. The other began yanking up the tunic.

Rúnin struggled, but the seax at his throat pressed hard enough to draw a trickle of blood. The material passed over his head, the blade only leaving his throat long enough for the tunic to come free.

This was it. He squeezed his eyes shut, preparing himself to meet the gods.

Harald inhaled sharply.

"What is that on his chest?"

The seax dropped from his neck to the spot right over his heart, prodding the marred flesh.

"It is a brand," one of the men said.

"But look at the edges. There used to be a tattoo underneath."

All three of the men cursed.

"*Outlaw!*" Harald hissed, the seax returning to Rúnin's throat. The other two men backed away, as if Rúnin would infect them with the curse of outlawry.

Harald's eyes flashed pure hatred. "You dared call us dishonorable, you sheep's shite!"

"Harald, let us be gone," one of the men said uneasily.

"Nei!" Harald shouted. "It is against the laws of all the Northlands to help an outlaw in any way. If we let him live, we will have given him aid of a sort."

Harald pressed the seax into Rúnin's neck until he could feel another trickle of warm blood down his chest.

Despite the fact that these men lived outside the law themselves, all those in the Northlands would see it as nigh a duty to rid the world of a proclaimed outlaw, for it was the punishment reserved for the worse, lowest of criminals.

After fourteen long years on his own, Rúnin was finally getting the reckoning that nigh all outlaws faced eventually. Death at the hands of strangers.

"It will be easiest to leave his body to rot. One less outlaw to share the woods with—all the better for us," Harald said over his shoulder to his two companions, his pale blue eyes keen on Rúnin.

Rúnin blinked up at the trees, taking his fill of the cloud-covered sky between the branches. He was no longer paying attention to the trappers. His leg throbbed where the arrow still protruded. The men likely would have let him live if they hadn't seen the brand. No matter now.

"Odin take me," he whispered.

He felt the seax at his neck twitch and he inhaled sharply, waiting to feel his blood spilling over his chest. But in the next moment, the seax fell away from his throat. He lowered his head to meet the startled stare of Harald's wide, unseeing eyes. Then Harald toppled backward and Rúnin registered the arrow protruding from the man's neck.

9

Time seemed to slow as his mind struggled to understand what was happening. The muffled shouts of the other two men filtered through his consciousness, along with the harsh shriek of battle. A *woman's* shriek.

Madrena exploded from the surrounding forest, sword drawn. The remaining two trappers seemed as stunned as Rúnin for a moment before one of them drew a short blade from his belt. He thrust at Madrena, but she easily blocked his attack. The second trapper had now gathered his wits and nocked an arrow into his bow, aiming at Madrena.

Without a care for the arrow protruding from his leg, Rúnin dove to the ground and snatched the seax from Harald's lifeless hand. As the second trapper drew back on his bowstring, Rúnin flung the seax. The blade landed in the man's shoulder. He screamed, the arrow and bow falling uselessly from his grasp.

Another scream snapped Rúnin's attention back to Madrena, but the noise was the other trapper's dying cry. As he dropped limply to the ground, clutching his throat as blood spurted between his fingers, Madrena strode purposefully toward the remaining trapper. She easily swept his legs, knocking him to the ground. With a boot pressed to his chest, she wedged the seax from his shoulder and quickly drew it across his throat. The man gurgled as the life drained from him.

Then Madrena turned on Rúnin, her sword in one hand and Harald's seax in the other, both dripping with blood. Keeping her eyes locked on him, she bent slightly and wiped her sword on the trapper's tunic, then slid the blade back in its sheath.

He struggled to pull himself upright. All he managed was to prop himself to a seated position. She closed in on him slowly, her unreadable eyes flicking to the arrow in his leg, then to his bare chest.

She faltered as her gaze landed on the marking on his chest.

"Madrena," he breathed. "Let me explain."

"Explain why you broke your vow to be my guide?" she said, raising the bloodied seax in her hand to point it at him. "Or explain the brand on your chest that marks you as an outlaw?"

He'd had the faintest hope that she wouldn't comprehend the significance of the brand. But apparently the practice of burning away a man's tattoos in order to mark him as an outlaw was the same in her part of the Northlands as it was in his.

"Let me explain both," he said, his eyes now following the seax as she stepped closer, leveling it at the scarred tissue on the left side of his chest.

"You are a coward," she spat. "You'll promise the moon if I let you live, just like you promised to take me to the east. You don't even know the man with the bear tattoo, do you?"

He swallowed the old ache that rose at her words.

"You're right about me. I am a coward. I have learned to be an oath-breaker, a murderer, and an honorless man. But I told you the truth about knowing the one you seek."

She dropped into a crouch before him so that her hard, colorless eyes were level with his. With the seax pointed at him in one hand, she reached out with the other and grasped the arrow shaft protruding from his right thigh.

He inhaled sharply, white spots swimming before his vision as a fresh stab of pain washed over him.

"I'm not sure why I saved you from those men," she said, her voice flat and quiet. He could barely hear her over the pounding blood in his ears.

"When I noticed you were gone from the pond, I decided to track you. At first I thought perhaps you'd gotten lost and that when I found you, we'd continue east with you as my guide. But then it became clear from your route, going west and then north, that you hoped to lose me. Is that true?"

Could he start telling the truth for the first time in fourteen years? He had to risk it. His life was now in Madrena's hands.

"Ja, that is true," he exhaled.

"Just as I thought after the first few hours tracking you. Then I kept going because I wanted to kill you for breaking your word to me. When I found these men hunting you, I didn't want them to steal the right to kill you myself."

"And now?"

"Now I can't decide if I want to let you die a slow and painful death alone in these woods for betraying me, or if I should kill you quickly and rid the world of your presence for bearing the mark of an outlaw." She flicked the seax's tip toward the brand on his chest.

His mind was sluggish with pain, but he reached for a plan. It was risky, but he had no other options. "You still need me, Madrena," he said, his words slurring slightly.

Her eyes flashed with frustration, so he went on. "You need me to find the man you're looking for. You'll never feel complete until you do."

A low growl emanated from her throat and she twisted the arrow in his leg once more.

As the blinding pain descended upon him, he wondered distantly if he'd misjudged this approach.

"I know the name of the man you seek," he gritted out through clenched teeth.

The edge of the seax was once again pressing against his throat. "If you are lying—"

"I'm not," he shot back, and for the second time in just a few breaths, it was the truth.

"Why should I believe you? Why should I believe a single thing you say, oath-breaker? You're an outlaw—you have been shunned from the world because you have no honor."

He swallowed and felt the seax bob against his neck. He'd sworn to himself to take this secret to the grave. Madrena waited, eyes hot and enraged, ready to cut his throat.

"Because I am from the village you seek."

"You'd say aught to save your life," she said with disgust.

Shieldmaiden's Revenge

"Look at the mark on my chest," he ordered.

"Why? I already see that you have been stripped of your tattoo."

It was true. The flat edge of the hot blade that had been laid against his chest as a boy of fourteen had nigh erased all traces of the tattoo that had been placed there only a few months before. But the outlines were still visible around the scarred flesh.

"Look at it," he bit out.

Her eyes darted down to the marred flesh again as if he were trying to pull some kind of trick. But then she paused, her gaze tracing the outer edge of the brand where the tattoo was still visible.

"Does it look familiar to you?" His eyes were locked on her, waiting for the moment of recognition he knew would come.

At last, she inhaled sharply. Her hand flew from the arrow shaft in his leg to his chest. Unconsciously, she let her fingers brush the edges of the tattoo. One of the bear's eyes was still visible, as was his lower jaw, along with a few sharp teeth. A segment of the intricate woven pattern that was identical to Jarl Bersi's trailed out from the far left side of the brand mark.

"It is the same…"

Her eyes shot to his, wide with confusion. For a fleeting moment, her face bore the same vulnerable look as it had when she'd screamed in her sleep, trapped in her nightmare.

"Who are you?" she hissed, her face hardening.

"As I told you, my name is Rúnin. I know the man you seek, for he was the Jarl of my village before…" He swallowed. Even after all these years, it was hard for him to form the words.

"Before you were outlawed?"

He nodded, holding her gaze.

That disgusted look came back in Madrena's gray eyes again. "I know what your Jarl did to me. You must have done something even worse to make that whoreson cast you out."

Rúnin's chest squeezed with a deeper shame than he had ever known, far more acute than the day his tattoo had been burned away before his weeping mother and all the villagers.

Though pain dulled his thoughts, a bell rung in the back of his mind again. What had Bersi done to her? Something about Madrena's words tugged at an earlier guess, one he suspected but hoped hadn't been true. He tucked her words away. Someday perhaps he would broach the horrifying subject with her—if he lived.

"I'll explain. But right now I need to get this arrow out of my leg." His hand shook slightly as he gestured at the arrow shaft protruding from his thigh.

Her eyes flashed as her mind worked over their predicament.

"You need me," Madrena said, her gaze falling to the arrow. "And I need you. By the gods," she muttered.

The rain that had been threatening all morning finally began to fall. Large drops slipped through the trees overhead to land on Rúnin's bare chest. The rain mixed with the little trickle of blood at his throat, creating a red rivulet over his skin.

Madrena stood and looked at him for a long moment. At last, she sighed and turned to the bodies of the three trappers. She snatched up Rúnin's boots, which had fallen next to the first trapper she'd killed, then gathered his tunic and cloak. She threw each article of clothing at him and he dressed quickly, the air suddenly much colder.

He fumbled lamely with his boots, unable to put all his weight on his right leg. The arrow wound spread a dull ache through his entire leg, but the pain flared sharp and hot whenever he moved. At last, Madrena came to his side and draped his arm over her shoulder while she crammed his feet into the boots.

By the time she straightened, he was gritting his teeth against the shooting pain. She eyed him.

"Come on, then. Perhaps we can find a dry spot higher in these hills." Without waiting, she grabbed his arm once again and put it over her shoulder, taking some of his weight on his right side. She didn't glance at the dead bodies as they shuffled to higher ground. They might not be outlaws like he was, but they were lawless, honorless men nonetheless. Thieves earned the same fate as murderers in the Northlands.

"Wait," he said, halting. He looked back over his shoulder, his eyes falling on Harald's bloody seax, which Madrena had discarded next to his body.

Madrena's eyes followed his. "The gods did not favor those men," she said. "If their weapons were worth having, they wouldn't be dead right now. 'Tis considered unlucky."

"I've learned to make my own luck," he replied. "The gods can watch and decide what my fate will be."

He turned and would have hobbled back to where the seax lay, but Madrena clutched a fistful of his tunic.

"You can have the arrow once I pull it from your leg," she said, narrowing her eyes. "Until then, you don't get a weapon."

He was in no position to argue. As she'd said, he

needed her, just as she needed him. It seemed they were bound together for the time being.

~

By the time Madrena had helped Rúnin up the increasingly rocky hillside, they were both soaking wet and panting for breath, she under his weight, and he for the obvious pain the arrow was causing him. The trees had thinned as they approached the hill's summit, which meant the rain hit them unfettered. Despite her stout wool cloak, Madrena could feel a trickle of icy rainwater running down her neck and along her spine.

At last she spotted what she'd hoped to find. The hill rose into a rocky peak, several slabs of stone lying against each other at odd angles. Beneath two such slabs she spotted a shadowy cave.

"There!" She pointed.

Rúnin only nodded in response. He was likely too focused on taking the remaining few steps to the rocky shelter to reply. As they'd stumbled along, he let her take increasingly more of his weight. Though he was all lean, hard muscle, he was still a large man. She grunted over the last feet to the cave, exhausted.

He put his hands on the gray stone that made the mouth of the cave, breathing heavily. She slipped past him to inspect their shelter. Water ran from the slabs over the mouth in little streams, but the inside was dry, the air cool and still. The cave would be only just deep enough for Rúnin to stretch out, and it grew narrower away from the mouth, but it would do.

With her help, Rúnin bent his good leg and sidled into

the cave. He collapsed on the dusty floor with a grunt. Without preamble, he wrapped one of his hands around the arrow shaft, holding his leg down with his other hand.

"Wait!" she snapped, realizing what he was about to do. "We need a fire and more water to tend to that. I think I saw some *hvönn* farther down the hill, too."

"I'll not leave this arrow in my leg for another hour while you wander the hillside, girl," he bit out.

"Fine," she barked back. "I am only trying to help save you from infection, but by all means, let's get this over with."

She pushed his hands out of the way and straddled his leg, gripping the arrow with both hands. Without waiting for him to give his assent, she yanked the arrow as hard as she could.

He roared in pain, bucking so hard that she was sent crashing into the cave's wall. But she had the arrow in her hands and in one piece, meaning it had come out cleanly. It dripped with his dark blood.

He lay on his back, panting and blinking at the cave's ceiling. "Did I hurt you?" he said through gritted teeth.

Madrena was so caught off guard that her mouth fell open. Here she was, brandishing the bloody arrow that had been lodged in his thigh a moment ago, and he was asking about her wellbeing.

"Nei," she said at last, feeling an uncomfortable heat rise to her face. This man—this outlaw—was strange indeed.

As he slowly propped himself on one elbow, she handed him the arrow.

"You've earned this."

Despite the tightness around his eyes and mouth, he raised an eyebrow. "Are you sure you trust me with it?"

Part of her wanted to wipe the teasing expression from his face with a slap, but another part stirred oddly. It didn't make any sense, but *did* part of her trust him? "Ja. I assume you'll be here when I return?"

He exhaled and it sounded like a half-chuckle. "There's a silver lining for you—at least you can now rest assured that I won't be able to slip away again." He winced as he tried to reposition his leg.

The smile that threatened to break her stony countenance faded.

"I'll not have you die of infection before you make good on your promise to see me to your village. And answer my questions."

He nodded and met her gaze, his eyes darker blue in the shadows of the cave.

"Ja."

10

By the time Madrena returned to the cave, she had a full waterskin and a handful of leaves and roots from the *hvönn* plant, but only a few pieces of wood dry enough to burn.

As she ducked back into the cave, she took in the sight of Rúnin splayed out on the ground. He'd fallen into a fitful rest. A dark red stain was spreading down his right thigh.

For a fleeting moment, she felt her bravery and pride leave her and she wished Alaric were here. He was so good at taking a seemingly impossible problem and finding a solution. And he could always make her smile with his wry sense of humor.

If Eirik were with her, he'd take charge of the situation, giving orders and making her feel like everything was under control.

And if Laurel had been there, she would have known what to do with the *hvönn*. She was such a quick learner. In her year living at Dalgaard, she'd already learned how to swim, fish, and weave in the Northern way. Most recently she'd begun learning about herbs and medicines from the healer who tended to her now that she was with child.

As it was, Madrena was alone with an outlaw. She had no needle with which to close Rúnin's wound, no pot to hold boiling water, and no idea what to do with the *hvönn* she'd found. All she had was some sodden wood, stream water, and a sickly looking man she needed to heal well enough to get her to his village.

She sighed. There was no point in dawdling or wishing things were different. Just as if she were in battle, she'd face each obstacle one and a time.

Noticing Rúnin's soaked clothing, she set about lighting a fire first. She gathered a few dry leaves that had blown into the back of the cave long ago and dug out her fire-steel and flint stone from the bottom of her satchel. Holding the curved piece of metal in one hand, she dragged the stone along its surface with the other. Sparks flared in the cave's dimness.

The leaves caught quickly, but the wet branches were slow to light. She had to hunch over and cup her hands around the little tendrils of smoke, blowing carefully. At last, a little fire glowed near the mouth of the cave, and the cold, damp air was cut somewhat.

She removed her cloak, overdress, and boots, laying them out near the fire to help them dry. The rain had grown sleety while she'd been out, the air turning increasingly cold. She feared worse weather was on its way, and they would both need to be dry to survive. With a quick glance at Rúnin to assure herself that his eyes were closed, she slipped out of her damp shift and hastily donned her spare shift and overdress.

Now she needed to see to Rúnin.

She approached cautiously, though he lay prone. She'd always sensed that he had secrets, that he was perhaps even dangerous, but she never would have guessed that he was an outlaw.

Being outlawed was practically a death sentence in the Northlands. Without the aid or shelter of another living being, few survived more than a year or two. And in case any of them tried to seek help, they were stripped of their markings, which were earned for battle or a sign of fealty to one's Jarl. The brand on Rúnin's chest signaled to all in the Northlands that he was a man without a home, without honor.

But the brand had long ago healed, indicating that Rúnin could have been living in the wilds outside the laws and protections of civilization for years. How had he survived so long? He'd said he'd learned to do what was necessary to live—he'd certainly lied to her and broken his promise to guide her to the eastern reaches of the Northlands. Yet he'd never threatened her, nor had he taken aught from her except the food she'd offered freely. What kind of heart beat in the mysterious man's chest just below the brand and the remnants of the bear tattoo?

She crouched next to him and he stirred, though his eyes remained closed. Was he simply exhausted and in pain, or had a fever already set in? She reached out an unsteady hand and brushed a few strands of dark hair from his forehead, then laid her palm against his skin. His brow was cool to the touch, though his skin was damp.

Her stomach clenched at the thought that she would need to undress him to remove his wet clothes and see to his leg wound. What a silly girl she was being. She was trying to help him, not bed him. And besides, he didn't have aught she hadn't seen before. But for some reason the thought only made her throat tighten.

How could she be drawn to a man she barely knew, a man who was an outlaw and a scoundrel, no less? She'd had a handful of infatuations both before and after the attack on the village five years ago. She'd even shared the pleasures of the body with a few.

In the months after that raid, she'd feared that she would never want to feel the stirrings of attraction and sensuality within herself again. But when a lad from the outskirts of Dalgaard caught her fancy a year later and they'd shared a casual companionship, she realized that the man with the bear tattoo's attack on her had naught to do with sex. Ja, he had violated her in the most horrifying way, but it had been more about power. Sex was meant to be about pleasure, not violence.

She wasn't one to shy away from the realities of the body—she was a warrior after all. But she'd only shared passing encounters with the village lads. Rúnin stirred something deeper within her, something she didn't entirely trust.

Hesitantly, she reached for the tie on Rúnin's cloak. When it was free, she pulled on his tunic. His weight pinned the material against the floor, however.

"Rúnin," she grunted, laboring unsuccessfully to work the tunic upward. "You need to sit up. You can't stay in these wet clothes."

He groaned and his eyes slit open. Grudgingly cooperating, he dragged himself up on one elbow. As she pulled the wet tunic over his head, he seemed to register the fire and her damp clothes spread out.

"Did you find the *hvönn*?"

"Ja, but…I'm not sure what to do with it." The heat of embarrassment flooded her cheeks. A warrior should have a better understanding of one of the most common and useful medicinal plants in all the Northlands.

"Did you find its fruit?"

Madrena turned to drape the tunic next to her overdress by the fire. "Nei, I think it's too late in the season. But I brought back some leaves and roots." She picked up the pile of plant matter she'd deposited next to her clothes and brought it to his side.

He considered the feathery leaves and rinsed roots in her hand for a moment, then glanced around the cave. "I don't suppose you have a pot in that bag of yours."

She snorted and shook her head.

"My luck," he muttered. He looked to be struggling to focus his eyes, but his next words came out clear and decisive. "We will use the leaves directly on the wound. I'll have to just eat the roots raw."

"*We?*"

He leveled her with a stare. "Unless you have a better idea?"

"How do you know how to use *hvönn*?"

"I've learned a lot of things over the years, especially when it comes to surviving alone in the forest."

"Just how many years?" Curiosity niggled at her despite the fact that she should be focused on getting him out of his trousers and seeing to his wound.

He stilled, his eyes drifting to the fire. "Fourteen come winter."

She inhaled sharply. "How…how did you…?"

"Later," he said, wincing as he lowered himself back onto the cloak spread underneath him.

She swallowed, torn between wanting to press him for answers now and aware of the toll the pain was taking on him.

"I shouldn't be helping you."

His gaze pinned her. "Nei, you shouldn't."

"I could be outlawed myself for aiding you."

"Ja. That is the risk you took in freeing me and setting off against your Jarl's wishes."

Her jaw clenched. This was what she needed—a reminder about why she was risking so much. She'd sworn to herself and to the gods that she would exact revenge on the man who'd raped her. If it meant aiding an outlaw, so be it.

"Take off your trousers."

He made a noise that sounded like surprised mirth. "You aren't shy."

"If you are going to live long enough to take me to your village, I need to see the wound." She forced her tone to be sharp even as she felt something twist deep in her belly.

As he dragged himself up enough to unfasten the ties on the front of his trousers, the muscles rippled in his chest and stomach. His skin glowed golden in the low firelight, the scar from the brand on his chest faintly lighter in color.

He bit down on a curse as he shifted his injured leg and began inching the tight-fitted trousers down his hips. Madrena glanced at the fire, then as casually as she could, she turned her back with the pretense of adding another piece of wood to the small flames. She waited until his curses died down and he stilled behind her.

When she turned to face him, his long, honed body was spread out atop his cloak. His eyes were closed and

Shieldmaiden's Revenge

he wore a grimace, but the fire made him look like one of the gods, forged in gold-covered iron.

Every line was ridged with muscle, with not a pinch of spare flesh on him. Her gaze trailed from the shadow-casting mountains and valleys of muscle down his chest and stomach to the dark hair between his legs. His manhood lay dormant but still impressive in size—just like the rest of him.

Her eyes darted lower, where her gaze snagged on the ragged wound in his leg, which even now oozed blood.

"Rip the *hvönn* leaves from their stems and crush them a little with your fingers."

She started at his voice, rough and low. His eyes were still closed, but he must have felt her heated perusal of every inch of his body. She fumbled with the plant, feeling foolish and incompetent—not the way a shieldmaiden should feel in tending to a battle wound.

Once she had pressed the leaves firmly between her fingers, she crawled toward him. At last, he opened his eyes, and their intensity was only slightly clouded with pain.

"Place them on the wound."

How had he learned so much about tending to a wound with naught more than a few leaves used as catch-alls by healers? She repressed a shudder at the thought of how many wounds he'd had to tend on his own in the wilderness over the course of fourteen years of outlawry.

She did as he said, placing several leaves carefully over the ragged-edged hole in his thigh. Her eyes flickered to his face, and she noticed a muscle twitching in his jaw as he fought for control.

"Do you have aught to bind it with?" he asked through clenched teeth.

She moved to her shift by the fire, which was almost dry. Mentally forming an apology to Laurel, who had given the shift to Madrena as a gift to demonstrate her improving embroidery work, she ripped a strip from the bottom of the garment.

Turning back to Rúnin, she scooted the strip of linen underneath his right thigh. Registering the fact that her hands brushed the skin a mere palm's span away from his manhood, she willed herself to remain focused. She wrapped the cloth carefully several times around the wound, then tied it off when she was done.

"Now bring me the roots." Even in the warm glow of the firelight, Rúnin's face looked pale and strained.

She hurriedly obliged, fetching the waterskin and what remained of the food she'd tied in a cloth as well.

He bit into a raw root and made a face, quickly snatching the waterskin from her hand and taking a swill. He ate all four root bulbs that way. When he'd finished, she pushed the remaining flatbread and fish into his hands.

"Eat the rest," she said.

"And what will you eat?"

"I'll go hunting tomorrow. You need your strength."

Though he ate just as ravenously as he had the first time she'd been with him, he refused half of the food, sliding it toward her. She ordered him and even tried to coax him to eat, but he flatly pushed the rest on her.

As she ate what was left of their flatbread and fish, she felt his gaze on her.

"How many times have you saved my life, shield-maiden?" he said quietly.

Shieldmaiden's Revenge

This mysterious man, an outlaw and a survivor, lay prone before her, completely bare and defenseless, and he owed her his life at least thrice over. He closed his eyes and his breathing dropped almost immediately into the rhythm of sleep.

She reached for her cloak and found that though the outside was still damp, the tightly woven wool on the inside was dry. She draped it over his form, battle hardened yet relaxed in exhaustion.

Icy rain continued to fall beyond the mouth of the cave. It would be a cold night. She sidled closer to the fire, wrapping her arms around herself and resting her head against one of the cave's stone walls.

She formed a plea to Odin in her mind to see Rúnin through this injury. But strangely, she wasn't thinking of her mission for revenge. Nei, she didn't know why she longed for the man to live, but somehow, some way, he *must*.

11

The nightmare was upon her again.

Rúnin was dragged from the numbing escape of sleep by her cries. She was curled on her side against the cave's wall, her voice muffled but urgent.

With a grunt for the pain, he brought himself up to his elbows. Madrena's cloak slid down his chest and he realized she must have covered him. In the low light of the sputtering fire, he saw that she wore her simple woolen dress, yet her feet were bare. Her boots were propped by the fire to dry.

She shivered and muttered something, but then her voice rose in a cry of panic.

"Madrena," he said loudly. "Madrena, wake up. It is only a dream."

How often did the night terrors plague her? And what had happened to bring them about? His mind went back to Bersi and a sickening feeling twisted his stomach.

Madrena screamed suddenly and thrashed, her legs

shooting out. She kicked over her boots, nearly knocking them into what was left of the fire.

He rolled onto his left side and reached toward her, careful of his leg.

"Madrena!" Like he had by the pond, he took her by the shoulders and shook her.

"Nei!" she shrieked, thrashing in his hold.

Her hands turned into claws and she swiped at him. Just before her nails would have raked his face, he caught her wrists, pinning her to the cave's floor. Her knee jerked up, looking to make contact. It bumped into his right leg, sending a surge of fresh pain through him.

He exhaled and grunted sharply but didn't loosen his hold on her wrists. Yet instead of calming her, his grip seemed to only hitch her panic higher.

"Nei, don't!" Her eyes popped open, but they gazed unseeing past his face. Tears streamed down the side of her cheeks.

"Madrena, it is Rúnin! You are safe!" he shouted, hoping that somehow his voice would crack through the nightmare's control over her.

At last she blinked, her eyes focusing on his face. Her thrashing stilled, yet her body remained tense.

"Don't," she said again, the panic still sharp in her voice. But this time he knew she was conscious.

He looked down at her in the light of the embers. Her hands were clenched into fists underneath his hold. His much larger hands easily circled each of her wrists, holding her firmly to the floor. His mind flew back to Bersi. Instantly, he let go of her wrists and pushed himself away from her.

Madrena released a shaky breath, a little moan of fear escaping past her lips. She scooted back against the cold stone slab of the cave's wall, but the space was small enough that it only put a few hand spans between them. She clutched at her arms, shivering uncontrollably.

Slowly, as if approaching a wounded animal trapped in a snare, Rúnin extended one hand toward her. Her eyes, glowing in the low light of the fire, darted between his outstretched fingers and his face. But she permitted the hand to keep advancing toward her.

He let his palm drop to one of her arms. With a pause to allow her to grow accustomed to his touch, he began running his hand up and down her arm, trying to generate some heat. All the while, she watched him with those unreadable gray eyes that seemed to absorb light and refract it back.

"The man you seek…" he said at last, his voice a husky whisper. "He…he hurt you, didn't he? He forced you."

Madrena squeezed her eyes shut for a moment, and he feared he had gone too far, pushing her to speak about something beyond words.

"Ja," she breathed at last, her voice thick with emotion.

Involuntarily, the hand that was running over her arm stilled and his fingers curled in rage.

Bersi.

The man who had turned Rúnin's peaceful village into a shadow land of fear and chaos.

The man who had given Rúnin the name Bersisson.

The man who had placed the bear tattoo on his chest, and who had burned it away with a hot blade months later.

The man who had banished him to outlawry was the same man who had spawned Madrena's nightmares.

"Rúnin?" Her voice tugged him back to the present, though his insides churned with hot fury.

"As I said, I know the man," he managed through gritted teeth.

Her gaze pinned him. "How…?"

He forced his fingers to uncurl against her arm and resumed rubbing her woolen sleeve. Suddenly he felt sick and weary, and it had naught to do with the dull ache in his leg.

"There has been enough pain for one night. I will explain in the morning."

She nodded slowly and exhaled. Despite his hand on her arm, another shiver stole over her and she tried to tuck her feet up under her skirt.

"Take your cloak back."

"Nei, then you'll have naught covering you. I'm fine," she said. As if to prove her lie, another involuntary shiver racked her.

He hesitated for a moment, choosing his tone carefully. "Then let me share my warmth with you."

He consciously didn't imbue the words with something suggestive, something sensual. Even still, the thought of her lithe, lean body curled up against him sent a coil of heat through his belly—and lower. He pushed the heat down. No matter how much he wanted to, he wouldn't burden her with his desire.

Nevertheless, her eyes widened. To his surprise, however, after a moment of consideration, she nodded.

She sidled closer, and he lifted the edge of her cloak to let her in. As she scooted next to him, he lowered himself onto his back once more. Her shoulder brushed against his as she lay down alongside him.

The cloak wasn't big enough to cover both of them side by side like that, though. Cold air crept in at the edges where the wool gapped.

Rúnin sighed. The gods were having fun with him again. When was the last time he'd lain completely naked with a beautiful woman, yet bound himself not to touch her?

He lifted an arm and looped it over her shoulder, pulling her toward him. She stiffened, yet she let him shift her so that the length of her body pressed against him.

At last, the cloak settled over them and Rúnin could no longer feel the wisps of cold air stealing in at the edges.

Madrena remained tense, her head perched on his shoulder and her hand balled atop his chest. Yet her desire to be warm must have won out—or could it have been that she sensed his guileless intentions and trusted him not to take advantage of the situation? He shouldn't let himself hope.

Either way, she slowly began to ease into his body. Her hand relaxed against his ribs. She drew up one leg over his good thigh, letting her icy toes draw warmth from his skin. And at last, the weight of her head settled against his chest—right over the brand and the remnants of the tattoo that had shown to the world his allegiance to Jarl Bersi.

What a mess he was in. He thought things had been dire when the slaver captain and Bjorn had taken him captive more than a fortnight ago. When they'd spotted the mark of his outlawry and deciding they could capitalize on it by selling him as a thrall, he'd thought his life was over.

Then the storm had seemed like a blessing. To be taken by Aegir and Thor in a violent squall was surely better than dying under the whip as a thrall. But he'd survived. The gods must have laughed when he realized he'd been dragged into a village, the most dangerous place for an outlaw.

But they'd granted him yet another reprieve by putting Madrena in his path. Now here he lay with her in his arms, his manhood stirring despite his attempts to will it not to. Her pale blonde hair brushed against his chin. She smelled of fresh air and wood smoke, with a hint of sweetness that likely emanated directly from her skin.

He wanted this moment, this night, to stretch forever. It didn't matter here with Madrena curled against him that he was an outlaw, a man without honor. It didn't matter that he had promised the impossible by agreeing to lead her to Bersi, for he had sworn never to return to Seterfell again.

All that mattered was that she grew limp against him, vulnerable in sleep and yet trusting him to act honorably. Was this what Valhalla would hold for those worthy enough to enter? He would never know. For in the morning, he would have to tell Madrena that the man who had violated her was the same man who'd once called Rúnin son.

12

Something was rustling Madrena's hair. Something warm.

The rhythmic ruffle at the top of her head slowly drew her out of a deep sleep. What could be causing it?

She must have shifted in her sleep over the course of the night, for the last thing she remembered, her head rested on Rúnin's chest, but now she lay on her left side, with her back against the cave's stone wall.

But that didn't make sense, because the stone behind her radiated heat. A heavy weight draped over her arm and torso, pinning her. And another hard length was pressed against her bottom.

She tried to sit bolt upright, but the weight of Rúnin's arm over her kept her in place. Rúnin groaned behind her, and she belatedly realized that her sudden shift may have caused pain to his leg. He sighed against her hair, confirming the source of the ruffling.

Heat suffused her face. This was all far too intimate. She wriggled again, trying to free herself from the warm weight of his body.

Rúnin suddenly stiffened at her squirming. "Gods," he hissed behind her, his voice tight. "Don't move like that against me."

If she thought her face had been hot before, now it raged like a bonfire. Impossibly, the hard length pressing against her bottom grew stiffer. Suddenly the knowledge that Rúnin was completely naked came crashing through her mind.

He was naked.

His manhood was rigid and long where it surged against her bottom.

Their bodies were molded together under her cloak.

She'd rubbed against him unknowingly, and now he lay frozen, holding himself motionless.

By the gods, could one die from embarrassment?

This time when she tried to bolt upright, he moved his arm to let her scoot away from him.

"I-I apologize," she said, though she didn't know why.

Rúnin sighed and shifted next to her. "There is no shame in sharing the comforts of the body," he said at last. "You were cold and scared last night. It was naught."

Her eyes darted to his. The cave was dim, with the weak, gray light of a cloudy morning barely reaching the recesses where Rúnin lay. But his eyes were bright and focused on her.

"And there is no shame in the body's...involuntary reactions," she said. Against her will, her gaze darted for the briefest moment down the length of his body and toward his manhood, which stood out against the folds of the cloak still covering him.

He said naught, but she felt his gaze burn into her

like blue fire. Heat crackled silently in the air between them for a long moment.

She had to get out of there, else her face would incinerate with embarrassment.

"I'll go look for more wood for the fire," she said tersely. "And for something to eat."

Without waiting for him to respond, she turned and yanked on her boots. As she reached for her bow and quiver, however, she realized that she needed her cloak—the cloak that was the only thing separating her from Rúnin's nakedness.

Before she could repress another wave of mortification, she heard rustling behind her.

"You'll want this."

The weight of her wool cloak thumped softly on the cave floor behind her. She snatched it without turning and scrambled headlong out of the cave.

The cold air helped douse the heat in her cheeks—and elsewhere in her body—as she stood and swung her cloak around her shoulders. A soft drizzle fell, and here at the top of this ridge, she felt like she was nigh inside a cloud. The outlines of the trees a mere stone's throw away were fuzzy and obscured by the mist.

Hunting in these conditions would require all of her concentration. Good. It was just what she needed—something to distract her from the tingling in her body where she'd been touching Rúnin.

~

It was hard to tell how long she'd been out, since the sun was completely obscured by the thick, damp clouds, but Madrena guessed it was a few hours. Long enough to shoot a mountain hare and gather a few more pieces of wood. And long enough to clear her head of the pounding blood and memories of Rúnin's body.

He was an outlaw.

She was endangering her life in several ways just by being with him.

Firstly, outlaws were widely known to have no code of honor. It was why they were outlaws to begin with. A year ago, Eirik had banished his uncle Gunvald, the former Jarl of Dalgaard. The man had killed his own kin and manipulated all in the village to secure the Jarlship for his son Grimar.

Some acts were so despicable that a man didn't even deserve a swift death. In those cases, outlawry was used. What had Rúnin done to receive such a punishment?

But worse, outlaws were a desperate sort—they'd do whatever was necessary to survive. Could she honestly expect Rúnin to be any different? He'd told her himself that he'd done terrible things just to live.

A part of her rebelled against the thought. Ja, he'd broken his word to her when he tried to desert her in the woods earlier. But he'd never threatened her or done aught to make her feel unsafe. By the gods, he'd even comforted her last night.

Her mind flew once more to the feel of his warm, bare skin against her cheek. He'd smelled piney, but there was also a clean, male scent to him.

She ripped her thoughts away from such trivialities as she climbed back the ridge toward their cave. Ja, he'd slept with her in his arms, and despite his obviously aroused state, he hadn't tried to lure or pressure her into…what had he called it? *The comforts of the body.*

But that was another danger. Something deep in her belly squeezed and her skin prickled all over.

She wanted him.

And he wanted her.

It was only a bodily longing, like an itch, she told herself firmly. Nevertheless, it was a dangerous desire, for at best it was a distraction from her mission. At worst… She didn't want to think about what could happen if she let her guard down only to be betrayed or hurt somehow.

She had to remain closed to him, closed to her own craving to draw nigh and lower her defenses. There were too many unknowns with Rúnin, too many unanswered questions still. But she planned to remedy that now.

As she neared the cave's opening, a flicker of moment caught her attention. Rúnin's large form, draped in his cloak, was bent and halfway through the cave's mouth.

Without thinking, she yanked her bow from her shoulder and snatched an arrow from her quiver. In one smooth movement, she nocked the arrow and trained it on his back.

"Stop," she commanded curtly from her position slightly farther downhill.

He froze.

"What do you think you're doing?"

"I was merely emptying my bladder," he said, still motionless.

She narrowed her eyes on him. Suddenly she realized that he'd been moving back into the cave, not slipping out of it. Her first reaction was to assume that he was attempting to flee again.

A chide for herself rose in her mind, but she pushed it down. She had every right to be suspicious of him. He hadn't earned her trust just yet.

Even still, she lowered the arrow. "Very well," she said flatly. Once she'd tucked away her bow and the arrow, she trudged the rest of the way up the hill.

His body relaxed at last. As he shuffled the rest of the way into the cave, it was obvious that his leg pained him. He was easing himself to the ground gingerly when she entered the cave.

"You managed to dress yourself," she observed. His trousers still contained a dark red stain down the right thigh, and there was a hole in the material where the arrow had been. "How is your wound?"

He winced as he shifted slightly. "I think the bleeding stopped. I changed the *hvönn* leaves, and it doesn't appear to be infected."

"Good," she said, putting on her flattest countenance.

She felt his eyes on her as she crouched and worked to revive the last embers of the fire.

"We'll still have to wait here for a few more days until I can walk on it," he said.

"Are you trying to talk me out of keeping you on as my guide?"

He exhaled, and she glanced over her shoulder at him.

"Mayhap," he said wearily.

"Don't think for a second that you'll escape me again," she bit out. The old anger stirred within her. "And don't try to talk me out of going after this man—you promised to—"

He held up a hand. "Hear me out. Perhaps then you will no longer wish to pursue Bersi."

She froze, a log halfway positioned over the fire in her hand. The wheels in her mind ground to a halt as she tried to make sense of what he had just said.

"Bersi?" she breathed. "Is that his name? Is that the name of the man who…" She had to swallow, for her throat suddenly constricted. Her head spun. "Bersi."

13

Rúnin's warm, large hand closed over her arm and she realized that he had moved to her side, though she didn't recall it. His dark brows were lowered, a look of concern and sorrow in his eyes.

"Madrena, are you sure... Are you sure you want to know?"

His low voice sounded distant through the pounding of blood in her ears. She'd waited so long, and now she had her first real piece of information about the man who'd haunted her sleep for the last five years.

She nodded. "Ja. I want to know everything."

He took the log from her hand and arranged it against another piece of wood in the fire. The water-resistant moss covering the log's bark caught first, and in short order the wet wood burned as well, though the flames were low and smoky. She watched him tend the fire for a long moment, then mutely removed the rabbit carcass from her belt. She'd already skinned and gutted it in the forest where she'd shot it, and she let Rúnin position it to roast.

At last he spoke again. "What do you remember of him?"

Madrena swallowed hard again. Normally she struggled to push the memories down. She'd never tried to call them up before.

"He was...big. Tall and thick in the chest. His hair was dark but with gray around the face, pulled back into many braids." She shook her head, but the worst of the shadowed memories rose up now. "He had...he had the bear tattoo on the left side of his chest. Once he left me..."

Madrena squeezed her eyes shut. Like a moment before, the warm weight of Rúnin's hand landed gently on her arm. The strength and comfort flowing from him was almost palpable. Her skin warmed beneath his soft touch.

"Once he left, I could hear him giving orders outside the hut. I knew he must be some sort of leader. Afterward, the village was in shambles. Their longships sailed away unobstructed, for they had torched our ships. No one recognized the sails, though from their cut we guessed they were from somewhere to the east."

She opened her eyes to find Rúnin's mouth tight and a muscle ticking in his jaw.

"What was the pattern on the sails?" Though he had seemed sure that he knew the man whom she sought, he apparently wanted to be absolutely certain.

"They had a white background with a red, hunched figure in the middle," she said. Suddenly it dawned on her. "The figure—it was a bear." She'd only seen the ships from very far off, but the memory rose to the surface, clicking into place now that she allowed herself to think about it.

Rúnin nodded, his throat bobbing as he swallowed. "'Twas Bersi," he said flatly. "The bear is his emblem, and he uses it faithfully." His hand dropped from her arm and unconsciously rubbed his chest where the brand scar lay over his own bear tattoo.

Madrena's mind swirled with dozens of questions. "Who is he?"

Rúnin looked to be struggling to answer for a moment. "He is the Jarl of Seterfell, my former home."

With a sudden horrible thought, Madrena had a vision of Rúnin on the raid that had destroyed Dalgaard —and shattered her life. But nei, she realized quickly, Rúnin had been outlawed these past fourteen years, and the attack had been five years ago. She never imagined that she would feel such a surge of relief over a man's long standing as an outlaw.

"Your village lived under his Jarlship?" she asked. "How?" If she went by her memories of him, he would make a savage, cruel monster for a leader.

Again, Rúnin's face flashed with tight pain. "He wasn't always our Jarl. He didn't take power until I was a child old enough to remember life before Bersi. Seterfell used to be a quiet, peaceful place. But when his ships came up the Gulf of Bothnia and he and his men were through ravaging the lowland villages, they turned their attention to the mountains."

His eyes grew distant as he stared at the fire. The hare's juices snapped and hissed, filling the cave with a mouthwatering aroma, but Rúnin seemed barely to notice.

"There must have been something he liked about Seterfell. Or perhaps it was simply that he'd burned and razed every other village he encountered to the ground and had no home to return to. Either way, he decided to make Seterfell his."

Her mind flitted back to the ruthless band of men who'd attacked Dalgaard. "I understand how he could lay waste to so many villages," she said. "But how could he appoint himself Jarl? How could he simply…take over?"

"Bersi arrived with two longships' worth of men—at least fifty trained warriors. Though Seterfell had warriors of its own, we were no match for his force."

She shook her head in disbelief. "And then? How could you all take orders from him? A Jarl's power is only as great as the will of his people."

Rúnin turned hard eyes on her. "Those are pretty words. Your Jarl must be even more noble than I thought if you believe that the only true form of power is granted, not taken."

Madrena felt a flush of angry heat flood her face. She opened her mouth to retort, but then her thoughts flew to that terrible night five years ago. Bersi was indeed a man to take power, not wait for it to be granted.

"What happened, then?" she said instead.

Rúnin dropped his eyes back to the fire. "His takeover didn't take long. Our warriors were killed quickly. My father died in that engagement."

Shame now replaced the quick flash of anger from a moment before in her gut. Of course she knew that the man who'd raped her must have harmed others in his life as well. But Rúnin's quietly spoken words reminded her fully that she wasn't the only one who had lost something to Bersi.

"Once our warriors were defeated, Bersi simply

proclaimed himself our Jarl," Rúnin went on. "Some in the village thought to overthrow him—not with force, for we were clearly outmatched in that regard. But by withholding our support and cooperation with him and his men. That was when the public beheadings of women and children began."

Madrena had to press her lips together to keep from gasping. As a shieldmaiden, she'd seen death in her life—she'd even killed in the heat of battle. But like most Northlanders, she held herself to a strict code of honor. She would never kill an unarmed man, nor would she raise a blade against innocent women and children. It shouldn't surprise her that Bersi was different, yet she felt sick all the same.

"The remaining villagers were effectively cowed after those first few terrifying months. But we never knew what would set him off. Sometimes his moods were exultant. In those times he'd shower the villagers with gifts of fine cloth or even rare figs and wine he'd collected on his raids in other lands. But when his moods turned dark, we never knew who would be put under the axe next."

Rúnin's voice was low but edged like a knife. "He ruled through fear and chaos. No one dared to stand up to him, not even his own men after a while. At first there were whispers that he was mad, but soon even those stopped."

Madrena released a breath she hadn't realized she was holding. "How…how did you survive?"

The hard lines of his face flickered in the low light of the fire. "As I said, I was just a lad. My mother and I kept our heads down and tried to stay out of the way, mostly. But when it came time for me to pledge my fealty and start raiding with him…" He shook his dark head as if the memories were too painful to speak of.

A long silence stretched, broken only by the crackle of the fire and the sizzling hare. Madrena knew Rúnin struggled with the memories, just as she did, but she had to know more. As gently as she could, she spoke again.

"You say you had to keep your head down and follow Bersi. How did you come to be outlawed then?"

His eyes sought hers, flinty and hard. "I stood up to him."

This time she couldn't suppress her inhale of surprise. "But…how…?"

He raised a hand, halting her fumbling. "Let us leave it at that for now. There has been enough dark talk for one day."

He dropped his raised hand to his right thigh, massaging around the arrow wound as if to alleviate some pain.

Madrena opened her mouth to prod, demand, cajole —anything to get more information. But at the strained look on his face and the stiff way he held his body, she let the words die in her throat.

"The hare is done," she said instead.

She drew her seax from her boot and removed the small dagger she'd given Rúnin earlier to shave with. Skewering the roasted hare with the smaller blade, she cut off hunks of meat with the seax and offered them to Rúnin.

He took the proffered meat and blew on it gently to cool it. She watched as his lips pursed, her mind still for a moment even as her body stirred. She'd shoved such feelings aside ever since meeting Rúnin, first because she sensed that there was more to the man than he appeared, and then because she'd learned he was an outlaw. What kind of Northwoman, and a shieldmaiden who lived for honor no less, was she to be drawn to an outlaw?

Yet Rúnin was clearly not like Bersi. She tried to picture Rúnin as a young man, old enough to swear fealty to Bersi and go on his first raid, yet still in essence a lad. His sharp, bright eyes would be the same, as would his dark hair. But he would be smaller, less layered with hard-won muscle, and not as tall and broad. He would be scared. Yet he'd said that he had stood up to Bersi. What sort of boy had Rúnin been? And what sort of man had he turned into?

He turned those blue eyes on her now and she started, shattering her trance.

"Will you not eat?"

She nodded quickly and turned her attention to the hare. She cut herself several pieces and the two of them ate in silence.

Though Rúnin was likely still hungry, she set aside half the rabbit for later in the day. She'd have to go hunting again in the evening, and she could only hope that she'd have better luck than she had this morning.

"You should rest," she said, breaking the somber quiet filling the cave. "But first, let me check your wound."

Rúnin only nodded wearily. He untied his trousers and shimmied them down his hips. Saving Madrena from flushing red again was Rúnin's tunic, which covered his manhood and draped almost as low as the wound on his thigh.

The makeshift bandage wrapped around his leg was tinged red, but the blood looked old. He unwound the linen and peeled off the *hvönn* leaves to reveal the ragged but healing hole in his leg. With a wince, he prodded the flesh around the wound, but the skin was healthy looking and no pus oozed from the arrow hole.

"No infection," he said, though his tight voice belied the discomfort he was in.

"Even still, we will have to rest here for several more days, as you said." She didn't like that idea, but what other option did she have? She needed him as they went deeper into the unfamiliar forests of the northeast. She ignored the voice that whispered in the back of her head that it was more than that—she didn't want to abandon him, even though every law of the Northlands said she should.

He nodded again, rewrapping his thigh and drawing up his trousers.

"You rest," she said, reaching for her bow and quiver. "I'll come back with a feast for us this evening."

He attempted a weak smile, but it didn't reach his pinched eyes. He reclined on the cave's dusty floor and pulled his cloak half over him. Before she even slipped out of the cave, he had drifted into an exhausted sleep.

~

BY THE TIME Madrena returned to the cave, it was long dark. The drizzling rain had stopped, but the temperature had dropped markedly and slate-gray clouds blocked out the moon.

It wasn't exactly a feast, but she'd shot three squirrels and two rabbits. She'd already skinned and gutted them, and once they were cooked, they would keep for a day or two—long enough for her not to go out hunting tomorrow.

As she ducked into the cave, her eyes landed on Rúnin's stretched form in the light of the fire's embers. Good. He needed to rest if they were to continue on their journey.

Though she'd tried to keep her thoughts from all that Rúnin had said while she hunted, she couldn't keep the numbing realizations and swirling questions at bay any longer.

Why had Bersi banished Rúnin fourteen years ago?

Could she trust Rúnin, as her instincts longed to?

Should she still be on this mission, knowing all the costs and dangers?

Aiding an outlaw was an offense punishable by death —or outlawry itself. To make matters worse, her outlaw guide was wounded. And though she prayed it would be otherwise, the air smelled of a snowstorm brewing. It was madness to continue on under these conditions, with over a sennight of travel ahead of them, if Rúnin's knowledge of these lands was accurate.

Despite all the confusion and overwhelming revelations of the last two days, she still had a clear answer to the last question—she wasn't going to give up. Bersi had to answer for the wrong he'd done her. He had too much to pay for to escape her revenge.

All the while her thoughts churned, she stoked the fire and roasted the hares and squirrels. At last Rúnin stirred and sat up. She tossed him a crabapple and a wedge of salty cheese from her supplies from Dalgaard, then passed him his remaining half of the rabbit they'd caten earlier.

As he licked the last of the rabbit's juices from his

fingers, he eyed the freshly caught animals roasting in the fire.

Madrena actually snorted. "Are you ever *not* hungry?"

He raised a dark eyebrow at her. "Nei, I doubt I've felt full these last fourteen years."

His words threatened to deflate Madrena's momentary flash of mirth, but then he went on.

"Once I brought down a reindeer and cooked all the meat over my fire. I ate the entire thing in one evening."

She scoffed, but she felt merriment playing around her mouth. "Nei, I don't believe it. An entire reindeer in one sitting?"

"Ja, indeed," he said, lazily licking his thumb for the last traces of juice. "I chewed on the bones for a while as well because I was still a bit peckish. After all, I'd only had four fish, a dozen wild onions, three handfuls of berries, and a rabbit or two that day."

"You need more practice at jesting," she shot at him, though she felt a smile struggling to break across her lips.

"Mayhap you're right," he said, his own merriment fading. "I find that I don't have very many opportunities to practice."

A somber silence settled between them as they shared the waterskin and Madrena set aside the newly roasted meat for tomorrow. As the fire died, she pulled her cloak around her shoulders, trying to keep the much colder air that filled the cave out of her bones.

A flicker of movement from Rúnin drew her eye. He was reclined but propped on one elbow with his cloak lifted at the edge. It was a silent invitation to share his warmth again, just as they had last night.

Madrena's stomach clenched, but not in fear—nei, it was something more like anticipation. She eyed him for a moment, warring internally over the wisdom of allowing herself the pleasure his large, hard body stirred within her.

"It will keep away the cold, and perhaps the nightmares as well," he said quietly, watching her face.

At last, she nodded, eagerness and trepidation fluttering in her belly like a flock of birds.

As she drew off her cloak, he rearranged his so that it would spread beneath both of them, cutting the chill from the cave's stone floor. She crawled to his side with her cloak in hand to use as a blanket.

Rúnin stilled and let her arrange herself at his side. Like the night before, she placed her head on his chest and let her hand rest on his ribcage. Careful of his right thigh, she draped one of her legs over his, fully entwining their bodies.

Instantly she was surrounded by his heat and scent, all pine and male skin. She stiffened, and a new heat washed through her, a combination of embarrassment and longing. If he had been one of the young men from Dalgaard, she wouldn't deny herself the pleasure of their shared company.

But Rúnin was nothing like those lads—in so many ways. He was a man whose body spoke of a hard life. As an outlaw, he had undoubtedly seen and done things that defied everything she held as honorable. But more importantly, he stirred something within her, something the lads of Dalgaard never had.

It was a visceral, primal longing unlike aught she'd ever known. Her body nigh hummed with awareness and yearning whenever he was close. His very smell shot heat coursing through her veins.

He must have sensed her tenseness, for he drew the arm upon which she lay around her shoulders. His hand absently ran up and down her back. Though his goal was likely to relax her, his touch had the opposite effect. Tingling pleasure shot through her, making her completely alert to every wave of sensation that rippled from the spot of his fingers.

Her skin tightened, especially around her breasts. With her leg slung over his, her womanhood was pressed against the outside of his left thigh. It throbbed deliciously, and she longed to press against his leg, though she knew it would only make the exquisite discomfort deeper.

As his hand slowed and his breathing dropped into a regular rhythm, at last exhaustion won out over her body. She felt the aching desire uncoil just enough to allow her to slip into sleep. Her last thought was of Rúnin as a lad, standing up to the tyrant Bersi—and paying dearly for it.

14

It felt too good.

Madrena's sleep-limp body tucked under his arm and draped across his chest.

The sweet scent of her pale blonde hair tickling his nose.

The gentle rise and fall of her breathing, which caused her soft, round breasts to push against his ribs.

His manhood throbbed as he stared at the slab of rock overhead. The weak, cloud-filtered light of morning had woken him. He thanked Delling, the god of dawn, for rousing him, for now he could savor this simple, blessed moment of Madrena sleeping in his arms.

How he ached to roll over slightly and settle between her legs. He'd kiss her awake slowly, letting her skin warm under his lips. She'd arch her back into him and he'd caress each of her perfect breasts until she welcomed him into her with his name on her tongue. And when they were joined, he would claim her just as she had already claimed him. Naught would be left between them but the ecstasy of the moment.

If it was possible, his manhood swelled even more at his heated thoughts. Yet instead of feeling elated to have this brief reprieve to relish her sleeping form and let his mind wander, a deep emptiness settled in his chest. For this was not the simple bodily longing of a man who was used to being on his own. Nei, it cut deeper than that—too deep.

He was afraid.

Madrena was so strong, so good. She'd lived through a nightmare, and yet she still sought to follow the path of honor by seeking justified revenge against Bersi. She lived by the code of a shieldmaiden, which meant that she carried righteousness in every action and thought.

And he would poison her.

He would poison her with the emptiness in his chest where his sense of honor and rightness had once blossomed. He would poison her with his cowardice. He would poison her even as he felt himself growing to care for her deeper and deeper with each passing moment.

What else could he call the admiration for her determination that had developed into respect for her strength? What else could he call the tug he felt deep in his belly at the mere sight of her? Nei, he didn't just care for her. But he wasn't brave enough to form the more apt word, even within the safety of his own mind.

He'd mistaken her for Freyja when he'd first seen her, for her beauty had arrested him. But perhaps she was actually Lofn, goddess of forbidden love. For where could this desire lead but to his own anguish and loss?

He had been alone for so long—nei, not just alone,

but lonely. Now the gods brought him to Madrena, a woman with the heart of a warrior, only to toy with him.

She stirred in his arms, drawing him out of his dark thoughts. He glanced down at her face, which she so often attempted to make flat and emotionless, as a warrior should. Yet in sleep, she looked younger, more vulnerable. And what dreams ran behind her eyelids such that her lips now parted on a little sigh of pleasure?

Her dark blonde eyelashes fluttered against her berries-and-cream skin. In the next instant, her pale, nigh colorless gray eyes impaled him.

She blinked several times, a rosy blush coming to her cheeks. "Did we…? Did we just…?" She fumbled for words, the blush deepening even as her wide eyes held him.

"Did we what?"

"Did we just…kiss?"

Now it was his turn to widen his eyes. "Nei."

She dropped her eyelashes, clearly mortified but trying to save a shred of dignity. "Forgive me, I…I don't know what I was thinking. 'Twas just a dream."

The last was muttered so softly that even with her head so close to his, he barely heard it. She'd been dreaming of kissing him? By the gods. Apparently he wasn't the only one whose thoughts had wandered into dangerous, if enticing, territory.

He hated seeing her look so humiliated, though. She wouldn't even meet his eyes anymore. Longing for those gray depths to pin him once more, he took her chin in his hand and tilted her face up to his.

As their gazes locked, he felt as though Thor's hammer had struck his chest. His breath left him, and his eyes involuntarily dropped to her full, pink lips.

Knowing that she had been dreaming of his kiss, he now felt the undeniable pull to test the reality of it.

The air suddenly grew thick around them. The cave and their rudimentary surroundings fell away from his vision and all he could see were her lips. She must have been just as hypnotized, for she leaned in until only a hair's breadth separated them.

Rúnin ached with every fiber of his being to close the gap between them. But nei. Madrena had to be the one to do it.

Just when he thought she would remain frozen, with the narrow space separating their lips seeming like the breadth of the entire sky, she sighed and rocked forward.

Her lips were even softer than he could have imagined. They melted into his like honey. A lock of her icy blonde hair brushed his cheek as she tilted her head slightly to bring their mouths more fully together. Her scent, of crisp, fresh air and earthy wood smoke, along with the naturally sweet smell that radiated from her skin, completely enveloped him.

She reached up and tangled her fingers in his hair, drawing him closer. He did the same, and her hair felt like silk as it slid over his fingertips. With another little sigh, her lips parted and the tip of her tongue brushed his mouth. He immediately gave her entrance and their tongues mingled, all velvet heat edged with a hungry urgency.

He realized that his other hand had turned into a claw on her back, so tightly wound was he as he tried to hold back the passion that threatened to erupt within him. He forced his fingers to relax and slid his hand down to that perfect spot where her lower back curved into her bottom.

She moaned softly into his mouth, telling him wordlessly that she enjoyed his touch. Her fingers flexed in his hair, shooting sensation from his scalp straight to his manhood. She was nigh on top of him now, with her breasts crushed against his chest and one of her legs between his. What he wouldn't give at that moment to draw her up so that she straddled him. Then he would have full access to her breasts, with the heat of her sex pressed against his erection.

Seemingly lost in the kiss, she rubbed her leg between his, bringing her womanhood fully in contact with his hip. As her knee rose, she brushed against his rock-hard shaft where it strained against his trousers.

Suddenly she gasped, but it sounded to be more from shock than pleasure. She jerked her mouth away from his, shattering their hot, wet contact.

"Nei," she breathed. "I shouldn't. We shouldn't."

As if it took all her strength, she pulled herself off his body and into a crouch at his side. Her cheeks were even brighter than before, but he wasn't sure if that was because of their kiss or her mortification for it. Either way, the sudden absence of her body left him feeling cold and even hollower than before.

"Don't," he breathed, reaching for her hand, but he didn't know how to find the words to tell her not to run away from their kiss—from *him*. She let him take her hand, but she kept her eyes downcast.

"You said before that there is no shame in the comforts of the body," she said at last. Her eyes flicked up to his. She'd dropped the flat, unreadable veil over her countenance, hiding her emotions from him. "That was all it was. Bodily comfort."

He nodded slowly, dropping her hand. Was that all it

had been to her, or was she just trying to protect herself? They had both been through enough in the last few days—gods, in the last several years—to long to retreat, hide, put up walls. After all, that was all he knew. And yet something deep in his chest rebelled against the impulse to flee from this.

"Ja," he said lowly. "Sometimes bodily comfort is all we have against the weight of the world."

She nodded curtly, the hardened shieldmaiden once again. As she turned toward the cave's mouth, however, she froze and muttered a little curse.

"What is it?"

"See for yourself," she replied, leaning out of the way. He sat up and got a good look at the landscape beyond the cave for the first time that morning.

Fresh white snow covered everything.

He echoed her curse with one of his own. The snow wasn't deep, but if it lingered for the next few days until they resumed their travels once more, the journey would be immeasurably harder.

"Pray that there is no more snow, and that this stuff melts quickly," she said grimly. "I'm going to head out and see if I can collect any last berries and mushrooms. If this cold snap holds, they'll all be ruined by tomorrow."

He tossed her the cloak they'd been using as a blanket and she slung her bag, bow, and quiver over her shoulder.

Just as she stepped out of the cave's mouth, he called to her.

"Madrena!"

She paused and half turned back to regard him where he lay.

"Was it as good as the dream?"

Her eyes widened infinitesimally and that pink color stole over her fair skin.

"'Twas better."

And with that, she vanished.

∽

MADRENA BRUSHED the snow away around the base of a clump of spruce trees with her foot. Though the snow was thinner underneath the spruces' boughs, nevertheless several inches dusted the forest floor.

When she saw a hint of the little brown caps she was looking for, she bent and dusted the remaining snow away with her hands.

She'd already plucked what were likely the last berries of the season—bilberries this time rather than cloudberries—from the snow-encrusted bushes lower down the ridge. She'd also found a cache of chestnuts nearby, and her bag was reassuringly heavy with the harvest she'd gathered. Now she would top the bag off with the bounty of stensopp mushrooms she uncovered carefully with frigid fingers.

She'd forced her mind to remain absolutely focused on the task at hand. The constant need to find food in the wild was exhausting and occasionally mind-numbing, but it was better to concentrate on such drudgery rather than let her thoughts wander to Rúnin.

She couldn't deny her longing for him. But that didn't mean she should act on it.

By the gods, she shouldn't have kissed him at all, and yet she'd nearly done even more than that.

Her lips tingled as if they'd been burned. She brought

one of her snow-dusted fingers up to her mouth and grazed her lips, imagining that his soft yet demanding mouth still pressed against her there. What would have happened if she had let her hand drop to his trousers to feel the hard, thick length of him? What if she had rolled on top of him, her legs open and her sex throbbing against him?

She yanked her hand away from her lips and cursed herself for the wayward thoughts. With a quick snap of her wrist, she decapitated several mushrooms and shoved them into her bag.

Her silly attraction to the man was a distraction at best and a liability a worst.

But her body whispered to her. It was only lust, a perfectly natural desire. What harm could it really do to indulge a little? It didn't have to mean aught more, and it didn't have to jeopardize her larger mission. Perhaps it would relieve some of the tension between them. Then she'd actually be able to focus better.

Madrena straightened and stomped away from the copse of spruce trees. Why couldn't she keep her thoughts straight? There were more important things to occupy her attention than simple bodily desire.

She tromped as fast as the snow would allow, her head down. Snow had fallen softly earlier in the morning, but now the gray sky overhead merely threatened. She would have to gather more wood to keep the chill out of the cave if they were going to be staying for—

Her head snapped up at a ruffle of motion between the trees ahead.

Something dark and rectangular flapped in the snow. Whatever it was, it wasn't naturally occurring in this forest.

Madrena quickly glanced around, but the woods were still and quiet. The only sound was the faint creaking of the trees in the whisper of icy breeze overhead. Slowly, she eased forward. The faint crunch of snow under her boots caused her to cringe, but there was no helping it.

With eyes and ears alert and one hand on her sword hilt, she drew closer to the fluttering object. As she stepped into a little clearing, something seemed vaguely familiar about the spot.

Her gaze locked on the dark object, which rose from a little mound of snow. Suddenly everything clicked into place. The flapping rectangle was a corner of cloak. Three snow-covered lumps lay motionless in the clearing. They were the bodies of the men who'd attacked Rúnin—the men whom she'd killed.

She'd had no qualms about killing them. Though they had every right to kill an outlaw on sight, they themselves were lawless and dishonorable men. Yet she felt a twinge of guilt at seeing their still forms in the snow. She herself was now lawless, for she'd aided an outlaw. By Thor, she'd *kissed* an outlaw, knowingly and willingly.

How did the gods weigh honor? She'd broken the laws of the Northlands many times over by saving Rúnin's life, sheltering him, tending him, and showing him affection. And yet she needed him to guide her to Jarl Bersi and avenge herself, thus rebalancing her honor. Would the gods see it that way, or would she fall from their favor, just as Rúnin had?

And what of Rúnin's integrity? By definition, an outlaw was stripped of all honor, yet all Madrena knew was that Rúnin had stood against a profoundly dishonorable man. What did the gods think of that?

She turned away from the little glen with a heavy heart and a head full of swirling thoughts. But just as she was about to return the way she had come, something snagged in the back of her mind.

Her eyes scanned the three bodies once again. She stepped closer, her instincts ringing bells of warning.

The bodies lay covered in a light dusting of snow, yet the snow on the ground surrounding them was thicker.

Realization struck her like a fist to the stomach.

The bodies had been moved.

Which meant that someone else was in these woods with them.

15

Madrena's eyes darted around the forest, but all remained still and quiet. Yet her gut churned with apprehension and her instincts were screaming at her to draw her sword.

Who had moved the bodies? And why?

She looked at the mound with the corner of cloak flapping lazily in the cold wind again to confirm her fears. The snow covering it must have been the lighter dusting they'd received this morning, not the heavier fall overnight. That meant someone had been here as little as an hour or two ago.

Her gaze quickly scanned the surrounding forest floor, but no obvious tracks or footprints were visible. She cursed. The same snow that had dusted the bodies in a coat of white had covered the tracks of whoever had been there.

But could it simply have been a curious—or hungry—animal that had shifted the bodies enough to knock the initial layer of snow from them?

Forcing her feet to move, Madrena inched closer to the bodies. Nei, no bite marks or other signs that the trappers had become some forest creature's meal. The fact that each of the bodies must have been rolled over and inspected indicated that the act had been done by a human. Possibly even someone who knew the men.

Dread laced through Madrena's veins. Again her eyes flickered around the woods. Where was the man now? Could he be watching her even as she stood in full view?

Her gaze landed on her own tracks in the snow, which trailed crisp and fresh behind her. Whoever was out there, she was leading him right to her.

And back to Rúnin, who lay injured and weaponless in the cave at the top of the ridge.

She clapped a hand over her mouth to muffle another curse. Her mind raced as she considered what to do.

Taking a deep breath of icy air, she willed her mind to concentrate. She'd been trained as a warrior, which also meant thinking like a warrior—strategically and calmly.

Where had she left footprints already? So lost in thoughts of Rúnin and his lips had she been that she'd likely wandered widely as she'd picked berries and gathered chestnuts lower on the ridge.

But, she reminded herself with relief, the earlier snows that had covered the unknown man's footprints had likely covered hers as well. She didn't have to worry about her wanderings as she'd foraged that morning.

Yet the snow had stopped before she'd begun collecting mushrooms. She'd left tracks from that spot to here, and she still had to get back to the cave through the blanket of white covering everything.

Thinking fast, she darted to a nearby spruce tree and grasped a thin branch toward the bottom that was almost as long as one of her arms. With a jerk and a twist, she broke the branch free. She winced as the snap echoed through the trees, cacophonous in the comparably quiet woods. But naught stirred to indicate that she'd been heard.

With one hand holding the branch and the other gripping the hilt of her sword, she slowly began walking backward over her own tracks. She lowered the branch's pine-needled end into the snow, lightly dragging it back and forth over her footsteps as she crept back through them.

She painstakingly retraced her steps to where she'd dug through the snow to collect mushrooms. With a careful sweep of the branch, the evidence of her presence was smoothed over.

Her back ached and her body crackled with tension as she simultaneously tried to cover her tracks and watch her back in case she was set upon. Walking backward and hunching over to keep the branch brushing delicately over the snow made her skin itch with vulnerability.

She had to go more than halfway down the ridge along the path she'd made between the berry shrubs and the copse of spruces. But at last her footprints began to fade as the snow from that morning had filled them in. Of course now she had to go back up the ridge and make her way to the cave, all the while erasing her tracks.

After what felt like hours of taut alertness and hunched strain in her back, she at last spotted the cave over her shoulder.

When she reached the mouth of the cave, she chucked the branch inside and paused to let her eyes adjust to the dimness.

Rúnin sat up, his face tight with worry.

"You were gone longer than I expected," he said. Before she could gather her thoughts to explain, he went on, his brow creased. "You need not fear me, if that's what this is about. I would never push myself on you. 'Twas only a kiss, as you said."

She didn't have time to consider the shadow of sorrow and regret that crossed his hard features. Instead, she held up a hand.

"There is someone in the area with us," she blurted out.

"What?" All traces of uncertainty vanished as his whole body tensed.

"I came across the clearing where the bodies of the three trappers who set upon you lay. They had been disturbed, rolled over, and then left in place. There were no tracks, but I'm sure it was a man—perhaps a companion of theirs."

"And you came back here? Your tracks will lead him right to us!" he snapped.

Madrena bristled. "Nei, they won't, for I covered every last one."

He stilled at her tone and his eyes settled on her. "Of course you did," he said quietly. "Forgive me."

She gave him a curt nod, some of the anger draining from her. But it was quickly replaced with apprehension as Rúnin tried to rise to his feet.

"What do you think you're doing? You are in no condition to walk."

He turned a disbelieving stare on her. "We have to get out of here—now. Whoever is out there is likely looking for the people responsible for the deaths of those three men. As you say, he could be their companion, a fourth trapper. What do you think he'll do when he finds us here?"

"So you think we can just run away, with you barely able to stand?"

She forced herself to stay rooted in place as she watched him struggle to gain his feet. He tested his injured leg by taking a shuffling step forward. But his face contorted in pain and he grunted through clenched teeth. He had to shift his weight almost immediately to his good leg.

He took a few steadying breaths and then met her eyes again. "What is the alternative? Wait here for him to find us? If he is a trapper, then he'll also know how to track. It won't take long, no matter how good a job you did covering your footprints."

She cursed under her breath and tore her eyes away to scan the cave's walls. But no answers lay in the cold stone.

"So this is the life of an outlaw, is it? Always running, always looking over your shoulder for signs of other humans? Fearing discovery at all times?"

"Ja," he bit out. The sharpness in his tone covered the sadness she found in his eyes when she met his gaze again.

Something pinched her chest. Was it simply the realization of how lonely and fearful the life of an outlaw must be? Or was it deeper than that, an ache for all that Rúnin held back in his eyes?

She pushed the twinge aside. She could think on it later. Right now, they had to act.

Without a word, she set about erasing the evidence of their presence in the cave. She cleared out the ashes from their fire and scattered the few remaining pieces of wood they'd planned on burning. Naught could be done for the smear of soot blackening the cave's roof near the mouth, so she left it.

Meanwhile, Rúnin bent with some difficulty and collected his cloak, fastening it around his neck.

Taking up the spruce branch once more, Madrena stepped aside and let Rúnin hobble out of the cave. She didn't comment, but she cringed internally at how badly he was limping. They wouldn't be able to move fast. She could only hope that Rúnin's leg was healed enough to stand the strain under which they were about to put it.

They circled around the cave and began descending the ridge on the east side, Rúnin limping in front while Madrena dusted over their footprints with the branch behind him.

She paused to look out across the lands that lay eastward. From their vantage point on the ridge, the snowy scenery unfolded like a blanket of the finest white wool at their feet. There was less snow in the lower lands in the distance, and she even caught a glimpse of shimmering water along the horizon. Between them and the lowlands with its waterway, however, lay several more ridges of snow-capped hills and mountains. The sea of trees, some completely clad in white and others the shadowy shades of deep green and black, was nigh unbroken as far as she could see.

Madrena swallowed hard. Their already difficult overland journey to Kvenland and beyond was now hampered by snow and plagued by an unknown man who was likely hunting them.

She sent up a prayer to the gods, but she wasn't sure if they would listen to her anymore.

16

Rúnin clenched his teeth against the pain he knew would come as he put his foot down.

There was a strangely lulling rhythm to the bursts of hot agony that flared through his leg with each step.

They had only been traveling for about an hour, but he had withstood hundreds upon hundreds of those flashes of pain. Madrena said naught about his slow pace and the occasional grunts that escaped from his throat. Even still, he could sense her tense frustration behind him as she covered their tracks.

He begged the gods for the dozenth time to unleash the snow that was pent up in the low, dark clouds overhead. If it would fall, they wouldn't have to worry about erasing their footprints and Madrena could lend him a shoulder to lean on. The scent of a storm hung in the air, and yet the snow wouldn't oblige. Here he'd been cursing the snow that morning and now he was praying for it in the afternoon. He turned his ire on himself for his fickleness.

Madrena sighed behind him, the first noise she'd made in the last hour since they'd left the cave.

Rúnin halted, shifting all his weight to his left leg, and glanced over his shoulder at her.

She'd stopped walking a few feet away and was arching her back against the stiff hunch she had to maintain to cover their footprints.

"Rúnin," she began, her voice weary. "This isn't going to work. You can't walk, and—"

"What have I been doing for the last hour, then?" he gritted out. He exhaled harshly. He shouldn't be taking his fear and frustration out on her. It wasn't her fault that he'd been wounded or that another man lingered somewhere in the area.

"There is no other alternative," he said, his voice now as tired as hers. "I will be fine. I've survived worse than this."

She eyed him, her blonde brows lowered. Her mouth opened, likely to form a question, but then she must have decided that now wasn't the time to probe him about what he'd lived through for the last fourteen years, or how he came into these circumstances in the first place.

Part of him wished he could explain all to her, but whenever he thought of speaking the words, shame and humiliation washed through him. He'd vowed never to speak of those events fourteen years ago. Luckily she hadn't pressed him on it—yet.

"Come on," he said, slowly turning away and lifting his right leg for another nerve-jolting step. "We'd better keep—"

The scent of wood smoke hit his nostrils, cutting through the cold, crisp air.

"Rúnin, what is—"

He threw up a hand to silence her and sniffed the air. The look of confusion slipped from her face as she watched him and inhaled as well.

There was no mistaking that smell—the scent of smoke meant that someone was nigh.

He cast his eyes around the forest in which they stood. They'd descended completely from the ridge into a thickly wooded valley. The trees in this area were mostly pines sprinkled with a few aspens and rowans that had been caught with brightly colored leaves still clinging to their boughs when last night's snow hit. They were close enough together to obscure any line of sight he might have.

As he shifted his gaze upward into the snow-laden branches overhead, he spotted what he was looking for. A sooty-gray thread of smoke wove its way through the trees, slightly darker than the clouds overhead. It was drifting toward them from the south.

Silently, he pointed to the trail of smoke and then lowered his hand toward the south. Madrena's sharp, pale eyes followed his gestures and she gave him a quick nod.

He began hobbling north, but he froze when he realized Madrena had turned south and had taken several steps toward the smoke.

"What are you doing?" she hissed lowly.

"What does it look like? I'm getting as far away from whoever's out there as I possibly can," he shot back.

She planted her hands on her hips and leveled him with a determined look. "I thought it would be obvious from the last hour that we aren't going to outrun anyone."

He pressed his lips together in frustration. "Mayhap not, but I damn well don't plan on going *toward* whoever it is either."

"I'm going to scout—carefully—and see what I can learn. Perhaps the fire simply belongs to…"

"Who? Who else would be out in these conditions besides outlaws and trappers?"

A pained look flitted across her eyes, and he realized that he'd just lumped her in with himself as an outlaw. But the horrible reality was that it was accurate. She would face whatever fate he did now that she'd aided him. He'd dragged her into this, he'd put her in danger, but there was naught he could do now—besides convince her to flee with him.

The hurt on her face quickly transformed back to the firm set of determination.

"Ja, you're right. It can't be anyone good. But if it is the same person who saw the bodies of the three trappers earlier, perhaps we can learn something of him, or throw him off our trail."

He shook his head slowly. "Madrena, this is madness. We must—"

"I'll not simply flee!" she snapped. Lowering her voice, she went on, though hot anger clearly still coursed through her. "It may be your way to run, to evade, but it's not mine."

Her words cut deep. Ja, he was used to turning tail and fleeing. It was how an outlaw lived. If the boy he'd once been could see him now, he would likely have the same look of disdain in his eyes as Madrena. Though she tried to keep her features impassive, her shoulders were stiff with frustration.

"I'm going," she said flatly.

He exhaled slowly. "I'll go with you, then."

Her eyes raked over him. "You don't have to."

"I'm not very well going to let you storm into some unfamiliar camp with an unknown number of men waiting for you," he said with annoyance. "You'll need help. I'm going with you."

A look of surprise, likely at his stubborn insistence on accompanying her, flitted across her face. "All right," she said, grudging acceptance warring with curiosity in her voice.

"I'll need a weapon."

All traces of receptiveness fell from her and she narrowed her nigh colorless eyes at him.

"If you are plotting to—"

"You're the one with the grand plan to scout around a strange camp, remember?" He raised an eyebrow at her. "I just don't want to have naught but two empty hands if we are surrounded and set upon by whoever's out there."

Now it was her turn to arch a brow at him. "You can barely walk. You think you can fight?"

"Ja, I do." He held her flinty gaze until she finally snorted and walked up to him. She bent and withdrew the seax from her boot. A close-range weapon—she still didn't trust him with the bow and arrows over her shoulder, but it was a start.

She held the long dagger in front of his face. "You'll be giving this back to me—handle first—once we are done scouting." Her tone brokered no arguments, though he wouldn't have made them anyway.

He took the seax with a little nod, then tossed it in his hand, getting a feel for the weight of it. She led the way, cutting south toward the source of the smoke. She no longer bothered to cover their tracks since they would retrace their steps when they were done scouting.

After a few minutes of walking in silence, she took hold of his wrist and drew his arm over her shoulder, taking some of his weight.

"Thank you," he grunted. Those were unfamiliar words for him to utter, but then again, it was an unfamiliar experience to be helped by someone. Yet Madrena had given him aid in countless small and large ways in the last sennight. Something low in his belly clenched at that thought—he couldn't let himself imagine for a second that he was worthy, redeemable. But by the gods, he wanted to be—for *her*.

He pushed the thought away. Now wasn't the time to indulge in fancies.

As they drew closer to the source of the smoke, Madrena separated their bodies and pointed for him to circle around to the left. He nodded and they both crept forward, she smoothly and silently and he with his awkward hobble, but he refused to make a sound.

The trees thinned slightly and Rúnin caught his first sight of the camp. He froze, his eyes scanning for any sign of movement. But the camp was quiet and appeared deserted—for now.

From a dozen paces away, Madrena nodded at him and motioned for them both to move forward. He kept his ears and eyes sharp for an indication of another presence in the area, but all remained still and silent.

At last, he and Madrena stood in the middle of the small camp. The fire smoked profusely but was nigh dead, left unattended likely for several hours. A small animal skin tent was propped up in the snow for shelter. Leaning against the tent was a stout pine walking staff.

Besides a few empty traps discarded on the ground and partially covered with snow, the camp was bare.

Madrena leaned over and placed her hand atop the smoking logs of the fire. "All but out," she said quietly, confirming what he'd guessed.

Rúnin pointed to the traps on the ground. "It looks like we were right—our trapper friends had a companion."

Madrena scanned the forest, her body tense. "Then where is he?"

"Likely out looking for us."

A shiver stole over her that probably had naught to do with the cold.

"Have you seen all you wish?"

She nodded and turned to go, but he paused before the little tent.

"What are you waiting for?" Discomfort mingled with urgency in her low voice.

Without responding, he ducked his head inside the tent. Just as he'd been hoping, the trapper had left some supplies inside. He'd likely been camped in the area the night before and had set out to check his traps and meet up with his companions. Instead, he'd found their bodies and was probably still out scouring the forest for their killers.

Rúnin grabbed a waxed cloth bundle he guessed was filled with food. A flash of red caught his eye when he lifted the cloth. Underneath lay a pile of red mushrooms dotted with white. Although Rúnin knew instantly what they were, he raised one in his fingers and inspected it. The mushroom had white gills and a rounded, blood-red and white-spotted cap.

He set the mushroom back in its pile and backed out

of the tent. He knew the power and potency of those fungi—and he wanted naught to do with it.

Once he'd emerged from the tent, he took hold of the pine staff.

Madrena stared at him with a look of barely-veiled unease. "What are you doing?"

He shrugged. "He can go back to Knorrstad in the south for more food if he needs it. But we cannot." He raised the walking staff. "And taking this may or may not slow him down, but it will certainly speed us up."

That cutting disdain flashed across her eyes again. He knew what she was thinking.

"This is how an outlaw survives, Madrena," he said, his words coming out harsher than he'd intended. "We steal. We flee. We do whatever it takes to live another day. You are welcome to leave me behind. Otherwise, this is how *you* survive now, too."

She swallowed and with visible effort molded her features into the look of a hardened shieldmaiden.

"Let's get out of here."

He held up his hand, pausing her mid-turn. Hefting her seax in his hand, he flipped it so that he gripped the blade and extended the handle toward her.

"As promised," he said flatly.

She considered the blade for a long moment before at last meeting his eyes. "Keep it for now."

Another sign of trust. But was he deserving? He would have to show her that he was.

He gave her a nod and slipped the seax into the outside of his boot. Without asking, he took the lead, retracing their footprints in the snow. Madrena trailed, carefully dusting her spruce branch over their tracks.

Rúnin walked easier now with the staff to lean on,

yet his unease was greater than before. As he'd warned Madrena, the trapper whose camp they'd just raided would know how to track. Even displacing their footprints, he might still be able to hunt them. Stealing his food could slow him down if he was low on supplies. Then again, it could add fuel to an anger likely ignited by the bodies of the three other trappers.

He hurried his steps, pushing his leg despite the pain. They were in danger, but not nearly as much as he would be once they set foot in Kvenland and drew closer to Seterfell. His face—or at least the face he'd had as a fourteen-year-old lad—was known in those parts. He'd made a promise to Madrena to guide her to Seterfell and Bersi. Yet if he did, he was a dead man.

17

The skies finally made good on their promise. Not long after they slipped away from the trapper's camp, a heavy snow began to fall.

They both drew up the hoods on their cloaks and continued on through the storm. Madrena discarded the branch she'd been using to obscure their tracks with no small amount of relief on her features.

As the hours passed, the pain in Rúnin's right thigh blessedly dulled to a stiff ache. He leaned on the pine walking staff as they trudged through the ever-deepening snow.

The tension from being in the trapper's camp lingered around them for the first few hours of walking, but slowly it melted away and the silence between them was relaxed. It would be nigh impossible for the trapper to track them through these conditions. Their footprints would fill quickly with the fresh, heavy flakes falling, and the man would have no idea which direction they were headed.

After a particularly arduous trek through a thickly

blanketed valley and over a steep hill, they paused, catching their breath. They stood close enough that their puffing white exhales mingled.

How used to being around another person—around Madrena specifically—Rúnin had grown in hardly more than a sennight. Strange. He'd thought during the darkest years of his outlawry that he would never know the companionship of another person again, that he was doomed to be alone for the rest of his days, however long those might be.

Yet it was different with Madrena. He glanced at her as her sharp gaze surveyed the landscape ahead of them. Her gray eyes seemed to absorb the diffuse light seeping through the clouds and bouncing off the snow. She was the fiercest, strongest person he'd ever known. Here she was traveling across the Northlands to face the pain of her past. The clarity in her sense of purpose was admirable.

A stab of shame sliced through Rúnin's belly. She was braver than he, for he would never risk facing Bersi or the events of his past again.

"Are we in Kvenland yet?" she asked.

The falling snow obscured the longer sightlines they'd had when they'd departed the cave earlier that day, but Rúnin was familiar with this series of ridges.

"Ja, on the western outskirts. Did you see water in the distance when we were leaving the cave?"

She nodded.

"That was the Gulf of Bothnia. Kvenland spans both sides of the gulf, and the lands to the north as well. We'll still have to skirt around the northeast side of the gulf to get to Seterfell, but we are less than a sennight away now."

The words should have been a relief to speak, and yet a stone of sadness sat heavily in his chest. In under a sennight, Madrena would be delivered to Seterfell and he would never see her again.

She would be killed by Bersi and his men.

Or she would kill Bersi, but he wouldn't be there to witness it. He would never set foot in Seterfell again. The knowledge weighed heavy.

"Madrena, there's something you need to know."

Her gaze assessed him for a moment, then shifted to the clouds overhead. The snow still fell steadily, but the light was fading from gray to the blue of rapidly approaching night.

"Let's get settled first," she responded at last.

He assented with a terse nod. Perhaps making camp would give him time to order his thoughts.

They descended the hill into thicker tree cover and began scouring the forest for a good place to hunker down for the night. Madrena spotted a fallen log leaning against an enormous spruce, creating a little sheltered spot underneath. She set about scooping away the snow that had drifted beneath the dead log to reveal a soft bed of old pine needles and leaves.

Meanwhile, Rúnin broke off several pine branches and propped them against the spruce and the log, making rudimentary walls and sealing off the shelter from further snowfall.

"Should we have a fire?" Madrena asked when their little shelter was complete.

Rúnin considered. "We'd be risking making ourselves a more visible target if the trapper somehow managed to track us through that storm. But then again, it will be a cold night."

Her eyes flickered over his form, and he knew she was remembering the way they'd stayed warm the last two nights. She tore her eyes away and he thought he detected a flush of color in her cheeks that had naught to do with the frosty air. Would she still look at him that way after he told her he wasn't going to Seterfell with her?

She went about making a fire, seeming to decide that the risk of detection was worth the extra heat. Though all the available wood was damp, after several tries with her fire-steel and flint stone, she managed to get a little blaze going at the entrance to their shelter.

Rúnin propped his walking staff against a tree and crawled into their little bough-walled nook. The space would only be big enough for the two of them, but the thought sent renewed heat into his blood. The dull ache in his leg drew his attention away from such thoughts, however.

A quick inspection of the wound revealed that it was still healing with no trace of infection. That was a gift, for they didn't have any more *hvönn* leaves to treat it. Rúnin had likely slowed the healing process with all the walking he'd done today, but the flesh looked more healed than it had yesterday.

He then took the opportunity to examine the pouch of cloth-wrapped food he'd taken from the trapper's tent. It contained a few slabs of flatbread, along with several hunks of smoked venison. As Madrena leaned back with satisfaction from their little fire, he showed her their cache.

"Perhaps you won't go to sleep hungry, for my satchel is full of berries, mushrooms, and chestnuts," she said with a little smile.

She passed him a handful of nuts and he quickly scored an X into them with her seax, then nestled them into the small fire to roast. Under the cover of their shelter, they shared a flatbread and ate the remains of the rabbit and squirrel that Madrena had hunted back at the cave while they waited on the chestnuts.

The nuts' shells at last started splitting, and Rúnin snatched them from the coals with quick fingers. He wrapped them in the trapper's cloth and rubbed them together, breaking away the roasted shells until only the flesh remained. They ate quickly to let the nuts' heat warm them.

When their bellies were full, they both held their hands over the flames, the crackling wood the only sound for a long stretch.

"What was it you wanted to discuss?" Madrena said at last, eyeing him sideways.

The air suddenly seemed to grow heavy in Rúnin's lungs, but he willed himself to speak.

"I will not be going with you to Seterfell."

She stiffened by his side. "I told you before—don't think to go back on your promise again."

"Nei, Madrena, I'm not. I'll lead you to Seterfell, as I vowed. When we are close enough, I'll show you how to get there, but I won't be going with you."

She turned her confused gaze on him. Her pale eyes glowed in the firelight. "Why?"

He sighed. All the time he'd had to gather his thoughts while they'd made camp hadn't been enough. "Because I was made an outlaw there. Because I swore I'd never go back. Because I could be recognized."

Madrena sat in stunned silence for a moment, but

then her eyes narrowed on him. "To whom did you swear never to go back?"

"To myself."

"But you are an outlaw—you can't go into *any* village. Why would you have to make a special vow about Seterfell? Why is it different?"

He exhaled slowly. Was it possible that she knew him better than he knew himself? He had to consider her question for a long moment before he was willing to speak the shameful answer.

"Because I cannot face Bersi," he said through clenched teeth.

"Why not?" she retorted. "I would have thought you'd leap at the chance I'm presenting you—a reason to go back to your village, and with someone who hates Bersi just as much as you do. Don't you want vengeance for his treatment of your people—and for yourself?"

"Nei," he ground out, his shame turning to hot frustration in his guts.

She continued to stare at him with disbelief. "From everything you've told me, Bersi deserves your hatred just as much as he deserves mine. He terrorized your village, murdered your people, and left you branded and banished. How can you not *burn* with the desire for revenge?"

"It doesn't matter," he said flatly, trying to end this dangerous conversation. "As I said, I'll make sure you can get to Seterfell, but then I'll be heading out on my own again."

He should have known that Madrena, with the determination of a great warrior, wouldn't let the matter go so easily.

"You still haven't explained why you were outlawed," she began.

He shot her a warning look and she held up her hand to calm him. "I am not asking you to tell me, for clearly you don't want to," she said quickly. "But from what you did say, you stood up against Bersi's tyranny fourteen years ago. You couldn't have been more than a lad."

"I was fourteen," he muttered, his mood darkening further.

"And yet you stood up to him," she prodded. "That took courage—and honor."

"Nei," he bit out, turning the full force of his blackened temper on her. He stuffed down all the pain, turning it into hot rage. A little voice whispered in his mind that it wasn't Madrena's fault, that he shouldn't be taking out his fury on her, but he ignored it, barreling forward.

"Don't you understand?" he went on, his voice tight with barely controlled anger. "None of that matters. It doesn't matter what my reasons were. I am an oath-breaker. I defied my Jarl's orders. I questioned Bersi publicly. I *deserve* to be an outlaw."

Madrena's eyes widened at his harshly spoken words, but she held his gaze, not backing down. "And so you'll just...*accept* Bersi's actions? You'll let him get away with all the wrongs he's committed against your village? How can you?"

"As I said," he repeated, trying to rein in the storm that raged within him. "I am an oath-breaker. I got what I deserved."

"But how—"

"Because I'm not you!" he snapped, the pain boiling

over at last. "Because I'm not just an innocent who was wronged by Bersi. I pledged fealty to him, and I broke that pledge. I am not an honorable man. Why would I charge into Seterfell looking for vengeance like some kind of hero from the Sagas? I'm not a hero, Madrena. I am an *outlaw*."

She stared at him wide-eyed for a long time, assessing him. He tried to calm his breathing and unclench his fists, but pain and anger still surged through him. Even the frigid night air couldn't cool the hot frustration coursing through his whole body.

At last she released him from her gaze and dropped her eyes to the weak fire.

"You're wrong," she said quietly. "You are not a man without honor."

'Twas as if someone had poked a hole in his anger and he felt it all drain from his body. What was left, however, was a deeper sadness.

"You've only known me for a sennight, Madrena," he said wearily. "You have no idea what I'm capable of —what I've done to survive."

"Ja, you're right, I don't," she said, the heat coming back into her own voice. "But I know what I've seen in this past sennight."

He tried to push the bitterness of so many memories down, but it rose in his throat anyway. "You've seen me steal."

"Ja. And I was the beneficiary of your theft, remember?" she retorted, pointing toward the trapper's cloth that still held food.

"You've seen me flee like a coward instead of fight."

"And we are likely both alive now because of it."

He leveled her with a stare. "I've killed men, just so

that I could live. Tell me, what makes my life more valuable than theirs?"

She met his gaze unflinchingly. "You've seen me kill as well, Rúnin. Those deaths were so that you and I could live. Self-defense is different than the kind of murder Bersi commits."

Slowly, she reached toward him and took one of his hands in hers. Her palms were callused from training to fight, and the backs were slightly weathered. This woman was no sheltered girl. She was a shieldmaiden, forged in pain and battle. And she was arguing for his honor.

"I've also seen you protect me," she said softly. "If you hadn't thrown that blade into one of those trappers, his arrow would be in my throat right now. And you know of my nightmares and…and their source…" Her voice hitched over the words, but she went on. "Yet I feel safer than I ever have before when I am asleep in your arms."

The air around them suddenly grew heavy with anticipation. She kept his hand in her smaller one, but raised her other hand to brush her fingertips along his bristled jawline.

"You have honor, Rúnin," she whispered. "Otherwise I would not desire you so fiercely. Otherwise I would not long for the feel of your lips again. Otherwise—"

He could take no more of her searching gray eyes, her feather-light touch, and her soft but assured words. His mind reeled with all she had said. She thought him worthy. Yet pain and doubt still laced through him. Though her words didn't erase his fear that he was past redemption, he yearned to believe her.

He needed to *feel* her words, to taste them on her soft lips and know the truth of them in the way her body moved against his.

In a moment of clarity, he knew what he wanted—what he so desperately needed. He closed the distance between them like lightning, his lips claiming hers in a searing kiss.

18

As Rúnin's lips connected with hers, a moan of relief rose in Madrena's throat.

She was trained to fight, to be brave, yet she'd never been more afraid than the moment she admitted that she desired Rúnin.

She'd feared that he would reject her, that he would brush off her words as nonsense—or worse, that he would turn a cold shoulder to her.

But even deeper than that was the fear that grew from her own feelings. She shouldn't want him. Everything he'd said to try to push her away was true, yet her body simply wouldn't listen to such reasoning. For she knew somewhere deep within her heart that she was right—he was a good man, whether he believed it or not.

But the nigh overpowering draw she felt toward him frightened her. Her desire left her vulnerable. The frustration and confusion she'd felt a moment before had transformed into its root—she cared for him. Ja, that was it. Deepest of all, she was afraid of the strength of her own emotions for him.

But what future could there be between them?

She didn't want to think on the future now, not with his warm lips melting against hers, his hands snaking around her back. His heat and scent enfolded her just as surely as his hands did as he pulled her closer.

He slanted his head, drawing her deeper into the kiss. His piney maleness overpowered her senses and her head swam. The velvety, wet heat of his tongue asked entrance against her lips and she readily parted them, meeting his tongue with hers.

His fingers reflexively curled on her back as their tongues mated in a heated dance. Without realizing that she'd moved, she found her own fingers twining in the dark hair at his nape, holding him close.

But it wasn't close enough.

She threw one leg over his, careful of his right thigh. At her movement, he pulled her closer until she was nigh sitting in his lap in their little shelter, their mouths still fused together. Ripples of heat emanated from where his tongue stroked and claimed her mouth. The heat drew her nipples taut beneath her dress and shift, but it didn't stop there. It traveled lower, pooling between her legs in a throbbing need.

Something hard and long pressed against her thigh, and she knew just how fervent his own desire was. That realization only flooded her with a more urgent longing. They both wanted this, against the odds and despite the insanity of it all.

One of the large, warm hands on her back drifted down to her bottom, holding her firmly in place in his lap. His grasp brought her thigh more directly in contact with his aroused manhood, and his fingers dug into the flesh of her bottom, giving her another jolt of pleasure.

His other hand slid to her waist and lingered there for a moment, his thumb brushing against the wool of her dress just below one of her breasts.

With a breathy moan of anticipation, she arched slightly, silently inviting him to claim her breast.

He complied almost instantly, cupping her in his large, rough hands. Madrena would have cursed the stout wool of her dress and the linen of her shift for separating her aching breast from his touch if her tongue weren't entwined with Rúnin's.

Another moan rose in her throat as his thumb swept slowly back and forth over the hardened peak of her nipple. She writhed on his lap, drawing a groan from him as well when her bottom rubbed against his manhood.

Suddenly, though, he ripped his mouth from hers.

"Gods, I want this—I want *you*," he breathed. "But...are you sure?"

Her lips ached from the absence of his kiss. The hot throb between her legs was growing more insistent by the second. The hard tips of her breasts were nigh begging for his touch.

Ja, she wanted this—desperately. Her body cried for his, and for the torrent of pleasure promised with every passing heartbeat. But it was more than that. She wanted *him*, too. She wanted to be enveloped by his strength. Somehow he made her forget all the darkness of the last five years. He chased away the nightmares. She longed for only him, only now.

"Ja," she panted in response. "I want *you*, too."

His lips met hers again, even more heated and

urgent than before. But now he took her hips in his hands and tilted her backward so that her back made contact with the soft, piney floor of their shelter.

Never breaking their kiss, his hand once again found her breast, and his caress sent bolts of sensation all the way to the soles of her feet. The weight of one of his legs draped over her.

He shifted again, rolling slightly so that one of his knees nestled between her legs and he came more fully on top of her. He was so big and heavy that his body nigh pinned her.

She tensed suddenly, fear stabbing her belly.

"Nei," she said, twisting her mouth away from his.

Instantly, he froze. She squirmed under his weight and he seemed to understand immediately. He rolled to the side, completely freeing her from his body.

"Madrena, I'm sorry. I shouldn't have…I know that we shouldn't…"

She pressed a hand to his lips to halt his apologies. She took a deep breath, trying to release the flood of dark memories and her instinctive response. "It's not that I don't want to…It's just…I don't like to be on my back."

To show him that the fires of desire still burned within her, she leaned in and captured his lips. He let her kiss him for a moment but didn't respond in kind. She placed a hand on his chest and felt the tension in his body. He was obviously holding himself back.

She took his bottom lip between her teeth, nipping it. He inhaled sharply and his hand instinctively shot out, clutching her hip.

"I still want you," she breathed against his lips. "Let me show you how."

She pushed on his shoulders until he lay flat on his back, his cloak splayed out beneath him. Crouching under the pine boughs of their shelter's low ceiling, she swung one leg over his torso so that she straddled him.

"I have dreamed of this," he whispered, his voice low and gravelly.

She started in surprise for the briefest of moments. She'd have to ask him about that later. But for now, her body demanded all her attention.

The cold night air caressed her heated skin when she twisted her skirts out from between them. Soft as a feather, his fingertips landed on her calves just above her boots. As he slowly trailed them up her legs, she watched him in the low light of the fire behind her.

His features were all hard lines and shadows, with dark stubble bristling his jawline. But his eyes looked nigh black in the dimness. He had the hungry look of a wolf about him. His jaw clenched and unclenched in barely restrained longing.

When his fingertips reached her knees, she rose up slightly so that he could tease the sensitive skin behind them. She let out a shaky breath as his hands skimmed higher, to the soft, delicate flesh of her thighs.

All the while he watched her with that same desperate hunger. What would this man do to her if they could strip themselves of their garments completely and leave naught between them? As it was, the air was too cold to discard their clothes.

As if in answer to her thoughts, he spoke, his voice husky. "I long to see all of you, Madrena, as I saw you by the pond so many days ago. What I wouldn't give to take each of your nipples in my mouth and lick you until you screamed my name."

She moaned in response as a fresh bolt of heat tore through her. Her nipples grew even harder against her dress. She twisted against the material, loving the sensation even as she wanted more.

His hands continued upward until they smoothed over her bottom and came to rest on her hips. His thumbs fit perfectly just below her hip bones, while his fingers splayed out along the curve of her bottom.

He pulled her down so that her sex came in contact with the hard column of his cock. Naught blocked the pleasure she sought now except the material of his trousers. Her hands dropped to the ties and she made quick work of them.

His cock sprung free, pulsing against her womanhood. They both froze for a moment, their sharp inhales echoing each other. Then he dropped his hands from her hips and reached between them, finding her slick heat.

"Gods," he breathed on another moan.

She rocked slowly back and forth against his hand as his fingers explored that nub of pure pleasure. Her hands landed on his chest and her fingers were like talons in the material of his tunic.

His cock was pinned between them, brushing her sex, yet Rúnin seemed content to stretch their aching torture. The tip of his manhood grew damp, either with her slickness or his own arousal, she didn't know.

While the thumb of one hand circled that perfect spot of pleasure, his other hand came up and resumed its earlier attention on her breast. With each pass of the thumb over her nipple, liquid fire shot straight through her to her sex. She let her head loll back as sensation built, threatening to wash her away completely.

But she wanted to share this exquisite pleasure with him. She rose up on her knees slightly, freeing his cock, which stood rigidly from his haphazardly opened trousers. She took him in her hand and he involuntarily jerked his hips.

Though she wanted to draw out his pleasure as well as hers, the torrent coursing through her could not be held back any longer. She guided his cock along the slick folds of her sex until he nudged her entrance. His hands stilled on her and a glance at his face revealed even in the low light that he was barely holding on to his control.

Her mind flitted away for the briefest of moments. What would it be like if Rúnin let go of his restraints and claimed her fully? What would it be like if she trusted him enough to cede control? Perhaps someday, somehow, she would know.

She guided him into her core, sinking down onto his length. She inhaled at the sensation of him filling her, stretching her. He ground out something that sounded like a curse. They both held themselves still for a long moment, she to adjust to his size, and he likely fighting not to come undone, if the muscle that jumped in his jawline and the tension in his chest under her hands were any indication.

Then slowly, she began to rock, easing him out and taking him in. His fingers dug into her hips, drawing her down his length firmly and aiding her in rising up slightly. Taut pleasure reverberated from her core throughout her entire body. Sensation ebbed and flowed with each withdrawal and thrust, but the tide was ever building, building.

One of his hands dropped from her hip and the pad

of his thumb found that spot of throbbing pleasure. The wave swelled. Just before it crashed over her, she let her head fall backward. She arched her back as the exquisite pleasure finally crested and broke over her. A cry of ecstasy rose in her throat as her whole being was flooded with sensation.

She vaguely registered that his own shout of release echoed hers a moment later. He thrust hard once, twice more, then their desire-wild rocking slowed to a lazy sway of their hips.

They remained fused together for a long, quiet moment, the only sound their slowing panting. Madrena lowered her head and locked eyes with Rúnin. The fire behind her had almost died, and his eyes looked like a depthless sea as they held her.

Slowly, she untangled herself and draped her head on his chest.

So much remained unspoken between them—why he had been outlawed, how to make sense of what they'd just shared, what would become of each of them once they reached Seterfell. But her mind was foggy with residual passion, and sleep beckoned.

Before she succumbed completely, she raised her head a little from his chest.

"Was it as good as the dream?"

He started slightly, but then actually chuckled at her words, which echoed his bold question after their kiss in the cave. The happy sound rumbled in his chest, reverberating through her body.

"'Twas better."

19

Rúnin woke in a warm cocoon filled with the scents of pine, wood smoke, and the sweet fragrance of Madrena's skin and hair. He lay on his side with her back nestled against his chest, her bottom tucked perfectly against his lap. Their cloaks tangled over them, somehow making one blanket that held in their warmth.

Memories of his fingers digging into her soft, supple flesh, her breathy moans of pleasure, the tight heat of her surrounding him, and her gray eyes sparking like flint flooded back.

His manhood stirred at the recollections. By the gods, no matter what hardships he had already lived through, no matter what trials lay ahead, he counted himself the luckiest man in the Northlands—nei, in all the lands, known and unknown. For to have a woman like Madrena share her body, her passion, with *him*? The gods must truly be smiling on him.

She shifted her head slightly on his bent arm. Her pale blonde hair spilled over it and slid like silk between his chest and her back. With his other arm, which draped over her narrow waist, he drew her closer still.

Madrena stirred again, this time arching her back slightly so that her rounded bottom pressed more firmly into his lap. If his manhood had been awakening before, it now stood at full attention, pulsing against her soft flesh through their layers of clothing.

"Mmm." She nestled harder against him, clearly coming awake herself now. She turned her head slowly, her hair sliding languorously along his arm. The pale, weak light of another cloudy morning filtered in through the opening of their shelter, illuminating her gray eyes as she cracked them open.

There was so much he needed to say, so much he needed to tell her. But all words vanished from his mind as her languid eyes focused on him. Her gaze, normally sharp as a flashing blade, held something entirely different as she pinned him wordlessly. The sleepiness burned away slowly to reveal a hungry fire in those gray depths.

She undulated her hips, causing her bottom to grind into his stiff cock. He inhaled sharply at the clear invitation.

He shifted the arm that supported her head so that his hand was free to skim down the front of her body. Now it was her turn to gasp. She arched so that her breasts came in fuller contact with his palm. Even through the layers of her shift and overdress, he could feel her nipple pebbling in pleasure against his hand.

She twisted her arm back to reach between them where his cock pulsed eagerly. Her hand ran up and down his length, coaxing him closer toward release, though he already struggled to hold back.

She must have sensed his urgency, for her hand slipped from him to twist up her skirts. He made quick work shoving aside the material of his trousers. He groaned when his bare, hard member came in direct contact with the smooth warmth of her flank.

Bending one leg, she placed it over his thigh, opening for him. He took himself in hand and found her hot folds already slick with pleasure. Ever so slowly, he eased himself inside her. He wanted to make this last, to make it good for both of them, but the hitch in her breath and the way she arched to accommodate his size nearly sent him careening over the edge of ecstasy.

Clenching his jaw at the torrent of sensation nigh boiling over within him, he forced himself to ease in and out at a torturously slow pace. Her fingers sank into his thigh, urging him on, but he didn't relent.

With a skim of his fingers along the neckline of her dress, he found a gap and slipped his hand within. The feel of her soft, smooth flesh in his palms threatened to shatter his resolve. His fingers found the round firmness of her breasts and grazed the hard buds of her nipples.

Just when he was about to lose his threadbare hold on control, he felt her tighten and spasm around him. She moaned and her body tensed, quivering with the release claiming her. At last he let go, and a thundering orgasm swept him, stealing his breath as it uncoiled deep within his belly and through his bollocks.

She went limp in his arms, her breathing ragged. His hand rested over her heart, and her heartbeat was erratic as it slowed.

At last, she turned her head slightly and pinned him once more with her pale eyes, but this time relaxed satisfaction filled them.

"I knew from the moment I saw you charge unarmed at your Jarl that you were a passionate woman, Madrena," he said huskily. "I never thought I would ever be lucky enough to taste it myself, though."

Her soft pink lips curved into a smile for a moment. All too soon, however, it faded.

"I meant what I said last night, Rúnin. I...I desire you." Her words were awkwardly spoken, but that made them all the more meaningful to him, for she clearly didn't say them often or lightly.

She went on, her blonde brows knitting. "And I believe you are a man with honor, no matter what you think."

Tightness stole over his chest, squeezing his throat. He had to swallow to be able to speak. "And for that I am humbled and grateful. But..."

"But it doesn't change aught, does it?" she breathed, her eyes holding his. "You will not stand against Bersi. You will not go with me into Seterfell."

"And you will not turn away from your mission. You will go to my old village and seek vengeance against Bersi, even though you don't have a plan and you will face not only him but his men as well."

She nodded slowly, never breaking their stare. "I will not give up."

He sighed and brushed a pale lock of hair the color of the winter sun away from her face. "Do not be a fool, Madrena."

She stiffened, her gaze hardening. "I'm not a fool to demand revenge for the crime Bersi committed against me. No man should be allowed to rape and go unpunished."

"I agree," he said lowly. The dark memories from

fourteen years ago flickered through his mind unbidden. He shoved them aside. Now was not the time to get lost in those waking nightmares. "I simply…fear for you."

She rolled to fully face him and jerked onto her elbow. "You are just like my brother and Eirik," she bit out.

"Ja, mayhap I am, for I care for you," he snapped. It wasn't how he should have told her, but fear and frustration churned in his belly, addling his wits. "You don't seem worried at all that you don't have a plan for when you get to Seterfell—what will you do? What of Bersi's men?"

At last she dropped her gaze, her lips tight around the edges. "I don't know. Mayhap I will set upon the village in the night and find him alone. Or mayhap I will lure Bersi into one-on-one combat with a challenge."

Her eyes darted up to him, revealing the pain pooling there. "It would all be easier if you were there with me. We could face him together."

He longed to reach out to her, to run the pad of his thumb over her lips until they were rosy and relaxed. But he couldn't. He had to close himself off to the desire to help her. It wasn't his fight. That was his way, after all—stay clear, flee trouble, avoid any connections. It was the only way to stay alive.

A cruel voice whispered in his head that there was little point in just surviving if his heart remained empty. Wouldn't he rather stay at Madrena's side, risk to his life be damned?

"Nei," he breathed. "I will not go with you."

He expected the same hot-headed anger he'd seen when she'd fought her Jarl, or when she'd told her brother she was leaving her village with a stranger regardless of the risk. But instead, she simply dropped her eyes and gave a curt nod. He felt her withdraw her heart even before she scooted away from him. Something in his chest cracked at the sudden, cold absence.

"I'll still need you to get me as close to Bersi as possible," she said flatly, her eyes everywhere but on him.

"As I told you, I'll keep my promise."

Her disbelieving eyes darted to his for the briefest of moments. Ja, he understood the irony of what he'd just said. But for some reason, he needed her to know that he would keep his word to her. In only the brief time that she'd bestowed her belief and trust in him, he'd grown to crave it. Now that it was gone, a frozen emptiness replaced it in his heart.

Again, she gave him a quick nod before she crawled out of their little shelter. She stood to the side and let Rúnin slink out as well. Madrena busied herself with straightening her dress and cloak while Rúnin discreetly refastened his trousers.

Fresh snow had fallen overnight, but the flakes had abated and the sun weakly fought to break through the pale gray clouds overhead. Their lingering in the shelter that morning meant that they'd lost at least an hour of daylight, which was growing shorter and more precious with each passing day. Even though it was still only midautumn, the gods seemed to have decided to hasten winter's arrival.

Without speaking, they moved about breaking down their little camp. Rúnin scattered the pine boughs he'd used to form the shelter's walls while Madrena dispersed the evidence of their fire the night before. They shared a hurried and silent meal of the trapper's remaining flatbread and some of the berries Madrena had gathered.

Then they pointed themselves east and began another day of arduous, snowy trekking. Rúnin still used the pine walking staff, though his leg felt somewhat better than it had yesterday—a good sign.

A tense silence hung between them as they trudged through the snow. Whereas yesterday they'd both been pulled tight as a bowstring for fear that the fourth trapper would set upon them, today it was different. The fresh snow put both of them at ease—it was nigh impossible that the trapper would be able to follow them.

But even with thoughts of the trapper banished, the tension hovered thick in the air. Madrena's hard, disappointed eyes floated before him in his mind. He tried to push away the remorse—why should he feel guilty? He was an outlaw, naught more. It was his lot to wander, to live alone, to do whatever it took to survive—even if that meant pushing her away.

He wouldn't have minded her anger in that moment, but all she had was flat coldness for him. He was used to silence, yet somehow this was so much worse than all the lonely days he'd spent in these mountains.

When at last the light began to fade behind the clouds, his nerves were brittle. From the hard set of her mouth and the strain around her eyes, she didn't fare any better.

The sound of rushing water had been drawing closer for the last hour or so. As they crested a little hill and the trees broke up, they caught a glimpse of the source of the noise in the blue haze of twilight.

A jagged, rapidly flowing river churned at the bottom of a ravine at their feet. While they'd walked up a gradually sloping hill, the earth sheared away in a steep embankment where the river cut a rough path through the landscape. Enormous boulders and fallen logs jutted from the roiling waters, generating foaming white water and shooting spray into the air. Beyond the river, the land flattened and the forests thinned into clumps and copses of trees.

"I know this river," he said. He had to raise his voice to be heard over the rushing water. "Once we cross it, we'll have to turn north to skirt the Gulf of Bothnia."

Madrena warily eyed the thrashing waters. "Is there a crossing place?"

"There is a well-used bridge about a day's walk south of here," he shouted back.

"That will set us back by two days." Her mutter was barely audible over the thundering river. She probably didn't also consider the fact that they could be spotted. He'd been a fugitive long enough to instinctively avoid people.

"Not far from here there is a fallen log that spans the riverbanks," he replied. "Or at least there used to be." He hadn't been in this area in several years. Judging by the force of the water cascading over tree trunks and rocks, the log could have been swept away long ago.

Her mouth turned down in frustration. She nudged a toe-full of snow over the high embankment on which they stood. The snow fluttered down to the riverbank at least twenty feet below.

"Very well," she said at last. "Where is this fallen log?"

He shook his head. "'Tis growing too dark to cross now—it will likely be dangerous, even in daylight."

Her eyes flashed with annoyance in the dying light. Could she really be so eager to get out of his presence?

"Let us find a place to spend the night," he offered,

trying to maintain the stiff distance that had grown between them since that morning.

"Fine," she shrugged, turning away from the embankment and the river.

They wound their way back down the hill into the cover of trees. There were no natural caves or conveniently arranged fallen logs here, though. They would have to sleep in the open. At least the snow hadn't resumed, he thought. Even still, the air held a biting chill.

Madrena set about clearing the snow from under a particularly large pine tree with her booted foot. Despite the fact that they were in lower country than they had been that morning, the snow still sat more than six inches deep, even beneath the trees.

Rúnin used his walking staff to uncover downed branches to be used for firewood. They'd need a long-burning fire this night to cut the cold. Madrena paid him no mind as they worked side by side in silence, though her stiffly held shoulders spoke of her awareness of his presence.

He paused and made himself look at her back. Her slim, long form moved underneath her cloak. In a few days' time, he'd be turning away from her forever. Selfishly, he longed to soak in the sight of her. The pale blonde waves of hair cascading down her back looked silvery blue in the twilit forest. Her limbs moved with an ease that revealed a familiarity with hard work, yet also hinted at the sensuality she'd unleashed last night.

If things were different, he'd go to her now, take her in his arms, and kiss the tight frustration from her lips.

But he'd made his choice. He couldn't go back on fourteen years of life as an outlaw, a man without honor, no matter how earnest her words and tempting her flashing eyes were.

She turned then and caught him staring.

"What?" she snapped. This was the hard-edged, hot-headed shieldmaiden he remembered glimpsing that first night through the high, narrow window in her village's smithy.

"Naught," he said, dropping his eyes.

She stomped up to him and snatched the wood he'd gathered from his hands. Retrieving her fire-steel and flint stone from her bag, she crouched in the little patch of forest floor she'd cleared of snow and set about trying to light a fire.

Once the flames took hold of the dead, sodden wood, they hunched over them, trying to capture the meager heat into their hands. They ate another silent meal of mushrooms and some of the trapper's smoked venison, which Madrena produced from her satchel.

As Rúnin added another log to the fire, careful to keep the flames alive, Madrena turned and without a word wrapped herself in her cloak and hunkered into the bare patch of forest floor.

He pulled up his cloak's hood and fisted the wool closed at the front. With a sigh, he eased himself down onto the remaining cleared patch of ground on the opposite side of the fire.

It was going to be a long, cold night.

20

Madrena bolted upright with a start. An icy sweat covered her brow despite the frigid night air. She glanced up through the pine boughs overhead. 'Twas almost dawn, judging by the lightening of the clouds to the east, yet bluish gray light still encased the forest.

The nightmares were becoming more frequent.

Nei, that wasn't entirely true. She'd had more in the time since she'd left Dalgaard over a sennight ago than she normally had in two or three moons. Yet they hadn't plagued her whenever—

She didn't want to finish the thought. But the truth was, she hadn't had the same night terror that had haunted her for the last five years on any of the nights that Rúnin had taken her into his arms.

Her eyes fell to the spot she knew he'd curled into last night.

The *empty* spot.

His large form was absent from the little bare area

she'd cleared last night. The fire smoked heavily. It had reduced itself to coals.

Her gaze darted around the forest, unease flickering in her belly. He'd likely gotten up to empty his bladder. Or perhaps he had gone to scout the crossing they would use that morning.

A darker fear stirred in the back of her mind. Had he simply left her, just as he'd done that first day by the pond?

Nei, she wouldn't entertain such a thought. He'd promised over and over that he would keep his word to her, and she believed him—mostly. She had been so sure of his true character just a day ago. But with his refusal to face Bersi by her side, his unwillingness to see himself as aught other than an outlaw and an oath-breaker, perhaps she couldn't be so sure.

The forest spread out silently all around. Her hands instinctively sought her satchel and the bow and quiver that lay next to her. Everything was where she'd left it the night before. Surely if he were truly fleeing, he'd see the advantage in taking their food and a weapon for hunting.

"Nei." This time she spoke the word out loud, a chastisement for herself and a denial of her deepest fear.

Just then, a flicker of movement in the trees off to the left had her whipping her head around, her hand clenching on her bow.

Rúnin's large, cloaked figure emerged from the forest. She exhaled sharply, relief flooding her.

But something about the way he moved sent bells of warning chiming in her head. He slipped around tree trunks silently, his body gliding through the shadows like some sort of animal of prey.

"Rúnin, what—"

His gaze collided with hers across a stone's throw of snow-blanketed forest. His bright blue eyes seemed to glow with a cold fire in the low light. He jerked a hand up to silence her. The hairs on the back of her neck prickled.

Rúnin closed the distance between them noiselessly. In the back of her mind, she realized his leg must barely pain him anymore for him to be able to move like that. But his strange behavior stirred more important wonderings.

When at last he crouched next to her, she whispered in her lowest voice. "What is going on?"

His eyes scanned the forest uneasily. "I don't know. I awoke to…something. More of a feeling than aught tangible."

He shook his head as if he couldn't find the words, but she understood. Sometimes a warrior's intuition tingled just before disaster fell. Her stomach turned to stone. What peril had he sensed?

"I went scouting, but I didn't find aught," he went on, his voice barely audible. The river raged faintly in the distance, but Rúnin was obviously on edge enough to not trust that it would hide their voices.

"An animal?" she breathed. They were deep in the wilderness here. Any number of wild beasts roaming the northlands could give them trouble, from bears to wolves—even a moose could be a threat if it had a calf with it.

His dark brows lowered. "I don't know."

They both turned their eyes back to the surrounding

forest. Madrena strained to hear something over the distant, dull roar of the river on the other side of the hill at their backs. She sensed it, too—something was off, but she couldn't put her finger on what.

"Do you think—"

"Down!" Rúnin bellowed. He threw himself at her, tackling her to the ground. His weight crushed her painfully, forcing the air from her lungs.

But a fraction of a second after they hit the forest floor, an arrow whizzed through the air right where her head had been.

Pandemonium broke loose inside her head as she struggled to breathe. Rúnin rolled in the direction the arrow had come from, keeping his body between the shooter and her body. She barely had time to gasp a sharp inhale before Rúnin grabbed her and flung them both behind the wide pine tree under which they'd slept.

"What in—" Her mind, sluggish from lack of air, ground slowly, trying to make sense of what was happening.

"The trapper," Rúnin panted.

"But how?" They'd been so careful with their footprints that first day, and then the heavy snow should have covered their tracks for them.

"I don't know." His eyes darted as if searching for an answer, but then he froze, shaking his head ever so slightly. He took a deep breath. "It doesn't matter now."

The sudden calm command in his voice gave her just enough reassurance to gather her wits.

"We can try to outrun him, slip away again," he said levelly, meeting her eyes. "But he's clearly more skilled than either of us anticipated."

"So you are saying we should face him?"

Rúnin opened his mouth, but just then another arrow landed with a deep thunk into the pine's trunk. The arrow reverberated where it had sunk into the bark.

Trepidation stole over Madrena as she stared at it. The arrow was only two hand spans from them on the far side of the tree. The trapper had already silently moved position and was inching around to their side of the tree.

"We have to move," Rúnin barked.

Madrena nodded quickly, but then her eyes fell on her bag, bow, and quiver of arrows lying on the ground just out of arm's reach. They'd lain there untouched when Rúnin had dragged her behind the tree.

His eyes followed hers and he seemed to sense her realization. They needed the bow and arrows if they had any hope of surviving the trapper's attack, and they needed the supplies in her satchel if they wanted to live more than a few days after that.

Without hesitating, Rúnin rolled low and came up several paces away with the bag, bow, and quiver in his hands. Though he moved quickly, he was terrifyingly exposed in that moment. He threw himself behind the tree trunk once more just as Madrena heard the nightmarish whirr of another arrow.

The arrow sank into the soft forest floor where Rúnin's body had been a breath before. He exhaled sharply as he collided with both her and the trunk. They were safe—at least for a moment.

Madrena took the satchel from him and slung it across her body. She glanced at the quiver and dread sank in her guts.

Some of the arrows had spilled out as Rúnin had rolled to scoop up the quiver. They arrows lay in their little cleared patch of forest floor, just a few paces away and yet in the trapper's line of fire. He followed her eyes and noticed the lost arrows. There was naught they could do about it now except hope the remaining arrows would be enough.

"If we move up the hill, we will be harder targets to hit," she said.

He nodded, his hand clenching around her bow. "Go. I'll cover you."

"Nei," she hissed. "I'll not leave you behind. And can you even shoot?"

Though it was absurd in that panicked, tense moment, he actually quirked his lips at her.

"Ja, I can shoot. I'll be right behind you. Go!"

Before she could respond, he took her shoulders and shoved her away from the tree trunk. A heartbeat later, he stood and stepped from the cover of the tree, an arrow nocked and drawn back in her bow.

She threw herself forward, her boots slipping in the snow as she scrambled up the hill. She didn't hear the telltale thwack of the bowstring, though. Rúnin must be trying to bide his time and save arrows. He was waiting for the trapper to fire again, thus revealing his position.

It was a dangerous gamble, and meant that another arrow would likely be flying at her head in a matter of moments. She bolted right, changing direction with the hope of avoiding the arrow that was probably training on her back at that very second.

The muffled thump of an arrow sinking harmlessly in snow sounded to her left, where she'd just been. A half a heartbeat after the arrow landed, Rúnin's bowstring twanged as he fired his own arrow.

Madrena bolted toward the trapper's arrow,

reaching for it even as she continued to angle herself uphill. She dared a glance over her shoulder as her hand closed around the arrow shaft. Rúnin had already turned and was scrambling after her as fast as the snow would allow. She changed direction again, hoping to draw the trapper's fire away from Rúnin's back.

A large tree rose before her, and she instinctively dove behind it. Another arrow sank into the tree's bark.

Rúnin closed in on her, and she scooted to make room for him behind the cover of the trunk. In one fluid movement, he latched his hand on the arrow protruding from the bark and slid behind the trunk, pulling the arrow free.

She extended her hand and uncurled her snow-filled fingers to offer the arrow she'd retrieved as well. He slid one of the arrows into the half-full quiver but nocked the other one.

"Did you land a hit?"

He shook his head, his brows drawn down. "Nei, but I think I know where he is."

Rúnin eased the tip of the half-drawn arrow around the tree trunk and aimed at a dense copse of young firs in the distance. Madrena followed the line of the arrow's shaft. The copse's overlapping boughs shifted slightly.

Suddenly an arrow cut through the air separating them from the trapper. Like lightning, Rúnin released his arrow. Madrena yanked on his shoulders, pulling him behind the trunk as the arrow whirred by a fraction of a second later.

"Thank you," he breathed even as he nocked another arrow.

"You think you can hide from me?"

The trapper's voice drifted to them across the wooded expanse.

Both Madrena and Rúnin froze, exchanging a look.

An eerie laugh filtered through the trees, but it held no mirth. The sounds sent shivers down Madrena's spine and icy fear into her belly.

"You already tried that, remember?"

The taunting voice echoed through the otherwise silent forest. Was Madrena imagining it, or had the voice moved?

"You think you can kill my friends and slink away? After I kill you, I'm going to skin you and make hides with your flesh!"

She hadn't imagined it—the voice was moving.

"He's circling us again," Rúnin said lowly. "We have to keep moving."

Madrena nodded. Her body tensed in preparation to bolt again as Rúnin drew back the arrow and bowstring.

"I'll piss into your skulls and shite on what's left of your—"

Rúnin jerked to his feet and whipped the bow toward the voice, letting the arrow fly.

Madrena lurched forward. The hill was steep enough now that she could put her hands in the snow in front of her, steadying her scrambling climb. Over her own pounding heart, she heard Rúnin release two more arrows, yet no roar of pain from the trapper indicated that any found their mark.

Just as she was about to make a darting zigzag, searing agony sliced through her left shoulder. She didn't have to look to know she'd been hit. But she had to keep moving.

She slipped and clawed her way higher, only able to

Shieldmaiden's Revenge

use her right arm, until she reached the crest of the hill. The trees at the top were thinner. None would be big enough to protect both her and Rúnin. The thundering of the coursing river below blocked out all sound, including her curse of pain.

Madrena darted behind a thin rowan tree, its red leaves fluttering in the cold breeze coming up from the river twenty feet below. She twisted to try to see her shoulder, only to be met with more stabbing agony. Yet she caught sight of the arrow bristling from her shoulder blade.

She cursed again. It was dumb luck—there was no way the trapper could have known that she swung her sword with her left arm. On almost anyone else, the arrow would be an annoyance, not a hindrance to using a weapon.

A flash of motion in the corner of her eye revealed Rúnin lurching to the hill's crest. She caught a glimpse of the quiver over his shoulder and her heart froze. Three more arrows left.

Rúnin's eyes fell on the arrow protruding from her back and he started to barrel toward her. But she motioned him off, pointing to a tree nearby behind which he could take cover.

"Come out, little rabbits."

The trapper's voice was closer still, taunting and soft.

Madrena could attempt to draw her sword with her right hand, but she'd be easier to disarm. Besides, the trapper would have to get close enough for her to use it. As it was, he seemed to be enjoying staying just out of reach, teasing them, drawing this out.

Instead, she withdrew the dagger strapped to her thigh. It was too small to do much damage, but perhaps a sure throw with her right hand would land it in the trapper's eye.

Rúnin nocked the third-to-last arrow and swung around the thin cover of the small pine tree. He loosed it, and at last the trapper howled in pain. She dared a glance around the rowan's trunk and got her first clear glimpse of the man.

Like his companions, he wore a tattered fur hat atop his head. His cloak was fur-trimmed, yet the material looked thin and ragged. He clutched a bow in one hand and had a quiver over one shoulder that still held more than half a dozen arrows.

But his other arm hung loosely at his side, an arrow protruding from his forearm. Blood trickled from the wound onto the snow at his feet.

Rúnin's aim had been true. Even without a clear shot, he'd managed to disable the trapper's arm to prevent him from firing at them.

Madrena stepped from the cover of the rowan tree, dagger in hand.

"You should have let us be," she said, her voice hard. "Now you'll join your companions."

The trapper's beady eyes trained on her. With a bellow of rage, he grasped the arrow from his arm and yanked it free. Blood spurted on the snow, but he didn't seem to notice.

As if from a nightmare, the trapper nocked the arrow he'd just ripped from his arm and fired it at Madrena.

Time seemed to slow.

Rúnin shouted something she couldn't understand. He let his own arrow fly and it sliced through the air right for the trapper's throat.

She twisted and lurched in an attempt to dodge the arrow fired at her, but her body was dull and slow from the pain in her shoulder. The arrow, aimed at her heart, drove into her side as she fell to the ground. Her hand unfurled and the dagger fell useless into the snow.

The trapper twisted also, somehow avoiding taking Rúnin's arrow to the throat, yet it landed just as lethally in his chest. Rúnin fired the last arrow in quick succession. It sank sickeningly in the trapper's stomach. The trapper doubled over and Madrena thought that at last he would fall.

But he rose up, monstrous and bristling with arrows. Wild-eyed. He grasped both arrows and yanked them from his body.

Horror and pain clouded Madrena's mind. The man was worse than a nightmare—he was like a berserker, mad with battle lust and numb to all pain.

The trapper nocked one of the bloody arrows in his bow and this time took aim at Rúnin.

Her eyes shot to him. Rúnin was frozen for a moment, likely just as shocked as she was at the trapper's inhuman strength. But then he dove toward her, narrowly missing the first arrow.

As he slid to her side in the snow, the trapper was already preparing another arrow. Rúnin grabbed her right arm and dragged her up. She struggled to rise from the snow where she'd fallen. Fresh waves of pain washed over her. She glanced down and realized distantly that the snow was red where she'd been lying.

"Madrena, focus!" Rúnin shouted. He was pulling her by the arm toward the hill's sheared off edge.

Another arrow flew by their heads, barely missing.

Perhaps Rúnin's shot to the trapper's arm had just saved their lives, she thought vaguely.

As they reached the cliff overlooking the river, her pain-blurred mind finally realized what Rúnin planned.

"We can't—"

Her words cut off as he wrapped an arm around her and pulled them both over the edge.

21

Rúnin shielded Madrena's body as best he could with his own as they slid and tumbled down the sheared-off embankment. Snow and ice clawed at them, twisting their cloaks and battering his body. 'Twas better than if it had been bare rocks, at least, he thought fleetingly.

He vaguely registered the sound of snapping wood as they descended. The cliff petered out and they slid to a halt at the edge of the raging river.

Rúnin eased Madrena away from him and looked her over quickly. His initial shock at seeing her hit not once but twice transformed into nauseating fear. Both the arrow in her shoulder and the one protruding from her side had been snapped off in their fall. He could only imagine the pain and further damage that must have caused. Two dark red stains were spreading where the nubs of each arrow remained buried in her flesh.

But the arrows breaking off hadn't been the louder splintering of wood he'd heard a moment before. He looked down at his hand and realized he only held half of Madrena's bow.

His eyes darted back up the hill. Partway down, the other broken half of the bow lay in the snow. A flicker of movement drew his eye to the hill's crest.

The trapper swayed slightly on his feet as he nocked another arrow.

With a prayer to every god he could think of, Rúnin stumbled to his feet, drawing Madrena up by the arm next to him.

"Take my sword," she said, her voice unnaturally flat. "Finish him."

"Nei, I need to get you to safety!" he barked. Even if he wielded Madrena's sword, the trapper would have the advantage of being able to fire on both of them from a distance until Rúnin drew close enough to stop him.

Without waiting for her protest, he dragged her upriver along the slippery bank. An arrow shot past them to land in the rushing water. Then a cascade of snow blossomed from the hill's steep embankment as the trapper followed them down.

Madrena's foot slipped and she half-fell into the churning river. He yanked her back even as he urged her to move faster. Another arrow whizzed to his left. If they could just hold off the trapper long enough for him to run out of arrows—or succumb to his wounds—Rúnin could face him knowing Madrena would be out of harm's way on the other side of the river.

"We've got to get to that crossing," he said, more to himself. He feared Madrena's mind was too hazed with pain to be able to help him form a better plan. His own thoughts screamed in a cacophony of fear and shock.

Madrena stumbled again but he quickly righted her, his grip firm on her arm. By the time they would reach the fallen log up ahead, the trapper would be out of arrows—assuming he didn't bury the remaining ones in Rúnin's back.

As if conjuring his thoughts, an arrow landed on the snowy riverbank in front of them. Rúnin tore his gaze from it and scanned the bank ahead. At last he spotted the old fallen log that bridged the surging river.

"Just a little farther!" he shouted to Madrena over the thundering water. "Once we reach the log, you'll cross and I'll—"

He heard the whirr a second before he jerked, the impact of the arrow in his upper arm making a sickening thunk. He dropped his grip on Madrena and she stumbled. Locking his jaw against the pain of moving his arm, he reached for her and took hold of her once again.

The fallen log loomed ahead as they lurched forward. Rúnin shot a glance behind him and saw the trapper nocking his final arrow. He grabbed Madrena and threw them both to the ground as the arrow flew where they'd just been standing.

The trapper cursed and dropped his bow, drawing a long, dirty seax from his belt and staggering after them along the riverbank.

As Rúnin dragged Madrena to her feet once more, she groaned in pain, her body lolling briefly. He scooped her up and began stumbling ahead. At last he reached the fallen log, even as the trapper's labored breathing grew louder behind him

He set Madrena down on her feet. She swayed. How would she be able to cross on her own? His mind swirled. Rúnin turned to gauge how far away the trapper was.

"I'll kill you slowly for what you've done!" the trapper roared. He was only a few paces away now, seax brandished overhead and blood darkening the entire front of his tunic. His dark eyes were wide with feral fervor and he seemed not to even notice his injuries.

There was no more time. There was no time to get Madrena across the bridge. There was no time to draw her sword. There was no time to form another plan or flee anymore.

"Madrena, go!" he barked over his shoulder at her. He sensed her stumble toward the log behind him and prayed that she had the strength to make it across. All he could do was buy her time, put his body between her and the trapper, and hope he could finish him off.

As the trapper closed the distance between them, Rúnin braced himself. At the last moment, he remembered that he still had Madrena's seax in his boot. He yanked it free and thrust it upward just in time to block the blade descending toward his head.

He jabbed at the trapper, but the man twisted out of the way. Just as Rúnin positioned himself to deflect the trapper's next attack, he heard a scream behind him.

"Rúnin!"

He barely evaded the stab at his throat and spun to find Madrena clinging to one of the log's long-dead arms, her feet thrashing in the surging river. She must have slipped or lost her footing, and now the river threatened to sweep her away.

"Hold on!"

Even as he shouted the words, the trapper bellowed

and raised the seax once more, battle lust burning in his eyes.

The blade arced across the cloudy morning sky. Rúnin could not meet force with force to deflect the blow, which had all the trapper's weight behind it. Instead, he dropped backward into the mud and slush on the riverbank.

The seax missed his head, but the trapper's belly was now exposed. With a swift thrust, Rúnin buried his blade into the trapper's gut. He jerked the seax sideways and then up.

The trapper roared as hot blood poured from him. He stood over Rúnin, his eyes burning and the seax frozen in his hand. At last, he went limp. Rúnin shoved him to the side to avoid being crushed, and the trapper's body splashed into the river, Madrena's seax still protruding from his belly.

The water snatched his body immediately, sending it slamming into boulders and dead logs. The river churned red around the trapper's limp form as he careened through the rapids like a fallen leaf.

That would be what happened to Madrena's delicate body if Rúnin didn't act fast.

She cried out again as he scrambled down the length of the fallen log. The wood beneath his feet was smooth and slick from years of being hammered by the river. He nearly lost his balance halfway to Madrena, but he righted himself before the river could snatch him.

Madrena clung with claw-like fingers to the branch, her left hand slipping away. She screamed in pain as her left arm dropped completely, useless from the arrow wound. Just as the fingers of her right hand lost their strength, he lunged forward, closing the distance between them.

His hand closed on her wrist as her fingers fell away from the branch. But the water still snagged and tugged at her feet. She twisted in his grasp and cried out again.

With all of his strength, he hauled her up by the wrist until he could grab her arm and drag her onto the log next to him. Taking her into his arms, he rose and inched across the log's slick spine until he reached the far side.

With shaking hands, he set her down as gently as possible a safe distance from the river. She was still conscious, but her normally bright eyes were dull in the weak morning light.

"You're hurt," she said flatly, her eyes going to his arm.

He'd all but forgotten the arrow that still jutted from his upper arm. Without a thought to the pain, he wrapped a hand around the arrow shaft and yanked it free. He didn't have time to worry about such a minor injury when Madrena lay bleeding before him.

He looked at her side where a dark red stain marred her dress. A half-inch of arrow shaft was visible, but no more. A quick look at her shoulder blade revealed the same of the other arrow.

"I…I am not sure I can get the arrows out," he said.

Her hand went to her side and fumbled over the wound as if she could simply extract it as easily as he just had with the one in his arm.

"Nei, don't. You'll hurt yourself." But the terrible truth was, she was in trouble, whether he removed the arrows or not. She was still bleeding, her face growing pale. And there was the ever-present risk of infection in the wild.

His mind spun as he fought to come up with a solution. He could try to dig out the remains of the arrows, but there was no guarantee he'd be successful, and opening the wounds further increased the risk of infection.

It was the best he could do at the moment. After that, he would have to face the problems as they came.

"Give me your dagger," he said, his voice tight. She shook her head slightly but winced at even that small movement.

"Dropped it," she said faintly. But then her paling lips curled slightly. "But I have another in the bottom of my satchel."

Leave it to her, fierce, clever shieldmaiden that she was, to have another little dagger tucked away for emergencies. He rummaged in the bag across her body, careful not to jar her, until his fingers brushed cool metal.

With the small blade in his hand, he drew in a steadying breath. He'd had to cut himself to remove a large, deeply embedded wood shard before, but he feared inflicting more pain on Madrena. As he lowered the blade toward her side, she stopped him with a hand over his.

"You realize you could have just left me behind, don't you? Or you could have let me fall into the river. Either way, you'd be free of this ill-fated mission of mine. You'd be free of your oath, and you could just slip away into the wilderness again."

He froze at her words. It had never crossed his mind in all the madness of their flight from the trapper that he would abandon Madrena just to free himself from his promise to her. A sennight ago, he'd fled her to avoid having to go near Seterfell and Bersi without a qualm.

A wry smile touched her fading lips. "But you didn't." Her gray eyes flickered with a shadow of their normal intensity.

"Nei, I didn't."

"Because you *do* have honor." It wasn't a question. It wasn't a veiled plea to get him to agree. She spoke the words levelly, as if they were the simple truth.

His heart twisted in his chest. Her belief in him shook him to the core. A seed of hope took hold deep within him, hope that he could be the man she saw in him.

"Hold fast," he said gently as he lowered the dagger to her side once more. "This will hurt."

As the blade slid into her skin, she inhaled and screamed through clenched teeth.

22

Madrena rested quietly, her features smooth in the warm glow of the fire.

Blessedly, she'd passed out back by the riverbank as Rúnin had burrowed into her flesh with the dagger. Both arrowheads had come out cleanly, though the wounds had bled profusely.

He'd carried her a little way from the river to a patch of trees where he'd set her down and built a small fire. The trees were sparser on this side of the river, and the landscape more flat. They weren't far from the Gulf of Bothnia now.

With the remains of her spare shift, he'd done his best to bind her wounds, though he could see even in the low firelight that the bandages on her waist were already tinged red. The injury to her shoulder was less severe, for the arrow had hit her shoulder blade and hadn't been able to bury itself very deep. But the wound in her side worried him. It could be a flesh wound, or it could be deeper—he had no way of knowing.

Her boots and the bottom half of her dress were wet

with icy river water. Yet another danger. He'd pulled off her boots and set them by the fire, but he feared that removing her dress would jostle her injuries too much. So he had to settle with positioning her as close to the fire as was safe and hoping she'd dry off.

He hadn't spared a thought for the old wound to his leg or the fresh one in his arm. His leg ached dully, but the skin had already closed. The pain in his arm had been sharper when he'd lifted Madrena, but it didn't impede him. He wouldn't let it—not when she needed him so badly.

As he stood to place another thin log on the fire, Madrena stirred. Her delicate brow lowered and she blinked a few times, her gray eyes clouded with pain and disorientation.

When she tried to sit up, Rúnin bolted to her side. But the pain stopped her progress before he could. She inhaled sharply through her teeth and clutched her side, easing herself back to the ground.

"Easy," he said lowly, handing her the waterskin. She took several swallows before clearing her throat and speaking.

"How long have I…"

"You've been resting for a few hours," he replied, glancing overhead. The sun was completely blocked behind a wall of gray, but the clouds were high enough that he didn't fear more snow. Although it was early afternoon, it might as well have been twilight for all the dimness.

She nodded. "We should still have a half-day's worth of light, then." She tried to sit up again, but this time Rúnin gripped her uninjured shoulder firmly, not allowing her to budge.

"Madrena, we aren't going anywhere."

"I can walk just fine, I'm sure," she shot back.

"Don't be foolish."

She bristled at his flat words, but he went on before she could interject. "Seterfell is still at least three days from here. You really expect to walk for three days with a bleeding hole in your side and storm the village by yourself?"

"Three days," she rasped through clenched teeth, more to herself than to him. "Three cursed days' walk from Bersi. I'm so *close*."

His chest squeezed and sank at the same time. She was still determined to have her revenge. Of course she was—she had every right. And yet it was another reminder that in three days their paths would diverge—forever.

"I know you've waited a long time for this," he said, softening his voice. "But don't let your impatience destroy what you've prepared five years for. You need to rest, to heal."

"I don't want to *wait*, Rúnin. I've been told to wait so many times, and now I'm so close! Curse that trapper to Helheim!"

Her voice was hard and urgent, yet it was also lined with desperation. Ja, Madrena was hot-headed and impatient—Rúnin had seen those traits on full display that first night when she'd faced her Jarl—but this was different. She had so much pinned on this mission. How could she ever live up to the pressure she'd put on herself?

Pushing his deeper fears for her aside, he focused on her present impediment. "How about this. Rest for the remainder of the day. We'll stay here for the night, since I've already made such a fine camp."

He swept his hand around their desolate setting. He'd cleared some snow, but other than that, the weak fire barely shed enough heat and light to extend more than a foot or two. The river roared dully in the distance, and the clump of trees under which they sat was one of the few breaking up the otherwise bleak landscape.

Though she fought it, Madrena's lips quirked slightly at his bravado. "Fine camp, eh?" She raised a blonde eyebrow at him.

Good. She must be feeling well enough to mock his attempt at a jest.

But then her features grew serious once more. "I want to keep moving," she said. "We can't waste an entire day, not when I'm so close."

He hardened himself in preparation for a new tactic. "You still need me. Remember, I could refuse to take you any farther, and then you'd be left out here on your own, bleeding and hurt, without anyone to show you the way to Seterfell."

She narrowed her eyes at him. If she was as sharp as he knew her to be, she would understand that his threat was hollow. He wouldn't go back on his word to her, nor would he abandon her—not after going to such great lengths to save her. But he needed to remind her that she still required his help.

Madrena at last broke their stare and muttered a curse. "Fine. I'll rest until tomorrow morning. But then we move."

He nodded. If she wasn't well enough to travel

tomorrow, he'd force her to stay put, but he'd already won a small victory. He wouldn't press his luck just yet.

As he began to turn back to the fire, she caught his arm, halting him.

"That trapper…" she whispered. "How did he find us? And how did he survive those shots?"

She shivered, her eyes drifting to the fire in memory. "I've only ever seen something like that once before, on the battlefield when we fought a band of raiding Northmen a few years back—berserkers. They fought like madmen without a care to their injuries. Some even turned on their own men, so blinded with bloodlust were they."

As if to rid herself of the disturbing memories, she gave her head a little shake.

"I've seen it before, too," Rúnin said, his voice low. "I found poisonous mushrooms in the trapper's tent when we snuck into his camp. Some of Bersi's men used to eat mushrooms like that before raids. They even did it once to prepare to fight a group of resistant villagers."

The memory of Bersi's large, grizzled hand, outstretched with one round, bright red mushroom, drifted to Rúnin's mind.

"Eat it, boy." Bersi's commanding voice washed over Rúnin's smaller frame. Rúnin looked up at his Jarl and shook his head.

It had been the first small refusal. Perhaps it had been a sign, a warning of things to come.

Bersi's hard, black eyes bore into Rúnin for a long moment. But then his fist closed over the mushroom and he shrugged.

"Perhaps it is better that you remember your first raid with a clear head," Bersi said with a little smile.

Rúnin snapped his mind back to the present. Even fourteen years later, the events of that day haunted him.

"The mushrooms could have given him the strength and focus to track us even through the snow. And he likely felt no pain from the arrows he took."

"So he was a berserker," Madrena said.

Rúnin considered for a moment as he gazed at the dancing fire. "I think it was more than that. I've seen men like that trapper before, and they didn't have to eat those mushrooms to go mad."

He felt her gray eyes resting on him. "What do you mean?"

Unease settled over him, but he shrugged. "Though I've avoided people as best I can, I've encountered other hunters, trappers—men who aren't forced into the wilderness, but who choose it over society. Some thrive on their own. Some grow lonely and return to their villages and towns. And some seem to lose themselves in the isolation. That trapper's only contact with other people was likely the group whom we killed. Take away the only thread holding him to humanity and…" He snapped his fingers and Madrena started slightly.

"So you're saying it was our fault—my fault—for that trapper turning berserker?"

"Nei, that's not what I mean," he said. "But…years of isolation change a man."

Rúnin let his words hang in the air as he continued to stare into the fire.

Her hand tightened on his forearm, drawing him out of his dark thoughts. "But *you* haven't become like that trapper."

It wasn't a question. Instead, she was trying to let him know yet again that she believed he still contained goodness. Though he desperately wanted her words to be true, he still feared the worst—he feared himself.

"I haven't gone mad, but I have lost something all the same from being out here too long," he replied quietly. "My honor, my humanity—this world, this life as an outlaw, has stripped them from me."

She pulled on his arm, drawing his gaze from the fire to her face. She was so beautiful—a combination of delicate vulnerability and lithe strength. The fog of pain had lifted slightly from her eyes, and they absorbed the dancing light of the fire as they held him.

"Honor is not like a sword, where if you break it or lose it in battle it is gone forever. Honor is a river and you are the source. The river cuts and curves over many paths that don't always make sense upon first glance. But the water knows how to flow and where it is going. Sometimes the river surges, sometimes the river dries up. But it can always spring anew from within."

As she spoke, she placed a hand on his chest, directly over his old tattoo and the brand scar that had obliterated it. His heart hammered against her palm, even through his tunic and cloak.

Her gray eyes turned sad suddenly. "I don't know why you try to stop the river within yourself, Rúnin. I don't understand why you've built a dam in your heart against the honor I know swells here." She pressed her hand more firmly into his chest.

He swallowed hard. It felt as though her gaze cut right through the exterior he'd hardened over the years and saw the boy he once had been, the boy who lived by honor.

"I...I don't know, either," he breathed, but that was a lie. Fluttering soft as an owl's wing in the back of his mind was the truth—he was afraid.

He was afraid to face what he'd done over the years

under the belief that he had not had honor. He was afraid to relive the horror of that fateful day fourteen years ago, the day that had made him an outlaw.

But most of all, he was afraid that if he let himself, he would love the woman before him, only to lose her.

At last, she released him from the captivity of her gaze. Though she didn't say more, she nodded ever so slightly. Did she somehow sense all the thoughts coursing through him? If she did, she wasn't going to push him further just yet.

A wince pinched her face as she tried to settle herself into a comfortable position on the ground. He'd used her bag to prop her up slightly and keep weight off her shoulder, but her side seemed to pain her more now.

"Too bad all the *hvönn* plants have been buried under this cursed snow," she grumbled sourly.

Rúnin would have snorted at her grumpiness if he weren't so worried about that very problem. Just as when he'd been injured, they had no needle or thread to close the wound. But at least he'd had the benefit of the *hvönn* to ward off infection and inflammation. He tried to hide his concern from her, though.

"You'll just have to heal completely by tomorrow morning," he said in his best attempt at lightness.

She grunted and closed her eyes, and within moments, her breathing deepened in sleep. She truly must be exhausted.

He stood and removed his cloak, draping it as gently as possible over her still form. Then he huddled closer to the fire. The thick wool of his tunic couldn't completely shelter him from the cold air pressing into him, but Madrena needed his cloak more than he.

Rúnin fed the fire and watched over her for the rest

of the day. As night fell, he ate but didn't rouse her to do the same. She seemed to need the deep sleep that claimed her. After building up the fire as best he could, he slipped under his cloak next to her, careful not to touch her lest he jostle her injuries.

Sometime in the middle of the night, he awoke to the feel of her arm landing on his chest with a thump. She muttered something incoherent and her arm flailed again, this time narrowly missing his face.

He sat upright and squinted at her in the dying light of the embers. Another nightmare?

Madrena's laugh cut through the still night, sending chills up Rúnin's spine. Nei, not a nightmare, but she didn't seem lucid either.

Something was wrong.

She flailed again, and he had to pin her arms to her sides to prevent her from hurting herself. Words spilled from her mouth as she babbled incomprehensibly. Underneath his grasp, her whole body shook in violent little quakes. She was shivering.

"Nei," he whispered, but his denial was useless and futile.

Fever had set in.

Though he already knew what his touch would reveal, he placed his hand on her cheek. Despite the frigid breeze ruffling the darkened trees overhead, her skin raged with fire.

Rúnin cursed roundly even as his mind spiraled in desperation. He could do naught and hope that the fever cured itself. Madrena was strong—her body might be able to fight it. He'd lived through a few fevers himself with no aid.

But this one had come on so quickly and burned so

hot already. The snow had covered or destroyed all the fragile plants Rúnin knew of to treat fevers and wounds.

Nei, he couldn't just sit here and do naught but watch as the fever racked her body.

The only alternative was to seek help.

But the closest village he knew of was Seterfell. His face—or at least the face he'd had as a fourteen-year-old lad—was known there. No one in their right mind would help him for it would be a death sentence at Bersi's hands. Anyone who aided him could be killed, along with both Madrena and himself.

Rúnin's heart pounded as if he were about to do battle, yet there was naught to strike, naught to lash out at. Hopelessness washed over him. If they stayed here, Madrena could die. If he sought help, he would likely be recognized and killed.

Something surged inside his chest. Madrena's words about honor returned to him. He had a choice, and honor lay in action. He would do whatever it took to protect this woman, his own fate be damned.

Even as new hope for himself bubbled deep in his heart, fear for Madrena stole his breath.

Seterfell still lay a three days' walk from here. With Madrena incapacitated, it would take even longer to skirt the Gulf of Bothnia and trudge into the hilly country in which Seterfell was nestled.

Another gust of icy wind sliced through his clothing. Had this freezing weather sunk deep enough into the landscape to give him another route? If he cut directly across the gulf instead of around the top, he'd save himself several days. But the ice would be thin and newly formed.

He glanced down at Madrena again. She'd fallen

silent and still, her hallucinations ebbing, but that worried him even more.

He had to risk it. He had to risk the gulf's thin ice, the inherent dangers of seeking out other people's aid, and the threat of recognition the closer he got to Seterfell. He could not lose Madrena—not when she had helped him find his honor at last.

23

Rúnin glided to a halt at what he guessed was the shoreline of the Gulf of Bothnia.

Before him swept an expanse of seemingly endless snow. That was a good sign, for it meant there was enough ice crusting over the gulf to collect a sheet of snow atop it.

He rubbed the bleariness from his eyes as he assessed the gulf. He'd worked through the rest of the night in preparation for this perilous journey.

Madrena stirred restlessly behind him. She reclined in the litter he'd fashioned last night. Beneath her prone form lay pine boughs woven together between two sapling trunks each as thick as his wrists. His cloak draped over her, but she still shivered and tossed her head from side to side.

The air was sharp and cold, yet he sweated with exertion, even without his cloak. Pulling the litter was taxing, despite the aid of the skis he wore. He'd used the axe Madrena kept on her belt to hack away at a young pine tree. After several hours of work in the dark, he'd managed to hew two rudimentary skis from the wood, each several feet long. He'd also made two shorter skis for the trailing ends of Madrena's litter so that her body wouldn't jostle so much.

He'd had to destroy the extra overdress she had in her satchel, but if they lived through this, he vowed to replace it. He tore shorter strips of wool to lash the skis to his feet and the makeshift litter, then a longer one to loop around his waist and secure to the top of the litter near her head.

It had taken many long hours during the cold, dark night and into the gray morning, but here he stood, pulling Madrena behind him in a litter, his feet gliding over the snow and ice smoother and faster than if he were on foot. It was the only way he could justify spending so much time in their camp by the river instead of being on his way to Seterfell—in the long run, all his work would save precious hours that could be the difference between life and death for Madrena.

Though his mind felt hazy with fatigue, he forced himself to concentrate. The closer he stayed to the gulf's shoreline, the thicker the ice was apt to be. But a more direct route straight across the gulf would shave off even more time from this journey.

Lowering his head in resignation, he pointed his skis straight toward the hills where he knew Seterfell was huddled on the other side of the gulf. He leaned his weight against the strip of wool that looped around his middle and attached to the litter. In another time, he would have bucked at feeling like a beast of burden pulling its load, but this was different—this was for Madrena.

The litter slid into motion and as his legs pumped

the skis over the ice, momentum kept them coasting at a comparatively easier glide. Rúnin let his eyes settle on the snow just a few feet in front of him. He only had to go a couple of paces, then a couple of paces more. Soon enough, they would be across the gulf and onto the safety of solid ground.

Madrena muttered again and he felt her weight shift in the litter. She had remained insensate throughout the night and morning, though the fever gripped her mercilessly. Before setting out, he'd checked her shoulder. The wound was clean and dry. But her side flared angry red. It still oozed, though now it was more pinkish pus than vivid blood.

With every thrash, with every roll, and with every hallucinatory jerk, he winced, for he feared she would only make the wound worse. He glanced over his shoulder to reassure himself that she was secure on the litter. Her cheeks flushed bright pink and her lips were unnaturally vibrant in the gray light of midday. But judging from the receding shoreline behind him, he was almost halfway across the ice-covered gulf.

Just then he heard a dreaded creak beneath him. His heart leapt into his throat even as his stomach plummeted.

As if in terrifying warning, the ice groaned and popped again all around him.

It would be worse if he stopped, he reminded himself as he pumped his legs faster, trying to get across the worst of the thin ice as quickly as possible.

But the ice crackled directly beneath him. His left foot suddenly jolted downward an inch as the ice partially collapsed beneath his ski. Freezing gulf water lapped at the sole of his boot.

He managed to pull his boot and ski free of the little sinkhole in the gulf's crusted surface. The more he could distribute the combined weight of his body and the litter containing Madrena, the safer they'd be.

With frozen fingers, he untied the strip of wool from one side of the litter and let the band of material fall from around his waist. He held on to the end he'd just untied and skied a few strides farther ahead, pulling the litter with one hand.

At last the ice fell silent. The only sound filling the frigid air was Rúnin's panting breath and the whistle of a cold wind across the gulf's bare surface.

Just as Rúnin let his gaze settle on the ice in front of him, a flicker of movement caught his attention. His head snapped up, his eyes focusing on the far shoreline.

Two black dots moved in the distance. From their narrow, upright outlines, they were no animals.

Men. His mind reeled as he struggled to decide what to do. He had likely already been spotted. Nothing along the gulf's expanse offered any cover. He could only pray to the gods that the men would move on and leave him alone.

He slowed the gliding of his skis and carefully altered his course somewhat. If he finished the crossing well behind them on the shoreline, perhaps they wouldn't bother to double back and greet him.

But wasn't he looking for help? He'd gone so long hiding from and evading others that he'd forgotten for a moment that for the first time in fourteen years, he actually *sought* others' aid.

With a readjustment of his skis, he pointed himself on his original path. Perhaps the two figures, who grew more distinct as he drew nigh, could help Madrena.

He'd thought at first that one of the men was substantially closer to him than the other, for he appeared larger. But as he drew nigh, he realized that the smaller one was actually a boy. The man raised his hand in silent greeting to Rúnin, even though they were still too far apart to make each other out clearly.

Rúnin lifted his arm to return the greeting.

Suddenly, a sharp crack shattered the air. It was as if the ground fell completely away under Rúnin's skis and he plunged into the icy water.

Cold slammed into his body, snatching the very breath from his lungs. His ears rang as his head dunked below the freezing water. The cold paralyzed him for a long moment until he willed his body to move, to struggle for life and heat.

He kicked the skis from his feet and clawed upward. His head exploded through the ice water, but the air felt like a cold knife against his wet hair and skin. He thrashed wildly for a second before he forced his mind to work again.

Thank the gods he'd unfastened his makeshift harness from the litter, otherwise he would have pulled Madrena's prone form under with him. As it was, his hand on the strip of cloth had yanked the litter dangerously close to the gaping hole he'd made in the ice. He sent up another thanks that his cloak still lay over her body, for if he had been wearing it, the weight of the sodden wool would likely be drowning him right now.

He struggled toward the shattered edge of ice lining the hole in which he swam. The leaden weight of cold was already settling into his limbs. If he didn't get out of this water fast, he would assuredly die.

Through ears still ringing with an icy ache, he

vaguely absorbed distant shouting from the shoreline. It would probably be too late by the time the man he'd waved to reached him, and the man was just as likely to fall through the ice himself.

"Faster, Jofarr!" The man's voice drifted to him, but he barely understood the words. His mind was growing sluggish from the cold.

Rúnin reached for the crust of solid ice as carefully as his wooden limbs would allow. His fingers wouldn't cooperate, and his hand came down like a stone on the ice, shattering it further. He tried again, easing the weight of his hand onto the ice, but it crumbled beneath him.

All of a sudden a small figure slid to the edge of the ice like a seal. The little figure's face popped over the ice's rim, and Rúnin was met with a young boy's wide-eyed stare. Rúnin would have started in surprise if he wasn't numb and growing muddled in his head.

"Help her," he rasped through a stiff jaw. He jerked his head toward where Madicna lay in the litter. The boy's dark blue eyes flitted to the litter but he didn't budge. Instead, he produced a coarse rope and threw it into the water at Rúnin.

Not trusting his hands to be able to grasp the rope, Rúnin wound it around his arm. But even through his cold-clouded mind, he knew the boy was too small to be able to pull him from the water.

"Help her," he said again. This time, the boy followed his command. He scooted on his belly around the edge of the watery hole and toward the litter.

As the boy took hold of the dangling strip of wool at the top of the litter, Rúnin's body stopped struggling against the icy pull of the water. She would have a chance of survival. He'd done his best, but it hadn't quite been enough for himself. But perhaps the gods would smile on him for trying to save her.

Just as his head slipped below the water, the rope around his arm went taut. In the next second, he was being dragged back to the surface. As his head reemerged, he saw the boy carefully pulling Madrena's litter toward the shoreline, but someone else must have been hauling on the other end of the rope.

His wet, stiff body slid onto the icy surface of the gulf once more. The ice groaned underneath him but held as he was towed further inland. He heard labored grunts echo with each yank on the rope, the sound growing nearer. Blessedly, Rúnin had lost feeling in his limbs, otherwise he imagined distantly that his arm would be screaming in protest.

At last he came to a halt on his back, his eyes fixed on the gray underbelly of clouds overhead.

"Is he alive, *Faðir*?" The boy's awed but doubtful voice filtered through Rúnin's hazy mind.

"Ja, Jofarr, you did well. And who is that?"

Rúnin tried to speak, but his lips and tongue wouldn't cooperate and his jaw began quaking with shivers.

"He told me to help her," the boy said.

Suddenly a man's face hovered in front of Rúnin's vision. "You need to move, else you'll die in those wet clothes," he said softly.

Something tugged at Rúnin's memory. Something… familiar about the dark blue eyes so like the boy's. Something about the square jaw under the brown beard. Or was Rúnin's ice-numbed brain playing tricks on him?

"Can you walk? I fear I cannot carry you, but my son can pull the woman."

Rúnin rolled onto his side and with effort shoved himself into a seated position. "J-Ja, I c-can walk," he stuttered.

Even the small amount of movement caused fresh, aching pain through his limbs, but he knew that it was a good sign. It meant his blood still moved through his body, weakly sending warmth to his frozen extremities.

The man helped him up and kept an arm under Rúnin's shoulder as the boy hurriedly rewound the rope. Rúnin's gaze immediately sought Madrena. She still lay in the litter, her body motionless now and her lashes resting against her flushed cheeks.

He felt the weight of the man's eyes on him.

"She is fevered," Rúnin rasped. "She has an injury to her side that has become infected. Please." His voice dropped low. "Please help her."

"My wife will know what to do," the man said, his eyes worried but kind. "You are both safe."

What strange words to hear after all these years. Something clenched in Rúnin's chest, and he glanced at the man to give his deepest thanks.

As he opened his mouth, the words froze in his throat. Realization clicked into place deep within Rúnin's memory.

Ketill. Ketill Petrisson.

The man had aged in the fourteen years since Rúnin had last seen him, but the eyes were the same.

Rúnin's stomach twisted even as Ketill helped him take several staggering, wooden steps forward.

"Hurry, Jofarr," Ketill urged his son over Rúnin's

shoulder. The boy took a firm grip on the litter and began gliding it after them.

"We aren't far from my home," Ketill said, shifting his gaze to Rúnin once more.

Rúnin tried to inconspicuously turn his head away. He nodded and kept his eyes on the snow in front of his feet.

Ketill Petrisson would recognize him.

And then Rúnin would be as good as dead.

24

"I am Ketill Petrisson."

Ketill still propped Rúnin up under one shoulder. Walking helped get the blood flowing through his body, but the price was first a dull ache and then sharp pain where his limbs fought to free themselves from the grip of the icy water in his clothes.

"And that is my son, Jofarr."

Rúnin glanced at the boy. Like his father, he wore a fur cap covering light brown hair. They shared the same deep blue eyes and spots of pink on their cheeks from the cold, though Ketill bore a thick brown beard whereas Jofarr's youthful face was smooth.

The boy couldn't be more than ten or eleven. Rúnin's throat tightened. 'Twas an innocent age, an age when a boy thought the world of his father. When Rúnin was Jofarr's age, he couldn't have dreamt up a monster as horrifying as Bersi. In a few years' time, would Jofarr have to swear fealty to Jarl Bersi? Would he be ordered to do what Rúnin had refused? Would he be flogged and outlawed, left to the wolves?

Rúnin squeezed his hands open and closed, bringing on a flash of new pain to distract himself from his dark thoughts.

He realized suddenly that Ketill was waiting for him to acknowledge the introduction he'd just made—and tell him his name.

"It is good to meet you, Ketill," he said, trying to hide the awkwardness of the words. He'd known Ketill all his life—or the first fourteen years of it, anyway. A handful of years older than Rúnin, Ketill had been someone he'd looked up to as a lad. And now he had to pretend to be a stranger.

Rúnin cleared his throat to buy himself time to form another lie. "I am Svein." It was a common enough name in these parts. Leaving off a family name would seem strange, but offering one could draw more questions for which Rúnin didn't want to form answers.

"And who is your…companion?" The unstated question hung in the air as Ketill glanced between Rúnin and Madrena.

"That is Madrena," Rúnin answered. No point in adding another lie that could cause him to slip up. But he still had to explain what they were doing here and how she'd gotten injured.

Lying had become a well-practiced and necessary skill over the years, but for some reason, it soured his belly to lie to Ketill, who'd always encouraged the goodness in Rúnin, especially after Rúnin's father was killed.

It was for Ketill's protection as well as Madrena's, Rúnin told himself firmly. Even if Rúnin's fate was sealed, Ketill and his family could still be saved if the truth were kept from them. Ketill had managed to survive Bersi's reign all these years, despite the fact that

Bersi had killed so many of Seterfell's men. Ketill must know how to keep himself and his family from Bersi's notice, and Rúnin's lies would help.

"Dare I ask what happened?" Rúnin could feel Ketill's gentle, curious gaze on him once more.

He took a deep breath of freezing air. "We are from Knorrstad. We were hunting on the other side of the Gulf of Bothnia when a wild boar attacked us. Its tusk gouged Madrena, and she fell ill. I had heard that there was a village in these parts and hoped that it would be closer than Knorrstad. I cannot tell you how grateful I am that you found us."

"Hunters, eh?"

Rúnin's head snapped up as he shot a glance at first Jofarr and then Ketill. He hadn't noticed it before, but Ketill had a bow and quiver over one shoulder and there was a white-furred hare dangling from Jofarr's belt.

The boy and his father had clearly been out hunting when they'd come across Rúnin and Madrena. Had Rúnin just made another crucial misstep? Would he be caught in his lie?

"My bow was destroyed in our flight from the boar," he said, lowering his eyes once more.

"Ah."

Had Ketill accepted the story, or was he now suspicious?

"We weren't expecting such strange weather when we set out from Knorrstad a sennight ago," Rúnin said in an attempt to change the subject.

"Indeed, 'tis unseasonably cold," Ketill said lightly.

"*Moðir* says that Loki must have tricked Höðr into bringing winter early this year," Jofarr piped up.

Rúnin swallowed. Was Jofarr's mother the same

woman whom Ketill had been courting when Rúnin was banished? Or had the sweet healer's apprentice died of some disease or in childbirth? Or at Bersi's hand?

"Your mother must be very wise," Rúnin said lowly. "For Loki is always fooling the god of winter to confuse the seasons in Kvenland." Rúnin's own mother had said the same thing when he'd been a boy. Winter could come early and linger late this far deep into the Northlands.

"You are familiar with these parts, then? Is not Knorrstad far to the south?" Ketill's voice was level, yet Rúnin's stomach clenched in fear. Perhaps he'd said too much.

"I follow the reindeer north in the winter," Rúnin lied quickly.

"Ah, ja. That's right. You are a hunter." Was Ketill toying with him? Rúnin risked a quick glance up and found Ketill's kind blue eyes searching him, his brows lowered but the corner of his mouth ticking up slightly.

Rúnin quickly lowered his gaze once more, forcing his eyes on the ground just in front of him. They had begun climbing into the hills almost immediately after leaving the gulf's shoreline. The snow was deep and fluffy beneath Rúnin's soggy boots. Thin clumps of pine and spruce trees grew thicker as they continued to trudge uphill.

A swift glance at the landscape told Rúnin that Seterfell was deeper in the foothills to the northeast. But assuming he remembered correctly, Ketill lived on the farthest outskirts of the village, if his homestead could be considered part of the village at all. It was nigh a half-day's walk from the village to Ketill's home—at least it had been with a young lad's smaller strides.

"And what of you, Ketill Petrisson?" Rúnin said, again trying to draw attention away from himself. "You said your home isn't far. You are from these parts?"

"Ja. Seterfell, the village you must have heard of, has been my home all these years." For the first time, Ketill's voice tightened and Rúnin got the impression that he was holding back. He couldn't blame the man. He couldn't simply tell a stranger that life under Jarl Bersi was a waking nightmare.

"Your wife..." Rúnin began. "You said she'll know how to help us?"

"Finna has learned a great deal about the healing arts," Ketill replied, his voice easy again. "You'll see soon enough."

Rúnin repressed an exhale of relief to learn that Finna was still alive and well. But just then, Jofarr shouted and pointed through the trees.

His gaze following the line of the boy's finger, Rúnin spotted a thin thread of smoke weaving through the tree tops farther up the snowy hill on which they trudged.

"*Moðir*!" Jofarr cried out. He began running uphill, still dragging Madrena's litter behind him.

"Careful!" Rúnin snapped before he could temper his voice. He didn't want to frighten the boy, but his composure would be torn to shreds if aught more happened to Madrena.

Jofarr instantly slowed somewhat and turned rounded blue eyes on Rúnin. But he kept up a quickened pace and began pulling away from Rúnin and Ketill.

"Forgive me," Rúnin muttered to Ketill. "I owe both you and your son my life—and Madrena's, gods willing."

"We only did what any decent people would," Ketill replied. Sadly, Rúnin knew that wasn't true. The Northlands were a hard place, and though some people helped strangers, others looked out only for themselves. But Ketill's words reaffirmed what he remembered of the man—he was still good-hearted, despite all he must have lived through under Bersi's Jarlship.

A flicker of hope stirred somewhere in the shadows of Rúnin's mind. Could he tell Ketill the truth? Would he understand all that Rúnin had lived through and still give him and Madrena aid and shelter?

Nei, he couldn't entertain such dangerous ideas. Rúnin's very presence here put Ketill and his entire family in jeopardy.

"*Moðir!*" Jofarr called again ahead of them. The trees suddenly opened into a little sloping clearing to reveal Ketill's homestead.

Carefully mortared stone lined the bottom half of a modest hut, atop which lay closely fitted wooden planks. A stream of smoke rose from the center of the tightly thatched roof.

Surrounding the hut were several pens of animals. Rúnin spotted a handful each of cows, sheep, pigs, and chickens in his quick perusal. Several different-sized wooden shelters stood to the back and right of the hut, under which the animals now huddled for warmth. Snow had been cleared from the hut to the animal pens, showing that the creatures must have been well cared for.

The hut's wooden door swung open and a woman stepped to the threshold.

"Do you plan on waking all the gods with your shouting, Jofarr?" the woman said, hands on her hips.

Familiarity once again tugged at Rúnin. Finna was slightly stouter in the hips and bust, but she had the same honey blonde hair and relaxed confidence about her that he remembered from all those years ago.

The woman stiffened as her eyes shifted from the litter Jofarr dragged to Ketill and Rúnin hobbling toward her.

"Ketill," she breathed. "What has happened?"

"*Moðir*, we caught a rabbit," Jofarr said proudly, holding the dead animal up from his belt. "And then we fished this man out of the gulf, and this pretty lady needs your help."

The words came out in a garbled rush. Perhaps the boy was younger than Rúnin had initially guessed. Or perhaps it wasn't every day that bedraggled and injured strangers appeared outside their homestead.

Finna's green-brown eyes shifted to Ketill for a better explanation.

"We came across these two while we were hunting," Ketill said, coming to a halt in front of the hut but keeping his arm around Rúnin for support. "They were crossing the gulf when Svein here fell through the ice. Madrena has been injured by a boar and needs help."

Finna nodded quickly, suddenly all business. "Bring her inside. I'll set the girls to making a tea and poultice. Svein, is it?" she said, glancing over Rúnin.

He kept his head down but bobbed a nod.

"You'll need to change out of those wet clothes and get warm—fast," she said, her gaze lingering on him. "Ketill can help you once we get the woman inside."

Rúnin nodded again, but Finna didn't wait for his assent. "Ingrid!" she called into the hut. "Get the water boiling." Then Finna poked her head around the corner of the hut. "Odny! Odny, come inside at once!"

As Ketill moved to Madrena's side to carry her into the hut, a streak of yellow caught the corner of Rúnin's eye. A little girl no more than five years old darted out of the covered stalls where the cows clumped together and chewed their cud. The hem of her dress was sodden with snow and mud, and her pale blonde hair, so much like Madrena's, streamed wildly behind her. She skidded to a halt when she saw the crowd in front of the hut.

"Odny, come inside now. These people need our help," Finna said to the girl.

The child's wide blue eyes took in the scene silently. Without warning, she darted into motion once more, slipping past her mother and into the dim interior of the hut.

Just then, Ketill lifted Madrena into a seated position on the litter, but Madrena groaned in pain. Despite the wooden stiffness in his limbs and the pain of moving so quickly, Rúnin shot to her side.

"Her left shoulder and her right side are injured," he said, carefully slipping a hand around Madrena's middle. Though his body felt filled with icy lead, he scooped Madrena into his arms and turned toward the hut.

Jofarr and Finna both stepped inside. Ketill walked next to Rúnin to assure that Madrena wouldn't be jostled.

Rúnin had to bend slightly to clear the doorway, but once inside, he realized the hut was surprisingly big. A large, inviting fire crackled cheerily in the center of the main room. The back wall had been made into a kitchen with a second, smaller fire pit built against the lower stone wall. Two darker alcoves stood slightly separated from the main room. Those must be the sleeping quarters.

An older girl was spreading several furs on the ground next to the fire pit in the middle of the room.

"You can put her here," she said softly, her hazel eyes, so like her mother's, flicking for the briefest moment toward Rúnin.

Rúnin stepped woodenly toward the pile of furs. As he bent, a grunt of pain escaped his lips, but he managed to set Madrena down without unsettling her. His cloak was still spread over her limp form. A glance at her face told him the fever continued to rack her.

He remained knelt by her side, gazing at her delicate features, which were twisted slightly in pain. A gentle hand on his shoulder had him jumping.

"We'll see to her," Finna said quietly. "But you must get out of those wet clothes before you are in worse condition that she is."

"Jofarr, fetch a tunic and trousers from my trunk. And some stockings as well," Ketill said.

The boy scampered to one of the darkened alcoves set back from the room. Soon Rúnin heard the sounds of rustling wool as Jofarr did his father's bidding.

Meanwhile, Finna and the older girl, who must be Ingrid, set to work in the kitchen. They plucked various dried plants from the walls and lifted clay lids on jars, sniffing the contents and talking quietly to each other. Odny, the towheaded girl, took a wooden spoon from a shelf and stirred the large caldron over the cooking fire.

The heat of the larger fire at Rúnin's side felt like it was singeing his skin, though he wasn't close enough to be burned. He held trembling hands toward the flames and ignored the prickling pain as the heat seeped into his damp skin.

Despite the pain, and despite his fears for Madrena, a lulling calm attempted to steal over him. Mayhap he simply couldn't be afraid anymore—mayhap he didn't have the energy to worry about all that could go wrong even still. Something about this warm, cozy hut and its kind inhabitants made him want to forget all the darkness, all the dread and distrust that had characterized his life for so long.

Jofarr emerged from the alcove, his slim arms overflowing with woolen garments. Through the soothing warmth of the fire and the gentle whispers of Finna and her daughters, trepidation leached back into his belly once more.

Rúnin would have to remove his clothes in front of these people. Surely then they would see his mark and know the truth. Would they kill him on the spot or simply drive him into the cold? Would they harm Madrena as well?

He would have to turn around when he stripped away his sodden clothes to hide the brand mark, but then they would see the scars on his back. Those scars would raise questions he didn't want to answer, but it was better than revealing the brand that marked him an outlaw.

"Here you go, Svein," Jofarr said as he handed Rúnin the bundle of clothes. Rúnin tugged off his sodden boots and leaned them close to the fire pit with stiff fingers. Then he rose and hobbled to the darkest corner near the doorway, turning his back on the cheery room.

Clenching his teeth against the stab of pain in his

arm where the trapper's arrow had hit him, he peeled his tunic off and dropped it to the floor.

Before he could slip the dry tunic over his head, he heard the gasp he'd been dreading.

"*Moðir*, why does he have white lines all over his back?"

"Odny, it isn't polite to stare," Ingrid hissed at her little sister.

"Back to your tasks, both of you," Finna said calmly, though Rúnin guessed she had been the one to gasp.

He shivered as the wool dropped over his back, barring his old scars from view. The tunic's length, falling almost to his knees, allowed him to modestly peel down his wet trousers and slip on the dry ones without drawing any more attention. Then he pulled the woolen stockings over his frozen feet.

Jofarr had brought him two leather strips with which to fasten the stockings. Rúnin had to shake his head in amazement. Somehow he'd forgotten that it was the style in these parts for a man to pull his stockings over his trouser legs and then secure them by crisscrossing bands of leather around them. It held the stockings up, but also provided extra warmth above one's boots. Plus, it kept the trousers' legs dry in deep snow.

His hands fell into the familiar rhythm of winding the leather around his lower legs. Though he hadn't done so for fourteen years, it came back to him as if he'd done it yesterday.

Suddenly he felt Ketill's eyes on him. Rúnin cursed himself silently. Yet again he'd given Ketill cause for suspicion. A man from the lowlands of Knorrstad shouldn't know how to wrap his stockings this way.

Rúnin wouldn't form another lie though— not under

Ketill's soft but curious gaze. Instead, he silently returned to Madrena's side.

He placed his still-cold fingers against her cheek. Her skin raged with fever. Although she was insensate, she unconsciously tilted her head toward his hand so that he cupped her cheek. Perhaps the coolness of his touch soothed her somehow.

"Give her this." Ingrid appeared at his side with a wooden mug full of steaming liquid. As Rúnin took the mug from her, he realized that Ingrid was almost more young woman than girl. She took after her mother with her green-brown eyes and dark blonde hair, though she seemed serious and watchful like her father.

Rúnin gave her a nod of thanks, and she instantly dropped her eyes and scurried back to her mother's side. Tilting Madrena's head up carefully, he positioned the mug at her lips.

The first few drops slid down her cheek. Then the next few had her instinctively coughing. But at last she swallowed a few mouthfuls of the brew.

"Now, let's see about her injuries," Finna said. She crouched next to Rúnin and gently drew back the cloak covering Madrena.

The strip of linen shift that Rúnin had wrapped around Madrena's middle was a bloody mess. Finna hesitated for a moment, but then reached out tentatively and untied the bandage.

"Shite." The word slipped past Rúnin's lips before he could stop it. "Apologies," he said quickly, flicking his eyes to Finna and the children. But the raw, festering wound on Madrena's side had his attention snapping back to her.

Through the hole in the material of her dress made

by the arrow, Madrena's skin was red and swollen. The open wound oozed yellow and white pus, the edges of the gash rising angrily.

Finna pressed her lips together, likely holding back her own curse.

"Jofarr, Odny, go outside and see to the animals," she said, her voice surprisingly level though her eyes were locked on Madrena's side.

"Why does Ingrid get to stay inside?" Jofarr whined.

"Because she is older than you and she is training to be a healer," Finna replied distractedly.

Ketill leaned over Rúnin's shoulder and caught a glimpse at the wound.

"Do as your mother says. Now," he said tersely.

Jofarr and Odny clambered to the door. Rúnin felt a brief blast of cold air before the door shut and the hut felt quieter and less crowded.

"We'll need more tea," Finna said to Ingrid. "Soak the bandages in it as well."

Ingrid nodded solemnly and set about her tasks.

"Help me get her out of this dress," Finna said, turning to Rúnin and Ketill.

Carefully, the three of them managed to shift Madrena's body a little at a time as Finna drew away the stout wool. When she was clad in only her linen shift, Madrena looked so much more frail and thin than Rúnin remembered.

Finna used a small dagger to simply cut away the shift near the wound. The garment was likely ruined anyway, soaked as it was in blood and torn by the arrow.

"I'll need to drain this before I can begin treating it." Finna handed Rúnin a small dagger. "Hold that over the flames for a count to fifty."

Rúnin had to swallow hard as he took the dagger from Finna. Unwanted memories threatened to overtake him.

The blade hovered in the fire until it glowed orange. He struggled against the two men holding him, but they were too strong. The radiant sword tip drifted toward him, hanging for a second near his face before descending to his chest.

He sank his teeth into his lower lip, trying to contain the scream of agony. But the noise ripped from his throat as white hot pain seared his chest, his very heart.

The stench of his own burning flesh filled his nose before darkness swallowed him.

"That's good enough," Finna said, her voice cutting through the memory.

He carefully handed her the hilt end of the now-hot dagger.

"Hold her, please."

Cognizant of her injured shoulder, Rúnin gripped her upper arms while Ketill pinned her ankles.

As the hot knife slit into her side, Madrena involuntarily jerked and flailed. But Rúnin and Ketill held her steady as Finna worked to free the wound of its infection.

At last, Finna leaned back on her heels and called for Ingrid to bring her a treated bandage. The girl carried over a steaming, dripping strip of cloth and handed it carefully to her mother. As she layered several soaked bandages along the wound, Madrena stirred.

"Bersi…" she whispered. "Bersi, nei." Her voice rose as she tossed her head from side to side. "Rúnin! Please help, Rúnin!"

Rúnin would have clapped a hand over Madrena's mouth, but it was too late. Dread sank like a stone within his chest. He snapped his head up, his eyes darting around the room.

Everyone had frozen and now stared at him. Finna's eyes were wide as her gaze darted over Rúnin's face. Ketill looked unsurprised, though his features were hard. Even Ingrid must have recognized her Jarl's name spoken on the lips of this stranger. She stared wide-eyed between Madrena and Rúnin.

"Ingrid, will you please step outside?" Finna said calmly, never taking her eyes from Rúnin.

Rúnin raised his hands slowly, though he doubted it would do any good. "I mean your family no harm. My only care is for Madrena."

"Ingrid." Finna's voice was more urgent. "*Now.*"

Ingrid hurried across the room. As the door opened and closed with her departure, Rúnin eased to his feet. He wouldn't raise a hand against these two, especially with their children right outside.

His time had come. He would either be killed by his former friends or turned over to Dursi. He let his hands drop in defeat.

25

Finna rose slowly to her feet and stepped to Ketill's side.

But to Rúnin's shock, neither one reached for a weapon.

"Rúnin. Such an unusual name," Ketill said, his dark blue eyes keen on Rúnin.

"Wasn't there once a lad in Seterfell named Rúnin?" Finna asked. "He was something like you, Svein. Tall for his age, dark-headed, bright, sharp eyes. He was a good lad."

Rúnin felt his brow lower in confusion. The two had obviously realized who he was. Why did they toy with him?

"What happened to that lad?" Finna said to Ketill.

Rúnin could sense Ketill's gaze burning into him, yet when he shifted his eyes from Finna to Ketill, he found the man's features were tight with pain.

"'Tis a sad story, Finna," Ketill said, his gaze boring into Rúnin. "When Jarl Bersi came to Seterfell and put himself in charge, the boy's father died trying to fight for the village's freedom."

Rúnin shook his head a little in warning. "What are you doing, Ketill?"

"Then his mother tried her best to protect the boy from the Jarl, but Bersi wanted sons. No matter how hard he tried, Bersi could not beget offspring, so he took the boy under his black wing, giving him the family name Bersisson."

"Stop," Rúnin hissed.

"Despite Jarl Bersi's cruel, vile ways, the boy remained true to the code of honor his mother and father had taught him. But when the lad swore fealty to the Jarl and went on his first raid –"

"Stop!" Rúnin bellowed. Pain surged through him, hot in his veins and sour in the back of his throat. He took a staggering step backward, but the hut suddenly felt too small. It was as if the stone and wood walls were closing in on him.

The hut was dim, though Rúnin could feel the children's eyes on him. The woman's scream pierced his ears. Bersi backhanded her again across the face.

"Do it, my son."

Rúnin swallowed, his wide eyes traveling from the terrified, bleeding woman to Bersi's hard features.

"I said do it!"

The woman whimpered and tried to shrink back, but Bersi grabbed her throat, giving her a little shake. The children in the corner moaned in fear.

Ketill's low, soft voice interrupted the nightmare, saving Rúnin from the darkness of the past. "The lad defied the Jarl's orders."

Rúnin squeezed his eyes shut. At least Ketill had taken pity on him and hadn't spoken the worst of it.

"So he was flogged in the village square. Never have I seen one so young, so small, take a beating like that. We all thought surely he would die, but the boy was strong. So Bersi increased the punishment. He burned away the mark of fealty on the lad's chest, then banished him to die alone in the wilderness, an outlaw never to see his mother or his friends again, and never to know companionship and safety again."

Rúnin's knees hit the hard-packed floor of the hut as he sank down. The memories threatened to overtake him once more, but he forced his tongue to work. "Why…why are you saying all this? You know who I am. You know you are doomed to my fate if you let me live."

Finna stepped forward and knelt in front of him. "Nei, Rúnin." His name came out choked through the thick emotion in her voice. "We could never turn you away or harm you."

She raised a shaky hand and touched his bristled cheek. Tears shimmered in her eyes. "It's really you, isn't it?"

"Ja," he whispered. "It is me."

"I suspected as much when I pulled you from the gulf," Ketill said, coming to his wife's side in front of Rúnin. "But when I saw your back, I was sure. No man should have survived that flogging, let alone a lad."

Shame burned in Rúnin's gut. "That lad *did* die, Ketill. The man you see before you may look like a grown version of the boy I once was, but that boy is long gone."

Finna took one of his hands in hers. Her fingers

were warm and callused from hard work—like Madrena's.

"We can only imagine what you've lived through all these years. We thought...we all thought surely you had died long ago. I suppose we should have known that the one who could survive the beating you took could survive the life of an outlaw as well."

"Nei, Finna, you don't understand," he said, his voice ragged in his ears. "I killed the honorable lad I used to be."

He tried to pull back his hand, but she held fast with surprising strength. "Listen to me, Rúnin!" she snapped, her eyes suddenly intense. "I, too, suspected it was you from the moment you set foot in our hut. But it wasn't simply your size and hair so like your father's, your eyes so like your mother's. It was because you demanded that we see to your woman first. It was because you looked at her with such protectiveness, without a care for yourself."

Rúnin opened his mouth to protest, but Ketill cut him off.

"And I heard you tell Jofarr to help Madrena instead of you, even though you were moments away from drowning."

"That is how you always were as a boy with anyone you cared for," Finna went on. "Remember when little Agnar kicked your family's dog? You threw yourself over the mutt to protect her, even though Agnar was bigger than you. You took Agnar's kicks yourself. You had bruised ribs for a sennight!"

His mother had chastised him lightly for the foolishness, and all over their mangy dog who stole scraps right from their table while they ate. But Rúnin's father had smiled slightly when he heard the tale, ruffling his son's hair without a word.

Rúnin felt a sad smile tugging his lips. He'd forgotten about that little show of valiance.

"You must love this woman a great deal to go to the lengths you did, to risk what you did," Finna said softly, her gaze settling on Madrena's now-still form.

Rúnin sobered instantly. His eyes darted to Madrena and his chest squeezed unbidden.

"I...I *do* love her."

They were the truest words he'd uttered in a long time.

Something clicked into place deep within him. Barely a fortnight ago, he'd opened his eyes and gazed upon her for the first time. He'd mistaken her for Freyja, but now he knew that she was so much more than beautiful. She was strong, yet she was brave enough to show him her vulnerability. She had a true warrior's heart—a noble, fierce, yet loving heart.

"A man who has room in his heart to love cannot be completely forsaken," Ketill said, flicking a warm look to Finna.

The seed of hope Madrena had planted budded in his chest, straining toward the light. Madrena had called honor a river. For the first time in fourteen years, he felt it surge within him.

But then he sobered as he looked at Ketill and Finna and thought of their three children outside. It didn't matter that they believed in him. They were all endangered by his very presence.

"I can't tell you how much your words mean to me," he said. "But you and your family are in mortal danger just by sheltering me. If Bersi were to hear—"

"He won't," Ketill said flatly.

"How can you be so sure? We all know what he is capable of."

Finna's mouth softened into an almost-smile. "Rúnin, things have changed since you left. Ja, there were many dark years after you were gone. Sometimes I think the only reason we survived was that we came out here, far enough from the village to avoid the worst of his rages. But in the last few years, Bersi has grown ill, weak."

"What?" Rúnin breathed.

"It started a few years ago. He had a cough that would keep him in bed for several days at a time. Though he tried to hide it from the villagers and even his men, there was blood in his lungs. I knew because I assisted Gunrud, the village healer, a few times before Bersi grew more secretive and private," Finna said.

It was almost too much to believe. "And now?" Rúnin asked.

"Now he is rarely seen, though it is whispered that he is on Odin's doorstep—or Hel's."

"Though some of his men have stayed loyal to him, many have slipped away on their own or in small groups," Ketill added. "They were always a bloodthirsty lot. They grew weary of waiting at Bersi's bedside instead of setting sail on raids. Only a few of his original band have remained in the village."

"So you see, Rúnin, we no longer fear him as we used to," Finna said, a gentle hand resting on Rúnin's arm. "Ja, he still has some power by proxy through the few warriors who'll do his bidding, but life has returned to something like normal in Seterfell. The random killings stopped. The demands for sacrifices and payments to prove fealty petered out."

"And so…and so you won't turn me over to Bersi? You don't have qualms about aiding an outlaw, even though it goes against all the codes of the Northlands?" Rúnin said slowly.

Ketill and Finna exchanged a look, and Rúnin sensed they were communicating without words.

At last, Ketill spoke. "You still do not fully understand, but we can try to explain it to you. All those years ago, every single person in the village longed to come to your aid when you were on the whipping post, and when Bersi branded you, and when he chased you off, still bleeding and semi-conscious from the flogging."

"We all wanted desperately to stand up to Bersi, to be as brave as a boy of only fourteen could be. Yet we were too afraid," Finna said, lowering her head.

"We didn't have the courage you had, Rúnin." Ketill's eyes bore into him, sharp and sorrowful. "But helping you now… It is as if the gods wished to give us a second chance to do the right thing, the thing we couldn't do all those years ago. It is our opportunity to atone for the wrong we did against you and against our own sense of justice."

"Helping you and your woman—it's the least we can do, and we thank the gods for the chance to right our past wrongs."

Rúnin's vision blurred as he looked between Finna and Ketill. "You believed in me…all this time?" His voice was gruff and thick with emotion. "All these years…"

He sank deeper into the floor, the energy draining from him even as he felt the unfamiliar stirrings of hope once more. "All these years I thought the village had shunned me just as Bersi had. I thought I was alone in the world, with naught left to cling to but my own dishonor."

Rúnin raised a shaking hand to his face and slid it along his mouth. "I could never have imagined…I never knew that all along, I wasn't truly alone."

Tears streamed down Finna's cheeks and emotion shimmered in Ketill's eyes as Rúnin brought his gaze up to them once more. Finna suddenly launched herself at Rúnin, colliding with his chest in a fierce hug.

"Nei, you were never alone, and you were never far from our thoughts, sweet lad," Finna whispered.

Madrena muttered and shifted in her sleep behind Finna, drawing her out of their embrace.

"Oh!" Finna said, wiping the tears from her eyes and standing quickly. "I've nigh forgotten myself."

She went to Madrena's side and cautiously lifted the moist bandages from the wound. With a nod to herself, Finna went to refill the wooden mug with the healing tea she'd made. But as she knelt before Madrena once more with the mug in hand, she froze, her eyes landing on Ketill.

"There is one more thing we need to tell you," she said, her gaze pointedly on her husband.

Ketill grew serious again and turned to Rúnin. "It is about your mother."

Rúnin's heart sank before the words were out. He'd feared that he would never know what had become of her after he was banished. But now the words he'd dreaded were about to be spoken.

"Aeleif…joined the gods a few years back," Ketill said quietly.

Rúnin's fists clenched at his sides. "Bersi?"

"Nei," Finna interjected. "A pox took her and several others from the village. It was…relatively quick."

Sadness replaced the flash of anger in Rúnin's chest, and he released the tension from his hands.

"She was strong, like her son," Finna added. "Bersi could never get the best of her."

With a nod, Rúnin slumped against the cool stones of the hut's base. His mother had tried to protect him from Bersi as best she could after his father died, just as Rúnin had tried to protect her from their mad Jarl. He'd known somewhere in his heart that he would never see her again after he was banished, but it was little comfort to know that she'd died only a few years ago.

Finna must have sensed the torrent of confusion and raw emotions tearing through Rúnin. "You need to rest," she said, glancing at him as she coaxed more tea down Madrena's throat.

Ketill helped Rúnin to his feet.

"We can make another pile of furs for you in the corner if you'd like," Ketill said.

"Nei," Rúnin replied, his eyes falling on Madrena. "I'll stay by her side. Sometimes she has…nightmares."

The unspoken explanation hung in the air for a long moment. Madrena had spoken Bersi's name in terror. Surely that had piqued Finna and Ketill's curiosity about how Madrena could know Bersi. Blessedly, though, they didn't press Rúnin on it.

Rúnin settled himself between the fire pit and Madrena's fevered body. She wasn't out of danger yet, but Rúnin felt a strange calm steal over him. She was under Finna's care, sheltered from the elements and in good hands.

Though he struggled against it, his eyes grew heavy as he watched Finna work quietly on Madrena's side. Though his mind reeled with all the revelations of the last hour, his body could not resist the soothing warmth of the fire.

Bersi's weakening illness. His mother's death. Finna, Ketill, and the other villagers longing to stand by him even though fear of Bersi's rage quelled them. And his love for Madrena.

It all swirled together into a tangled brew in his mind as his eyes drooped.

Sometime later, he heard the door open quietly, then Finna giving Ingrid instructions. But he could no longer fight the pull toward sleep. Oblivion dragged him under.

26

"*Moðir*, it's not fair!"

The little girl's voice drifted to Madrena through the shapeless fog of the underworld.

"Odny, lower your voice indoors, please." A woman's voice, but Madrena didn't recognize it.

"But Jofarr killed Helgi!"

Nei. No more death. No more violence, not against women and children. Madrena's mind filled with the image of Bersi looming over her. The bear tattoo swirled before her, its maw wide and its teeth clamping down on her.

Nei. No more. She struggled to fight Bersi off, but her limbs felt like they were made of iron.

"How could he kill a bit of stuffed wool?" This was a new female voice, younger than the woman's, but filled with an adolescent's biting scorn.

"He swung his sword at her until her head popped off!" The little girl's voice was filled with the threat of tears.

"Jofarr! Jofarr Ketillsson, come here please!" the woman called.

Cold air washed over Madrena for a moment and then was gone. In the back of her mind, she heard a door thump closed.

"Jofarr, you have upset your sister. Did you hurt her doll?"

A long pause followed, but at last a young boy's voice mumbled almost inaudibly. "Mayhap."

"Speak up and answer your mother when she asks you a question, son."

Madrena would have jumped at the deep male voice nearby filled with stern command.

"Ja, *Moðir*, I used Helgi for practice," the boy said reluctantly.

The girl's voice rose in a wail.

"Odny, hush," the woman ordered. "And Jofarr, you will repair Helgi until she is…healed. And you are not to train on her anymore."

"But how am I to become a great warrior if I cannot practice with my sword on something?" The boy's voice pitched higher in desperation.

"Perhaps Rúnin will let you wield your sword against him." Now the deep male voice held a note of teasing.

Rúnin.

He was alive, but was he safe?

A deep, rough chuckle reverberated in her ears. It was a shocking, warm sound.

"And risk being beheaded like Helgi? I think not."

Rúnin's voice was barely recognizable, yet Madrena was sure it had been him. He sounded so…relaxed. So content. So close.

Madrena tried to move her tongue to call out to him, but it felt like wood in her mouth. She cracked her eyelids open and winced against the light. It was dim wherever she was, but even firelight seemed bright compared to the dark oblivion from which she'd just emerged.

She blinked a few times, lowering her brows against the dull pain as it receded and her vision cleared.

Furs tickled her neck as she rolled her head to the side slightly. She lay on her back, the warmth of a fire to her left.

As her eyes opened fully, they landed on a young girl of perhaps five. The girl stood a short distance away, her pale blonde head cocked to one side and her dark blue eyes staring quizzically at Madrena. In her hand she held a lump of wool that had been sewn to have arms and legs. A bit of wool fuzz trailed where the doll's head should have been.

The girl took a step toward Madrena, her eyes wide and curious.

Vaguely, Madrena heard the boy beg Rúnin and the other man to help him in his sword practice. The woman and the older girl chimed in. No one seemed to notice the little towhead's sudden rapt attention on Madrena.

She took another step and then knelt on the ground so that she was almost at eye level with Madrena.

"Hello," the girl whispered. She reached out a cautious hand and plucked a lock of bedraggled hair from Madrena's forehead. "You have hair like me, but your eyes are strange."

Madrena couldn't help but smile weakly. She swallowed with difficulty and tried to prop an elbow beneath her, but pain tore through her side. A dull ache echoed in her left shoulder.

"Madrena!" Rúnin's voice was unnecessarily loud

given how close he was. All the mirth was gone, to be replaced by urgent worry.

Suddenly his large, calloused hands were wrapped around her arms, easing her back down to the furs. She blinked up and there he was.

Several days' worth of bristle darkened his firm jawline. His deep brown hair was pulled back at his nape. Those bright, sharp eyes scanned her, clouded with concern.

Madrena tried to speak, but it turned into a cough. She winced as her body's convulsions shot fresh pain through her side. The skin there felt pulled tight, as did her shoulder.

A cup appeared in Rúnin's grasp. He slipped his other hand under her neck and carefully lifted her head to help her drink. The cool water was like a balm to her dry mouth and rough throat.

As he pulled the cup back, several more faces crowded around Rúnin's head. Her gaze darted between them, suddenly wary.

"Where are we?" she whispered

"We are safe," Rúnin said quietly. "I'll explain, but you should rest more."

"I've been resting for a day already," she shot back. She made another attempt to sit up, but Rúnin's hands held her down.

"What does she mean, a day, *Móðir*?" The little boy looked down at her curiously.

Rúnin's dark brows drew together. "What do you remember, Madrena?"

Though her mind was still foggy with sleep and she felt strangely weak, she forced herself to think back.

"Crossing the river. The trapper. Our conversation about honor."

He waited as if she should remember more. At last, he spoke. "That was five days ago."

"*What?*" she croaked.

The little towheaded girl giggled loudly.

"Outside, children." The woman's voice brokered no argument, and three of the faces over Madrena quickly vanished. The door a few paces from her feet opened and closed hastily.

"Madrena, this is Ketill." Rúnin gestured toward the other man, whose thick beard was a shade darker than his light brown hair. His eyes were the same dark blue as the little girl's—and just as curious.

"And this is Finna. She saved your life."

Madrena's gaze shifted to the woman. With her kindly hazel eyes and honey hair, she bore a strong resemblance to the older girl who'd just departed. Or rather, the girl bore a resemblance to Finna, who was clearly the children's mother.

"Thank you," Madrena said slowly, her mind still turning with frustrating sluggishness.

"You must have many questions," Finna said. "Don't mind me or my husband. As Rúnin said, you are safe with us."

The woman shooed her husband back a little way and then pulled back the fur that lay atop Madrena.

"You remember that I removed the arrows from your shoulder and side, ja?" Rúnin said, his gaze drifting from her face to her side. Finna was unwinding some sort of bandage around Madrena's middle.

"I remember waking up after you did it," she replied cautiously.

"We talked, and then you fell asleep."

She nodded. "And you're telling me that was five days ago?"

"You fell into a fever that night. I made a litter for you and skis for myself and headed toward Seterfell. I crossed the Gulf of Bothnia instead of going around, which was almost a deadly mistake. But Ketill found us and brought us to his home."

She narrowed her eyes at him. "That doesn't even *begin* to explain things." She inhaled to go on, but it turned into a gasp of pain.

"Forgive me," Finna said as she prodded the aching skin on Madrena's right side. "I think you pulled out a stitch when you tried to sit up. But that is easily repaired. The skin no longer looks inflamed, and the wound has at last stopped oozing."

Rúnin leaned over her and she caught a whiff of his familiar scent—male skin, pine, and fresh air. He inspected her side for a moment and nodded, most of the worry at last fading from his eyes.

"And may I just add," Finna said, giving Rúnin a sharp look. "I knew from the second I saw this wound that no boar's tusk did this. I simply didn't want to press you for the truth when you were so distressed."

Madrena's eyes jerked to Rúnin, scanning as much of him as she could see from her position on her back. "Why were you distressed? Were you hurt? Are you all right?"

"Oh, nei, Madrena!" Finna said with a shake of her head. "It's not that. It's just that he has had to watch the woman he loves hovering on Odin's doorstep for the last five days."

Now Finna was the recipient of Madrena's sharp gaze. "What was that?"

Finna's mouth dropped open and she looked between Madrena and Rúnin. "I only meant…that is…I thought you had already…"

Madrena felt her eyes round as she turned her stare back on Rúnin. For the first time since she'd known him, he actually seemed flustered. But he quickly smoothed his face, apparently gathering his wits.

"I was very worried about you," he said softly. "Finna recently reminded me that I have always been that way about people I care for deeply—people I…love."

Madrena blinked. Curse her slow mind and her suddenly clumsy tongue for not being able to form words. There were too many questions, too many swirling pieces of information crowding her mind.

Ketill cleared his throat loudly in the corner. "I'd best see to milking the cows. Would you assist me, sweet wife?" Without waiting for an answer, he lifted Finna from the floor by her elbow and tucked her arm under his. With a thump of the wooden door, Rúnin and Madrena were suddenly alone.

She had grown accustomed to his presence over the course of their journey, and yet, something was different now. It wasn't just the crackle of bodily awareness she felt, even through the weakness and pain in her limbs, for she had become used to the pull he had on her. Yet suddenly it felt awkward to be alone with him.

"Let me make sure I understand," she said carefully. "I have been unconscious these past five days. The wounds from the trapper's arrows became infected."

"Ja. Well, just your side. Finna stitched your shoulder, but it is already on its way to being healed."

"And you dragged me to Seterfell. The place you swore never to return to."

"Ja."

"Because..." Her throat caught. "Because you love me?"

He nodded slowly, his eyes piercing her. "Ja."

Despite the spark of pain in her side and the pinch in her shoulder, she reached for his face. Her hands cupped his bristled cheeks. A look of surprise flitted through his bright blue eyes before she pulled him to her.

At the first brush of contact, something shifted deep within Madrena's chest. Her heart squeezed even as her stomach dropped into weightless euphoria. His words moved her, but his actions shook her to her core.

He had risked his life in order to save hers. She'd known deep down that although he didn't think so of himself, he was a good, honorable man. He'd never tried to hurt her. His embrace chased away the nightmares. And he had saved her both from the trapper and the raging river over which she'd dangled helplessly.

But this was different—this was more profound. For as an outlaw, he'd risked himself—and not just in any village, but in the one place where he could be recognized.

His lips softened against hers, his hand coming to the back of her head to cradle her. Slowly, purposefully, their tongues met and caressed each other. Though their bodies had already matched the sensual entwinement of their tongues when they'd had sex a sennight ago, this kiss was somehow more intimate.

In fact, it was like nothing Madrena had ever felt before. Her body gradually came awake. Warmth rose to her skin that had naught to do with the fire to her left. But it wasn't the effect on her body that had her reeling.

She pulled her mouth away on a panting breath.

"How can you love me?" she whispered in wonderment. "You've only known me for a little more than a fortnight."

His eyes, unfathomable blue, penetrated her. He brought a hand to her cheek and slowly trailed a fingertip from her ear to her chin.

"Because in that short time, you've shown me how strong you are. You have shown me how true your heart runs. I love your passion and intensity. I love your stubbornness and determination. I love the fire in your veins. And I love the way you see me, the way you believe in me."

Madrena swallowed hard. The weakness and vulnerability stealing over her were so unfamiliar that they frightened her for a moment. But she realized with a jolt what the word was for those feelings of exposed defenselessness.

"I love you, too."

A flood of something like relief washed through Rúnin's eyes as he continued to gaze at her. With another brush of his fingertips along her heated skin, his voice dropped low into a tease.

"How can you love me?" he said, echoing her words. "You've only known me for a little more than a fortnight."

But as she looked up at him, she saw a shadow of doubt and fear cross his features. She grazed her palm over the dark stubble on his jawline.

"Because in that short time, you have shown me *your* strength. You have shown me the honor that cannot be snuffed within you. I love your protectiveness. I love how your embrace wards away the nightmares. And I love your trust in me."

His mouth descended in another searing kiss, this one more urgent, more demanding than the last. Her hands shifted to his shoulders, and she could feel the pent-up strength bunched in his muscles, the barely restrained need under her fingertips.

A new fear rustled in the back of her mind as she processed one of the many revelations of the last few minutes. She pulled back again.

"You clearly trust these people. But Rúnin, they *know* you. You must be in great danger here."

"Nei," he breathed on an exhale. "For once, I believe we are safe."

"But how?" She tried to sit up and this time managed to prop herself on one elbow with minimal pain. "How can we possibly be safe so close to Bersi? If everything you told me about his reign over your village was true, our presence will be discovered soon enough. We are like sitting ducks here."

"There is so much to explain," he said, his brows drawing together.

She listened in silence but with increasing agitation as Rúnin told her what Finna and Ketill had said about Bersi.

"And you believe just because he is ill that he no longer poses a threat?" Her question held a harder edge than she'd intended, especially after their confessions of love, but she couldn't seem to temper the frustration welling in her.

Rúnin leaned back slightly and ran a hand through his hair, though it was already bound and pulled away from his face. "It's not that simple, Madrena. In truth, I haven't given Bersi much thought. I was more worried about you."

That softened some of her anger, but not all of it. "He still has men loyal to him, men willing to do his vile bidding."

"Ja."

"The serpent can no longer poison its victims with its head removed," she said softly. "I'm still going after him."

"Like this?" He swept a hand down her body to indicate her injuries and proneness.

"Nei. I'll heal. I'll rest. I'll prepare myself. But then I'll have vengeance."

"That's your right," Rúnin said carefully. "But from what Finna and Ketill told me, Bersi isn't much of a threat anymore. Life in the village has returned to nigh normal."

"And because he has been weakened and can no longer terrorize them, he should be allowed to live peacefully?"

"Nei, that's not what I'm saying. You have every reason to seek revenge. All the laws in the Northlands are on your side. All I mean is…" He cast his eyes around the hut's thatched ceiling. "I just…couldn't bear to lose you."

The anger that threatened before fizzled into tenderness. "I don't plan on dying, Rúnin," she said softly.

"I know. You are a skilled shieldmaiden. I believe in your abilities. Call my concern the worries of a coward."

She felt her brows draw together. "You still won't go with me to face him?"

He dropped his head. "I've never desired vengeance for what Bersi did. All these years, although I would choose the same course of action, I have always believed I deserved his punishment."

"I don't understand," she whispered, "and I wish you would let me."

His rough, warm fingers brushed a strand of hair from her forehead. "I've fought against the memories for so long."

She seized his hand and gripped it in hers with all the strength she could muster. Her gaze held him, trying to communicate silently that he could at last speak of the pain that haunted his eyes.

He squeezed her hand back, a subtle war waging on his hard features.

At last he took a deep breath and began to speak.

27

Rúnin's whole body was wound tight as he held Madrena in his gaze. All the shame, all the self-loathing from the last fourteen years threatened to make him turn away, to build up the walls around his heart once more.

But in Madrena's gray, fire-lit eyes, he allowed himself to hope that he would find understanding and redemption.

"I told you how Bersi took over my village and proclaimed himself Jarl."

She nodded.

"I was only a couple of years older than Jofarr when it happened."

Madrena's eyes flicked toward the hut's door and recognition flashed in them. "Finna and Ketill's little warrior son?"

"Ja," he said, a sad smile tugging at his mouth for a brief moment. "Once the villagers' resistance had been mostly quashed, Bersi set about making himself a family. He took a wife, but when several months passed without getting her with child, he had her killed."

Madrena stiffened, the slim hand in his clenching.

"He took up with several other women, but none of them produced a child."

"Your mother?" The question came out clipped, her mouth tight with fear and disgust.

"Nei, she was spared his attentions. After I was born, she bled greatly. The village healer managed to save her, but she was never able to have a child after that. I remember it being a source of sadness between my parents, but after my father died and we were left to Bersi's madness, my mother came to believe that the gods had been protecting her."

Madrena exhaled slowly and nodded. "But Bersi was never able to have a child of his own?"

Every few months, another one of the village's women. Strung up in the village square, head lolling limply. Or bloodied and beaten, left in the mud, blank eyes staring in death.

Rúnin gritted his teeth against the memory. "Ja. After more than a year, he gave up, blessedly. But he still wanted an heir, a son."

Madrena's eyes widened slightly as realization dawned, but he went on anyway.

"My mother tried her best to protect me, to keep me hidden from notice, but as a young boy, it was time that I started training to be a warrior. Bersi must have noticed me during our practices. Mayhap it was because I was bigger and stronger than the other lads my age. Mayhap it was because I had dark hair like him. I don't know why, but he decided that I would be his heir."

Now Madrena's nails dug painfully into his palm, but she didn't speak as she waited for him to go on.

"He stripped me of my father's name and gave me his instead. I became Rúnin Bersisson—Rúnin, son of Little Bear. He pulled me aside from the other lads and taught me how to fight with a sword, a bow, an axe, everything. His style was brutal, but so was life in the Northlands, so he said. At first I only practiced on wooden dummies. But then he had me train against his men. Sometimes it was clearly practice, with me squaring off against one of Bersi's weaker warriors. But other times Bersi ordered us to keep fighting until only one of us was left. I killed my first man when I was thirteen."

"But you obeyed," Madrena said softly.

Shame surged through him at her words. He'd warred with himself ever since he'd been banished if he should have defied Bersi sooner. Could he have saved those lives? Could he have saved himself?

She must have read the pain on his face, for she quickly went on. "You didn't have a choice, Rúnin. You were just a boy at the whim of a madman. All I meant was...you told me that you eventually stood against Bersi. What caused you to do something so dangerous?"

Rúnin forced himself to unclench his fingers, which he hadn't realized were beginning to squeeze Madrena's hand like a vise.

"By the time I turned fourteen, I had done many terrible things, things that would have shamed my father if he still lived. Bersi decided that I was old enough to go on my first raid. But first I had to swear my fealty to him—not as a boy frightened of his Jarl, but as a man, pledging my unquestioning loyalty and obedience."

"Why are you here before me today, Rúnin Bersisson?"

Bersi's voice thundered over the heads of the silent villagers gathered to see the ceremony.

"To swear fealty to you, Jarl Bersi. To pledge to give you my life if you so request it, to obey your commands without hesitation, and to defend all that is yours."

Rúnin glanced over to where his mother stood hunched in the crowd. Silent tears streamed down her face before she turned away and was swallowed by the masses.

"Let this arm band be a reminder of to whom you belong," Bersi said as he clamped the gold band around Rúnin's slim forearm.

"And let your chest carry the mark of your Jarl, so that all will know that you are the son of a bear!"

"He gave me the bear tattoo," Rúnin went on. "Just like the one he has. Then we set out on my first raid. We sailed down the Gulf of Bothnia to a small village on the southeast shore. The village was easily taken."

He knew his flat words cut Madrena, for her eyes flickered with rage and revulsion. But what he had to tell her next was far worse.

"There was hardly a fight to be had before the village's meager loot was secured. But Bersi's battle lust wasn't sated. He took me to one of the few huts that hadn't yet been burned. We found a woman with two young children huddled inside."

The stench of smoke and the sound of screams faded slightly as Bersi closed the door behind them. Three sets of eyes gazed in terror at them. The woman tried to shield the children with her body, but Bersi was more focused on her than the little boy and girl.

He grabbed her by the hair, twisting until the woman screamed in pain and fear.

"Bersi ordered me to…"

"Nei," Madrena breathed.

275

Rúnin fought against the bile rising in the back of his throat. Madrena had wanted to know his darkest secret, the reason he had been banished. It was this memory above all others that tormented him, this waking nightmare that had defined every moment of his life since.

"He ordered me to rape her."

"Nei," Madrena said again on a sob. "Please tell me you didn't, Rúnin."

He took a deep breath. "I didn't."

Madrena squeezed her eyes shut for a long moment, likely trying to ward off her own black memories.

"I didn't," he said again gently. "Bersi had controlled me through fear. Even though I hadn't wanted to become his heir, and I hadn't wanted to kill and maim in his name, I did so because I was a frightened boy. But in that moment, I saw those children's fear, and the woman's fear. I thought of my own mother. The children were not so different from me—only a few years younger. Despite her fear, the woman was brave in attempting to fight back against Bersi. I longed for that kind of bravery."

The fire crackled in the pained silence that stretched for a long moment.

"He ordered me to rape her, but I refused. He commanded me, struck me across the face, but again I refused. I wanted to be brave for once, to stand up to him. But what I didn't anticipate was that he would take out his rage at my defiance on the woman and children. He struck my head with the pommel of his sword and I fell to the ground. Yet I was still semi-conscious. I had to watch as he raped the woman, then ran his sword through both her and the two children."

Shieldmaiden's Revenge

Madrena brought a shaking hand up to her mouth. Tears welled in her eyes. "And...and that is why he outlawed you?"

"Ja, though I think he initially meant to simply kill me instead. He dragged me from the hut and threw me on his longship. I came back to my senses when we reached Seterfell. Bersi ordered that the villagers be gathered, and I assumed based on his past fits of violence that he would behead me for my transgression against him. Instead, he tied me to a pole and flogged me."

"The scars on your back," Madrena whispered. "You got those when you were just a boy?"

Rúnin nodded, his jaw clenched.

"The flogging went on for more than an hour, or so I assume. I lost consciousness and awoke still tied to the post several hours later. I was left there overnight, and then the flogging resumed the next morning. By the third morning, I should have been dead. For some reason, I lived on, though."

Madrena's eyes reflected the horror that he had lived with all these years. Strangely, speaking about it left him numb, as if he were telling someone else's story.

"Bersi's bloodlust must have cooled somewhat, but he wasn't done with my punishment," Rúnin went on. "He ripped the arm band representing my fealty from my arm and threw it into the fire. Watching the metal heat up in the flames must have given him the idea to brand and outlaw me. Blessedly, by that point I was mostly insensate to the pain. I vaguely remember my mother's crying face before I was cut down from the post and thrown outside the village."

"How...how did you possibly survive?"

He thought back to that hazy fortnight when his back had bled, then crusted over. He hadn't possessed a shirt, a weapon, or a crumb of food. But somehow he'd found the will to live.

"I did what it took," he said, his voice hard and rough.

Madrena's gaze drifted to the fire, her face tight with pain and sadness. He caught himself holding his breath and forced himself to exhale slowly. Although he'd learned a long time ago not to believe in hope and redemption, he still found himself praying that Madrena wouldn't turn away from him in disgust.

"I still don't understand," she said at last, her eyes searching the fire.

His stomach sank, but before he could draw his hands away, she went on.

"I don't understand why you have taken Bersi's dishonor on as your own."

"What?"

Her gray eyes locked on him, and he saw compassion and sorrow shining from them. "You told me before that it didn't matter why or how you defied your Jarl, just that you were an oath-breaker, a man with no honor."

"Ja," he said carefully, unsure of where she was going.

"But what about the oaths that you no doubt made to your father and mother? They taught you about honor, did they not?"

Rúnin's mind drifted to the fuzzy memories of his father, the smiling face behind the dark beard. His mother's quiet strength. Their love for each other and their pride in him.

"Ja, they taught me to stand for what is right."

"And you have made oaths to the gods, surely. To fight well and true for Thor, to respect the Allfather, Odin. To use your life and your death to prove your worthiness to enter Valhalla."

"What are you saying?"

Madrena clasped his hands, her grip surprisingly strong all of a sudden. Her eyes flared with urgent insistence.

"I'm saying that to refuse a dishonorable command can actually be an act of honor. Have you never heard of the tale of Eyjólfr and Hávarðr?"

Rúnin blinked at her and she made a tsking noise.

"Eyjólfr was hunting for Gísli, who was outlawed for a murder he didn't commit. Eyjólfr came across Gísli's wife and demanded that she tell him where her husband was. But Gísli's wife remained true to him and refused to divulge his location. Eyjólfr was so enraged that he ordered his men, led by Hávarðr, to murder Gísli's wife. But Hávarðr stood up to him, telling the men not to harm the woman, for to do so would be a grave injustice and a dishonor on all the men. Eyjólfr was shunned by the gods for ordering something so heinous as killing an innocent woman, whereas Hávarðr was smiled upon for doing the right thing, even though it meant defying the order of his superior."

When Rúnin continued to stare at her, she shook her head in amazement. "You truly haven't heard the tale before? I thought all young warriors in training were taught that defying an order can be a just act. Perhaps Bersi kept it from you for fear that it would give you ideas."

Rúnin nodded slowly. "I understand what you're

trying to say. You wish to convince me that I have honor despite everything. Finna and Ketill are working on me as well along those lines."

He dropped his gaze to the fire. "I want to believe you all," he said, his voice low. "Just know that you are working against fourteen years of shame and isolation. You are working against the twisted power Bersi still has over me."

Madrena took his face in her hands once again and drew his eyes back to her. The depth of the emotion he found there riveted him.

"I know," she said. "But I need *you* to understand that your actions have only made me love you more. You did the right thing, Rúnin."

Tears welled in her eyes, clouding the gray light shining from them.

"I am working to accept what you and Finna and Ketill are saying," he whispered. "I…I hope to believe in myself again."

Her voice caught on a sob in her throat and she drew him to her once more. He carefully wrapped his arms around her back, longing to crush her to him but fearful of hurting her.

"I have lived the life of a coward all these years," he said into her hair.

She shook her head in denial, but he went on.

"Nei, it's true. I stood up to Bersi once, but after that I gave him control over my life. I should have been free from his poison the moment he banished me, but instead I carried the weight of my broken pledge like an anchor on my leg. I wish I had been brave like you. I wish I had gone after him, faced him for all his wrongs."

Madrena pulled back, a look of vulnerable hope

transfixing her features. "There is still time, Rúnin. You can still stand up to him. Fight at my side. Fight for justice."

He felt like he was standing on a precipice. Behind him lay the life he'd known—the life of an outlaw, a coward, a man who accepted Bersi's reign of terror. Before him lay the unknown—a life of honor, of acting on what he knew to be right in his heart. And Madrena was at his side, holding his hand. He felt himself lean over the edge and into the future with Madrena.

It was as if the anchor weighing him down was at last cut away. He'd shared his darkest memories and secrets, and love still shone in her eyes.

"Ja," he whispered. "I will go with you. I will go *anywhere* with you, my love."

"I'll never let you doubt yourself again," she breathed just before her lips met his.

The kiss stole his breath, stole his very life force. His heart surged with a love he'd never known, never thought he'd deserve. The seed of hope reached toward the sunlight, unfurling leaf by leaf as it grew stronger.

As he tilted his head to deepen the kiss, he felt one of her tears moisten his cheek. He pulled back slightly to swipe away the tear track with his thumb.

"Don't cry, my beautiful, strong shieldmaiden," he said gently.

"These are tears of joy," she said through the thick emotion in her throat. "Something I haven't experienced in a long time."

He brought his head down to her once more, capturing her mouth and inhaling her sweet scent. His arms tightened and he felt his manhood stir to life at the feel of her breasts pressed against his chest.

Suddenly her body stiffened and she inhaled through her nose.

He released her instantly, but a wince of pain marred her features.

"Curse this wound," she muttered, clutching her side.

"I've overextended you," he said.

"Nei, I'm fine." But her voice was laced with sudden exhaustion.

He lowered her gently to the furs. "You need to rest and heal."

"Ja."

His eyebrows shot up unbidden. "You truly must be tired to agree with me so readily."

She snorted as she let her eyes drop closed. "I have waited so long, and the time is almost here."

As she drifted off to sleep, unease settled in his chest. Ja, he would stand by her side against Bersi. But Madrena had focused the last five years of her life on revenge. He only hoped that once she had it, she could free herself of Bersi's poisonous grasp. He knew better than anyone what a life under the madman's control turned into. Once she had her vengeance, would Madrena truly be free?

28

Rúnin straightened and wiped the sweat from his brow. Despite the cool air, it felt considerably warmer than a sennight ago.

He propped his wooden rake against the slats of the animal stalls and paused to soak in the late afternoon sun slanting through the trees. Overhead, the tops of the firs and pines sparkled where the weak sun touched the clumps of dazzling white snow still clinging to the boughs. Where he stood, the ground had been churned into a muddy, slushy mess. 'Twas an apt representation of the difference between the lives of the gods and the lives of men.

Just as he grasped the rake to continue to scrape out the muck from the cows' stalls, he heard Jofarr's voice soaring in a whine.

"But why does *she* get to train with us?"

Madrena's voice was authoritative and clear. "Because girls can be warriors too, Jofarr. Odny could become a great shieldmaiden someday."

"Ja, I want to be a shieldmaiden like Madrena!"

Odny's high-pitched voice piped up.

"But—"

"Jofarr Ketillsson!" Ketill straightened in the pig sties a few paces away from Rúnin. "Warriors do not wail and complain. Only little children do that." Though Ketill's voice was firm, Rúnin was close enough to see the merriment tugging at the corners of his friend's eyes.

Madrena appeared from around the side of the hut, trailed by Jofarr and Odny. She stepped into the little cleared area in front of the animals' pens.

"That's right," she said sternly. "And I don't train little children. I only train warriors. So what will it be?"

Jofarr sulked for a moment, toeing a lingering patch of snow. Meanwhile Odny stood straight and silent, her little shoulders thrust back and her eyes solemn as she waited for Madrena's command.

"Fine," Jofarr muttered at last, giving his little sister a sideways glare.

"Good, let's get on with it, then," Madrena said. She produced two small wooden practice swords from behind her dress. She had borrowed one of Finna's, and though the fit wasn't perfect, the dark blue shade was becoming on her.

Each child took their wooden sword gravely, though Odny's was far too big and heavy for her. Rúnin heard a muffled noise coming from Ketill and looked over to find him struggling not to laugh.

"Before you ever face an enemy, real or imagined, you must first learn to handle your sword properly," Madrena said, pacing in front of the children. "Your sword is an extension of your arm, and thus you must treat it like a limb—beloved and essential to you. You must give it a name befitting its power and importance."

"What is your sword's named, Madrena?" Odny asked, eyes wide.

Madrena patted the pommel of her sword, which was belted to her hip. "I call her *Hárfagri Maer*—fair-haired maiden—for when I draw her out she flashes like the sun itself."

Now it was Rúnin's turn to repress a smile. By the gods, he loved Madrena.

"Show us!" Jofarr said eagerly.

"Nei, for you must remain focused on your own blades. Never let yourself become distracted in battle."

Rúnin hadn't realized he'd tensed at the thought of Madrena drawing her sword, but he relaxed now. She'd been healing quickly this past sennight, but he didn't want her to risk reopening the wound or overextending herself. Though she would never admit it, she was still weaker than she had been before. She'd regained her appetite quickly and slept long and soundly, but she still wasn't ready for what lay ahead.

"Feel the weight of your sword," Madrena went on. "Get used to its length and heft."

Jofarr brandished the wooden sword in front of him, but Odny nearly toppled over when she tried to hold hers out.

Ketill didn't manage to repress his chuckle this time. Odny, a fierce little warrior already, shot him a scathing look as she righted herself and kept a firm grip on the wooden handle.

"Now sheathe your sword."

Both children struggled to slip their wooden training swords through the empty leather loops attached to their belts that stood in for their sheaths. Jofarr's sword tip caught on his belt and refused to budge, whereas

Odny's slipped right out of her hands and into the slush.

Rúnin coughed to cover the laugh that rose to his throat.

"What's so funny, Svein-Rúnin?" Jofarr said, deeply offended. Finna and Ketill had explained to their children that Svein's real name was Rúnin, and that he'd told them it was Svein to protect them. The children had taken to calling him Svein-Rúnin, and Rúnin wasn't sure if it was a tease or an endearment.

Madrena shot Rúnin a mock-chastising glare. "All warriors must start somewhere," she said.

At last, both children managed to slip their swords in their imaginary scabbards.

"Now, sheathe and unsheathe your weapon one hundred more times," Madrena said calmly as she strode toward the animal pens where Rúnin and Ketill worked.

Odny squeaked in devastation and Jofarr groaned, but they both set about yanking their wooden swords from their hips and threading them back through their leather loops.

"I hope you plan to bathe tonight after all that mucking," she said with a raised eyebrow at him.

He leaned against the cow pen's slats toward her. "Mayhap you will join me? I can take over Finna's duties, I'm sure."

Finna had been helping Madrena bathe for the last sennight. The woman feared Rúnin would be too clumsy and hurt Madrena's injuries. She was probably right, for if Rúnin beheld Madrena naked, slick with water, and lathered in the piney juniper soap she'd been using of late, he would likely lose all control.

After speaking words of love to each other, they both longed to express themselves with their bodies as well. But thus far, Madrena's injuries had prevented it. It was growing increasingly difficult for Rúnin to sleep by her side on the pile of furs next to the fire, or watch the sway of her lithe hips as she gave lessons in swordsmanship to the children. Even simply being near her sent his manhood hardening.

Madrena's eyes flashed heatedly as she closed the distance between them and leaned against the other side of the pen. "Mayhap," she said lowly, a sultry promise in her voice.

Ketill cleared his throat loudly a few paces away.

"I take it you are feeling better than ever this day, Madrena?"

"Ja," she said, lowering her gaze and breaking the sensual spell hanging between them. "I cannot thank you and Finna enough. And Ingrid. She is truly skilled."

Madrena was right—Rúnin had watched these past several days as Finna and Ingrid had tended to Madrena, changing her bandages, checking on her stitches, and rebuilding her strength one bowl of stew and cup of special tea at a time.

As Finna and Ingrid worked diligently on helping Madrena heal, Rúnin had busied himself outdoors with Ketill and occasionally Jofarr and Odny. It was a pure joy to work side by side with Ketill. Rúnin knew that since autumn had been interrupted with the early arrival of winter, his and Madrena's presence was an extra strain on the family's limited resources. He was grateful to help in any way he could—even if it meant mucking out the animal stalls.

Jofarr helped with the manual labor and also accompanied them on their occasional hunting trips. Odny never had a problem entertaining herself. Several times in the last few days, Rúnin had found her in the animals' stalls whispering into the cows' ears or petting the chickens' feathers as she fed them. She was a strange, merry child.

"Ingrid will be Seterfell's healer one day, I believe," Ketill said with obvious pride. But then his eyes dimmed somewhat. "If only Finna had gotten such an opportunity."

Madrena's brows drew together slightly. "What do you mean?"

Rúnin had only told her the basics about Ketill and Finna—that they had been his family's friends, that Rúnin had always looked up to Ketill, who was a handful of years older than he was, that they were trustworthy and loyal allies now. But Madrena didn't know much of their hosts beyond that.

Ketill's eyes softened with memory. "Finna spent some time training with Seterfell's healer many years ago. But as Bersi's violent fits grew worse, she was wise to withdraw from the practice. She has always had a passion and talent for healing, though."

"Which Ingrid has inherited," Rúnin said quietly.

Ketill smiled warmly. "Did you know, Rúnin, that you almost met Ingrid before?"

He felt his brows draw together in confusion.

"You remember that Finna and I were courting when…when you were banished."

Rúnin nodded.

"Well, Ingrid came along only half a year after you were sent away. Finna and I were married before her birth, mind you," Ketill said with a conspiratorial waggle of his eyebrows at Madrena. "But not before her conception."

Madrena snorted and rolled her eyes. Rúnin let a deep chuckle rumble through his chest.

Ketill held up his hands defensively. "I'm only saying—"

"—That you want every man in the Northlands to settle down with a beautiful wife and raise many happy children on their own little farmstead," Rúnin finished dryly.

"You might give it a try sometime, Rúnin. Who knows, you could become a farmer yet." Ketill's merry eyes danced as he turned back to cleaning the pig sty.

Madrena snorted again and turned back to Jofarr and Odny. Rúnin took hold of the rake and began mucking out the stalls once more. Madrena's commanding voice, along with the children's excited questions, filled the cool afternoon air.

For the first time he could remember, Rúnin felt content.

~

As darkness fell that evening, Rúnin straightened and arched his back against the ache of bending in the stalls all day. The children had long ago tired, though Madrena had remained outdoors. She'd carefully drawn her sword and worked the blade in slow arcs until the air grew blue with twilight.

Though he knew he should trust her, he couldn't help watching out of the corner of his eye. He saw her flinch and wince several times when she tried to bring the sword overhead. Her side still pained her, yet the urgency to seek out Bersi remained a hot flame inside her. He could only hope that she wouldn't push herself too hard, too fast.

Yet his eye was drawn to her for another reason besides worry. Watching her move, all fluid lethality and deadly grace, his manhood awoke and strained against his trousers. She'd braided her pale hair away from her face, but the braids loosened around her shoulders and the silken lengths of icy blonde cascaded down her back, swinging as she moved.

With every crouch, with every elegant turn, with every twist of her body, he grew more entranced until Ketill's laugh startled him back to work.

When the light faded, the hut's door swung open and Ingrid poked her head out.

"My *Moðir* bids you come inside for the evening meal," she said.

Rúnin was all too eager, and not just because the hut's cozy warmth and a hot meal called to him. The family's wooden table and benches were only big enough for the five of them, which meant that Madrena and Rúnin had taken their meals seated on the furs by the fire, their legs brushing as they ate.

Rúnin followed Ketill and Madrena indoors, but once inside, he froze.

The now-familiar pile of furs on the floor in front of the fire pit was gone. His heart sank. He knew they were a burden on the family, especially given the need to carefully ration supplies through the impending winter. He and Madrena couldn't stay forever. Mayhap Ketill and his family were finally indicating that they could no longer extend their hospitality.

"Don't look so downcast, Svein-Rúnin," Finna said,

using the children's name for him with a mischievous glint in her eyes. "We are not kicking you out—we've simply moved you."

"Oh?" he said cautiously.

"Ketill and I were talking last night, and it seems that you two would do well with more… ahem…privacy."

Madrena glanced at him. One pale eyebrow arched sardonically, but a telltale flush came to her cheeks.

"Ja, that's right," Ketill jumped in. "We moved your furs to the grain loft. Now that it isn't so bitterly cold, you should be able to enjoy your…privacy there."

Even as a hot flare of anticipation ignited within him, he caught sight of little Odny looking up in confusion at her parents.

"Why do Madrena and Svein-Rúnin need privacy?" she asked, her blonde brows knitted together.

Ketill grinned broadly and winked at Madrena and Rúnin. Ingrid flushed bright red and turned, pretending to busy herself in the kitchen. Jofarr looked just as confused as Odny as Finna slowly began forming an answer.

"I think we'll get settled in the loft," Rúnin said quickly.

"Ja, we can eat out there as well," Madrena added. She snatched a slab of buttered and honeyed flatbread and a small clay jug holding some of the day's milk.

Rúnin eyed the roasted vegetables and slices of juicy venison also set out on the table, but he had a greater hunger for something else.

He and Madrena hurried to leave. Just as Finna was explaining what men's and women's body parts did, Rúnin closed the hut's door firmly behind them. The night air was crisp, though it was mild enough that even with the sun down, Rúnin could hear the steady dripping of the melting snow.

They made their way by the light of the nigh full moon through the mud and slush to the back of the hut. The grain loft's hazy outline slowly materialized.

It was raised on four wooden poles that stood slightly higher than Rúnin's head. That way the winter's stock of grain for the family and feed for the animals could never mold or spoil in a flood. The loft also stood a stone's throw away from the hut and animal pens. If, gods forbid, either the hut or the grain loft caught fire, at least the family wouldn't be left with naught.

A wooden ladder rose toward a little door cut into the loft's tightly fitted wooden slats. Rúnin took the jug of milk from Madrena so that she could climb with one free hand. Once she'd pushed open the door and slipped inside, he followed her up the ladder.

The comforting scents of dry hay and grain surrounded him as he crawled into the loft. A few narrow window slits allowed both fresh night air and moonlight to filter into the dim interior. The back of the loft was stacked high with hay for the animals and sacks of grain, likely barley and rye for flatbreads and porridges—and ale.

But just inside the loft's door, a little space had been cleared on the wooden floorboards. The furs they'd been sleeping on this past sennight made a thick nest, perfect for two.

Rúnin settled in the furs next to Madrena and leaned back against a bale of sweet, earthy smelling hay. He removed the stopper from the milk jug and took a swig, the cool, creamy milk sliding down his throat.

Silently, he passed her the jug and she handed him half of the flatbread she'd taken. The fresh bread was slathered thickly with butter and drizzled with honey.

He tried to focus on the simple pleasure of eating and all the comforting scents surrounding him, but as they ate in silence, the need building deep in his belly—and below—coiled hotter.

As Madrena took the last bite of her flatbread, a bead of honey clung to her lower lip. Mesmerized, Rúnin slowly leaned over and touched his finger to the drop of sweetness. Locking eyes with her, he raised his hand to his mouth and deliberately sucked the honey from the pad of his finger.

Never taking her gaze from him, she put the lid on the milk and set the jug aside. Her eyes sparkled in the moonlight. Normally they appeared to reflect light, so pale were they, but now they looked slate-dark and unreadable.

"Madrena," he whispered. "I have wanted you from the moment I first saw you."

Her mouth twitched. "You were so out of your head that you mistook me for Freyja."

"I was mistaken," he breathed, tracing his finger once more around her soft lips. "You surpass her."

The pink lips under his finger arched into a smile. "And I wanted you, too, even though you looked more like a piece of battered driftwood than a man."

He would have chuckled, but he was too riveted on her mouth. Slowly, purposefully, he leaned toward her. She remained in place, waiting.

At last, his lips brushed hers. They tasted of honey and her own sweetness. She inhaled at the contact, drawing him in. Her fingers brushed his bristled cheek, then his nape. As they deepened the kiss, their tongues met and mated slowly, sensually.

The heat of her mouth sent another pulse rushing to his cock. It throbbed insistently against his trousers, but Rúnin was determined to take his sweet time.

"I want to taste every inch of you," he breathed against her lips. "I want to see you."

Though they had already entwined their bodies in lust more than a sennight ago, he hadn't gotten to brush his lips against the bare skin of her breasts, or taste her pleasure, or gaze upon the perfection of her body. Tonight would be different.

In silent answer to his whispered words, her nails sank into his neck and twisted in his hair, pulling him closer and sending another wave of tingling sensation rippling through him.

His hands dropped to the brooches holding the straps of her overdress atop her shoulders. As he fumbled with the brooches, her hands slipped down the front of his chest to the belt over his tunic. While their hands worked, they both kicked off their boots.

With deft fingers, she unclasped the belt and slid underneath the wool tunic. Her fingertips traced over his abdomen and to his chest, teasing him lightly with the graze of her nails.

At last, the brooches came free. His palms brushed her shift-covered breasts as he drew down the overdress. She inhaled even at the light contact. Careful of her side, they both eased the dress past her waist and over her hips. He tossed the dress onto a nearby hay bale when it was free of her long legs.

Ever so lightly, he skimmed his hands over her hips and trim waist until he reached the swell of her breasts.

Her nipples were already pebbled against her shift as he cupped each one.

He'd wanted to go slow, but he was a fool to think that he could contain the raw need hammering in his body. Breaking their kiss, he trailed his lips down her slim neck, trying to savor the taste of her skin even as he longed to flick his tongue against her breasts.

Her head fell back and she moaned as his lips played along her neck and to her collarbone. He made quick work of the ties at the front of her linen shift, and the material slid open with a whisper.

Moonlight slanted down on her, landing atop her head and making her hair look like silver. The cool light settled on her shoulders and brushed the perfect roundness of each breast. Lowering his head, he trailed kisses between them, then shifted to brush his lips against one taut nipple.

Her gasp of surprise followed by the low moan in her throat told him all he needed to know. He let his tongue circle her nipple, teasing and flicking it lightly.

She arched, bringing her breast more fully against his mouth. He was happy to oblige her unspoken plea. Once he had laved one nipple, he shifted to the other. Her fingers curled in his hair, urging him on. Then she fisted the material of his tunic at his shoulders and pulled up.

Their contact broke for the briefest moment as the tunic slid up his body and over his head. When he closed the distance between them again, his chest rubbed against her breasts. He inhaled sharply at the feeling of unobstructed skin on skin.

Slowly, he drew her down to the furs with him, making sure not to lean atop her and make her feel like he was overpowering her. Instead, they faced each other, she on her good side with an arm bent under her head, and he propped on one elbow.

She pulled him to her once more, their mouths connecting in a heated kiss. Her hands slid down his chest, over the banded muscles of his stomach and to his back. He tensed for a moment as her fingers ran over the old scars there, but her touch was passion-filled, not fearful or disgusted.

Once again, she arched, rubbing her breasts against his chest. The movement also brought her hips flush with his. As she circled her hips against him, his cock pressed into her low belly. He groaned as the need to be inside her hitched higher. But nei, he still wanted to see her, to taste her.

Pulling back slightly, he took hold of the hem of her shift and began slowly dragging it up. His hungry eyes devoured each inch of newly exposed skin. Her legs were lithe and long, each one toned from hard work and yet still womanly in their gentle curves.

As the shift crossed the apex of her legs, he stilled for a moment, mesmerized by the patch of darker blonde hair there. Her hips flared delicately and then he saw the still healing wound in her side. The stitches were clean and straight, the skin smooth if still a little pink where it hadn't fully healed yet. She would be fine, though, thank the gods—and Finna.

The flat planes of her stomach gave way to the curving underside of her breasts. Then the shift slipped over her head and she was completely free of the material.

He sat up to set the shift next to her dress nearby, but froze when he turned back to her.

Moonlight now gilded every inch of pale, smooth skin as she lay in the pile of furs. Her hair spilled in a pool beneath her head. Her normally creamy skin looked like the finest silver he'd ever seen. Truly, she was more beautiful than any goddess.

He could have sat there drinking in the sight of her indefinitely, but she reached for the ties at the front of his trousers. Her fingers brushed the long, hard length of him and he feared that he would come undone right there and then.

Cool air caressed his heated skin as the trousers loosened and his cock sprang free. She paused in drawing the material down his hips, boldly perusing his shoulders, chest, abdomen, and his manhood, which stood rigidly out from his body. The hunger in her own gaze only thickened the lust coursing through his veins.

He helped her draw the trousers down his legs and kicked the material free. But instead of lying down next to her once more, he raised one of her feet in his hands and placed a kiss on the arch.

She shivered, but he doubted it had aught to do with the cool air around them. Gripping her leg, he kissed her ankle next, and then her calf. When his lips brushed the skin on the inside of her knee, she bucked and moaned. Unbidden, her legs sagged open slightly, inviting him higher.

His lips brushed the sensitive skin of her thigh, then higher still until he was nearly at the crux of her legs. Her knees fell apart even more, making room for his shoulders to settle between them.

At last, his mouth descended on her sex. She was already hot and slick with desire. His tongue flicked over her and she jerked again, her back rising off the furs even as her head twisted from side to side.

He teased and flicked, caressed and stroked until every one of her breaths was a moan of pleasure. When he slipped a finger inside her tight heat, her hands clenched in the furs at her sides. He could feel her begin to shudder even before she whimpered his name. Spasms of pleasure shook her, but his tongue lingered on her sex, savoring the taste of her desire for him.

He rose from between her legs as the last trembles faded. Though his cock throbbed nigh painfully, he began to lie down at her side once more.

But her legs clamped around his hips, halting him.

"It's all right," she breathed, her voice thick with passion. "I want you like this."

She splayed on her back beneath him, looking sated but still lusty. Yet when he met her eyes, he saw vulnerability in their gray depths.

"You're sure?"

"Ja," she whispered. "I trust you."

A new surge of heat tore through him, but it was different than the lust raging in this body. His heart swelled and his throat tightened. She trusted him. Love entwined with lust in every fiber of his being.

With great care, he lowered himself slightly until his cock brushed the damp folds of her sex. He placed his hands on either side of her and her fingertips snaked up his arms, lingering over the contours of corded muscle there. He held her gaze, watching for any signs of fear, but only raw longing met him.

She lifted her hips slightly, inviting him in. With deliberate gradualness, he eased the head of his cock inside her womanhood. He had to clench his teeth against the blinding pleasure and the almost overwhelming need to plunge into her. She moaned beneath him and rolled her hips.

He nearly lost his threadbare hold on control then, but somehow he held on. He pressed deeper into her tight wetness until little by little their bodies were fused together.

Although he was forcing himself to go slow, her own impatience got the better of her. Her breathing hitched and she writhed urgently beneath him.

"Don't tease me," Madrena panted. "I want you—now."

Her words snapped the last threads of his resolve. He withdrew but sheathed himself fully almost immediately. Their groans of pleasure mingled as he repeated the motion.

Heat coiled low in his belly, tightening his bollocks. With each thrust, her panting moans hitched higher until once again she was crying out his name. As he felt her tighten around him, he erupted in blinding ecstasy.

As he drifted down from the heights of pleasure, he rocked their hips slowly together. Reluctantly, he withdrew and collapsed by her side.

"I love you."

He barely heard her over his still-pounding heart.

"I love you, too," he breathed.

She rolled toward him and his arm slipped around her as if it had always meant to be there. Before they fell into an exhausted sleep, he pulled one of the furs over their naked bodies.

Whatever lay ahead, they could face it together. That was his last coherent thought before sleep pulled him under.

29

They were so slow to rouse the next morning that the sun slanted brightly through the loft's narrow windows before they reluctantly donned their clothes.

"Do you suppose Ketill will be mad that I have kept you from your morning chores?" Madrena asked as she watched Rúnin dress. The hard lines and bunching muscles on his lean body stirred memories of last night. She felt her skin flush with the simple pleasure of looking at him.

He tugged his trousers up his legs, regrettably barring the sight of his manhood from her.

"Did you see how he teased us yesterday? Nei, I don't think he'll be upset in the least."

Rúnin stuffed his arms in his tunic and she took one last, long look at the rigid bands of muscle along his stomach.

"How do you suppose Finna explained things to Odny?"

He shrugged but then shot her a heated look. "Sex is

simply a part of life. The girl must already have an inkling—she lives on a farm, after all."

Madrena felt a smile curling her lips. "I remember once Alaric and I came upon our parents while they thought to have a moment alone. We must have been about Odny's age, for we found the whole thing strange and disgusting."

Rúnin chuckled lightly. As his bright eyes studied her, however, he grew serious. "You have never spoken of your parents before."

The smile slipped from her face. "They died many years ago. A fever took both of them. Luckily, Alaric and I were old enough to take care of each other. We've been on our own ever since then."

Rúnin smoothed a strand of hair away from her face with his warm, callused hand. "You must miss your brother very much."

Suddenly a lump tightened her throat. Alaric was never far from her thoughts. Some said because they were twins, they would be able to sense things about each other, even from far apart. Madrena had experienced strange tickles in the back of her mind before, only to learn later that Alaric had felt the same thing at the same time. But she hadn't felt aught since she'd left Dalgaard with Rúnin.

"Ja, I do miss him."

An unspoken question hung in the air between them for a long moment. What did the future hold for her and Rúnin? Once they had faced Bersi, would they return to Dalgaard together? Would she trek back by herself to be with her family and friends while he remained here with Ketill and his family? Or would he continue on alone in the wilderness, living out Bersi's sentence of outlawry?

Rúnin opened his mouth, his brows lowered. Before he could speak, however, Odny's high voice drifted up to them.

"Are you ever coming out?" she squeaked from below the loft.

Madrena had to clap a hand over her mouth to avoid laughing out loud.

"Ja, Odny, here we come!" Rúnin replied.

As Madrena tugged on her boots, Rúnin cracked open the small door and poked his head outside. Cool air and sunshine flooded in around him.

"Did we miss the morning meal?"

"Ja," Odny replied indignantly. "*Moðir* saved some porridge for you, but 'tis cold now!"

"I'm sure we will survive," Rúnin said gently. He began descending the ladder and Madrena followed. She glanced around their little nest before closing the loft door. Once again, her skin heated as memories from last night flooded her.

When Madrena stood in the slush at the bottom of the ladder, she was met with Odny's frown. The girl's hands were fisted on her hips, her blonde hair rumpled.

"Is there something else, Odny?" Madrena asked patiently.

"Nei," the little girl huffed. "*Moðir* just wanted me to tell you about the porridge." With that, Odny bolted toward the animal pens, but Madrena caught a mumbled string of words about boy parts and girl parts.

Madrena raised her eyebrow at Rúnin. A smile threatened his normally flat mouth.

As they stepped inside the cozy warmth of the hut, Madrena noticed an unusual stillness and quiet. Finna turned from her work in the kitchen and nodded to them, a broad smile on her face.

"Ah, there you two are!" she exclaimed even as her eyes twinkled knowingly.

Madrena felt her eyes rolling upward but halted herself. She wasn't normally one for the frivolities and hubbub surrounding coupling, but she realized with a start that for the first time, she shared a sliver of the giddiness Finna seemed to be enjoying on their behalf. Madrena wouldn't deny herself the truth—it was different with Rúnin. Wonderfully different. Besides, who was she to dampen Finna's joyful spirits?

"Where is everyone?" Rúnin asked. Madrena attempted a casual glance at him. Though he, too, avoided Finna's overt excitement, his normally hard features were relaxed in contentedness.

"Ketill and Jofarr set out to the gulf to catch fish. They are hoping the ice is melted by now. And I sent Ingrid to the village healer to get more supplies—dried *hvönn* and the like. If the gods smile on us, we won't need them this winter, but we must be prepared."

Madrena sensed Rúnin stiffen at her side.

"You sent Ingrid to the village—by herself?"

Finna's brows drew together but she smiled softly. "Of course. The healer's hut isn't so far from here. Besides, I sent her only after the sun had risen. You may not have noticed, but dawn was several hours ago." The tease was back in Finna's light voice, yet Rúnin remained tense.

Finna half-turned back to the flatbread she was preparing, but then her gaze rested more carefully on Rúnin.

"It is not like the old days anymore, Rúnin," she said

gently. "She'll be fine. And she knows not to speak of your presence here."

Rúnin frowned but gave Finna a nod. How protective he was, Madrena thought, her chest swelling. But a darker thought sobered her. How much he must have lived through to fear that a girl walking a short distance near her own village wouldn't be safe.

"She'll likely be back in an hour or two, depending on how long Gunrud bends her ear," Finna went on.

As Madrena and Rúnin settled themselves with a bowl of cold porridge each at the empty wooden table next to Finna, the woman continued on about the old healer.

Gunrud had been the same woman to train Finna for a brief time. Finna seemed to take pleasure in recounting stories of the elderly healer's strange smelling hut and odd, ever-changing collection of dogs and cats. Even when Finna had been a girl, it seemed that Gunrud had been on death's door, often making strange requests of Finna to leave loaves of bread in the woods or pull back the furs on the windows even in winter.

They lingered in the warm hut long after the porridge was gone. Madrena hadn't realized how comforting it was to be around true friends. Once again, her heart tugged toward Dalgaard. Her chest squeezed as she settled into a decision. Once her business with Bersi was done, she would return to her village, her family, her friends. But what of Rúnin?

At last, Rúnin stood. "We'd best make ourselves useful before the sun sets again," he said to Madrena. A twinkle of promise lit his vivid blue eyes—a promise of what they would do once the day's work was completed.

Reluctantly, she stood in preparation to leave the

warm comfort of the hut. With the children occupied, she'd likely join Rúnin in the animal stalls today.

She stretched her arms overhead as she considered mucking out the stalls. A sharp twinge of pain in her side had her inhaling through her teeth. She drew a hand to the still-healing wound and touched it lightly.

Rúnin frowned. "Perhaps you should rest today."

"Nei, I'm fine."

He continued to eye her. "You've been pushing yourself too hard. Training with the children was too much, just as I feared."

"You didn't seem to have any worries about my wellness last night," she said with one raised eyebrow.

Finna tried and failed to muffle a giggle in her sleeve as she worked the flatbread dough, her back turned to them.

Rúnin leveled her with a hard look. Madrena held up her hands in concession.

"Fine, I'll rest in the loft. But I'll be joining you in the stalls this afternoon."

Rúnin only grunted, and Finna chortled again.

As they made their way outside, Rúnin followed her to the loft's ladder and planted a searing kiss on her lips before turning and heading toward the animal pens several paces away.

She watched him for a long moment before reluctantly climbing the ladder and settling herself in their little nest of furs. Though her side ached dully, after a kiss like that, she doubted very much that she would be able to relax enough to sleep.

Despite the fact that there was plenty of work to keep him busy, Rúnin kept finding himself pausing to look at the grain loft. Madrena lay there, her head likely pillowed on her arm and her pale blonde hair spilling all around her. Mayhap her lips still tingled from the kiss he'd given her, as his did. Mayhap her mind was filled with lusty images of what they had shared last night and what they would share again tonight.

He shook his head and brought his attention back to his task for the dozenth time. But just as soon as he had resumed mucking, his head snapped up at the sound of a breaking branch.

He froze, his eyes scanning the surrounding forest. Now that the snow had begun to melt, the sound couldn't be attributed to a branch bending and breaking under the snow's weight.

"*Moðir!*"

Rúnin recognized Ingrid's voice and relaxed a hair's breadth. But unease slid over him at the girl's urgent call.

A flicker of movement caught Rúnin's eye in the dripping forest.

Ingrid's youthful frame stumbled through the trees. She popped out into the farmstead's little clearing behind the hut, just beyond the grain loft.

Rúnin dropped his rake and sprinted toward her. She appeared unharmed but flustered and rumpled.

"What has happened, Ingrid?" he said when he reached her.

Her cheeks were flushed, which could have been from the cold, but some instinct told Rúnin it was more than that. Ingrid, normally so careful and tidy, had dead leaves and twigs in her hair, and the hem of her dress was soggy.

Something was very wrong. The hairs on Rúnin's neck bristled.

The girl's hazel eyes were wide with fright.

"I went to Gunrud's hut," Ingrid said, her voice dazed.

"Did something happen to you? Are you all right?" Fear and revulsion twisted in Rúnin's belly. His mind darted to Madrena. An image of her as a young and innocent girl like Ingrid was suddenly soured with the knowledge of what Bersi had done to her. Bile rose in the back of his throat.

"I am fine," Ingrid said with a quick shake of her head. "But Gunrud told me… She said…"

"Speak," Rúnin snapped. He didn't intend to frighten the girl more, but he needed to know the cause of the distress filling her eyes and the dread lacing through Rúnin's veins.

"She said that Jarl Bersi…"

Time seemed to stretch impossibly as he waited for Ingrid to finish speaking. He wanted to yell at the girl to speak again, but he felt frozen in anticipation.

"…Jarl Bersi is *dead*."

30

Rúnin's skin prickled all over, but it had naught to do with the cool midday air.

"What?"

"Jarl Bersi is dead," Ingrid repeated, her dark blonde brows drawn together and her eyes filled with confusion and fear.

Rúnin had to swallow the tight sourness rising in his throat. The man who had once called him son was dead. The man who'd nearly killed him for not raping a woman was dead. The man who'd outlawed him, cutting him off from everything he'd known to presumably die in the wilderness alone—was dead.

"How?" he heard himself croak. He blinked several times, forcing his mind to come back to the present.

"Gunrud said that she had been called into the village three days ago." Ingrid trembled slightly as she spoke. "Jarl Bersi was worse than ever, coughing up blood and struggling to breathe even just lying in his bed."

Rúnin tried to picture Bersi, weak and frail, lying abed with a blooded rag to his mouth. But no clear image would materialize. The Bersi he remembered, the Bersi who still haunted his nightmares, was strong—harder than stone, wide with knotted muscles, eyes cold and sharp.

"Gunrud gave him the tea that normally eases the cough, but it didn't work this time," Ingrid went on. "The cough grew worse until…until the following morning. He just…stopped breathing."

"And what of Gunrud?" Knowing Bersi and his men, the old healer risked her life to be in the presence of the dead Jarl's body.

"Two of his warriors were with the Jarl and Gunrud the entire time, so she didn't fear being accused of killing the Jarl. They let her go home. Gunrud said the village is preparing for Bersi's funeral now."

Rúnin's mind spun sickeningly as he tried to digest this information. What would it mean for the village to no longer live under Bersi's mad rule? Would one of his men, battle-hardened and twisted into a warped mold by Bersi, take his place?

And what of Madrena?

Something in Rúnin's chest cracked open at the thought of how she would react. She had made it her life's mission to exact vengeance on Bersi with her own hands. Now she had been robbed of that.

"I have to tell my *Faðir* and *Móðir*," Ingrid said, cutting into his churning thoughts.

"Ja, of course," Rúnin replied dazedly.

He led Ingrid to the hut and stood next to the fire as Ingrid told Finna what had happened. Though it was his second hearing of the story, disbelief and shock still clung to him.

Ingrid's hands shook as she held them over the fire as she concluded her explanation. Finna tried her best to smooth her daughter's dark gold hair.

"I'll go to the gulf and look for Ketill and Jofarr," Rúnin offered. "They should know, and we should all remain close to the farmstead until after the funeral. There is no telling what the remainder of Bersi's men will do."

Though he half-expected Finna to reassure him once more that times had changed and things in Seterfell were different, she only nodded, her eyes filled with worry.

That only deepened the dread in Rúnin's belly as he ducked out of the hut. He began trudging down the little hill on which the farmstead perched. But even before he'd entered the thicker stretch of trees separating the hut from the Gulf of Bothnia, he froze.

It was true that Ketill and Jofarr needed to be found and told of Bersi's death. But the deeper truth was that Rúnin was trying to avoid telling Madrena. How would she react? Would she collapse into tears or fly into a rage? Would she be able to let go of her profound, unerring desire for revenge?

He had to tell her. No matter what her reaction, he couldn't keep this from her, even for an hour. He turned on his heels and strode purposefully toward the grain loft.

As he climbed the ladder, he pictured her sleeping, the last moment of peace she'd likely know for a long time. Lead sat in his belly. However hard this was for her, he vowed, he would stay by her side. He'd help her through the anger and frustration, the sadness and loss.

At the top of the ladder, he eased open the small wooden door to the loft. As his eyes fell on the dim interior, he froze.

Madrena was gone.

31

Madrena felt her body falling. Her descent was cut abruptly short as she connected with the soft pile of furs in the grain loft. The furs and the loft's wooden floorboards might as well have not been there, though, for she felt herself continue to sink down and down endlessly.

"Nei." Her whisper was deafening in her own ears.

Rúnin's deep, rough voice came through the loft's slats, sounding just as shocked as she felt.

Ingrid's answers were pinched and high but still easy to make out, even through the roaring in Madrena's ears.

She shook her head a little, but it made the loft spin.

Bersi was dead.

The man who had raped her, stolen her innocence and her happiness, would never face the justice of her blade.

Bersi was dead.

His wrongdoings would never be paid for in his own suffering and an honorless death at her hands.

Bersi was dead.

She would never have her revenge.

Madrena felt hot denial surge through her all of a sudden.

"Nei," she said again, but this time with more conviction.

He couldn't be dead, for that would mean the last five years of her life had been meaningless.

Her mind raced as she searched the words she overheard for some mistake, some loophole through which Bersi could have escaped death.

Ingrid said that Gunrud had told her all this. But Ingrid hadn't seen it for herself. From what Finna had said about Gunrud, the aged healer was hardly in her right mind all the time.

But Madrena knew she was grasping at straws.

For the first time since that terrible day five years ago, she actually wished Bersi was alive—so that she could kill him herself. What kind of cruel games were the gods playing with her to bring her so close, practically on Bersi's threshold, only to snatch him away with some old man's illness?

Rúnin and Ingrid's voices dropped off and she heard the soft thud of the hut door as it closed behind them.

Her breaths came shallow in her chest, her palms suddenly damp with sweat. Bersi was supposed to die under her blade. That was the only way to make sense of what she had suffered at his hands. It was her responsibility to see that honor be served and Bersi be made to answer for his crimes. And it was her way to restore what Bersi had stolen from her—her belief in the justice of the world.

She couldn't simply accept third-hand word that Bersi was dead. Bersi was a survivor—she wouldn't believe he'd died until she saw it for herself.

And if he truly was deceased—her mind rebelled against the very thought—she wouldn't let him go quietly to the gods. Nei, she would destroy any chance he had at a peaceful afterlife. She would exact her revenge on his dead body, for her blade could still mar the eternal form that he would bear in the afterlife's realms.

To reach Bersi's body, she would have to cut through the warriors still loyal to him. No matter. Any man who'd aligned himself with Bersi was just as culpable for his crimes. She could only hope that she could take them on alone.

Even as her head swirled with all the implications of what she'd just overheard, her hand reached for the belt with her sword and axe attached to it. She had to act. Now.

A dark thought descended upon her with horrifying clarity. Her hand froze on her belt.

Rúnin would try to stop her.

He'd always been resistant to joining her in facing Bersi. Now that she knew the truth about his life under Bersi and as an outlaw, she understood his hesitation. But he'd vowed to stand by her side against Bersi at last. He seemed to finally accept that Bersi was the only one at fault in the horrors of his early life.

But if he believed Bersi was dead, he would try to talk Madrena out of going to Seterfell to settle the matter once and for all. And she didn't have time to convince him to let her go.

She winced as the belt brushed against her wounded

side. She was still weak and injured. What chance did she have?

Viciously pushing the voice of warning away, she dragged up the memory she so often fought—of Bersi looming over her, wrenching her legs apart, and tearing her body in two.

She'd killed him a thousand times in her mind, but after five years of waiting, training, and the last grueling fortnight of searching, he could not escape so easily. He had to pay, one way or another.

She'd already opened the loft door and climbed halfway down the ladder before she realized she'd decided. She would go to Seterfell herself. If Bersi truly was dead, she'd still have her revenge on him—or on anyone who'd helped him in his violent lunacy.

The farmstead's clearing remained quiet as she slipped into the woods, heading northeast.

This is madness.

The whisper came to her in her brother's voice, so soft and yet so clear that she started. Those were the words Alaric had spoken when he'd found her sneaking out of Dalgaard with Rúnin.

Madrena choked back the sudden sob that rose to her throat.

Bersi was dead.

But this couldn't be the end of it. It just *couldn't*. Not after all she'd been through, all she'd planned and struggled and overcome. She refused to accept that her life's purpose had been stolen from her so swiftly, so cruelly.

She willed her feet to move once more in the direction she believed Seterfell lay.

It was fitting that she was alone in this after all. Her brother and Eirik had tried to convince her that revenge wouldn't ease her pain. Rúnin had just as much reason as she did to seek vengeance, but he didn't seem to burn for it the way she did.

It would come down to her, as it was always meant to be.

~

RÚNIN CURSED the gods and himself as he stared at the empty loft. A quick scan of the little space told him what his heart feared most: Madrena was gone, and so were her weapons.

He leapt down from the ladder and sprinted to the hut. Both Finna and Ingrid jumped as he yanked the hut's door wide open.

"Rúnin, I thought—" Finna began.

"Madrena has disappeared," he interrupted. "I fear she overheard Ingrid's news about Bersi."

Finna's eyes rounded in shock. "What would she do?"

Rúnin dragged a hand through his hair. "I don't know. She likely won't want to believe that what Ingrid said was true. Bersi…hurt her many years ago."

Finna's eyes widened more as she took in Rúnin's unspoken implication. Luckily, Ingrid seemed not to comprehend what he alluded to.

"That is why she muttered his name in her fever dream," Finna said almost to herself.

"She has made it the focus of her life for the past five years to prepare herself and then hunt him down to exact vengeance," Rúnin went on. "She won't be able to accept that Bersi has evaded her."

"And when she reaches Seterfell and finds his body laid out for the funeral pyre?" Finna asked.

"As I said, I don't know. She is an honorable, just woman, but she is also hot-headed and tempestuous. She's likely not thinking straight. Mayhap she will try to take on what remains of Bersi's men. Or mayhap she won't be satisfied until she has Bersi under her blade, alive or dead."

As he spoke, he sensed the truth in the words. Madrena was a warrior. She had trained her body and mind relentlessly these past five years, if her skill was any indication. She would need to extract a warrior's revenge, which meant that someone had to pay in blood.

Finna recoiled slightly. "She would...mutilate his corpse?"

The suggestion was repulsive, but not because Bersi was already dead. Nei, if Madrena was bent on revenge, she could still extract it from Bersi's corpse. Doing so would assure that he would never rest whole and at peace in one of the nine realms of the afterlife. Mutilating the dead was one of the worst offenses in all the Northlands, as Madrena well knew. If that was what she planned, perhaps she was too far gone for Rúnin to save.

Rúnin's guts knotted to think of Madrena, so honor-bound and sure of right and wrong, doing something so unforgivable. What was she willing to sacrifice to have her revenge at last? Would she compromise her honor to destroy Bersi's?

"And what of the innocent villagers?" Finna asked when Rúnin remained silent, a hand coming to her mouth. "What if they get in her way?"

Rúnin felt something shift into place in his mind. His head had been swimming with possibilities, fears, and doubts—what did Bersi's death mean? What would Madrena do? And what should *he* do in response?

But now it was clear.

He had tried to build a dam against his impulse toward honor for so long that it felt foreign to let it course through him unimpeded. Yet as the old pathways opened in his heart, he knew he had to go after her.

And he had to stop her.

"Does Ketill have a sword?" Rúnin asked, his mind racing.

"Ja—in the trunk just there. But why, Rúnin? What will you do?" Finna said.

Rúnin was already kneeling in front of the trunk Finna had indicated. He yanked back the lid and pushed aside the folded clothes and trinkets.

"I'm not going to let her do this to herself," he said absently. At last his fingers brushed a leather scabbard and he pulled the sword free.

"To *herself*? I don't understand."

As he stood and fastened the sheathed sword to his belt, he spared a glance at Finna. She stood next to Ingrid, the mother and daughter's hazel eyes mirrored in wide confusion.

"She'll never forgive herself if she hurts an innocent in her blinded state of mind. I won't let her lose herself to the pain and rage she must be feeling now. I won't let her become like Bersi."

Finna stepped in front of him as he moved toward the door. She gripped his arm, her eyes desperate.

"Rúnin, I know…I know that Ketill and I, and likely Madrena as well, pushed you to remember your honor. You have and will always be a champion of good. But… but you are in an impossible situation. You cannot harm your love." Her voice was low and pleading. "I know you want to do what's right, but if you would wait for Ketill, perhaps the two of you could think up something—"

"Nei, there's not enough time for that," he replied as he strode toward the door. "This all ends once and for all—now."

32

Madrena slipped behind the thick trunk of a spruce tree as the outlines of Seterfell's scattered huts materialized through the trees.

Just as she'd hoped, the village had only been a little more than an hour's rapid hike upward into the higher foothills to the northeast. Though her side ached as she caught her breath from the trek, she pushed the discomfort aside.

Through the trees, she could see men and women walking between huts. Yet the village was quiet, held in a somber embrace. Did they mourn their Jarl's death, even after all he had done to them?

Madrena forced her mind back to the task at hand. She'd kept her rage high as she'd made her way through the forests to Seterfell. The white-hot fury that burned in her veins helped her stay focused. She would see Bersi's dead body with her own eyes. And naught would stop her from getting her vengeance, one way or another.

She scanned the village until she found what she was

Shieldmaiden's Revenge

looking for. A longhouse was just visible between several other, smaller huts. That would be where Bersi resided.

A handful of unmoving figures stood before the longhouse. They must be Bersi's men guarding him—or his body.

Madrena's fingers wrapped around the hilt of her sword. The blade hissed softly as it came free of its leather sheath in one smooth motion.

"Do not fail me, *Hárfagri Maer*," she whispered. The weight of the blade was comforting. This was how it was supposed to be—weapon in hand, she was ready to face her enemies.

Sliding from behind the spruce tree, she walked with long, purposeful strides into the village.

At first, no one seemed to notice her. But then, a woman with a young child trailing behind her halted abruptly, staring wide-eyed and open-mouthed at Madrena. A wordless scream rose in the woman's throat and she snatched up her child's hand, dragging him away to the shelter of one of the huts.

Madrena flicked challenging glances at the other villagers as she continued to stride. They were mostly old men and women. That was Bersi's doing, and his legacy—so many young men dead, and so few strong villagers left to defend him.

Villagers backed away from her, fright in their eyes as she strode directly toward the longhouse. Many quickly ducked into nearby huts or cowered behind whatever cover they could find. These people were used to terror and knew that their best chance of survival was to stay out of sight.

She wondered distantly what she must look like to those who peeked around corners and from behind stone walls at her. She'd braided her hair back from her face, as she always did when she was entering battle, and she'd tucked her skirts between her legs and into her belt to allow greater movement. Her hand tightened around her bared sword, her axe swinging at the ready on her hip.

Her gaze locked on the longhouse as she drew nigh. The five men standing in front of it must have sensed the rising panic and flight at her appearance, for they turned. Some of them visibly shrank back as she bore down on them. One even scurried for cover. The remaining four held their ground, though Madrena could see fear in their eyes even from this distance.

None of the men drew weapons, however. Unease tickled the back of her mind, but she ignored it. Anyone who would stand to defend Bersi would face the consequences.

She came to a halt several paces away from the longhouse, eyeing the men. They were older than her—perhaps even older than Finna and Ketill.

"I have come for Jarl Bersi," she said lowly. "Step aside."

One of the men, tall and thin with hair turning from light brown to gray, stepped forward cautiously.

"Perhaps you have not heard, friend," he said carefully. "Jarl Bersi died two days ago."

Her hand ached as she gripped the hilt of her sword tighter. She had to force her jaw to unlock so that she could speak.

"Then let me see his body."

"Why?" The man's dark blue eyes filled with unease. The others behind him exchanged wary looks.

"So that I may take out his eyes, one by one,"

Madrena said. Hot pain shot through her body, spilling from her mouth. "Then remove his hands so that he may never wield a weapon in the afterlife. Lastly I will cut off his manhood so that no pleasure will await him in any of the nine realms."

The men before her looked aghast, but she didn't bother hiding her intent or the rage radiating from her.

"Nei!" one of the others shouted. "We'll not allow you to desecrate the dead."

"Because you have so much love in your heart for your Jarl?" Madrena spat, raising her sword so that it pointed at the men. "Because you are so loyal to him, even in death? You can join him then!"

The man who'd spoken first raised his hands defensively in front of him. "We are not Jarl Bersi's men!" he said. "They've all left—the last of them yesterday."

Madrena narrowed her eyes on him. "Why would they leave?"

"The few that remained said they were bored of this village. Without Bersi holding their fealty any longer, they went north in search of more adventure."

Madrena pressed her lips together in frustration. "Then why do you stand here guarding Bersi's body? Let me pass."

"We are merely following the proper traditions for his funeral," the man said. "Not out of love for Bersi, but in fear of him. If we do not treat his body properly, we risk his *draugr*, his cursed presence, haunting us forever. Surely you can understand that."

A flicker of doubt stole over her. These villagers were still living in fear of Bersi, even now that he was dead. His spirit could haunt them and bring disaster if they didn't treat his body with respect.

But she couldn't give up now. She had to have revenge, or else—

She hardened herself against the aging, weaponless man before her.

"If you defend Bersi, you are my enemy," she said, ice forming around her heart. "This is your last chance to get out of my way, or face the consequences of standing between me and my revenge."

The men's eyes widened as she slowly raised her blade. They braced themselves even though their hands were empty.

Madrena swallowed the shame and guilt rising in her throat. Her rising sword flashed dully in the weak sun.

∽

"MADRENA, NEI!"

The words ripped from Rúnin's throat even as he sprinted through his old village toward her.

Just as he'd paused to catch his breath on the outskirts of the village, he'd seen her raise her sword and feared he was too late.

As he tore through the huts toward the longhouse, she froze. The blade remained motionless in the air, her back still turned on him.

Rúnin skidded to a halt next to the little group of men Madrena faced. At last he got to look at her, and what he saw shook him to the core.

He hardly recognized her normally beautiful features, so twisted in rage and pain were they. She looked every bit the fierce warrior ready for battle—except that she had no enemy. Something clearly warred across her face—anger clashed with agony, and did he see a flicker of fear in her hard gray eyes?

"Get out of here, Rúnin," she hissed through clenched teeth.

"Nei, I won't. I won't let you do this, Madrena."

"Rúnin…" He felt the men at his side dart their gazes from Madrena's raised sword to him as one of them spoke his name slowly. "Rúnin…Bersisson?"

A low groan rose from behind Madrena's clenched teeth at the name Bersi had bestowed upon him. Rúnin wished he could snatch up the spoken name and throw the words far away, for they were only bringing Madrena closer to her breaking point.

Rúnin dared a glance to the man who had spoken. Recognition flickered in the back of his mind.

"Halladr? Halladr Stone Foot?" Halladr had been Seterfell's shipbuilder, known well beyond the village as a skilled artisan and a good man.

"By the gods, Rúnin, you're alive!" Halladr said, emotion pinching his voice.

"Enough!" Madrena cut in. "Rúnin, step aside. The rest of you as well."

"Nei, Madrena," Rúnin said levelly. "I will not let you hurt these men. They are innocent of Bersi's wrongs."

Her gray eyes flared with renewed frustration. "Move and no one has to get hurt. I *will* have vengeance."

Grim apprehension settled into Rúnin's stomach. He had guessed right. "You cannot desecrate Bersi, Madrena, unless you want to subject these villagers to more of Bersi's wrath in the form of his *draugr*."

"Then you would have him step into the afterlife

unscathed?" she bit out, her voice rising. "He has to *pay*, Rúnin!"

"And what of the innocent villagers who have endured him all these years? Will you have them pay as well?"

She actually bared her teeth at him, and he feared his attempts to talk her down were crumbling.

"Do not stand against me in this, Rúnin," she said, her voice a low threat.

Slowly, his hand moved to Ketill's sword on his hip. Her eyes darted down and widened slightly at his movement.

"You would choose *him* over me?" she hissed.

"Nei, Madren—"

Before he could explain, a battle cry tore from her throat and she lowered her blade at him. He had just enough time to yank Ketill's sword free of its scabbard and block the blow aimed at his arm.

Somewhere in the back of his mind, he registered that her first swing hadn't been intended to sever his head from his body. Perhaps he could still get through her rage-clouded mind and reach her heart.

"I don't want to fight you!" he shouted. He angled himself slightly and took several slow steps sideways to draw her away from the longhouse and the unarmed men.

"But you reach for your sword in Bersi's defense!" she shrieked.

"Madrena, listen to me! I'm not defending Bersi. I'm defending this village, *my* village—and *you*!"

She growled and swung again, but he managed to jump out of her range.

"I know this is hard for you. By Odin, 'tis a shock to

me, too," he panted. "But we must find a way to accept it. Bersi is dead. You have to let go of your desire for revenge."

"Stop talking and fight me!" She thrust her blade forward and he barely had time to deflect the blow with his sword.

"I know you, Madrena," he said as she circled him. "I love you. I love you because you live by honor."

"Stop it!"

"If you hurt these innocents, you will be no better than Bersi."

Her eyes flashed with pure fury and she screamed, charging at him. As Rúnin struggled to evade and repel the hail of blows she rained down on him, he feared he'd made a terrible error. What if he couldn't reason with her? What if he truly would have to hurt her to stop this madness?

She shrieked again and swung her sword in a whistling arc at his torso. He didn't have time to dodge the blade. All he could do was block it.

The impact was so great that he felt the reverberations of the blow all the way up his arms and into his teeth. Their swords were locked together for a long moment, her wild, rage-fueled energy waging against his checked, defensive strength.

He looked into her eyes and in that moment saw the years of hurt, the pain masked by anger, the invisible scars she hid so well with her tough exterior.

But the pain wasn't just from the old wounds Bersi had inflicted. Betrayal lay in their gray depths. *His betrayal.*

In a flash of clarity, he realized that by fighting her, he was cornering her, leaving her naught but her own rage to feed upon, naught but pain and hatred to fuel her.

She was like a wounded animal—the more penned in she felt, the more aggressive she became. But the aggression was only a sign of her desperation, of all her hopes and goals, her sense of purpose and justice, being stripped away from her.

Madrena would kill him if he kept fighting her. And she would destroy herself when her rage dissipated and she realized that she had chosen hatred over love, death over life.

Rúnin knew what he had to do.

He stepped back so that their blades slid along each other, disengaging.

With a mighty heft, he threw his sword to the muddy ground.

33

Madrena felt her jaw slacken in disbelief.

Rúnin chucked his sword into the churned mud and slush several paces away. He held up his hands, his bright eyes pinning her.

"Bersi is gone." His ragged voice grated her.

"Pick up your weapon!" she shouted.

Blood pounded in her veins, her whole body humming with the need to fight. But it was different than the other times she'd felt the euphoric surge of power within her limbs. Something twisted the feeling, poisoning it. She was supposed to experience the enthralling battle lust with *Bersi* at the tip of her sword, not Rúnin.

"Bersi is gone," he repeated.

"Stop saying that!" She closed the distance between them, her blade poised atop his shoulder, right at the juncture where the strong column of his neck rose. With a press of the flat side of the sword, she forced Rúnin to lower to his knees before her.

"Madrena. Bersi is gone." This time his voice was a low whisper.

"Nei," she breathed, faltering under the weight of his repeated words. "Nei."

A wedge of truth finally cracked into her resolve. But if he were dead, then what did her life mean?

"You didn't get to put your blade to him," Rúnin said softly. "You never will."

Pain tore through her, hot and sharp. She gritted her teeth against it, but it still choked her throat and stabbed her chest.

"Stop it!" she hissed, her voice so thick with emotion that she barely recognized it in her own ears.

"But you reaped your vengeance."

"Don't toy with me, Rúnin," she warned, pressing the blade more firmly into his shoulder.

"I'm showing you the truth, just as you showed me the truth about honor." His eyes were bright, urgent, yet they silently entreated her to listen.

As he continued to gaze up at her, the crack in her heart widened. A new pain leached over her as she looked down at the man she loved under her blade. Yet the fire still raged in her veins. The need to fight, to destroy and kill, clawed desperately in her belly.

"You had your revenge, because you survived Bersi," Rúnin said, never taking his eyes from her. "You survived his attack. You lived. And you became strong. So strong that you allowed yourself to love."

His eyes cut her like the bluest knife. It was as if he could see to her very core. The tip of her sword wavered against his shoulder and she realized distantly that her hand trembled like a leaf in an icy wind.

"And you became so strong that you rescued me as

well," Rúnin went on. "You pulled me from the brink. You saved me from Bersi, just as you saved yourself."

Her mind flitted back to the man she'd met less than a month ago in Dalgaard. He'd been secretive, evasive, cowardly. Now she looked at that man, on his knees and under her blade. Despite the fact that he had the same strong, bristled jaw, the same dark hair settling around his shoulders, the same vivid eyes as the man she'd pulled from the sea, Rúnin was now a man of honor, a man freed of guilt and secrets.

"But if you keep going down this path, you will never be truly free of Bersi."

She shook her head a little as if she could escape his words, but deep in her chest she knew them to be true.

"If you cannot let go of your quest for vengeance, Bersi might as well have killed you five years ago in Dalgaard. And he might as well have killed me, too, for standing against him."

Ever so slowly, Rúnin raised one of his hands and placed it atop the balled fist that held her sword.

"Let go of Bersi, Madrena. Let go of revenge. Set yourself free. Love me, as I love you. *Live*."

Madrena inhaled sharply. Something shattered within her. Something crumbled. Something fell away. Something broke under the weight of Rúnin's words and his gaze.

But something also flooded into the place where rage and pain had knotted inside her for so long—love.

She collapsed to her knees, the sword slipping from her grasp to fall with a muted thud to the ground.

Rúnin's hard arms came around her, pulling her against the solid wall of his chest.

A keening wail rose in her ears and she realized it

was her own. At last, all the anger, all the rage, all the fury fell away and all that was left was raw pain.

Another cry tore through her and her head fell onto Rúnin's firm shoulder. Grief that she'd repressed for so long erupted violently. Her whole body shook as sobs racked her. Tears flooded her eyes and poured over her cheeks onto Rúnin's warm neck.

She shook and sobbed, moaned and wept against his neck for she didn't know how long. All the while, Rúnin simply held her in his strong embrace.

When at last the light began to fade to twilight blue, her quaking tears ebbed. He scooped her up wordlessly, cradling her against his chest, and carried her out of the village.

Partway back to Ketill's farmstead, she found her legs and walked through the melting snow at Rúnin's side. Though neither of them spoke, she interlaced her fingers with his. Through the darkening forest, Rúnin's warm hand anchored her as they left Seterfell and Bersi's silent body behind.

34

"Are you sure you want to do this?" Rúnin cupped Madrena's soft cheek in his hand and held her eyes for a long moment, searching for any signs of doubt or hesitancy.

But he found none in their gray depths. All he saw was strength.

"Ja, I'm sure," she said.

He lowered his head to capture her lips in a gentle kiss. Though he longed to wrap his arms around her and kiss her more fully, the sun was already slanting at a sharp angle through the trees. Once it slipped behind the snowcapped mountains to the west, the funeral would get underway.

"Are the others coming?" she asked as she opened the little door to the grain loft and began descending the ladder.

"Ja."

"Even the children?"

Rúnin closed the loft's door behind him and followed her down the ladder. When his feet reached the soft ground, he turned to her. "Ketill and Finna think that witnessing the Jarl's funeral will help the village heal from all that Bersi put them through. The children should be part of that as well."

Madrena visibly swallowed and nodded. That had been her reason for wanting to see the funeral as well. Rúnin only hoped that watching Bersi's body burn on the pyre would give her the peace she deserved.

It had been five days since he'd confronted her in Seterfell. She had been quiet since then, for she was obviously still raw. He woke frequently in the night to her quiet tears, and her red-rimmed stare during the day belied the grief he imagined churned within her.

But for the first time since he'd known her, it was a pain not concealed with anger or hot-headedness. Every once in a while, he got a glimpse of the old Madrena when she rolled her eyes at him or snorted at the children's bickering. She was still the strong shieldmaiden he'd met back in Dalgaard. But rage no longer choked her, and vengeance no longer ruled her.

She was on the path toward healing once and for all from Bersi's poison. Rúnin prayed that attending Bersi's funeral would be another step on that path.

Just then the hut door opened and Odny and Jofarr spilled out, followed by Ingrid, Finna, and Ketill. Everyone was swathed in cloaks and fur-lined boots, for they would be outdoors for much of the ceremony.

The younger children were full of energy and questions as they began the trek toward Seterfell. But as the sun dipped low, they seemed to pick up on the somber mood of the adults and quieted.

How strange—and wonderful—that these children had survived Bersi's reign and would now live free of him. Hope swelled in Rúnin's chest. The gods were good to watch over this family.

By the time they reached Seterfell, the bluish light of twilight had fallen, though the village was well lit with several torches stuck into the ground. The dark shadow of the funeral pyre loomed beyond the longhouse. Rúnin's hand tightened around Madrena's.

As they approached the longhouse, Rúnin's attention was tugged to a tall, thin man organizing the gathered villagers.

"Halladr," Rúnin called. The man turned and his warm gaze fell on Rúnin. But then the man's eyes shifted to Madrena and he visibly tensed.

"Halladr Stone Foot, I'd like you to properly meet Madrena," Rúnin said as they halted in front of the longhouse. Finna and Ketill drew their children deeper into the crowd of gathered villagers, for Rúnin had already told them Madrena wanted to speak to Halladr in private.

Halladr nodded cautiously at Madrena. Clearly he wouldn't easily forget the incident five days ago.

Madrena took a deep breath. She'd practiced her apology with Rúnin, but she seemed to struggle to bring forth the words in Halladr's presence.

"I...I want to tell you how sorry I am for threatening you," she managed at last. "I know now that you are not to blame for...for everything. And," she swallowed hard, her hand squeezing his. He squeezed back, trying to give her strength.

"And I apologize for threatening to defile Bersi's corpse. Doing so would have sated my own thirst for vengeance, but would have brought more harm to the innocents of this village."

Halladr relaxed somewhat. "I'm glad you understand why I defended his body. Jarl Bersi has brought enough pain and suffering to these people without having him return as a *draugr* to haunt and curse us."

Madrena nodded, casting her eyes to the ground. Halladr watched her in silence for a moment. He seemed to decide something and the tension fully left him. Carefully, Halladr raised a gnarled, work-knotted hand and placed it gently on Madrena's shoulder.

"I know Bersi's destruction extended beyond Seterfell. Many others bear the scars of his reckless violence." Halladr's dark blue eyes flicked to Rúnin for the briefest of moments. "But after tonight, when we send him to the afterlife, he will never return to this world again."

Madrena lifted her head and met Halladr's kind eyes. "Thank you," she said softly.

"Madrena wishes to make a request," Rúnin said.

She hesitated for a moment but leveled her chin. "I wish to see Bersi's body for myself."

Halladr faltered, but before he could refuse, Madrena went on. "I will not dishonor myself by ruining this funeral. And I'll have Rúnin at my side to assure that. But I wish to look upon his lifeless form so that I'll know I never have to see him again."

Halladr again considered her in silence for a long moment. "Ja," he said at last. "You can see him."

Madrena's body went tense beside Rúnin, her nails digging into his hand. It had been her idea, and though Rúnin had been against it at first, he agreed that she should ask Halladr. They'd both assumed, though, that after her near-attack on the longhouse, she would be denied.

"We will light the pyre soon," Halladr said. "If you truly want to see his body, you'd best go now."

As Rúnin began leading Madrena toward the pyre, Halladr caught his arm. "Rúnin, you have been greatly missed in Seterfell."

Rúnin's chest swelled. He'd been shocked at Ketill and his family's acceptance of him, but in the last sennight, he had allowed that acceptance to ease his fears about his outlawry. Yet he never expected others in Seterfell to welcome him back. Halladr's words gave him hope.

"There is much to discuss," Halladr said. "But know that you are safe here."

"Thank you, my friend," Rúnin replied, gripping Halladr's arm briefly.

Rúnin guided Madrena past the longhouse and through the small gathering of villagers. A pensive air hung heavily around those gathered. The villagers had endured much, yet they could not truly celebrate the death of their cruel Jarl until after his body had burned.

Once they were through the crowds, Rúnin halted in front of the pyre. At his feet, several large stones ringed the stacked wood in the outline of a longship. The villagers—likely with Halladr's craftsmanship in mind—had decided not to burn one of their few longships. Instead, the stones represented the longship pyre fit for a Jarl.

The pyre itself rose well above his head and was two arm spans wide. Several stumps of increasing height had been placed along the side of the stacked wood as rudimentary stairs.

"Are you ready?" Rúnin asked, turning to Madrena.

Her eyes shimmered darkly in the torchlight, her face unreadable. "Ja."

"I'll be with you the whole time."

She nodded and inhaled deeply. Then she stepped onto the first stump and began her ascent to the top of the pyre. Rúnin followed closely.

She stopped at the highest stump, but there was enough room to join her. As he came to her side, he took in the sight onto which her eyes were already locked.

Bersi's lifeless body lay motionless atop the carefully stacked wood of the pyre. A red cloak splayed beneath him, dark as blood in the low light. Around his body and atop the cloak lay baskets of grain, dried flowers, and other small trinkets. On his right side lay an elaborately wrought sword, and on his left a long wooden spear.

His eyes were closed, with a gold coin placed over each one. His hair was much grayer than Rúnin remembered, but it was braided back from his face as he always wore it. He might have been asleep, except for his pallor and unnatural motionlessness.

Madrena let out a long breath through her teeth, her eyes riveted to Bersi's corpse.

"I have thought of seeing him dead for so long," she whispered. "But it was never like this."

"Ja, I know," Rúnin replied softly.

She raised a shaking hand and reached toward Bersi's corpse. Rúnin caught her wrist. "Nei, Madrena, don't."

"I need to see it one last time and know that it cannot haunt me anymore," she said.

He released her wrist, and her trembling fingers went to the ties on Bersi's tunic. Once she'd loosened the ties, she carefully lowered one flap of material to reveal the skin over his heart.

The bear tattoo was motionless, though its yawning mouth and sharp teeth still forced Rúnin to swallow. The mark on his own chest had been identical.

He watched as Madrena's face flitted with fear, then disgust, then hatred. But at last her features smoothed.

"It still seems wrong that he should be allowed to enter the afterlife whole and unmarred," she said, her eyes still on the tattoo.

"But he is not going to Valhalla, where he would be granted all his strength and ability to make battle," Rúnin said. "His men truly must not have cared for him beyond fearing him, for none of them offered Bersi a weapon to hold as he died. His death was just as dishonorable as his life. He will be going straight to Helheim."

"There is comfort in that," Madrena said. She muttered a quick prayer to Hel, goddess and overseer of Helheim, the realm where no Northman wished to spend eternity.

"We had best step down," Rúnin said quietly. "They will want to light the pyre soon."

Madrena's eyes suddenly grew brighter in the torchlight as she focused on Bersi one last time. She seemed to be trying to memorize his lifeless form. Perhaps she was attempting to replace her earlier memories of him, terrifying and strong, with this image.

Rúnin turned his gaze on Bersi as well. This was the man who'd called him son but who had slayed his true father. He had destroyed Rúnin's life, and yet he'd inadvertently brought Rúnin into Madrena's path. Bersi had been a source of death and destruction while he lived, but his passing gave Rúnin hope for the springing of life anew.

Madrena turned away at last, her eyes still shimmering with emotion. He followed her down the stump stairs without a backward glance.

Just as they stepped into the crowd, a drum began to beat, loud and slow. A narrow, hunched figure emerged from the longhouse cloaked and hooded in red. The villagers parted as the ancient priestess made her way toward the pyre. A hushed silence fell over the gathering, broken only by the drum.

Rúnin wondered distantly if the priestess was the same as when he'd been a boy. She'd always seemed impossibly old, yet also ageless because of that. He couldn't make out the priestess's face in the shadows under her red hood, but he imagined that she could be the same—she had survived far more than Bersi.

The priestess slowly ascended the stumps until she stood at the top of the pyre. She withdrew a gnarled hand from the cloak and sprinkled something over Bersi's body.

The drum stopped abruptly and the priestess's voice rose reedy yet loud over the crowd.

"Hear me, Hel, goddess of Helheim. Drag Jarl Bersi, Little Bear, across the river of the dead. Leave him along Náströnd, the shore of corpses. Close your heavy gates behind you so that Bersi may never return again. And then join the living for the celebration of Bersi's death. Drink with us the *sjaund* and then depart from Seterfell."

The priestess beckoned with her hand, and a villager came forth with a chicken and a sharp blade.

None of Seterfell's few thralls, most of whom had

been brought there after being captured by Bersi, had volunteered to join him in death so as to be able to serve him in the afterlife. It was a great insult to Bersi, but everyone in the village knew he was going to the place all Northmen feared. So the sacrificed animal—only one chicken—would be Bersi's sole companion as he traveled to the afterlife.

The priestess swiftly cut the chicken's throat and drizzled its blood over Bersi's body. Then she dropped both the dead animal and the blade onto the pyre and stepped slowly back to the ground.

Another villager handed the priestess one of the torches and she lowered the flames to the pyre. The wood was dry and caught quickly. In a matter of minutes, the flames engulfed the enormous pyre, sending a black column of smoke into the dark night sky overhead.

Rúnin reached for Madrena's hand once more and gave her a reassuring squeeze. Glancing sideways, he saw the fire reflected in her glistening eyes. Tears streamed unchecked down her cheeks as she watched, transfixed. Yet her normally hard features were smooth.

She had found peace at last.

35

As the fire died and the pyre disintegrated, the villagers slowly filed into the longhouse. Their murmurs rose to excited chatter as the solemn air of the funeral lifted and the celebration began.

Rúnin stayed close to Madrena's side. She remained quiet, but she'd wiped her tears and her eyes had cleared to their normal sharp gray.

Inside the longhouse, Ketill waved to them. He'd already secured a spot for himself, Finna, and Ingrid at one of the long tables that were pulled out for such occasions. Jofarr and Odny played with several other children at one end of the longhouse.

Ketill pointed to the empty seats across from them and they settled themselves on the wooden bench. Servants wove their way around benches and tables as the longhouse grew crowded and loud. Food and ale were passed around, and everyone shared in a meal, though anticipation still coursed through those gathered.

At last, a sharp whistle pierced the air. The longhouse grew quiet and Rúnin spotted Halladr standing not far away.

"Seven days have passed since Jarl Bersi's death," Halladr said in a booming voice. Rúnin felt his brows rise. He remembered Halladr as a kind, hardworking shipbuilder, not an organizer and leader in the village.

Ketill must have seen Rúnin's surprise, for he leaned over the table toward him. "Halladr is much respected, even beyond his skill and craftsmanship," Ketill whispered. "As Jarl Bersi grew weaker, Halladr quietly took on more responsibility around the village."

Rúnin nodded as Halladr's loud, clear voice continued.

"We have sent Jarl Bersi into the afterlife without issue. No *draugr* will haunt us."

The villagers stamped their feet and pounded the wooden tables in agreement.

"And now it is time to drink the *sjaund*!"

This time the villagers added their shouts of approval and excitement to their pounding.

A horn of the special *sjaund* ale was handed to Rúnin. Drinking it would mark the true end to the funeral and the beginning of the celebration. Though all funerals were cause for celebration, since they marked the passage of a Northman to one of the nine realms of the afterlife, the villagers of Seterfell had extra cause for festivity, for now they were completely free of Bersi.

Rúnin took a long swig of the ale, then passed the horn to Madrena, who also drank deeply. As others around them drained their horns, they lifted them into the air with a cry of elation.

The longhouse filled with a deafening din that only quieted because Halladr whistled again.

"We have much to celebrate," he said in that booming voice. "Including the return of one of our own." Halladr's dark blue eyes swung over the longhouse and landed directly on Rúnin.

Fear suddenly twisted his belly. He shook his head slightly at Halladr, but the man only smiled softly.

"Some of you may remember Trygg and Aeleif. Trygg died many years ago, but Aeleif was with us until a few years back."

Several people in the longhouse murmured and nodded their heads.

"Trygg and Aeleif had a son."

Rúnin's palms broke into a sweat. There was no way for him to slip from the longhouse unnoticed. What would this crowd do to an outlaw in their midst? Even if they had despised and feared Bersi, it didn't mean they would go against the laws and customs that regulated the Northlands.

"His name was Rúnin, and he was known throughout the village as an honorable, good lad. He was strong and tall even before he was old enough to make a pledge of fealty, and he used that strength to protect the weak and defenseless. But when Bersi came and made himself Jarl, the boy was swept into Bersi's cruel embrace."

The longhouse now fell silent. Distantly, Rúnin guessed that they thought they were hearing a tragic story, one to remind them of their former Jarl's many brutalities. In a way, he supposed they were right.

"But the lad was even stronger than we had all imagined, for he defied Bersi's orders and did what we all wished we were brave enough to do."

To Rúnin's disbelief, another wave of nods and murmured agreement swept through the longhouse.

"Rúnin, son of Trygg and Aeleif, was outlawed. But he lived. He lives even today."

Confusion replaced approval in the noises rising from the crowd.

"In fact, he is here with us this night," Halladr said, his eyes boring into Rúnin. "Stand, Rúnin."

Gritting his teeth, Rúnin slowly rose from the bench. Cries of shock and surprise filled the longhouse. He refused to flinch from them, even though the weight of it all was nigh unbearable.

Rúnin waited for the mob to set upon him.

But the mob never came.

The stunned faces of the villagers, some vaguely familiar, others new, slowly transformed before his eyes.

"By the laws of the Northlands as imposed by Jarl Bersi, Rúnin should be cast out," Halladr said levelly. "But Bersi himself was a lawless man, a man who broke the codes of honor of both men and gods."

For a fleeting moment, Halladr's penetrating gaze flicked to Madrena before returning to Rúnin.

"One deranged, ruthless man forced Rúnin into outlawry, but that is not the way of the law in the Northlands. That is why I am putting it to you all—should we accept Rúnin Tryggsson back into Seterfell, and back into civilization?"

The longhouse fell into a dead silence and Rúnin's heart stopped beating.

"Ja!" someone in the back shouted.

Suddenly the longhouse was filled once more with

rumbling feet, pounding fists, and shouts of approval. The very thatched roof seemed to reverberate with the joyous noise.

Rúnin staggered under the crashing waves of support. Suddenly Madrena was standing at his side, her arm around him, giving him strength.

Halladr held up a hand and the cheers quieted somewhat. "Then Rúnin Tryggsson, you are once again one of us."

Another cacophonous swell filled the longhouse. Rúnin's chest enlarged until he felt sure that his heart would burst. At long last, the nightmare was over. Bersi was dead, and he was a free man.

Halladr had to whistle again to gain enough quiet to be heard.

"Now that the *sjaund* has been drunk, there is one more matter to attend to. Rúnin, although you are the son of Trygg, you once had another name."

All the elation that had filled Rúnin a second before drained away. "Ja," he said carefully. "I was called Rúnin Bersisson for a brief time."

"Jarl Bersi never had heirs, but he claimed you, giving you his name," Halladr said. His words were for the benefit of the villagers who hadn't known of the events fourteen years ago. Rúnin, however, already sensed where Halladr was headed, and he dreaded his next words. Madrena must have guessed as well, for she tensed by his side.

"You can lay claim to Bersi's inheritance if you wish," Halladr said, though he spoke gently, as if he knew such a suggestion would pain Rúnin.

The longhouse fell completely silent. Even the children quieted, clearly sensing something important was transpiring.

"All the Jarl's men have abandoned the village, thank the gods," Halladr went on. "And Bersi never sired a child. If it is your desire, you can claim the wealth he amassed, his thralls—and his Jarlship over Seterfell."

Rúnin's blood hammered in his ears. He had never let himself hope to be welcomed back into society after being banished. And yet he was not only being received by his old friends and neighbors—he was being offered the opportunity to lead them as their Jarl.

But all the wealth, all the power, meant naught to him unless he had the one thing he wanted most.

He turned to Madrena, searching her with a silent question in his eyes.

Her blonde brows were drawn together and her gray gaze reflected a deep well of sadness.

"I cannot stay in this village knowing that Bersi lived here for so long," she said, her voice barely audible even in the silence hanging around them.

She swallowed, struggling with her next words. "My place is in Dalgaard," she managed at last through the thick emotion in her throat.

Rúnin cupped her cheek in his hand, running his thumb along her soft skin. He saw with perfect clarity what he wanted, what he had to do.

"Then my place is in Dalgaard as well," he whispered.

Her pale eyes clouded with tears, yet her brows rose in hope. "Truly?"

"Ja, truly. I want to be at your side for the rest of my days, Madrena."

A tear slipped down her cheek, but he knew it was

borne of joy. Brushing the drop away, he raised his voice to be heard by everyone in the longhouse.

"I will never be able to express the depth of my gratitude to you all for accepting me back." He let his eyes fall on Ketill and Finna, who sat gazing up at him with emotion shining in their eyes. His gaze swept over those gathered before landing on Halladr.

"Bersi's wealth shall be distributed among the village as a small token for the lives lost and altered by his cruelty. His thralls shall be freed. And as for the Jarlship…I think perhaps there is someone better suited for the honor."

Rúnin held out his hand to indicate Halladr, and a low rumble of approval built in the longhouse until it was once more deafening.

Madrena laughed and clapped beside him. The sound of her joy thickened his throat until it was hard to swallow. He would make sure to draw out her laugh more often.

Halladr raised his drinking horn at Rúnin. "In the morning we will make decisions. But now it is time to celebrate!" he shouted. Somehow, the villagers grew even louder at that. More ale was passed around, and several drums and pipes struck up.

As Rúnin and Madrena settled back down onto the bench, Ketill leaned forward. "So, you two will return to the west?" He had to shout to be heard over the din, but he wore a grin on his face.

"Ja," Rúnin said. "Ketill, Finna, we can't thank you enough—"

Ketill held up a hand to cut him off. "No need, my friends."

"Just promise to come visit us in the future," Finna

said, her eyes bright with emotion. "Will you be leaving soon?"

Rúnin exchanged a glance with Madrena. "A few days of rest would be nice, but after that?"

Madrena nodded. "It would be good to head out before another storm blows through."

"Mayhap this time, though, we will travel by ship. It might make the journey…smoother," Rúnin said, raising an eyebrow at her.

Madrena's laugh once again filled the air, hearty and unrestrained. As she leaned against him in the din of merriment, he decided that he would make it his mission to hear that laugh every day.

EPILOGUE

A muscle in Rúnin's jaw twitched as he clenched his teeth against the pain.

"Must you be so slow about it, Alaric?"

Madrena's twin brother lifted his golden head and chuckled, a wicked light in his green eyes.

"What would be the fun unless I inflicted a bit of extra pain on the man spending his nights with my sister?" Alaric said mischievously.

Madrena snorted. "Since when did you become my *Faðir*, Alaric?"

"Since you showed up a fortnight ago alongside the man with whom you escaped Dalgaard, proclaiming you now love each other," he replied smoothly, settling his attention once more on his task.

Rúnin reclined bare-chested in their hut. It was still technically Madrena and Alaric's hut, but Alaric had been gracious enough to sleep in the longhouse while Madrena and Rúnin decided where to live—and enjoyed each other's company in private until then.

Despite the wintery air outside, Alaric had pulled back the furs on one of the high, narrow windows to let in more light. He leaned over Rúnin, a needle and dye pot in hand.

As Alaric resumed pricking Rúnin's brand scar, Rúnin flinched and the muscle in his jaw ticked again.

"I think you are enjoying this far too much, brother," Madrena said as she watched Alaric form the sun tattoo that both he and Eirik bore. Perhaps she would get one as well. Eirik didn't require it of those who swore fealty to him, but she liked the idea of matching her friend and her brother—and her love.

Alaric chuckled but grew serious as he continued to work on the tattoo.

"Mayhap this is my own twisted way of saying thank you," he said quietly to Rúnin.

Rúnin raised a dark eyebrow at him. "If this is how you show gratitude, remind me never to do you any favors."

A wide grin split Alaric's face as he pricked Rúnin especially deep. But then the smile slipped from his mouth once more.

"I mean it," he said softly. "Thank you."

Rúnin seemed to sense Alaric's mood and grew somber as well. "For what?"

"For bringing my sister back."

Madrena's brows shot up and she turned to Alaric. But before she could speak, Rúnin chuckled.

"You know as well as I that Madrena doesn't go anywhere she doesn't want to," Rúnin said with a wry twist of his mouth. "I didn't bring her back. She came back on her own, and she let me tag along."

Alaric gave her a sideways glance from where he

perched on a stool at Rúnin's side. "Ja, you've got that right."

Madrena would have punched him in the arm if it didn't risk ruining Rúnin's tattoo.

But Alaric's vivid green eyes lingered on her. "I thought I'd never see her again when she left Dalgaard those months past—especially considering she was taking a secretive shipwreck survivor with her. And yet here she is. But that's not what I'm thanking you for."

Alaric paused for a long moment, his hand stilling above Rúnin's chest and his eyes sinking into her. "I am thanking you for bringing my sister back to *life*."

Madrena's vision blurred as she held her brother's gaze. He continued to speak as if only to Rúnin, yet his eyes remained steady on her.

"These last five years, some part of her has been dead. That...*man* took the light inside her." His voice hardened for a moment, but then he went on. "But something has changed. I see the fire in her once more, and not just the fire of anger or revenge. I see my true sister again."

At last Alaric shifted his gaze to Rúnin. "And you clearly had a part in it, so I thank you."

Rúnin slowly extended his hand to Alaric, who set aside the dye pot, and they clasped arms silently.

Madrena blinked back the tears threatening to spill over. Alaric was right. She had come alive again—and it was because of Rúnin's love.

Just as Alaric resumed his work on Rúnin's chest, the door to their little hut swung open and cold air flooded inside. Eirik filled the doorway.

He stepped into the hut and quickly closed the door

against the wintery air. With a few strides, he was leaning over Alaric's shoulder, inspecting his work.

"The scar and the remnants of the bear won't even be noticeable," Eirik said. "Very good."

"Thank you, Jarl," Rúnin said.

Eirik shook his head a little. "Just Eirik is fine, as I've said."

"That will take some getting used to," Rúnin said ruefully. "Things are very…different in Dalgaard compared to where I grew up."

Madrena had explained everything to Eirik and a few others, including Laurel and Alaric—with Rúnin's permission. They all knew what his life had been like and what he'd survived. To Madrena's relief, they had all welcomed Rúnin into their lives. Eirik even said it was a boon to have someone as hardy as Rúnin join the village.

"Have you just come to watch Rúnin squirm, Eirik, or is there something else," Alaric said, once again pricking Rúnin with the dye-dipped needle.

"Actually, I need to speak with Madrena—alone." Eirik motioned her toward the door and followed her out.

The air was crisp now that winter had more fully settled upon them. Snow crunched beneath her boots as she walked with Eirik toward the longhouse. Though the sun hid behind low clouds, the village was bright with a thick blanket of snow.

Once inside the longhouse, he guided her to one of the alcoves built into the walls for more privacy.

She felt her brows crease. "What is this about, Eirik?" she said, suddenly wary.

He crossed his arms over his chest, which indicated

that he was assuming the role of Jarl rather than friend at the moment.

"I haven't brought this up in the fortnight since you've returned to Dalgaard because I thought you needed time to get settled."

She nodded cautiously. "Thank you."

"But the fact of the matter is, you defied my direct orders when you left Dalgaard. And to make matters worse, you helped Rúnin escape."

Madrena's stomach sank. She'd been dreading this conversation, but she had to face the consequences of her actions.

Eirik ran a hand through his hair distractedly. "Never mind the fact that Rúnin wasn't with those slavers. We didn't know that at the time."

"What did you end up doing with those men?"

Eirik smiled wolfishly. "We gave them our smallest boat and sent them on their way—with the threat that if we ever saw them near Dalgaard again, we wouldn't be so…hospitable."

Madrena chuckled, but Eirik resumed his cross-armed stance and she sobered.

"You have made so much progress in your training of late, Madrena. The men respect you, look up to you even."

She tried to prevent her chest from swelling with pride at Eirik's rare praise, for she knew he would still punish her for her blatant disregard for his order not to travel east.

"You were doing so well that I had planned to make you captain of next summer's voyage westward."

Madrena felt her eyes round. "Captain?" she breathed.

Shieldmaiden's Revenge

"Ja," he said wryly. "You would have had a crew of twenty men and a longship under your command. But…"

Her excitement fizzled, yet she knew it was only what she deserved.

"But in light of your actions, I cannot give you such an honor. I have decided that Alaric will captain the voyage. He has expressed great interest in the lands to the west."

Madrena's heart sank even lower. Indeed, both she and her brother had been taken with the western lands during their brief encounter the summer before last. Yet it stung to know that he would see those rolling emerald hills and misty shores again while she remained in Dalgaard.

She felt Eirik's pale blue eyes sharpen on her. "Did Alaric tell you how miserable he was during the time you were gone?" he asked carefully.

Madrena snorted ruefully. "He would never admit such a thing to me, but ja, I imagine he missed me as much as I missed him."

Eirik rubbed his jaw in a show of contemplation. "You two are not used to being apart from each other, are you?"

"Nei," she said, narrowing her eyes slightly. What was he up to?

"That is a shame, for I have a different kind of voyage in mind for Alaric next summer. I have heard rumors from elsewhere in the Northlands that some Jarls are sending their warriors to the western lands or the south, but not simply to raid—to settle."

Madrena's jaw slackened as her mind worked to

comprehend what Eirik was saying. "Northlanders settling in those strange lands? Among the locals?"

"Ja—strange, isn't it? Some encounters have been bloody, but others have ended with Northlanders and locals living in harmony, mingling even."

"And you would have Alaric settle in the western lands?"

Eirik's brows lowered and his voice dropped. "These last few winters have been hard. Disease, weak crops, and of course the threat of raids has left us weaker than I'd like. It is time to expand, to find new lands. And I have seen none more fertile than those to the west."

Madrena nodded slowly. Even as Eirik's words stirred something in her, her heart sank.

"Alaric will do well by you and Dalgaard, Eirik," she said, trying to keep the disappointment from her voice.

The corner of Eirik's mouth twitched. "But I am back to the same problem, Madrena. I fear Alaric will be distracted by your absence if you remain in the village."

A sliver of hope widened. "What are you saying?"

"I'm saying that although you won't be leading the voyage, I'd like you to go as Alaric's second in command."

Madrena whooped and barreled into Eirik in a rough embrace. It wasn't the most respectful response, especially toward her Jarl, but she knew he would understand.

She stepped back, another thought occurring to her. "What of Rúnin?"

"He can go with you. As I've said, a man like that, a survivor, is much needed in these hard times. I expect he'll do well in a new land."

Without hesitation, she plowed into Eirik once again.

"Will you tell them, or shall I?"

Madrena withdrew. "I will." A smile split her face, but she didn't care to hide her uncharacteristic display of joy.

As she made her way back toward her little hut, her mind swirled with possibilities. They would sail to the west once the weather was reliably good—but who knew when they'd return to Dalgaard? Mayhap Eirik and Laurel and their soon-to-be-born child would travel west someday. Or mayhap she and Rúnin and Alaric could return to the Northlands when the seas were calm.

She stepped into the warmth of the hut just as Rúnin and Alaric stood.

"Not bad, eh, sister?" Alaric said, pointing to the now-completed sun tattoo on Rúnin's chest, just above his heart.

Emotion rose in her throat as she gazed at Rúnin. No matter what the future held, as long as he was by her side, she would be happy.

"Ja," she said. "It is perfect."

The End

AUTHOR'S NOTE

As I mentioned in my note for *Enthralled* (Viking Lore, Book 1), the only surviving accounts of the Vikings came from the victims of their raids and attacks. For that reason, Vikings have become synonymous with pillagers, rapists, and plunderers. But historians and scholars have developed news understandings of Vikings and their complex social and legal structures, including ideas about honor, vengeance, and outlawry.

Honor was extremely important to Vikings. Because Vikings believed that nothing in life was predetermined by the gods except the time of one's death, it was of paramount importance to build a "good name" in whatever time one had — to live on in legend, pass on a good name to the next generation, and impress the gods. Those who had honor were brave, noble, generous, fair, respectful, and had the strength to do what was right. Those who were dishonorable, on the other hand, were cowardly, treacherous, and untrustworthy (as seen in acts like breaking one's oath or killing kin, for example).

The tale Madrena tells Rúnin about the honor to be

Author's Note

had in disobeying one's superiors comes from chapter thirty-two of the *Gísla Saga*. This tale illustrates Vikings' nuanced understanding of honor. In the tale, Eyjólfr orders his men to kill a woman for protecting the location of her outlaw husband—despite the fact that killing or harming women was considered a despicable act. Hávarðr stands up to him, telling the men not to do the work of a dishonorable man, even though by doing so he is breaking his oath of fealty to Eyjólfr. Ultimately, each person must answer to the gods for their honorable (and dishonorable) actions.

When a person's honor was besmirched, vengeance had to be sought. Vengeance was not meant to punish the person causing dishonor, however. Rather, it was meant to repair the honor of the person wronged. This conception of honor and dishonor helped me mold Madrena into someone so myopically focusing on revenge, and who is initially devastated when the opportunity for vengeance is taken from her.

In researching *Enthralled*, I became fascinated with the concept of outlawry in Viking society. That research led to the way I portray Rúnin and outlawry in this story —except for the use of the brand to remove tattoos and mark an outlaw. Though there is some evidence that Vikings had tattoos, perhaps to show their fealty to a Jarl or King, branding to remove tattoos as a way of identifying an outlaw was my own invention.

As Robert Wernick puts it in his book *The Vikings*, outlaws are "unfeedable, unferriable, and unfit for all help and shelter." An outlaw could be killed without penalty by anyone who saw him, at any time—and some people sought to kill outlaws just for the extra honor it would garner them. Aiding an outlaw was grounds to be killed or outlawed yourself. In imagining how lonely and terrifying the life of an outlaw would have been, and how hard it would be to survive in the cold Northlands without any aid, Rúnin's character materialized. A man who could survive outlawry for fourteen years would have been very rare indeed.

Probably just as rare were shieldmaidens, unfortunately. Although they are mentioned in the *Sagas*, scholars don't agree on whether or not there were actually women warriors in Norse society. Some believe that shieldmaidens only existed in myth as Valkyries or as legendary women like Brynhildr (Brunhilda) and Lagertha. Others contend that some women could have fought alongside men as real shieldmaidens. The Vikings immortalized real heroes—both men and women—in the *Sagas*, after all. For the purposes of this story, I am siding with the latter view. Graves of Norse women have been found with weapons and animal bones, indicating a warrior's burial.

Speaking of burials, while some Vikings buried their dead (or some of their dead, like thralls), pyres were favored. For someone important, like a Jarl, an entire longship (or just an outline of a longship in stones) would be used to hold the pyre. Things that a person might need in the afterlife, like food, weapons, and even thralls, were added to the pyre and burned with the body. If everything was conducted properly, the deceased would be carried to one of the nine realms of the afterlife.

All Vikings wanted to go to Valhalla, with its endless feasting and joyous battling, but not all Vikings were warriors (and only one who died a warrior's death, with a weapon in hand, could enter Valhalla). There were

Author's Note

other peaceful afterlife realms that a Viking could enjoy, but Helheim was considered the least desirable. Although it is not as horrific as the Christian version of Hell, Helheim was a place for those who had died dishonorably, or led a dishonorable life. No feasting, no pleasure, and no fun awaited in Hel's realm.

But if a funeral was not conducted properly, or if the body of the deceased was treated poorly or desecrated, the Vikings believe the deceased would not enter one of the realms and instead linger as a haunting *draugr*—their version of a zombie. Literally translated as "again-walking," a *draugr* would have a physical form and would haunt and cause destruction to anyone who wronged him in his previous life. As if there wasn't enough in the Viking era to worry about!

*Draugr*s could be avoided if all the proper funeral ceremonies and rites were observed, though. This included the ritual drinking of the funeral ale, *sjaund*, seven days after a Viking's death. Only after the *sjaund* was drunk could the deceased's inheritances be divvied up.

Two quick notes on plant life in Viking-era Scandinavia. I mentioned the *hvönn* plant because it was used as a catch-all during Viking times against fever, colds, cough, infection, and more. We know the *hvönn* today as angelica or wild celery. Vikings also used it to flavor food as well as treat illness.

Lastly, I incorporated the *Amanita muscaria*, the red mushroom with white spots, because some scholars believe that berserkers ate it before going crazy in battle. Historians have long debated why berserkers were so fierce in battle, seemingly immune to pain and so out of their minds that they would even turn on their own men in the haze of their bloodlust. Some have guessed that a crazed, hallucinatory state of mind was achieved by eating such poisonous mushrooms. That possibility made for an interesting twist in writing about the trapper pursuing Madrena and Rúnin.

Though this is a work of romantic fiction, I aimed to capture some of the struggles, complexities, and pleasures of the Vikings' way of life. I hope you enjoyed traveling back to the Viking Age with me! Thank you!

Make sure to sign up for my newsletter to hear about all my sales, giveaways, and new releases. Plus, get exclusive content like stories, excerpts, cover reveals, and more.
Sign up at www.EmmaPrinceBooks.com

THANK YOU!

Thank you for taking the time to read *Shieldmaiden's Revenge* (Viking Lore, Book 2)!

And thank you in advance for sharing your enjoyment of this book (or my other books) with fellow readers by leaving a review on Amazon. Long or short, detailed or to the point, I read all reviews and greatly appreciate you for writing one!

I love connecting with readers! Sign up for my newsletter and be the first to hear about my latest book news, flash sales, giveaways, and more—signing up is free and easy at www.EmmaPrinceBooks.com.

You also can join me on Twitter at:
@EmmaPrinceBooks.
Or keep up on Facebook at:
https://www.facebook.com/EmmaPrinceBooks.

TEASERS

FOR EMMA PRINCE'S BOOKS

Viking Lore Series:

Step into the lush, daring world of the Vikings with **Enthralled (Viking Lore, Book 1)**!

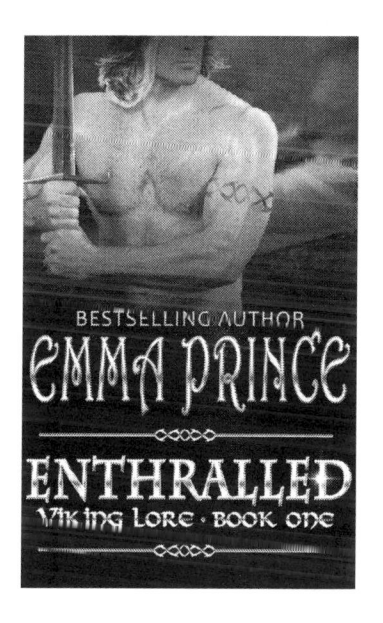

He is bound by honor...

Eirik is eager to plunder the treasures of the fabled lands to the west in order to secure the future of his village. The one thing he swears never to do is claim possession over another human being. But when he journeys across the North Sea to raid the holy houses of Northumbria, he encounters a dark-haired beauty, Laurel, who stirs him like no other. When his cruel cousin tries to take Laurel for himself, Eirik breaks his oath in an attempt to protect her. He claims her as his thrall. But can he claim her heart, or will Laurel fall prey to the devious schemes of his enemies?

She has the heart of a warrior...

Life as an orphan at Whitby Abbey hasn't been easy, but Laurel refuses to be bested by the backbreaking work and lecherous advances she must endure. When Viking raiders storm the abbey and take her captive, her strength may finally fail her—especially when she must face her fear of water at every turn. But under Eirik's gentle protection, she discovers a deeper bravery within herself—and a yearning for her golden-haired captor that she shouldn't harbor. Torn between securing her freedom or giving herself to her Viking master, will fate decide for her—and rip them apart forever?

Taste the sweetness of blooming first love in ***The Bride Prize*** (**Viking Lore Novella, Book 2.5**)!

With his family lost to illness, Tarr leaves the only home he's ever known with nothing but a dream—to sail across the North Sea to the mysterious lands in the west. In order to earn a spot on his Jarl's voyage, he must compete against his fellow Northmen in games of strength and skill. But when he learns that the prize for winning the competition is the hand of the dark-haired beauty he met only days ago, will he be forced to choose between his dreams and his heart?

Eyva wants nothing more than to train as a shieldmaiden, but her parents refuse, hoping to yoke her to their Northland farm forever. When they put her up as the bride prize for their village's festivities, she fears she will never escape the fate of a grueling life on her parents' farm. But Tarr's longing gaze and soft kisses just might give her the courage to fight for herself—and for their budding love.

Get swept away by the passionate tale of the Vikings' encounter with the Picts in ***Desire's Hostage* (Viking Lore, Book 3)**!

She is his hostage...

As the daughter of a proud Pict chieftain, Elisead's duty is to make a marriage alliance for the betterment of her people. Yet the forest spirits whisper to her, calling her into the woods to carve in stone the long forgotten markings of the old ways. But when she witnesses a terrifying band of Northmen land on the shores of her village, she senses that her fate lies with the golden leader who entrances her with his dancing emerald eyes and claims her with his forbidden touch.

Desire binds them together...

Alaric sets sail from the Northlands with the weighty responsibility of making a permanent settlement in Pictland. To build an alliance with a local Pict chieftain, Alaric agrees to exchange hostages—and claims the chieftain's daughter as his leverage. Now, his greatest challenge is to resist Elisead, the auburn-haired beauty who captivates him completely. When the fragile negotiations turn deadly, Alaric must choose between his mission and his desire to protect Elisead from the mysterious forces working against peace between their peoples.

Highland Bodyguards Series:

The Lady's Protector, the thrilling start to the Highland Bodyguards series, is available now on Amazon!

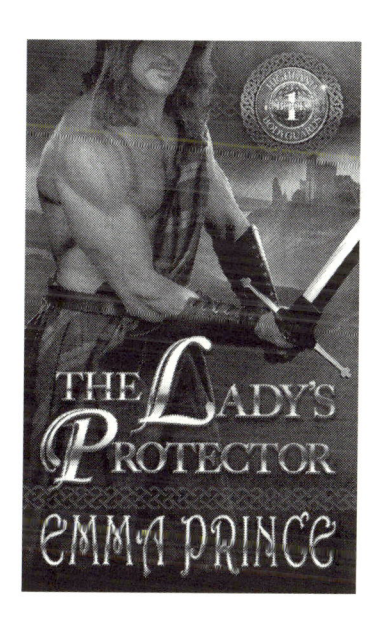

The Battle of Bannockburn may be over, but the war is far from won.

Her Protector...

Ansel Sutherland is charged with a mission from King

Robert the Bruce to protect the illegitimate son of a powerful English Earl. Though Ansel bristles at aiding an Englishman, the nature of the war for Scottish independence is changing, and he is honor-bound to serve as a bodyguard. He arrives in England to fulfill his assignment, only to meet the beautiful but secretive Lady Isolda, who refuses to tell him where his ward is. When a mysterious attacker threatens Isolda's life, Ansel realizes he is the only thing standing between her and deadly peril.

His Lady...

Lady Isolda harbors dark secrets—secrets she refuses to reveal to the rugged Highland rogue who arrives at her castle demanding answers. But Ansel's dark eyes cut through all her defenses, threatening to undo her resolve. To protect her past, she cannot submit to the white-hot desire that burns between them. As the threat to her life spirals out of control, she has no choice but to trust Ansel to whisk her to safety deep in the heart of the Highlands...

The Sinclair Brothers Trilogy:

Go back to where it all began—with Robert and Alwin's story in ***Highlander's Ransom***, Book One of the Sinclair Brothers Trilogy. Available now on Amazon!

He was out for revenge...

Laird Robert Sinclair would stop at nothing to exact revenge on Lord Racf Warren, the English scoundrel who had brought war to his doorstep and razed his lands and people. Leaving his clan in the Highlands to conduct covert attacks in the Borderlands, Robert lives to be a thorn in Warren's side. So when he finds a beautiful English lass on her way to marry Warren, he whisks her away to the Highlands with a plan to ransom her back to her dastardly fiancé.

She would not be controlled…

Lady Alwin Hewett had no idea when she left her father's manor to marry a man she'd never met that she would instead be kidnapped by a Highland rogue out for vengeance. But she refuses to be a pawn in any man's game. So when she learns that Robert has had them secretly wed, she will stop at nothing to regain her freedom. But her heart may have other plans…

ABOUT THE AUTHOR

Emma Prince is the Bestselling and Amazon All-Star Author of steamy historical romances jam-packed with adventure, conflict, and of course love!

Emma grew up in drizzly Seattle, but traded her rain boots for sunglasses when she and her husband moved to the eastern slopes of the Sierra Nevada. Emma spent several years in academia, both as a graduate student and an instructor of college-level English and Humanities courses. She always savored her "fun books"—normally historical romances—on breaks or vacations. But as she began looking for the next chapter in her life, she wondered if perhaps her passion could turn into a career. Ever since then, she's been reading and writing books that celebrate happily ever afters!

Visit Emma's website, www.EmmaPrinceBooks.com, for updates on new books, future projects, her newsletter sign-up, book extras, and more!

You can follow Emma on Twitter at:
@EmmaPrinceBooks.
Or join her on Facebook at:
www.facebook.com/EmmaPrinceBooks.

Made in the USA
Lexington, KY
03 January 2019